The sheriff pulled the Blazer over to let me off where the road branched toward the rig. "Miss Hansen, before you go, might I make a suggestion?" His voice was caustic, sarcastic.

"Yes sir?" I glanced sideways at him. His face was impassive, devoid of emotion under the reflective sunglasses. I clutched the door handle tightly.

"Don't ever try to make your living playing poker. You don't have the guile. Now run along and stay out of trouble."

Fury filled my veins. I had every right to care about what happened to Willie and Bill. I had every right to want to be involved, to make a difference. I wanted to know who or what had killed these two men, and why. Lengthening my stride and squaring my shoulders I walked to my trailer.

The sheriff's words had backfired: instead of leaving go of the investigation, I was now determined to have my part in it.

TENSLEEP

SARAH ANDREWS

A SIGNET BOOK

SIGNET
Published by the Penguin Group
Penguin Books USA Inc., 375 Hudson Street,
New York, New York 10014, U.S.A.
Penguin Books Ltd, 27 Wrights Lane,
London W8 5TZ, England
Penguin Books Australia Ltd, Ringwood,
Victoria, Australia
Penguin Books Canada Ltd, 10 Alcorn Avenue,
Toronto, Ontario, Canada M4V 3B2
Penguin Books (N.Z.) Ltd, 182–190 Wairau Road,
Auckland 10, New Zealand

Penguin Books Ltd, Registered Offices:
Harmondsworth, Middlesex, England

Published by Signet, an imprint of Dutton Signet, a division of Penguin Books USA
Inc. This is an authorized reprint of a hardcover edition published by Otto Penzler
Books. For information address Simon & Schuster, Inc., Rockefeller Center, 1230
Avenue of the Americas, New York, N.Y. 10022.

First Signet Printing, December, 1995
10 9 8 7 6 5 4 3 2 1

 REGISTERED TRADEMARK—MARCA REGISTRADA

Cover art by Bob Guisti

Printed in the United States of America

PUBLISHER'S NOTE:
This is a work of fiction. Names, characters, places, and incidents either are the
product of the author's imagination or are used fictitiously, and any resemblance to
actual persons, living or dead, events, or locales is entirely coincidental.

BOOKS ARE AVAILABLE AT QUANTITY DISCOUNTS WHEN USED TO PROMOTE PRODUCTS OR
SERVICES. FOR INFORMATION PLEASE WRITE TO PREMIUM MARKETING DIVISION, PENGUIN BOOKS
USA INC., 375 HUDSON STREET, NEW YORK, NEW YORK 10014.

With love to Damon:
Still *it* and always will be.

ACKNOWLEDGMENTS

My thanks to Robert J. Bowman, Marilyn Wallace, Marcia Muller, Clint Smith, and Pamela Jekel, who critiqued early drafts of this manuscript, and to J. David Love, Scientist Emeritus, U.S. Geological Survey, who proofed it for geological and geographical errors.

And to my folks, for drop-kicking me through school, and for littering the bathroom with paperback mysteries.

And to Deborah Schneider, agent without peer!

And to Kate Stine and the rest of you at OPB. How'd I get so lucky?

1

The night the geologist died I was asleep, wrapped in the suffocating flannel of my sleeping bag on the narrow bunk in my trailer. I was hoarding my rest until midnight, when I had to start a twelve-hour shift.

The sounds of the vehicles that came to attend to Bill Kretzmer's death didn't wake me, muffled as they were by the rumbling, incessant roar of the drilling rig's enormous Allis-Chalmers motors. People come and go at odd hours from a drilling rig anyway, around the clock, day after day, until the oil well is completed. My ear is tuned to alert me to different sounds, like changes in the rhythm of the drilling brake, or an abrupt crescendo in the roar as the draw works hoists the drill string skyward into the thin Wyoming air.

As it was, a ruckus right underneath my window woke me that midnight: the frantic protest of the engine of our company truck as Howard over-revved it and missed the gears. I rolled over and squinted at my watch. As usual, he had neglected to wake me in his hurry to keep his date with a bottle in town. I gritted my teeth and got up, cursing as I pulled the cold denim of my blue jeans over my legs.

I stumbled about, putting a fresh pot of coffee on to brew in the trailer's kitchenette. I was staring out the window, just starting to wonder why there were so many cars and trucks parked around the base of the rig, when Johnny Maxwell, the tool pusher, came by to tell me the bad news. He pulled off his gimme cap and brushed aimlessly at the salt stains on its brim with thick, calloused fingers. He couldn't bring himself to look at me. His usually smiling mouth was drawn into a tight line, and he spoke bluntly.

"Bill Kretzmer's dead, Emmy. I'm sorry. I know you were friends."

There suddenly wasn't any air in my lungs.

Johnny continued, filling my silence with words. "I found him on my way back from town a couple hours ago. Seems he missed that bad curve where the road is all built up across the wash. Damned thing's banked the wrong way. These clay roads, they're too slick by half anyway." He paused, now watching me carefully to see how I was taking it, his hands beginning to twitch back and forth at the wrists like he didn't know what to do with them.

I still didn't say anything. I realize now I was staring bullets at him, mutely accusing him of treachery for being the messenger of such disaster. He shifted uncomfortably and started to talk again, to say more than he otherwise might, his voice taking on a note of confession. "It was dark, Em. I slowed for the curve. I didn't notice anything at first. But then I saw some of the sagebrush along the top of the bank was ripped up. I thought, Someone's finally missed the turn. I stopped, shone my headlights over the edge, and got out to take a look. Things were ripped up all the way down the bank. Hell, the smell of all that sage was . . . then I saw the underside of his car. I was too late, Em. He was hanging there by the seatbelt, upside-down. I touched him, and he just—" Johnny set his jaw. "Emmy, he was already gone. His neck was broken. I'm sure he didn't suffer."

My mind had caught on one detail of what Johnny had said. "Upside down?"

"Yeah. The seat belt held him in place."

My head began to ring. Johnny and the rest of the trailer faded, everything far away, his pale blue eyes the last to vanish as memory shifted me three hundred miles distant and ten years back in time. My heart was pounding. It's spring break of my senior year, I'm on my way home from a dance at the high school, driving my daddy's truck, wishing I wasn't alone. I'm being careful, taking each curve real careful to avoid the ice from the late spring snow. In the headlights I see the marks where a car has left the pavement. I stop, set the brake, get out, follow the tracks. There's my mother's car, upside down. I'm scared. There she is: she's out there, walking aimlessly through the sage and rabbit brush, cursing at the moon. I call to her. She won't answer me, only stamps her feet and curses louder. I run to the car. I reach in past the steering wheel. My uncle's body hangs in the embrace of the seat belt, his skin already growing cold in the night air.

I looked at Johnny, whispered, "Why?"

Johnny sighed. "Well, Em, these things happen. You remember Bill saying how that car kept stalling on him when he hit the brakes hard, and he'd lose the power steering and brakes. The rent-a-car agency was supposed to swap it for a new one. I guess they didn't get to it soon enough. The sheriff went over the whole scene pretty careful, measured the skid marks and all. He figures Bill went into that turn too fast, hit the brakes, and lost control."

No, I mean why—I forced myself to look around the room, get my bearings, remember where I was, remember that ten years had passed since Mother missed that turn on another ranch road at the opposite corner of Wyoming. My uncle was long buried. It was over.

And now Bill was gone. No. My mind raced, trying to find a loophole in reality. I said, almost shouted, "I want to talk to the sheriff. Bill wouldn't have gone into that turn that fast."

Johnny sighed again and laid the tips of his rough fingers on my arm. "I know this is hard for you, Em, but try to just accept—"

I stiffened. "I'm not just saying this, Johnny. I rode back and forth to town with Bill dozens of times, and he was a very careful driver. He always slowed for that turn. And that car only ever stalled on him when he was stopping, like here by his trailer, or one time when he braked hard for a cow."

Johnny let go of my arm. "Well, Em, maybe when he had you with him he was just being careful for your sake."

I stalked back into the bunk room and closed the door, and stayed there until I heard Johnny leave the trailer.

It was a long night. I sat staring into my coffee until long after it was cold. Bill was the only thing that had made the job bearable. *This damned job,* I thought. *This irritating job sharing this cramped trailer with Howard the drunk, this God-forsaken job on the edge of the earth with these loud-mouthed roughnecks, this son-of-a-bitching job where Ed Meyer can come into my trailer and slop his brand of filth on me any time he gets in the mood. This . . .*

At three a.m., I was still just sitting there, when out of the corner of my eye I noticed a faint light coming from Bill's trailer across the way. It had the odd, bobbing quality of a fairy dancing about. At first I thought I was dreaming, maybe hallucinating the spirit of Bill come back to pay a visit. Then I remembered that Bill's papers and personal things were still in that trailer, and I was on my feet and out the door before I knew what I was doing. I threw my trailer door open so hard it banged back against this heavy little four-inch drill bit I use to keep the door from slamming into the plotting table. The rig motors had been idling quietly, and the crash sounded enormously loud and close.

The light stopped moving.

I lunged across the short distance to Bill's trailer and yanked open the screen door.

The light went out.

I opened the inner door, slipped a hand inside, and flicked on the lights.

A tall, gangly boy stared pop-eyed at me in the sudden blast of light, and dropped abruptly to the floor.

"Willie?" I said, recognizing his ruff of red hair.

"Please, Em, turn it out," he whispered, his green eyes shining with anxiety.

"Shit, Willie, what are you doing in there?" I wanted to

grab him by his scruffy denim jacket and hurl him out onto the ground.

Willie squeezed his eyes shut and pressed his face to the floor. I could see he was trembling. Something about the softness of his freckled cheek against the filthy linoleum derailed my anger. I turned out the light and stepped inside the trailer. "This looks pretty strange, Willie," I whispered into the darkness. "What the hell are you doing in here? Haven't you heard?"

"Please leave, Em. This is no place for you right now," he urged, his voice heavy with sadness and fear.

I waited, uncertain what to do.

A moment later the trailer shifted as Willie slipped past me into the night. Over the renewed roar of the rig motors, I thought I heard him say, "It's too late, anyway."

I gave Willie a moment to disappear, and then turned the lights back on. I wanted to make sure he hadn't tampered with any of Bill's possessions, like his maps and files. But in the cold glare of the lights, I could see that the trailer had already been stripped clean of any sign of Bill Kretzmer.

2

My shift ended at noon. Howard lay snoring fitfully on the lower bunk. "It's time, Howard," I shouted, hoping my voice would shatter his hung-over eardrums.

Howard emitted an involuntary snort, opened one bloodshot eye, and stared at me through the open door.

Scraping my chair back with as loud a noise as possible, I reached for the keys to the company truck. I suppose I intended to go to town for my ceremonial mid-day bowl of chili, maybe take a break from the mawkish looks of sympathy I had begun to draw as I went about my chores, but as I headed out the door, I realized that for the first time, I was leaving for lunch without Bill Kretzmer. My friend. My mentor. Tears suddenly pooled in my eyes. I prayed that the men on the rig wouldn't see.

I hurried to the truck and roared away from the rig, but then in no time I was bearing down on the curve where *it* had happened. "Damn you, Bill," I muttered as I braked to a stop, tears now blinding me. I cried for Bill. I cried for my uncle. I even cried a bit for my damned mother, big wracking sobs that drained the energy from my body like water out of sand.

By and by I found myself just sitting there looking around, kind of gathering up an impression of the place where my friend had taken his leave of this world. It was sunny, and a warm breeze was blowing out of the west, carrying the sweet scent of burgeoning life, not death.

I shook my head, remembering the day I'd met him, remembering the excitement that had shined from his dark eyes. Eyes that more recently had radiated an angry, almost paranoid glare when people asked him neighborly questions like, "How's the well going, Bill?"

But nerves and excitement or no, the Bill Kretzmer I had known had been too methodical a man to get to hurrying and roll his car. Besides, what had Willie, the young pumper who tended the oil field's peripheral wells, been doing creeping around in Bill's trailer in the middle of the night only six hours after Bill's death?

I stepped out of the truck to survey the scene. Perhaps I could see something by daylight that the sheriff had missed by night that would explain what had happened to my friend.

Beyond the hills to the west lay the town of Meeteetse, where Bill had gone each night at eight-thirty to phone his wife. To the east lay badlands, with little valleys of empty prairie, leading to the rig.

I crouched down and stared at the dust. So many cars and trucks had been over the road since the evening before that I could make nothing of the marks on the hard-packed clay surface. Down in the wash, there surely was one mess of ripped-up sagebrush and gouged soil where Bill's car had left the road and flipped down the bank, and where the wrecker had backed down the grade to drag it out. I wandered down through the brush to one side of the disturbed ground, leaving my footprints in the soft adobe soil. Cattle tracks abounded where a herd had moved down the draw. One shoeless horse had passed through. There were tracks from last night's mice and ground squirrels, and the coyote that wanted them for dinner. In the damp mud at a seep in the bottom of the draw, I could even make out the fine lines of a raccoon's bristly fur around the prints of his paws. But where Bill's car had come to rest, I found only a confusion of boot prints left by men too late to help.

A wren called from an unseen perch. Overhead, the wide Wyoming sky rolled on blue and clear forever. I rested for a while on a low rim of sandstone and picked through the rounded pebbles and other small treasures that the wind had winnowed from the bottom of the wash. There were scattered flakes of chert and reddish jasper the size of my thumbnail, relics of some long-dead Indian's efforts to chip out arrowheads. I sat running my thumb over the smooth curves of their faces, wondering what that Indian had found there, before the advent of white men and their rifles, their cattle, and their automobiles. The stone remained mute.

A soft white cloud ate the warmth of the sun. I chose three of the most colorful chips and a fossil snail to hold in remembrance of my departed work mate, silently said my good-byes, and left.

As I ate that bowl of chili in town, I began to feel better. Food is good that way. The tourists at the next table were a welcome distraction, carrying my mind to other places and other lives. The man wore pink slacks. He read the entire menu to his patient wife, regaling her with every nuance of its profound novelty. "Look here, Barbara, they have chicken-fried steak. They surely don't have that back home. I think I'll try some. And just look here at the breakfast menu. Biscuits and gravy. Have you ever. And how about these commemorative plates on the wall, you ever see anything like it? I'll bet there's one for every cow-chip tourney and pie-eating contest they've held in the state."

Barbara eyed the plates, adjusting her head to find the right lens in her trifocals. "Looks like state capitols to me, Fred. And presidents."

Even after they left I dawdled, munching down every last saltine and herding the crumbs into a pile on the Formica with my fingers as I tried to decide whether to try to talk to the sheriff or not. I hadn't found any physical evidence to report, and what had seemed an urgent certainty in the dark of night seemed a touch overly dramatic by day. *Bill might truly have just been unlucky,* I reasoned. *Like most people killed in car crashes, right? One more sad statistic testifying to the limitations of the human animal piloting a ton and a half of hurtling steel and upholstery.*

I loaded the cellophane wrappers from the saltines into

my bowl and added my much-twisted paper napkin, uncertain what to do next. My doubts were no longer gnawing at me exactly, just kind of drifting around like a rank breeze. I didn't like the sensation. It was too much like that time when Mother rolled her car and no one would talk about it, and I was expected to accept my uncle's death as just one of those things. I sure didn't want to open myself to that kind of frustration again, but I didn't know what would make it go away faster, tilting at it like a windmill by telling the sheriff what I knew, or getting on with carrying the load of resignation that gives life its special tang.

As the waitress brought my tab, I decided I'd have a little chat with Willie Sewell the next time I saw him, but decided otherwise to put these concerns out of my mind.

By the time I returned to the rig, I had begun to adjust to Bill's absence. I did feel a certain twinge of guilt about going on working without him, so I appointed myself executor of his vision for the well, telling myself I'd make sure everything went as he had intended.

The drilling crews talked about little else than the accident for a day or two, but soon a new topic of gossip occupied their minds. Blackfeet Oil, the exploration company that was drilling the well and had sent Bill Kretzmer to "sit" it, had chosen his replacement.

Rumor had it that the new geologist was a woman.

3

Let me tell you, a woman is not a common sight on a drilling rig. The oil boom of the 1970s opened the way for a few of us to find jobs as mudloggers and even roughnecks, and the exploration companies that contract the drilling jobs had just begun to send women out as geologists and engineers when the crude oil price collapse of the 1980s brought the disaster of massive layoffs. I was lucky to get work, however intermittent, and in four years, the only women I'd met on the rigs were one tough roughneck, a courier who'd come to pick up drill core, and a rookie engineer at a field office. So we're still rare as hen's teeth in the oil patch, and the men for the most part still look on us as aliens, or perhaps as some sort of third gender, like we can't bake pies or have babies like the girls they marry.

So the day Alix Chadwick arrived from Denver, things were in a bit of an uproar up on the rig, and I was catching more than the usual amount of flak. I tried to avoid everyone, but to get my drill cuttings samples, I had to keep going up on the rig.

The drilling mud that is pumped down the inside of the drill string to lubricate the drilling and lift the rock cuttings back up the bore hole is drawn from a holding pit the size of a small swimming pool. To get to where the drilling mud flushes out of the bore hole, I had to cross the parking yard, climb about a dozen feet up a steel staircase to the level of the drilling floor, pass through the doghouse (the metal shed where the men keep their coveralls and where they go to warm up) on the side of the rig and through the Dutch door that opens onto the drilling floor, dodge around the great rotating drill pipe that extends through the top of the borehole and then climb out onto the catwalk that runs around the outside of the canvas windbreak surrounding the drilling floor. There the mud gushes out over a sieve called a shale shaker. The boys were pretty excited and, shall we say, noticing me more than usual. It was like running the gauntlet.

I tried going around the other way, taking the short cut through the pipe yard and up the back stairs by the skids where the draw works pull the pipe off the storage racks, but one of the hands was doing maintenance of some sort on those stairs.

We were drilling at about four thousand feet depth by then, making maybe ten feet an hour, and I was catching a cuttings sample every five feet and taking them back to my trailer, where I'd examine them and note the findings in my log. Each time I crossed the drilling floor I overheard snippets of conversation—speculation about what a "girl" geologist was going to look like—and the guys watched me with bright eyes. As I crossed the floor in search of sample number whatever, that damned Wayne hollered, "Is she gonna be ugly like you, Emmy?" I hunched my little hard hat down and tried to ignore him, but the wolf calls started anyway, Wayne leading the pack, sauntering toward me with his grimy hands planted on his swaggering hips, the zipper of his coveralls open down to the nickel-plated bucking bronco on his belt buckle. Frank Barnes, the driller on that shift, bellowed at the men to cut it out and get back to work.

Johnny Maxwell was moved to lecture them as well. Not long before Alix was due, he dropped by the drilling floor to remind them that, woman or no, the geologist was the Company Man, and he expected them to treat her accordingly.

"Then will she be as ugly as Bill?" howled Wayne.

Trying to ignore this, I grabbed a big piece of blue chalk and marked the drill pipe five feet above where it emerged from the drilling floor, holding the chalk at chin level as the pipe turned. The drilling brake would lower the drill pipe through the floor a millimeter at a time, letting the bit grind into the earth at a measured rate, and when my blue chalk reached the floor, I'd know it was time to catch another sample.

I replaced the chalk on its ledge on the side of the derrick and headed back to my trailer, focusing my mind away from the wolf pack by calculating exactly when Alix would arrive on the rig. Her flight from Denver would arrive up in Cody at eleven. I figured a half-hour drive down from the airport, plus whatever time to pick up her baggage and rental car, not long in an airport with only three or four scheduled flights per day. I gave her until noon to show her face.

At eleven-fifteen, I heard a particularly raucous round of guffaws as I climbed the stairs to the rig to catch the next sample, but this time when I stepped into the doghouse all conversation stopped, and the guys stared at me with smirks and smiles on their faces. They were a bunch of dogs ready to spring, eyes alight, breathless, waiting for the lead dog to make the first move. The silence stretched on until Wayne jumped up and said, "Hey, Emmy, you know how turtles make love?"

I knew damned well how turtles made love, but I wasn't fast enough. As I bolted for the Dutch door, he yanked off his hard hat, flipped it upside down, and rapped it on top of mine. Hard. Peals of laughter.

Frank stormed in off the drilling floor. "Come *on,* boys. What you think, it's play time? Get back to work, damn it!"

The truth was, I was excited about the impending arrival, too. I had it in my head that having another woman there would sort of balance things out. This Alix Chadwick and I could sit around and make *our* wolf calls and tell *our* scathing jokes, and she would know some good ones, too. She had to be tough or she wouldn't be working in the oil patch. Yeah, this was going to be good.

At eleven forty-five, Alix Chadwick's rented Buick

pulled over the rise toward the rig. All hands except Frank were arrayed along the forward catwalks, polishing things that didn't need polishing, straining to be the first to get a look at her. God bless him, even Howard was awake.

The Buick pulled to a stop below the stairs. I rose from the plotting table in my trailer and stepped out to greet her, relishing the moment, shoulders squared, chin high. *The women greet each other as comrades,* I dreamed. *The men draw back in awe. A new age dawns.*

Alix was still sitting behind the wheel folding up a map when I reached the car.

I stopped a few feet from the car door, waiting for her to open it. She didn't seem to notice me. Her head was bowed in concentration and she took her time straightening up her kit.

I smiled, contemplating a cheery "Hi there," but as time squeezed out into an uncomfortable dimension, my smile began to congeal into something more appropriate for Halloween.

At last the car door opened. Alix Chadwick swung out a pair of long, slender legs swathed in very expensive chinos and stood up. And up. And up. She must have been nearly six feet tall, and every inch relaxed, assured, and pure class.

My brain lurched frantically into gear, measuring her, reaching desperately for some point of communality. Okay, she was about my age—mid-to-late-ish-twenties—and there was no doubt she was female, but that was where the similarities ended. She was elegant where I was plain, smooth where I was lumpy. She looked like someone who had found life's ladder an easy climb, probably skipping the rung on which I stood. She swept aside a lock of her dark, glossy hair and observed me calmly, saying nothing.

"You must be the new geologist," I said, for lack of a more clever opener.

"Yes. And you are?"

"Em Hansen. One of the mudloggers."

"I see." Her voice oozed with the subtle shadings of privilege, reclining comfortably in a sightly drawling Massachusetts accent.

Just then, Johnny Maxwell materialized and introduced himself. I noticed he had changed into a clean pair of jeans, and his wiry hair was combed back neatly under his hard hat. "Hello, Ms. Chadwick. Welcome to Bar Diamond Field," he said. "I'm Johnny Maxwell."

"Ah," Alix said, "you're the tool pusher. Please show me which trailer is mine. Then I'd like a tour of the rig."

And that was that. What a let-down. She let Johnny help her into Bill's—her—trailer with her gear, but I was dismissed with, "I'll see the mud log in about an hour."

I sat in my trailer and sulked while Alix did whatever it was she was doing in her trailer. But when she headed up onto the rig, I followed, suddenly unable to resist watching her take her lickings from the boys.

The boys were still decorating the forward catwalks. Every eye was on Alix as she mounted the steel steps. She took her time. She took in the view of the pipe yard, of the badlands, and of the great blue Wyoming sky like royalty gazing upon her kingdom. With an absentminded toss of her shining hair, she stepped into the doghouse.

I hurried across the yard and took the steel stairs two at a time, reaching the doghouse just in time to see all hands collide with each other in an effort to be the one most casually draped across the standing desk the driller uses to record his job. Wayne shot a look at the girlie calendar above the desk and stifled a smirk.

Alix Chadwick fixed her gaze on everyone, giving them a cool, regal smile that made them each about *that* big. As her gaze swept past Wayne, he suddenly shifted his eyes to the floor.

Silence reigned. Wayne took his hard hat off, but he didn't pop her with it. No, he held it in front of his chest and jerked his head in a little bow. I about shit.

And that was that.

As the hours and days went by, Alix stayed cloistered in her trailer, coming out for little more than to drive her

Buick into town for a meal. I was beginning to think I had dreamt her.

Then on the fourth day Chet Hawkins came along, and a whole new side of Alix Chadwick emerged.

It was the first really warm day of spring. Chet Hawkins, son of the owner of Bar Diamond Ranch and heir apparent to all the lease-hold royalties of Bar Diamond Field, came riding up to the rig on a beautifully groomed Appaloosa. He sat so much at ease on his horse that he didn't even look down as it picked its way through the obstacle course of pipes and trucks that surrounded the drilling rig. A black and gray mutt trotted along beside the horse's hooves.

Alix had stepped out of her trailer and paused for a moment in the sunshine, making one of her interminable notes on her officious little clipboard. Chet looked at Alix. She looked back. He rode over closer to her trailer and stopped a decent distance away, far enough that his horse wouldn't crowd a stranger's sensibilities, and tipped his hat back at a friendly angle. His face emerged from the shade of his hat brim, fully visible to her for the first time.

Alix's mouth opened just barely, but her jaw may as well have hit her knees for the volumes spoken by that little lapse. Miss Butter-Wouldn't-Melt-In-Her-Mouth had lost her cool at last.

Recovering quickly, Alix floated a hand up to her brow to shade her eye. And smiled.

Chet rode over closer to her, dropped the reins, swung his far leg up, hooked the knee over the saddle horn, and started to roll a cigarette, just as cool as if he was sitting in an easy chair. It was the sexiest damned move I'd ever seen.

From where I sat, I couldn't hear what Alix and Chet were saying to each other. The window of my trailer was open only a crack so my papers wouldn't blow around, and the wind was from the wrong direction, and, well, you can never hear much over the rig engines anyway. I had to make my inferences from the lingering qualities of their smiles and eye contact.

I forced myself back to work, staring down at the trays of cuttings I was describing. The next time I looked up, Chet was gone. Well, it was time for me get the next cuttings sample anyway, so I got up from my desk and grabbed my hard hat and set out for the stairs to the drilling floor. As I stepped out my door, Alix's gaze dropped abruptly from the rig to her clipboard and she started writing something.

Chet's horse was tied to the railing at the bottom of the stairs. Chet, it seemed, was up on the rig talking to Frank Barnes. As I scurried across the drilling floor, I sneaked a look at Chet. I grew up in Wyoming, and he was the type of guy with the expensive Stetson, the one who through some quirk of fate was born on the ranch with the oil under it rather than the one next door that had to scrape a living running cattle or growing sugar beets. Chet's daddy Garth didn't have to slave away repairing the fence line like my father did; he could sit back on his Barcalounger with a highball and hire it done. Heavy Wyoming crude oil was his crop.

I cracked a mental whip at myself to quit ogling Chet and get my mind back on my work. As I leaned over the shale shaker, I concluded with bleak envy that Chet had ridden out here just to get a look at the girl geologist.

Abandoning all pride, I turned and squinted at him. He had one of those healthy, high-cheekboned, smiling faces that are easy to look at for long periods of time, like his features were all the best of friends. He wasn't yet thirty, but the years of riding the fancy horses that Garth raised had creased his face early, giving him a worldly puckishness that just improved the effect.

Chet stood out like spun gold next to Frank. Frank was all darkness and gravity, more bear than man, the kind of thickly muscled guy who looks like he's always wearing a heavy jacket even when it's just a T-shirt. Chet's gaze wandered around to me, so I smiled hello. I got a minimal response. I wondered, *What is it, is something caught in my teeth?*

I grabbed my cuttings, stuffed them into their muslin

sample bag, hurriedly marked them, "Hawkins no. 4-1 Tensleep, 4010 feet, April 17," and squeezed the excess mud out through the muslin, trying to rivet my mind on how miraculously warm the mud was as it came out of the hole.

Emoting over drilling mud isn't much of a cure for rejection. Cursing myself for spilling the damned stuff down my pant leg, I hurried down the metal steps two at a time, snapping my mind off Chet and Alix and every other little worry that tried to cram its way into my head. It was noon and I could shake Howard awake and do as I pleased for twelve hours, get the hell off the rig.

To my surprise, I found Alix in the logging trailer, talking to Howard who was, by some miracle, awake. He sat stiffly upright at the plotting desk, proudly pointing out what I had plotted that morning as if the work were his. He was saying, "Yep, you can see that drillin' break plain as day, an 'en 'ere's the shale again," blurting out what was obvious. He had the boiled flesh of the alcoholic, and flat eyes that looked like they were painted onto the front of his cylindrical head. As he spoke, his mouth opened and shut like a slash in an inner tube, sputtering fetid gases.

The trailer moved slightly with my weight as I stepped in.

Alix looked up. "So, are we through the Frontier Formation?" she asked, nodding at my sample bag.

"Yeah, no sandstone in the cuttings. This sample is all shale," I answered, plopping the mess down beside Howard. He let out a barely audible sigh, his spare tire deflating further.

"Fine," Alix said. "I'm going into Meeteetse. Would you like to come with me, Emily?"

Her sudden friendliness stopped me cold. What did she have in mind? And I didn't like being called Emily.

"Sure," I muttered. "Right now?"

"Yes, I want to beat the luncheon rush at the Blue Ribbon Cafe," she said.

I stiffened at her slight sarcasm and was immediately furious with myself for caring what some gold-plated bitch from the East thought of any inch of Wyoming. And why had she chosen this moment to notice that I was alive?

Alix made a gesture toward the door.

I took a red pencil and marked the bottom of the chart, noting where I had left off so I wouldn't get blamed for Howard's slothful work. Howard stared out the window at nothing. Grabbing my keys, I barked, "I'll drive."

Alix followed me out the door, catching up to me easily on her long legs, without seeming to increase her stride. She said, "Are you sure you wouldn't like me to drive? My car's right there."

"Yeah, I'm sure," I snarled, jumping in and cranking the truck's big engine to a roar.

As we pulled onto the dirt road that led away from the rig, I automatically reached up to adjust the rearview mirror from where Howard had left it, and caught the reflection of Chet coming down the steps from the rig. It was just a passing image until I saw that Alix was looking steadily into the mirror on her side of the truck. *Caught you,* I thought.

We topped a little rise and turned right onto the bigger dirt road that served the main part of the Bar Diamond Field. Pumpjacks moved slowly up and down on the wellheads, their heavy counterweights rotating with every draw. Alix and I rode along for a while in silence, bouncing on the seat springs.

After a while, Alix made some conversation. "Did you log any of these wells, Emily?"

"Yeah, the 17-1, Bill's other new one, last summer."

"I see. So is this all Bar Diamond Ranch land?"

"No, most of the oil field is under Bar Diamond Ranch, but those wells along the hills to the east are on BLM land—Bureau of Land Management. Government. Oil fields don't know about things like property boundaries."

"Of course. I understand the Tensleep Sandstone is particularly thick here."

"Yeah, nearly three hundred feet." The Tensleep Sandstone is one layer of a vast sheet cake of sedimentary rocks that have been deposited across western Wyoming. In places, the Tensleep is over four hundred feet thick, but its surface was eroded into shallow hills and valleys before the next layer of the cake was deposited on top. Later, the whole works was warped and wrinkled as mountain ranges thrust upward through it. And here and there where the Tensleep buckled into domes, oil seeping through its myriad pore spaces boiled upward and was trapped. "That's a lot of oil reservoir. Of course, people have been pumping from that horizon since the 1940s, and from shallower horizons since the 1920s. The field was starting to decline before Bill Kretzmer came along."

Alix changed the subject. "Are those the Hawkins' cattle?"

"Yeah." That struck me as a somewhat stupid question, but I magnanimously make allowances for these Eastern dude types.

"Oh. Well, how many head do they have?"

"Don't know. Takes about ten acres a head in these parts. Drylands ranching." I watched a golden eagle rise from the ground over to the right, riding a rising shaft of air in effortless delight.

"How many acres do they have, then?" Alix continued, making a detailed study of the back of her right hand as she spoke.

I'll be damned, she's pumping me about Chet Hawkins! My mind raced through the implications. *Quick departure for town. Smooth. Don't hang around and look impressed. And take a chaperone along, and better yet, another woman with information. How slick.*

I riffled through my mental file cabinet for something that would really knock Alix off her gilt-edged pins. "They measure it in sections out here," I answered, referring to the mile-square system of surveying used in Wyoming. "Six, maybe eight."

Alix didn't seem to have much to say the rest of the way into town.

4

When we returned from town, I found Ed Meyer, Blackfeet Oil Company's chief operations engineer, in my trailer. I cursed my luck, wishing he'd go the hell back to his office in Denver and stay there.

No luck. Ed Meyer didn't vanish in the puff of mental smoke I willed upon him. He sat in the tiny kitchen area talking with Howard, who sat right where I had left him, the soggy sample bag still by his foot, unopened. With Ed were Merle Johnson, who runs the service company that does most of the maintenance at the field, and two of Merle's roustabouts, Hank and Tim. Merle nodded to me, his aging face as mute and impassive as granite on the side of a mountain. Hank appraised me frankly through insolent bedroom eyes, his unshaven jaws working rhythmically over a wad of gum. Tim didn't look up.

"Well, if it ain't my favorite girl mudlogger, ha-ha-ha-ha-ha," Ed cried through his flashy, tooth-filled smile. "You been out gettin' a bean with my favorite girl geologist, I see."

I froze. My eyes focused on Ed's right hand. The son of a bitch was fiddling around with the fossil snail I picked up when I was saying my good-byes to Bill. I contemplated squishing his head. I said "Hi," out loud and inside my head I allowed myself a good, *Fuck you, asshole, and don't call me girl,* as I struggled to control my facial muscles, pursing my lips so I wouldn't bare my teeth and snarl. One does not mouth off at the Chief Operations Engineer. Not if one wants to stay employed. Everyone else, the drillers and roughnecks, the tool pusher, the mudloggers, you name it, we're all subcontractors to Blackfeet Oil, working like so many communal peasants to get a job done; but Ed, like Alix, is the Company Man, the lord of the manor. The Geologist is the wizard with the dowsing rod, ultimately answerable only to the success or failure of her technical decisions. But the Chief Operations Engineer makes all the purchasing and contracting decisions—the money decisions—on all of Blackfeet's drilling projects. Ed had contracted this whole job; every nut, every bolt, every inch of pipe. On this rig, he *was* Blackfeet Oil.

Ed squinted at me as he leaned back in his seat by the kitchen table and spread his knees apart. He tipped his head back and hoisted his cigarette to its lofty roost above his chin, took a drag and exhaled, holding the cigarette away from his lips. Smoke formed a veil around his face, dimming the polished glow of his store-bought tan, lingering near the artfully combed tendrils of his thinning hair. As his hand wavered beside his face, the light caught the facets of a large diamond set flush in a heavy gold ring and glimmered off the expensive fabric of his jacket, which he wore pushed up from his wrists. He smiled at me appraisingly, puffing on the cigarette and pulling it away again, showing me his teeth several times. His other hand described a lazy circle on his stomach, which was starting to sag and spread with the ravages of his forty-some-odd years. He started to jiggle one foot up and down in its highly polished snakeskin cowboy boot. "So, what you girls been up to?" he asked, in a voice that seemed to curl around my neck. He extended his foot out toward my feet.

Hank sneered.

I prepared to make myself scarce. "Oh, gosh," I said, snapping my fingers and looking as preoccupied as I could, "I knew I forgot something!" I spun around and hurried out of the trailer.

I heard Ed mutter, "Spacy little number," to The Boys as the door swung shut. They laughed.

I holed up in my truck, but I could still hear Ed's voice

booming out of the trailer. The monologue he was treating his captvee audience to turned quickly to the subject of Bill Kretzmer. I heard Ed say, "Well, who needs geologists anyway. All's they do is stick their shitty little noses into all the good work we're tryin' to do here, messin' things around with their 'what-ifs' and 'about-thats.' I tell you, I ain't got much use for 'em. Bunch of rock jockeys. Pebble pimps, ha-ha-ha-ha-ha. And shit, he wasn't so much of a geologist, anyhow. The Tensleep Sandstone reservoir here at Bar Diamond Field is about played out, but to hear him, the 17-1 here we drilled last summer was going to be a barn-burner. 'Come in at virgin pressure,' he says, like he thinks he's an engineer or something. Old fools at the Board meeting sat there sucking it up like it was gospel. So I says, 'Leave reservoir pressure predictions to the engineers, fool; that old Bar Diamond Field's a good old cow, but she's about milked out.' So we drill the goddamn well, and what happens? She's a dud, just like I said. Lucky if she pays out. Forget it. God knows how he sold the Board of Directors on this well we're drillin' here now. I just wonder who he had to sleep with."

My blood didn't just boil, it steamed, it vaporized. I couldn't stand hearing Bill spoken of in that way. Bill was one of the best geologists that ever hit Wyoming, and no one knew the Tensleep better. As Ed griped on and on, I thought longingly about how Bill brooded over his maps and well logs, glowering out from under his heavy eyebrows, fiddling with those long brush mustaches of his, pawing back and forth through the file boxes he brought with him to the rig, refiguring this and scratching his head over that, making his little cryptic notes as he read and reread every paper ever written about the Tensleep Sandstone.

I rolled up the window so I wouldn't have to listen. It was past time for me to turn in, but tired as I was, I knew better than to sack out in the truck. It would have been too obvious, guaranteed to draw more flak. And there was no way I was going to climb into a bed with Ed Meyer in the

next room. In desperation, I set out for Alix's trailer, and
tapped lightly on the door.

"Come in," I heard.

I hadn't been inside that trailer since the night of Bill's
death, when I had encountered Willie Sewell and his phantom light. I pulled the door open, hoisted myself up the
steps, and looked in. Inside I saw the familiar pseudo-
wood-paneled, claustrophobic space with lumpy synthetic
curtains half covering chest-high windows. Alix sat
sprawled across the settee at the end of the trailer, cradling
a coffee mug against her stomach. A paperback lay open on
her lap. One long leg rested up on the cushions and the
other stretched toward me on the floor. Her boots were set
neatly by the door, and I could see her toes through the thin
spots in her gray socks. She raised one eyebrow, like a
schoolmarm.

"Um," I began, with my usual articulate flair, "well, Ed
Meyer's in my trailer and, well, he looks like he's going to
be there a while, and I was wondering if I could stretch out
here for a few minutes and get some sleep." I struggled to
squeeze my voice out, cursing myself for having emotions.
If I had been wearing a cap, I'm certain I would have
doffed it and clutched it humbly to my chest. People do certain things for each other in the oil patch, but I had never
made such a request of a Company Man before, even one
who was a woman.

"Say no more," Alix replied, smiling a faint smile. She
made an elegant gesture with her hand, one fluid motion
taking in the room and all its contents, the room beyond
and its bed, bestowing them all on me. She looked pointedly at my feet. I smiled and stepped out of my shoes.

"Thanks," I said.

"Pull the door shut and take the lower bunk. I'll wake
you at midnight."

I did as she said, pulling the flimsy fake-wood door shut
against the protestations of its skewed frame. Alone in the
dim closeness of the sleeping room, I stretched my arms up
with pleasure, pulling my spine up to its full five foot five-

and-a-half and then rising onto my toes. My knuckles hit the ceiling. I climbed onto the foam mattress of the lower bunk and, burrowing under the musty sleeping bag that lived there, I found that there were sheets on the bunk, and a pillow to put my head on, one that had a pillowcase on it. It was even clean. I sighed. *Alix, I owe you one,* I thought, as I sank into deep sleep.

Sometime after dark, loud voices in the outer room wakened me. One was Alix's. She spoke very loudly and clearly, enunciating her words sharply as if speaking with someone old and hard of hearing.

"I said no. I have work to do here. Do go on to dinner without me."

At first, the other voice was indistinct and muffled. It rose and fell in pitch. The sense I got from its tone was one of cajoling, now ha-ha funny, now with a slight edge to it.

"So kind of you to think of me," Alix's voice went on, in powerful, hearty tones, expertly changing the subject. "Will we have to change muds when we drill through the Sundance Formation?"

"FUCK the Sundance," came Ed Meyer's voice, clearly now. There was a short silence, and then his voice came again, back down at a more normal volume: "Can't leave a lady without a friend on a Friday night! Aw, c'mon, Alix. Ha-ha-ha-ha-ha." His volume dropped further, his tone more rich and vibrant. I missed a sentence or two, then the volume rose again: "Y'know, we have a real nice professional relationship established here. That's real nice for both of us. Course, now, what we have for a *personal* relationship could be a whole lot more . . . You never know. Could be real, real nice. It's all in what we want to make of it."

Alix's voice came back, in the same declarative tone. "I've heard that some drillers have had really bad problems in the Sundance about a township south of here. The rock is very poorly cemented. You may want to heavy up the mud."

"You come to dinner, sister! Or are you sick of this job?"

"Of course, the Sundance probably is well cemented here and won't give us a problem, judging by past wells, but we won't know until we get there, and I *could* point out to the Company president that you're drunk on site."

Two heartbeats later I heard the front door crash outward against the metal siding. The trailer lurched as heavy footfalls rang off the metal steps and thudded away into the night.

5

As I leaned over the shale shaker on the catwalk on the side of the rig to catch the sample for 4380 feet, the sun rose over the distant badlands, spilling out golden across the stiff prairie grasses, kindling each tuft of sagebrush into stark relief against its blue-gray shadow. The banded hills to the east showed muted tints of the strong maroons, creams, and blues I would see at mid-day. To the west, a waxing moon was setting beyond the crests of the Absaroka Mountains. The season's first meadowlark pierced the morning air with its melody, lifting its heart in competition with the moan of the rig motors.

I walked back along the catwalk to the drilling floor, where business went on as usual, the great Kelley bushing turning the drill string under the power of the deafening motors. The upper end of the drill string fed slowly through the Kelley bushing—a two-foot wide by one-foot tall doughnut of metal turned by the rig motors—as the bit, thousands of feet of drill pipe beneath my feet, gnawed steadily into the earth, chattering now and then as it hit hard spots. The entire rig, with its 120-foot-tall derrick, its five diesel-electric motors, its monstrous draw works, its thirty-foot-long doghouse warming hut, and its web of railings, catwalks, and ladders, vibrated steadily in the still morning air.

I swung open the Dutch door of the doghouse and bellied up to the standing desk. Above it, there was a bulletin board with the obligatory government announcements concerning employees' rights, thrice-Xeroxed cartoons, and that raunchy Ridgid Tool calendar with its well-fleshed, tool-loving babes who wore bathing suits year-round. Next to that was the radio telephone. Bud, the driller for the midnight-to-eight a.m. tower (the word they use for "shift" in the oil patch), stood at the desk, supporting his considerable girth against its front edge as he updated the driller's log. I compared my depth record to his.

"Don't drip that slop on my foot," Bud rumbled from deep within his mammoth innards. He flashed me an incomplete row of stained teeth as he laughed at the absurdity of being careful with his filthy boots.

I laughed and made gestures of embarrassment, offering to clean his toe off with my cuff.

"Right!" he roared, pulling his rubbery lower lip tight over a wad of chewing tobacco. Laughter made him cough, and he spat tobacco juice into a Styrofoam cup. "I got another pair to home needs cleanin', too. You charge reasonable rates, sweetie?"

The morning light slipped through the canvas bunting that shrouded the sides of the drilling floor, growing stronger and stronger, washing out the banks of fluorescent lights that had glared against the moonless night during the pre-dawn hours. Bud cuffed a switch with one of his great fleshy hands, killing their greenish glare for another day. I walked back across the drilling floor and went down the stairs by the main draw way to the pipe yard, jumping down the final short flight onto the muddy ground.

Johnny stood in the doorway of his trailer, his face lit up orange in the dawn. He beckoned me over to join him. I dropped the sample bag on the step of my trailer and did so.

"They're having a memorial service for Bill today," Johnny said. "Fine day for it. Fitting."

My heart lurched. Maybe it would be in the afternoon, and I could attend. "Where?"

"Denver."

To cover my disappointment I asked, "How do you know?"

"His widow said. Nice lady."

"A lady? Bill was married to a lady?"

"First class."

That was hard to imagine. Bill had been a pretty rough-cut individual. "How do you know her? I don't remember her ever visiting him here."

Johnny's voice grew husky. "I met her in town, when she came for his body. I took her Bill's things from the trailer."

"So you were the one who cleaned out Bill's trailer?"

Johnny shot me a look of sharp curiosity, his leathery skin tightening at the corners of his eyes. "Yeah."

"Oh. Where did you put his papers?"

"His papers?"

"You know, his files, maps, and stuff."

"I don't know. There weren't any papers. Just his personal effects from the sleeping room. You know, clothes and so forth."

"When did you take his clothes?" I hadn't looked in his sleeping room that night. Perhaps they had still been there when Willie and I met at three a.m.

"The next day." Johnny's eyes narrowed further. "Why do you want to know?"

"Just wondering. Did you notice anyone—"

"Slow down, Em. Maybe one of the guys from the Cody office took them."

"Were they there that night?"

Johnny stared at me. "What are you talking about?"

I tried to downplay it. "Oh, nothing."

"Bull." The jovial, nice-guy-but-not-overly-smart persona that Johnny usually showed the world vanished. I contemplated making some excuse why I just had to break off our conversation—a nature call, something like that—but Johnny had turned full toward me. I knew that posture: It meant he would have his answer, thank you, and *now*.

"Okay. I just noticed that the papers were gone."

"When?"

"Oh, three a.m., when I sort of um, stopped by. They say Bill died at, what, nine or something. I mean, that's pretty fast work."

Johnny sighed in exasperation, and I wasn't quite sure what he found so exasperating, me or the subject. "Those were Blackfeet's papers. Proprietary stuff. They wouldn't leave them lying around."

Now it was my turn to say *bull*, but I decided to say it in my own way. "Bill never locked that trailer. Those papers were lying around every time he went into town. And it seems strange whoever took them didn't clear it with you, Johnny."

Johnny replied, "I reckon you're right, Em." But that was all he said. He turned away. I went back to my trailer and prayed I hadn't pushed things too far. I was banking on the delicacy of Johnny's position to keep him quiet. A tool pusher is on the rig to keep things running smoothly, not to help foment controversy.

A few minutes before eight, the peace of the site was shattered as Frank and the rest of the day crew arrived, wrestled into their coveralls and slammed their lunch pails into their lockers in the doghouse. Thus the rotation of eight-hour drilling tower continued, 'round-the-clock, day-in-day-out, until the well would reach completion. Acceptance of this fatiguing schedule lived in the quiet pride in each man's face. *We have jobs,* their faces sighed. *Thank God we have jobs.*

The night crew dragged their gear out of their lockers and headed for their trucks, and their six packs, and their long drives home. As they were maneuvering and clashing gears in the pipe yard, Ed Meyer topped the rise in his company Oldsmobile, charged into the yard, slammed on the brakes, then turned off his motor and lounged behind the wheel smoking the rest of his cigarette. Hank Willard, Merle Johnson's hand, sat in the seat beside him, sipping coffee from a Thermos cup. After fifteen minutes, Ed gunned the engine, backed out of the yard, and drove away. It was a classic Ed Meyer strafing run. "*In*specting what you *ex*pect," he always called it.

The grind and roar of the rig motors went on and on.

I went on about my business. The drilling crew went on about theirs, moving pipe, maintaining the rig, mixing drilling mud from fifty-pound sacks, moving up and down the stairs and ladders and along the catwalks like so many ants maintaining their ant hill.

At nine o'clock I was at my desk in my trailer, peering at the latest sample of drill cuttings under the binocular scope, confirming ad nauseam that we were indeed still drilling through foot after foot of drab gray shale, listening to Howard snoring softly in the back room as his body struggled to pump the alcohol out of his system quick before he woke up and sluiced some more in, when a dark blue pickup rolled into the yard. Chet Hawkins got out, wearing his Sunday-go-visiting hat, a black Stetson with a handsome array of pheasant feathers forming a half-disc above the brim in front. He knocked on Alix's door, and she stepped out to chat.

This time the breeze was from the right direction, and I heard almost all of the conversation.

"Hello there, Alix," he said, "Just passing by, thought I'd see what was what." He put one boot up on the back bumper of her car, skewing his athletic frame so he could lean an elbow on one knee. He looked as if he had just stepped out of the shower, his good looks and high coloring gleaming pure health and good intentions.

Alix shifted her clipboard from dead center to one side of her breasts and smiled. "So, what is what?" she asked. They smiled at each other, and then both broke into charming laughter over nothing and everything.

Chet grinned. "So, Alix, about that horseback ride you were wanting. I think I might have found you a mount that won't throw you off into the first prickly pear cactus."

"Sounds do-able."

"How about tomorrow morning?"

"Hmm, that's Sunday. I think I might be able to get off for a bit."

"Good. I'll take you out to that BLM land. Maybe we'll see those wild horses I was telling you about." He straightened up and shifted his weight to the other foot, showing his muscular thighs and flat stomach off from another attractive angle.

"Sounds good," said Alix, straightening her spine prettily. "And you must take me to that sage grouse drumming ground, too."

"Well, awright. I expect they'll be drumming, Alix." He leaned his head toward her, smiling broadly. "Alix. I like that name."

Shit, Alix, I thought, *sage grouse isn't all you're gonna find drumming out there. Sounds like the hominids are in rut, too.*

As the everyday pace of my shift wore on, time began to drag. The soft colors of early morning grew harsher as the sun climbed higher in the sky. The irritation of too much coffee blighted my capacity to concentrate on drawing the shale symbol on foot after foot of the log, and I found myself dreaming of the day we would punch through the carbonate rocks of the Phosphoria Formation and on into the lovely sandstones of our objective, the Tensleep Sandstone. That day would spell release for me, an end to a well that wasn't any fun anymore. We'd drill out the Tensleep, and there would be nothing left for me to do. I'd be towing my company's trailer out of the yard as the casing pipe rolled in on the flatbeds.

The roar of the rig motors began to invade my mind, tearing at me, gnawing like a chain saw. The reek of solvent from my cuttings trays, mingled with the cloying odor of Howard's stale cigarettes, threatened a headache. It was getting to be one of those days when I truly hated my job.

I stared at the cuttings, all cleaned up and laid out in the sample trays by ten-foot depth intervals beside the binocular scope. I willed them to turn magically into Tensleep chips. If the first Tensleep sample had a good stain of oil that streamed when I hit it with solvent, I'd drive into town and buy a round for the house at the Elk Horn Bar, in Bill's memory.

Bill. What happened to you out there, my friend? What

made you miss that turn? It was going to be sad, biting into the Tensleep without Bill. He had been so excited about it. He had planned to run in with a core barrel when we reached the top of the Tensleep, the pay target. A core was the ultimate peek at the beast, a four-inch cylinder of living rock. As the draw works raise it from the bore hole, the sample is still steaming from the warm depths of the earth, oil oozing and bleeding from its fractures, vugs, and laminations. It is marked and wrapped and hot-shotted to a laboratory, where men stay up into the night to plug it and test it for permeability, porosity, and saturation. For the geologist, who must usually rely on indirect clues like well logs or distant outcroppings of the rock formation, a core is like a love letter from Mother Earth herself.

But we probably wouldn't cut a core now. Ed Meyer would declare that it was too expensive.

Nostalgia overtook me. I remembered an evening Bill had pulled a thin book out of his file box and showed me maps of the way the geography of Wyoming looked three hundred million years ago, when the Tensleep Sandstone was a blanket of sand dunes beside an ancient sea. "Have you ever seen the Tensleep where it outcrops near Hyattville?" Bill had asked me. "Over there against the Big Horn Mountains, where it's been pushed up and eroded out to the surface. It's like a fucking time machine, like you're walking around there by the sea, strolling among the sand dunes. A sea of sand beside the sea. You can see the crossbedding from the dune slipfaces, where the layers of sand lapped one on top of the other as the dune migrated downwind, just like it happened yesterday. We'll be able to see the same cross-strata in the core . . . at least, until all that oil oozes out and covers it up!" He had cackled maniacally, mustaches flaring, then leaned back in his chair and sighed. "The Tensleep is a beautiful sand sea," he'd mused, slipping unconsciously into the primordial past as only a geologist can. "Imagine, sand dunes from here to Colorado. Do you know how she got her name?"

"There's a town of Tensleep, right? Was it named for the rock, or the rock for the town?"

"The rock for the town. There's a little spring in a canyon over in the Big Horn Mountains. The Indians used to camp there on their way through to Laramie. The spring was ten camps—you get it?—ten sleeps from where they were headed."

As Bill spoke, my mind had slipped back also, flying back past the long-abandoned Indian camps, back through hundreds, thousands, then millions of years, his words changing in my mind's eye to a blanket of sand hundreds of feet thick and hundreds of thousands of miles square, now thousands of feet thick and hundreds of thousands of miles square, now thousands of feet beneath us, buried under ages of other deposits. *What secrets does she hold?* I had wondered. *What riches of understanding will emerge when we awake the Tensleep and tap her ancient hidden soul?*

The peculiar suite of grinds and squeals that heralds the connection of a new stand of pipe to the drill string brought me crashing back from the Pennsylvanian Era into the present day. Automatically, I marked the log, recording the connection. *Ninety more feet of pipe in the hole. How boring. What a bad pun. Fuck me.* Presently the sound of the motors changed again as the Kelley bushing started to turn the pipe again.

Then a scream of metal snapped me to attention. I jumped up and ran to the door. Outside, the rig's guy wires lashed violently. The derrick trembled. I saw the roughneck named Emo hurrying down the ladder from the derrick, shouting something I couldn't quite make out. I hurried onto the rig.

I found Johnny and Frank encased in a terse debate. Not much was being said but a whole lot was being communicated. They stared bitterly at the Kelley bushing, which lay motionless, indicating that the drill string was at a standstill. I collared Wayne, who muttered something like, "That fuckin' mud."

Right, Ed was running a strange mud. That, and the fact

that there was an emergency right after a pipe connection—a time when the drill string would have been hanging dead still in the hole without moving for several minutes—told me that the mud must have dropped its solids from suspension while the pumps were shut down for the pipe connection. The solids had set up like concrete, freezing the bit, and Frank had found this out the hard way when he started the Kelley bushing turning again to turn the drill string. I found out later, by asking Johnny, that the elasticity of the four-and-a-half thousand feet of drill string had absorbed three rotations of the Kelley bushing before its torque translated to the bottom, at which point something had broken free with a violent snap.

I edged closer to the driller's brakes. Frank's eyes were wide with worry. Johnny murmured, "I ain't kidding. I never seen a bastard let go that hard. Well, come on, Frank, you think it broke?"

Frank's jaws worked with tension. After several moments he replied, "I don't know. Only one way to find out. Why the fuck did Meyer have to run this fucking weird mud?"

"Yeah, another Ed Meyer special."

Frank eyed the big dial across the drilling floor which indicated how much weight was on the bit, and how much of the drill string weight the draw works were holding up so that the string wouldn't collapse under its own weight. "If it broke, it's pretty far down," he said. "That's about what she weighed before it happened."

Johnny shook his head in worry. "Oh well, start her up, Frank. Let's see what we got."

I held my breath. We couldn't afford a broken drill string. The previous well had gone over cost, and its production rates were so marginal that Blackfeet had almost canceled this second one. Suddenly this job I'd come to hate mattered terribly to me. It mattered not only because it was Bill's well, but because everyone out here depended on its success for their continued employment. Things were bad in the oil patch; investors were scared, and rigs that had enjoyed back orders for years were stacked up in contractors' yards. Here in northwest Wyoming, where times were already hard for cattle and wheat, this new drilling at the Bar Diamond Field had been a tremendous boon. This one well employed nineteen people full-time: three five-man drilling crews, two mudloggers, a tool pusher, and a geologist. It contributed mightily to the incomes of the myriad employees of companies that supplied the rig, as well those of mud and pipe salesmen, drill bit suppliers, surveyors, backhoe operators, cement contractors, and wireline loggers. It increased the flow of cash through the tills of the motels, laundromats, cafes, saloons, filling stations and shops in town, not to mention those of the cattlemen and truckers who supplied them; and it would provide future work for every field engineer, roustabout and pumper in the area.

Frank put his big hands on the brake. He bowed his head. There was nothing for it, no way to find out if the string had broken except to start the Kelley bushing turning again, and the longer he waited, the more firmly the mud would imprison the bit. His shoulders tightened as he gingerly eased off the brake. The Kelley bushing turned once, twice, three times, four. The weight on the bit held steady. Frank caressed the brake, his eyes closed. All was well.

6

Just after noon I was handing the work over to Howard, who sat heaped in his chair, observing the charts through bloodshot eyes. The door banged open against my drill bit doorstop, and in stepped Ed Meyer and Merle Johnson. "Hey, hey, it's that cute little girl mudlogger!" Ed whooped. "So, whatcha doin', sweetheart? Crossin' your T's and dottin' your I's? Ha-ha-ha-ha-ha."

I said, "Hi, Ed. Hi, Merle." You already know what I was thinking.

"Hey, ain't this a cute one," Ed chortled, bending to heft my bit. Right then I truly wanted to kill him. A four-inch completion bit is a badge of honor in the oil patch. They don't just hand them out like gimme caps; they're rare and prized. And this one was mine; the foreman of Bar Diamond Field had given it to me as thanks for helping him get his truck out of a ditch. Now Ed Meyer had his perverted hands all over it. I looked daggers and shrapnel at his paltry brain case until he put it back where he had found it.

Merle nodded to me and sat down, his thick torso and legs settling into their customary quiet. He examined me through his pale eyes for a moment, then shifted his gaze to the window and contemplated the day outside.

Gesturing toward the chart on the work table, Ed sneered, "So, little girl, what you figure out for us this morning?"

Howard lurched onto his feet by sections, holding the chair back for support, concentrating, his cigarette shaking in his mouth with the effort. He smiled a tiny bit of poison at me and indicated with a sweep of his hand that the hot seat was all mine, winked unctuously at Ed, staggered aside, and summarily dropped his bulk in the seat next to Merle. I sat down at the desk and cleared cigarette ash off the chart.

Ed moved over behind me. He leaned so close to me that I could feel the heat of his breath against my ear, and the reek of used tobacco smoke assaulted my nostrils. He squeezed my shoulder.

Saliva went thick in my mouth. I tried to swallow but couldn't, and hated myself for not knowing even a little what to do to stop him. Fighting to control a tremor that was developing in my hands, I pointed out the changes in lithology on the mud log, cross-correlating it with the drilling speed break where we had come into the shale.

"Real nice, honey," Ed cooed.

"Thanks, Ed." Tension forced my voice to crack and boom out much louder than the situation warranted, surprising us both. Ed abruptly backed away and sat down, sprawling his knees left and right. He started telling a joke, something about women with "tits the size of eggs. Fried eggs. Ha-ha-ha-ha-ha." I quit listening. I'd heard him tell that so-called joke before.

Merle coughed quietly. He was a grayish-looking man of about fifty. His gnarled hands and sturdy build spoke of heavy labor on the rigs and in starting up his oil field services company. Feeling my eyes on him, he shifted quietly in his seat, crossing his cowboy boots at the ankles and leaning forward onto his left elbow. He rested his face in one meaty hand and clasped his mouth, twisting the seams in his face into a new arrangement, and trained his sky-colored eyes on mine.

Johnny Maxwell stuck his head in the doorway from ground level. "Ed, got a minute?" he called.

Ed got up with a sigh. "Back in a sec," he said, striding out the door with his brow knitted in a look of fatigued importance.

"Could you use a cup of coffee, Merle?" I asked, nodding my head toward the percolator on the counter.

"Sure." He got up and poured, sipped with concentration.

I fished around for something to talk about, finally commenting on his belt buckle, which was a large silver thing with a saddle on it. It was old enough that I couldn't quite make out the engraved inscription on it. "That buckle a rodeo trophy?" I asked.

"Mm-hm." He nodded, and gazed out the window, unsmiling.

Having ridden the barrels myself, I know quite a bit about rodeo, but I just couldn't get Merle talking. He seemed such a mannerly guy that I found myself feeling sorry for him, having to put up with Ed's adolescent bombast to make his living, but something about him suggested it all just flowed past him without getting him wet.

As I was thinking this thought, Ed burst back into the trailer. "Just can't do nothing without me around here," he said. He sat down again and sighed, emphasizing the extremes of effort he suffered for his job. He lit up another cigarette and started telling dirty jokes again.

About four jokes and accompanying machine-gun laughs later, there was another knock at the door. I hollered, "Come in," and in stepped Willie Sewell, all bristly red hair, coppery freckles, and startling green eyes. He stared defiantly at each person in the room in turn, and when he got to me, his eyes looked a question, too. I shook my head as subtly as I could, to reassure him that I hadn't told anyone that I had seen him in Bill's trailer that night.

Willie took off his cap. He was covered with crude oil and dirt, and kinked himself around awkwardly to fit into the low room, exaggerating his spindly, narrow-shouldered build. "Oh, ah, Mr. Meyer," he said, "ah, I'm havin' a bit of trouble with well number 17-1 again, you know, the one we drilled last summer. Ah, that metering valve went down again last night. I don't know how much got pumped while it was out. I don't know how long it wasn't registering." He tucked the forefingers of each hand into his hip pockets.

"Aw, hell, Willie," said Ed. "That's twice this week. Shee-it. Can't you keep that sumbitch goin'?" He inhaled and blew a long thin stream of smoke in Willie's direction.

Keep it going? I thought, appalled that Ed would automatically blame the problem on Willie. *Why don't you stop
to ask yourself what makes the metering valve on a brand-
new wellhead assembly go out? We only drilled that well
last summer—*

Willie's face clouded. "Well, I got it running again,
that's not the problem. It's just that I rebuilt it good as new
three days ago, after the last time it went down. It was right
as rain. So I can't figure out—"

"Like hell, Willie." Ed put the heel of one boot on the
opposite knee, stuck out his chest, and leaned back.

I almost rose from my seat. *This guy's asking the right
questions, Ed,* I wanted to say. *Don't be so fast to muzzle
him, you self-serving asshole.*

Willie's posture tightened. "I was thinking someone
might be—"

Merle stood up. "Come on, Ed, Willie's a smart boy.
Let's go get a look-see at what he's trying to tell us."

And then come back and tell me. Just what was Willie on
to?

With great ceremony, Ed took one last drag from his cigarette and flicked it into the sink, all the while raking Willie
with a cold stare. Then with a sigh of irritability loud
enough to carry to the back row of the biggest theater on
Broadway, he heaved himself to his feet and headed for the
door, snarling, "Awright Willie, let's go see what's up with
your goddamn meter."

Merle followed Ed out the door.

I followed them with my eyes, wishing I could slip unseen into the back of his truck and get a glimpse of what
ailed that metering valve. Did this have something to do
with Willie's appearance in Bill's trailer? What could be so
important about a broken metering valve that a lowly
pumper would risk the wrath of the head man?

I sat there fidgeting, wondering about Willie. He was
very young. His heavily airbrushed high school graduation
portrait graced the wall of the A&W Root Beer stand in
Meeteetse, along with those of the seven other members of

the previous year's senior class. He stared formally at the camera, mortarboard straight, tassel dangling beside his set jaw. Underneath the photo, a piece of paper was neatly tacked up, "Valedictorian" printed in curly letters. The portrait next to his was one of a slightly plump girl with her hair combed at an extreme slant across her forehead, a battery of braces decorating her nervous smile. Between the two pictures was a third, smaller one of Willie and the girl hunched together, he in a tuxedo with the collar gaping, she in a wedding gown, poorly fitted and dripping with cheap, machine-made lace. The slip of paper underneath this one read, "Willie and Dinah, August 10." Still another photograph, smaller yet, showed Dinah in front of a Christmas tree, holding a tiny baby, smiling so brightly that her braces blasted the flash-bulb glare right back out of the picture.

Pumpers like Willie are a lonesome brand of oil field worker. They spend most of the day alone, far down a dirt road at the edge of a field, pumping the crude oil from the tanks by any wells that aren't hooked up to a pipeline. They fuss and fume over their charges, pleading and screaming at the disintegrating equipment on these outback units, wielding wrenches and twisting baling wire to keep them going. I'd heard Willie was fanatically proud of his beat, coming out to check on his wells evenings and weekends, sometimes with Dinah and the baby riding shotgun in the pickup truck and a favorite hound standing braced in the back, tongue rolled out and panting.

I watched out the window as Willie's truck scrambled out of the parking area, whip antenna thrashing, Ed at the wheel. I was glad I hadn't told anyone about seeing him in Bill's trailer, but now more than ever I wanted to know what he'd been looking for.

I resolved not to wait any longer for chance to provide me a meeting with Willie. Ed Meyer might have him now, but Sunday at noon, when I got off shift, I would search him out and have that talk.

7

Sunday morning, Chet Hawkins drove up in one of his daddy's shiny new pickups, all smiles, pulling a trailer carrying the Appaloosa and a nice bay mare. The mare was even more beautiful than the appaloosa, and between the horses and Chet I was a goner. I chanced a fantasy that Alix would be busy, and Chet would ask if I wanted to go riding instead.

But then Alix Chadwick, famed ingenue of oil patch and points east, stepped from her genteel forty-foot fully trailable bower wearing the very latest in Levis and Izod casuals, and a brand-new straw cowboy hat.

Chet laughed at the cowboy hat, Alix laughed at her cleverness, he helped her into the truck, and they were off down the back way to the BLM land, the horses' round rumps swaying as the trailer lurched over the uneven road.

About an hour and a half later, I was still sitting there eating my heart out when I saw the pickup returning, fast, without the horse trailer. Chet skidded it to a stop by the rig and jumped out. Stonefaced, he ran up the steps two at a time and rushed into the doghouse.

The other door of the pickup opened more slowly. I saw Alix climb out, her hands on the door, first one foot to the ground, then both. She pulled herself up to a standing position like a woman of ninety, as if she had forgotten how to do it and had to invent each movement anew. But it was the look on her face that got me on my feet, into my shoes and out the door: she looked haunted.

"Alix!" I yelled. "Are you all right?"

Alix turned and watched me for a moment, her brow knotted in confusion.

Out of the corner of my eye, I saw the men on the rig converging on the doghouse, fast.

"Alix," I repeated, "what is it?"

Her face twisted with pain.

"Alix?" I took her arm and began to lead her toward her trailer.

The men came off the rig running, eyes rich with excitement and worry. They ran as a pack, calling orders back and forth, dividing up some important task that had catapulted them from the ordinary. Chet came briefly to Alix, touched her face, and said, "You okay?" then to me he said, "You take care of her, Em. I can depend on you, right?"

Of course you can depend on me, I thought, managing to mumble, "What happened?"

Chet's eyes flared with a mixture of excitement, anger, and perhaps—what was it?—fear. He suddenly gripped me by the shoulders, surprising me with unexpected intimacy, and stared closely into my eyes. "Dead man," he said, then just as suddenly he was off to his truck, firing the engine, two roughnecks climbing in beside him. "Frank's getting the sheriff on the rig phone," one of them hollered out the window to me as Chet wheeled the truck around, then, "Check see if he needs any help, Em."

I felt dazed, yet oddly, amplified by shock and Chet's attention. Changing plans, I steered Alix over to my trailer, coaxing her up the steps and inside. She lowered herself onto the settee.

I pulled back a smudged panel of the wallboard I wasn't supposed to know was loose and grabbed one of Howard's secret bottles of hooch, unscrewed the cap, and poured a dash into a coffee mug. I put the mug into Alix's hands. She knocked it back, coughed violently, and winced. Then her eyes reddened with tears.

I dampened a length of paper towel in the kitchen sink and blotted her face with it, first her forehead, then both cheeks, dabbing away until she fought the towel off with a confused hand.

"Tell me," I said.

Alix yanked the towel out of my hands and sank her face into it. At last she began to speak, her voice muffled through the sodden paper. "I'd—I wanted to see the wild horses on the BLM land. He—Chet—took me there. We followed tracks from the horses, but then we saw a truck. And a body. It was, he was crushed. Trampled by the horses. His head was caved in. His chest—"

"Who was it?" I asked.

She put down the paper towel and rocked herself gently, hugging herself, eyes squeezed tightly shut.

"Chet said, um, somebody Sewell."

My mind spun away amidst thoughts of red hair and freckled skin spoiled by clotted blood, of green eyes staring unseeing at the vault of the heavens. Of a young wife with braces on her teeth and a baby in her arms, trying to understand why she was suddenly alone.

Alix ripped a fresh towel off the roll, straightened up, and blew her nose. It was time to leave her to herself. I told her I was going to check on Frank up on the rig.

She nodded abstractedly, as if we were strangers finishing a casual conversation while waiting for a bus. I left her alone to recover her pride.

When I reached the doghouse, I found Frank hollering into the radio telephone. Duane and Emo, the two hands who had not gone with Chet, were doing their best to pace the floor in the narrow room. Emo muttered, "Poor Dinah" under his breath. "Poor Dinah. Poor Dinah." Like it was a mantra.

Frank was shouting, "Yeah, it was on BLM land, but get me the sheriff." Struggling to hear the reply, he pressed the earpiece farther into his flesh and jammed a thumb into the opposite ear. "Damn it, Cheryl, we got a problem out here by the rig, and I want the sheriff. No, I don't want the Federal nitwits. Now, you get your officious little ass off the line and get Ben Lewis on."

Duane and Emo nodded in agreement. Duane took a mock swing at the telephone.

"Ho, Ben," Frank went on, "got a problem out here at Bar Diamond by the Hawkins 4-1. Yep. Can you come? No, I'm afraid we don't need no ambulance. Been a while I guess, but you might bring the coroner. Yep. Yep. Oh. No, I think it best not to name names over the air. Yeah, I got a couple men out sitting with the body. No, Johnny Maxwell's up in Greybull, won't be back 'til this afternoon. Yep. Okay, see you soon." He hung up the receiver and looked around at us. He said, "There's work to be done, fellahs," and signaled me to follow him onto the drilling floor.

I followed him through the Dutch door and over to the brakes. He grasped a lever and yanked it, resetting it from idle to automatic, turned back toward me, and tagged my arm with the tip of one finger as he headed for the stairs to the pipe yard. In one of those moments of hyper-awareness that come with the shock of emergency, I found myself sharply aware of the place where he had touched me, and realized that it had been a very long time since anyone had touched me in friendship.

On the catwalk we could hear each other without raising our voices. Frank studied my face with concern.

"She okay?" he asked.

"Alix? Yeah, I think so," I said. "She's pretty tough, or at least self-contained."

Frank nodded, absorbing the information like a doctor listening to a recitation of symptoms.

"She had a good cry, and I gave her a good snort of Howard's poison."

One corner of Frank's mouth twitched.

It startled me how easily the words tumbled out of my mouth. I had never before let myself speak as candidly with any member of this rig or any other, let alone felt this fully invited to do so. I chatted with Johnny a lot, but that was all it was, chatting, swapping information for the advancement of the job. He was the tool pusher. It was his job and his professional disposition to shmooze comfortably with every and any member of the assemblage of riffraff subcontractors necessary to make the job go. But this was Frank, a driller for heaven's sake. I heard myself saying, "So I hope she's let the worst of it out. But I don't know, maybe she pulled herself together a little too fast. I wonder. I guess there's not much more can be done for her now. I guess it was a pretty bad sight."

"Hm," Frank murmured, his lips tightening. He looked away for a moment. When he looked back again, I had the sensation of looking into a deep well, so deep that I couldn't see the bottom. "Sheriff's on his way," he said. "I'll need your help when he gets here."

"Sure."

"You could help him with Alix. Kind of ride along so she can show him where Willie's body is, see he doesn't get too rough with her with his questions. He doesn't always think." Suddenly awkward, Frank said, "He was in Viet Nam with me. He's seen too much." He glanced away again. "And, um, please just see they look after Willie right." His jaw muscles bunched up fiercely and his brows drew tight, his eyes fixed on the western horizon.

I wondered what he saw: perhaps the mountains, but I thought also that he stared at something in his mind's eye, something much farther away, years removed; a dark and troubling something that reached for him still, from a hot, humid jungle more than an ocean away.

I said, "Sure, I'll look after Willie."

Frank let out a caged breath. Presently he nodded and went back up the stairs.

Despite Frank's attempts at discretion, news traveled fast. By the time the sheriff arrived, thirty minutes later, two more pickup trucks had pulled up to the rig with citizen's band radio whip antennas flailing. The first man out from town was Elmer Tripp, who stepped out of his truck and locked his eyes on me, the first person he could find, and said, "It's Willie Sewell, ain't it." More a statement than a question.

I nodded.

"I heard he gone missing," he went on. "Been hearing it on the CB all morning. Ain't like him to be away without tellin' nobody." He slid his hat off into one hand, revealing an almost hairless white scalp that changed abruptly to brownish red an inch above his brow. He sagged sideways against the door of his truck and stared at the ground. "Shit," he muttered, under his breath. I could just hear the sibilance of the *s* and the stop of the *t*.

The next truck to arrive was brand new, its polished dark paint and absence of dents bragging that it was a Bar Diamond Ranch truck long before it pulled up close enough that I could see the logo on its door. Garth Hawkins himself stepped out and pulled himself up tall, his back as straight as a Marine Corps colonel's. He smiled a mirthless smile of greeting at Elmer, showing a row of teeth too perfect to be his own. *The boss is here,* his actions said, *you all relax now.*

Then Sheriff Lewis rolled up to the rig, sitting high and stiff in the seat of a Chevy Blazer with a large Sheriff's Department badge emblazoned on the door. Having never seen the sheriff before, I braced myself for an even bigger man, maybe six feet three or four, guessing by the height of his head and shoulders in the cab. So I was surprised when he stepped down out of the cab and kept on going down, his long torso mounted atop a pair of legs better suited to a much shorter man. The long band of his uniform necktie exaggerated the effect, and he walked stiffly, elbows out sideways and arms braced away from his body to make room for the thick tooled leather of his Sam Browne belt. His eyes shot this way and that, like he was daring anyone to snigger.

Maybe it was just a reaction to the stress of the moment, but as he walked toward me, I fought to repress a smile. Even with his cowboy boots and rod-up-the-ass posture, I was looking right over the brim of his hat. I couldn't see his eyes until suddenly, as he moved closer to me, he snapped his chin up to take me in. I involuntarily looked him up and down, my mouth a thin line against impending mirth.

Luckily, Frank came down from the rig and drew his attention. He said, "Ben, thanks for coming."

"Sure thing, Frank. Now, how about you tell me what's going on."

Garth Hawkins drew near the conversation, half-blocking me from it as he turned his back to me and folded his arms across his out-thrust chest. "Right, what's happening here, Frank?" he said, his voice resonant with the expectation of a central part in the conversation.

Frank raised an eyebrow briefly at Garth, turned back to the sheriff, and said, "I don't know much. Garth's boy Chet took our geologist out riding this morning."

"Chet did what?" Garth demanded.

Frank went on, turning his attention more squarely on the sheriff: "And it seems they come across a body."

"Where's that boy now?" Garth sputtered, but Frank talked across his interruption:

"It was Willie Sewell. He was pretty bad, I guess. Chet says he looked like he been trampled to death by some horses. Chet took two of my hands and went back out to keep the birds off. The geologist's here, in the logging trailer."

The sheriff said, "Let me talk to him."

Frank raised one hand and waved it ineffectually back and forth. "Ah, our geologist is a lady, Ben, and she's okay, but she's, ah, had a bit of a shock."

The sheriff glanced back and forth between Frank and the trailer a couple of times, and once at me. "Oh."

Frank said, "This here's Em Hansen, one of our mudloggers. She'll go along with you and Alix—that's our geologist—and kind of help out. Show you the way."

Garth Hawkins cut in again: "See here, Ben, you all just come on back to the ranch. I'll get on the radio to Chet. He can manage—"

Decisively, the sheriff said, "No, Garth, that's just not how we're doing things here." He swiveled from the waist like a doll with only one point of articulation, back and forth from me to Frank to Garth twice, staring at us intently, his eyes bugging. "Thank you, Frank. I'll let you get back to work now." To me he said, "Now, Miss Hansen, could you go get this geologist? Elmer, I think it best you stay here. You get people to stay off these here radios 'til I can notify the next of kin."

As I started for my trailer, I heard Garth assert, "I'm coming along. I got my stock to consider, all you people racing around all over my range, and that boy don't know what he's gone and got hisself into."

"Thank you no, Garth," the sheriff ordered.

"On my land—"

"It ain't your land they're on," Frank interjected, with a trace of vinegar. "BLM. And not your lease range, neither. Belongs to all of us." I wished I hadn't missed the face that went with that voice; Garth struck me as a horse's ass, too.

I knocked on the door before I stepped into the trailer. Alix was sitting right where I had left her, quiet but composed. "The sheriff's here," I said. "Think you can show us how to find Chet? I'll be going along to help."

"Right." She stood up quickly and came outside.

Garth Hawkins already had his truck rolling out of the yard toward the ranch, his speed suggesting a certain lack of respect for its springs.

Alix strode across the yard to where the sheriff stood and stopped at a distance I figured was calculated to be far enough back that her height wouldn't crowd him. No innocent, this girl. "Hello, Sheriff, I'm Alix Chadwick," she said, extending her hand.

The sheriff stared at Alix with his lips pursed, his eyes once again beginning to bulge. Hesitating just a blink, he lifted one hand off his hip, stepped forward, and shook the tips of Alix's fingers. His head tipped back and his eyes grew even wider. "Pleased to meet you, Miss Chadwick, I'm sure," he said. Then he swept his hand toward the Blazer. "This way, ladies."

8

It was almost a half hour's slow drive over a faint, disused road to the place where the horses had trampled Willie. There were a few false turns in the track, but it wasn't hard to follow the earlier tire marks and the trail of bent stalks through the thin prairie grasses. Horned larks flew up from our path, and the sun climbed overhead. Cumulus clouds built steadily in the west over the Absaroka Range, gorging on the warm air, threatening an early thunderstorm.

The sheriff drove along stiffly, back to being a tall man now that he was sitting, his eyes almost level with long-legged Alix's.

"Now, Miss Chadwick," he was saying, "you were out riding, were you, with the Hawkins boy?"

"Yes."

"And you came across the body. Can you tell me the circumstances? Was it just laying there in the grass?"

"Yes."

"On its face or on its back?"

"On its . . . we rolled him onto his back, to see . . ." She clutched her hands together and looked about on her lap for something to concentrate on.

"You *moved* him?" The sheriff glared at Alix.

"Yes, Chet did."

The sheriff shook his head, his eyes starting to bug out. "Well, you say he'd been trampled. How do you know that?"

Alix's voice tightened. "How else could it have happened? His face and chest were caved in. There were hoof prints all around him on the ground."

I reached forward from where I sat in the back seat and put a hand on her shoulder. She was trembling ever so slightly.

"What exactly do you mean, 'caved in,' Miss—"

I broke in. "I guess we'll see pretty soon for ourselves, Sheriff. I can see the fellows up on that next rise. Can't it wait, please?"

The sheriff turned his long torso far enough around in the seat to stare at me for a moment. I held my breath, frightened he'd roll the Blazer.

The men were to one side of Chet's pickup, sitting on the ground. Adrenaline had long since worn off, and they were quiet, fiddling with stalks of grass and talking. They rose to meet us. Chet stepped forward.

"He's over the other side of the truck," he said. "We found his pickup down the other side of the rise here. Keys are in it. We found a blanket in it, so we covered him up."

The sheriff and I climbed out of the Blazer and followed the men around the truck. I noticed that Alix stayed behind.

Willie's fallen form lay under a frayed old army blanket, the shape of his nose and his belt buckle faintly discernible through the worn olive drab wool, his scuffed and cracking boots protruding from the far edge. All around in the powdery dirt was a confusion of tracks: horses' hoof prints, men's boots, and beneath them all, the faint remnants of the marks of balding truck tires.

The sheriff held a hand out to keep everyone back and walked over to the body. He squatted down, his short legs folding abruptly, and tugged up the edge of the blanket, lifting it high for a good look. He reached his hand out and I could have sworn he caressed the body.

I drew near, caught a glimpse of crusted blood and orange hair and looked away. Chet and the others shifted uneasily, jamming their hands deeper into their pockets.

"You rolled him over?" the sheriff bellowed.

"Yeah," said Chet, his lower lip beginning to protrude.

"We couldn't see the blood from the other side. Didn't know right away he was dead."

"These your boot marks, Chet?" the sheriff demanded.

Chet stepped forward. He leaned and looked, and then straightened up and lifted one foot, checking the sole and the print. "Yessir, they are."

"And these big rubber soles, that looks like yours, Wayne."

One of the roughnecks nodded grudgingly.

"And these here ones with the nails in the heel. Yours, Darrell? I can even see where you had 'em half-soled," the sheriff mocked, lightly touching the fine dirt.

Darrell clumsily lifted a boot. "Yep," he said.

"Well, now, you're a fine pack of half-wits, stamping all over the ground right next to a body. You don't even know how this boy died! Shee-it, boys, how's a man supposed to do his job, anyway?"

The roughnecks shifted uncomfortably and looked at each other.

Color rose in Chet's face. "Aw, hell, Ben, we all know he's probably up here rustling them wild horses. Look at them hoof prints. He must've gotten crosswise with that stallion, is all. Look at them marks on his chest! What the hell else was I supposed to do? I for one am sure as hell not going to leave a man uncovered, to get ripped up by animals!"

The sheriff shot him a stringent glance and then dismissively went on with his inspection of the ground. He peered closely at the shoeless patterns of the hooves, then walked over to where the horses were tied to the end of the trailer. He lifted each horse's four shod hooves in turn and studied them at length. Then he straightened up, squared his shoulders, and glared at Chet from under the brim of his hat. He was some distance uphill from Chet, forcing him to stare eyes at a level. With a voice dripping with irritation, he said, "I am inclined to agree with you, Mr. Hawkins. But now, let me make it damn clear to you that in future, you don't never touch a body 'til I'm here. You understand me, boy?"

"Yeah, Ben, I do," Chet spat.

"All right then, let's get him into the Blazer."

Chet's eyes narrowed. He said, "Well, now, Ben, don't you think we should wait for the coroner? I mean, if this is such a big fucking deal, why don't we do it to the letter?"

The sheriff narrowed his buggy eyes at Chet, staring him down for what became a very tedious half minute, then sneered, "He'll get his look later. Now, let's get to it." Turning on one heel of his cowboy boots, he unlocked the Blazer's tailgate to prepare a space for the body.

Alix sprang out of the Blazer and hurried over toward Chet's truck like she was chased by wasps.

I remembered then what Frank had asked me to do for Willie. Instinct told me that it was something no one else would do quite right, that this was somehow a woman's job. *Otherwise why would Frank have asked me?* I reasoned. *Chet has more authority here, and Wayne is older.* But now that I thought about it, Frank's request rattled me, because it might just mean he had noticed I was female. I felt somehow undressed, exposed—and a little irked. *What is it with these guys?* I wondered as I moved toward Willie's body. *First they demote me from womanhood to eunuch buffoon for having the gall to look for work in "their" territory, and now, when things get just a teensy bit sticky emotionally, I'm supposed to spring up like the great earth mother and do the dirty work.* I'd worked damned hard to become one with the wallpaper on this job, and it had cost me plenty. It was a damned limited existence, as confining and hard to account for as waking up one morning packed in cotton wool in a locked trunk.

Summoning courage and trying to sound assured and authoritative while keeping my voice low enough that the sheriff wouldn't notice what I was doing, I said, "Okay, let's get the blanket beside him and roll him onto it." Chet and Darrell and Wayne knelt quickly to help me.

I knelt beside the blanket, wondering what else I was

going to see beneath its dusty contours. I had to force my hand toward it, implore my fingers to close into a grip. I tugged. The blanket slid sickeningly off the quiet form.

My first impression was that Willie was sleeping. I worried that I might be disturbing him. Then a cloud slid away from the sun, bringing out the stark pallor of his skin. My stomach lurched. I thanked my stars that his head was rolled over onto the damaged side. Avoiding looking at his chest, I concentrated on laying out the blanket quickly beside him, spreading it methodically on the ground, tugging it up close to him.

The roughnecks gathered around and we hitched the body quickly onto the blanket. It came stiffly except for one arm, which flopped from the shoulder like a club.

I directed Chet and Darrell over to the far edge of the blanket and motioned for Wayne to grab the corner next to me. Bunching up the edges in our hands, we lifted on the count of three. Willie didn't weigh much for his height.

As we carried Willie's body to the Blazer, I thought thoughts of peace and deliverance, trying in vain to remember any prayer I might have heard the few times I had been to church as a child.

All this time, the sheriff had been wrapped up in the task of rearranging the materials in the Blazer and folding the back seat forward. When he at last turned around and saw what we were doing, he jumped at us, screaming, "Just whose clever idea was this?"

We stopped in our tracks, the blanket suddenly heavy in our hands. "Mine," I said.

The sheriff spoke slowly, his voice low and insinuating, weaving around me like a snake. "Well, this is lovely, Miss Hansen, just lovely. I've always been as ready as the next man to give a girl a chance, but now maybe you can see what the problem is. They just don't understand, do they, what their job is and where they ought to just wait for orders. I do believe we have a little ego problem here, boys."

My throat tightened with rage, and I clamped my jaw muscles. The blanket grew heavier and heavier, and shame built in me with the thought that I might lose my grip and drop my corner.

I may have been intimidated into silence, but Chet wasn't. "Oh for Christ's sake," he said. "Will you get off Emmy's case so we can set this down, *Mister* Sheriff Sir? She's just trying to do the decent thing." With that he shifted forward again, forcing us all to shoulder our way past the sheriff.

We slid the body in kitty-corner and tucked the edges of the blankets around it. I tried to bend the legs up slightly at the knee so the tailgate wouldn't crush the feet, but they were rigid and wouldn't go. In the struggle we realized that though the knees wouldn't bend the hips would, so we rolled the body as gently as possible onto its side and swung the legs across at an angle. Still scowling at me, the sheriff cranked the motor, said, "Just remember, young lady, it's always the maverick as gets cut out of the herd." Then, barking at Wayne and Darrell to bring Willie's truck, he waved me toward Chet's pickup with a gesture like a slap, and drove away.

Exhausted, I stood looking at the place where Willie's body had lain. The marks left in the dust looked to me like some great enormous bird had raked the earth with its wings and talons as it snatched its prey up into the sky.

9

The clouds from the west grew black and loomed closer, consuming the vast blue sky. It was time for me to get some sleep, but I knew I would lie awake fighting a mounting sense of foreboding in the claustrophobia of my trailer, seeing dead bodies on the backs of my eyelids. Instead, I stayed up and sat by myself on one of the racks at the far end of the pipe yard, watching the clouds move in over the badlands, alone and miserable.

The pack of pickup trucks gradually thinned out as ranchers left the gathering by the rig and headed back to their stock and hay fields. The wind picked up, blowing dust and bits of dried grass.

Alix and Chet came out of her trailer, heads bowed in somber communion, and stood talking for a few minutes by his truck, close together. He took her hand and held it for a moment. She lifted it and touched his cheek. Then he climbed into his truck and left.

I could see flashes that spoke of lightning beyond the hills. The wind grew cool and fresh.

Alix tarried in the parking yard for a few minutes, her arms folded tightly across her chest. Then she stretched her neck, raising her head to its usual loft, and looked around. When she saw me, she came over to where I was sitting.

"Hellish business," she said.

"Yeah."

"Chet was just telling me about the way Bill Kretzmer died. I hadn't known much about it. At the office, all they knew was that he rolled his car. Kind of makes me squeamish, two deaths so close together."

"Yeah," I answered again. *Hell, one death makes me squeamish.*

I was growing to admire Alix in spite of the sense of competition I felt with her. Now we were moving inexorably past business-only contact into the kind of relationship that is born between two people who have shared suffering; but much as my thoughts and feelings about the day's events itched for release, I was too unsettled to put them into words. Talking about thoughts and feelings had never been my favorite pastime, anyway. It seemed that every time in my life I'd stated an opinion about anything, someone had been right there to let me know how stupid and ignorant I sounded. And about the last person I would have volunteered an opinion to anyway would have been some Eastern gilt-edged princess who Always Has It Right. Instead, I stuffed my upset down as far as I could and said nothing. I watched the clouds.

Presently Alix spoke again, her thoughts coming out in scraps and pieces. "I guess life goes on," she said. "I didn't know Bill well. I've only been with Blackfeet eight months. There are—were—five geologists with the Company. We worked different areas. I did Colorado and Oklahoma, Bill did Wyoming. But I liked him. He was quiet, kind of moody."

I sighed. This much I could talk about. "I liked Bill, too. He was a really good guy."

"Yes, he was," she said. "A bit hot under the collar sometimes, though. Impatient. Chet says that's what killed him. He says he took a turn too fast."

Here it was, the perfect opening. My chance to lance the boil of my feelings. I could say what I had to say, the very thing I had avoided even thinking ever since Bill had died. All I had to do was say, "I don't think it was an accident," and I'd feel better. But I kept my mouth shut.

"And now Willie, too," she went on. "It's weird, having two right together like that."

I bit my lip.

Alix looked me sharply in the eye. "Emily," she said, "do you think this Willie fellow was really trampled by horses? I mean, do horses do that kind of thing?"

My God, I thought, *she sees it too!* My reticence finally burst. "No, I don't think it looked right either," I began, but then stared at my hands, as if not looking her in the eye made my words less powerful. The words tumbled out easily now that they had started. "And I think the same about Bill. I've had this feeling all along, like it didn't make sense. Sure, he was a hothead, and he was impatient, and he was driving a bum car, but he wasn't tired of living. I saw him take off out of this pipe yard a dozen times and he never hurried, he always slowed for the bumps. You know what I mean?"

"What?" she said. I looked up and met her eyes. Alix was standing straight with her feet planted flatly on the ground, looking at me squarely. When she spoke, she tipped her head slightly to one side. "Emily, I was just asking about Willie because this has all been hard to digest. Understand that I've never seen a man dead before. It was a shock. But you can't mean you really think—"

Shit, now I've done it! I clutched my arms around my ribs in protection and drew away, furious with myself. I had let my need to unburden my foolish feelings seduce me into opening my big fat mouth. And I was angry. I was sure Alix had led me on. But the cat was out of the bag. My thoughts whizzed around like punctured balloons, spitting ineffectual worries. *What will she do, now that she knows what I think? Will she think I'm nuts? Will she tell anyone? What if I'm wrong?* Anxiety swelled my throat shut.

Rallying, I forced a very unconvincing smile and tried to lie: "Aw . . . come to think of it, Chet's right. Yeah. Say, just forget what I said, okay? I'm just feeling kind of rocky, you know?"

Alix said, "You don't strike me as the rocky type, Emily."

If you only knew, Alix. I looked away to the horizon,

scrambling to hurl the focus of the conversation as far away as possible. "Nice clouds," I whined.

"Come on," Alix insisted, "what's this stuff about Bill?"

"What stuff about Bill?"

"I believe you were telling me you don't think it was an accident."

"Who am I to say?" I whispered, closing my eyes in an attempt to make Alix disappear. To me she remained the alien, patrician being from another culture, one of the lucky ones who are not deeply touched by tragedy or hardship. I thought bitterly that the shock of the morning's events would evaporate off her skin like ether, the strength of her breeding repelling unpleasantries before they scarred her.

"Come on, Em. I won't tell anyone."

Shit, this woman's clairvoyant. Okay. Okay, why not tell her? "I just had a feeling, was all. Something in his eyes . . . a fear. Foreboding. Anger. Something wasn't right. And then he's dead." I shrugged. *Not much to go on, when I think about it.*

"And Willie?"

"Yeah and then Willie." I stopped, instinctively keeping the story of Willie's appearance in Bill's trailer from Alix. This was somehow not her business. I continued instead in a more general vein, trying to make a case on his character rather than this specific deed. "I know these country boys, Alix. I may have gone away to school and gotten educated, not stayed home and gotten knocked up like the other girls, but I know how things are. Willie had a wife and kid. Some of these guys get married because they figure that's how life is, you got that girl pregnant and you get married. Or maybe they even do it the other way around. They don't necessarily give a shit. They go on being whoever they were, taking chances, but under it all they take things seriously. The responsibility is real to them, because that's how life is. They get a job and work themselves until they're old and bent as a fence post, never letting on if they've got another thought in their heads. I barely knew Willie, but it looked like he was trying especially hard."

Alix seemed to consider what I was saying. "Maybe the bills just stacked up on him, and he decided to try rustling just this once. I understand it's not considered such a bad thing to do here. Chet says that people rustle wild horses all the time to sell as dogfood."

I shook my head. "Yeah, but you don't do it alone, and not on foot. You just try roping wild horses from a pickup truck some time. It takes two men, at least, on specially trained horses. No, it doesn't stack up right, and there's a million other things could have happened out there."

Alix persisted. "Chet says that Willie probably had a horse with him and it ran off. He could have trotted the horse in there tied to his back bumper and planned to trot a whole string of horses out. That's what Chet said he might do, if he was alone and didn't have a horse trailer. He could keep them under better control that way. That's what Chet said."

Chet this, Chet that. "I guess that proves Chet's never rustled wild horses," I said, fighting a little self-satisfied twist off of my lips. "Chet's had it *easy,* Alix; he's never had to work a day in his life. He wouldn't understand how rough feral animals can be." As I said this, I realized that I had argued myself in a tight circle, now arguing that Willie might indeed have been trampled by horses. Like I say, I hate telling anyone my opinions. It just screws me up.

Alix cocked an eyebrow at me, pursing her lips wryly at my uncharacteristic assertiveness. "Maybe you're just tired," she said. She rolled her eyes. "It's been quite a day."

I laughed one of those little self-deprecating ain't-I-silly laughs. *God, when I try to lie, I get nowhere. When I try to tell the truth, no one believes me.*

"Come on," Alix said, "I'll make you a cup of chamomile tea before you turn in. The very least I can do after all your help with Sheriff Highpockets."

"Thanks, no," I mumbled. "I'm just going to sit here a while longer."

Alix shrugged and started to walk away.

"Alix—"

She stopped.

"You will keep this conversation between ourselves, right? Don't tell Chet or anyone? I—I feel silly." My voice went shrill on the last word.

Alix ran a thumb and forefinger deftly across pursed lips, zipping them shut, smiled, and walked away.

I found that my hands were clenched into fists.

I stared at the towering thunder clouds, wishing they would sweep across the drilling yard and cleanse the scene of my fears, but they seemed to have stalled over the hills. I closed my eyes and let the cool wind wash my face. *Yes, Alix is right,* I decided. *I'm just overwrought. They were just bad accidents, and I'm letting my imagination get the better of me. Maybe I just need a vacation.*

I sat under the darkening sky for a long time, easing into the comfort of these thoughts like a hot bath, my mind drifting along with the rumble of the rig motors.

But little by little my anxieties returned, and I started worrying about the two deaths all over again. I thought I saw a pattern, but there was a piece out of place. It was a slippery and annoying sensation, like seeing something out of the corner of my eye that disappears when I look at it straight. *Cut it out,* I told myself. *Get reasonable. Stay out of trouble. Besides, what teeny little shred of hard evidence do you have that says these weren't just two ordinary accidents that happened to two people working in the same oil field and in the same week?* I jumped down off the pipe rack, ready to call it a day.

As my feet hit the ground, it came to me. The ground. When I had rolled the body onto the blanket, the ground had been dry, entirely lacking in bloodstains, and there had been no grass stuck to the front of the body where it had supposedly rested before Chet rolled it over. I knew then that the body had been moved there from somewhere else.

10

Just as I had supposed, I lay awake in the claustrophobia of the trailer's sleeping room, seeing dead bodies on the backs of my eyelids. Now that I was certain that Willie's death was no mere accident, my uneasiness over Bill's death doubled, and I sensed trouble all around. I tried my damnedest to put the whole thing out of my mind, but the full moon of Easter reached its glaring fingers through a gap in the curtains, prying my eyes open again and again. I got perhaps three and a half hours sleep.

When I went on duty at midnight, I was one cranky mudlogger. Fortunately, none of the men on the midnight to eight a.m. tower questioned me about what I had seen on the prairie. Frank Barnes nodded to me when he came on at eight, and watched me for a while with his usual brooding gaze, but I resisted the temptation to talk to him.

Alix rolled out a bit later than usual. She glanced my way through puffy eyes as she read the driller's log and conferred with Johnny over the details of the morning report to be phoned in to Denver. The roughnecks on the day tower tried to strike up some chatter with her, but after croaking "good morning" to them, she staggered back to her trailer and didn't show her face again for another two hours.

My conscience, or some such organ, began to kick me in the butt, needling me to report my odd meeting with Willie and my observations about the blood to the sheriff. By the time I got off at noon, I had argued myself from *Mind your own business* to *Better make sure the sheriff noticed* and back again at least six times. Willie's late-night visit to

Bill's trailer had seemed terribly private, for all its obvious implications, and I felt a hesitancy to dishonor the dead. With my usual incapacity to avoid trouble, I decided on the compromise of going into town on a fact-finding tour, rationalizing that I would just put an ear to the gossip mill and of course be reassured that the sheriff had noticed the lack of blood on the ground, that he had already declared foul play, and that the cavalry would arrive any minute and straighten out the whole weird mess. As further rationalization, I told myself that I needed to see if I had any mail in General Delivery at the post office. Losing the argument with myself, I headed for town.

It's a handsome drive into town. On that particular Monday, there were extra-nice cloud formations over the Absarokas, and I saw a pair of marmots on a rock outcropping quite near the road. Presently, I bumped across the cattle guard between the dirt road and the pavement of Highway 120 and continued north over the swells and swales of grazing land and sandstone bluffs, crested the last hill, and dropped down past the filling station and the Pioneer's Museum and into the pocket that held Meeteetse's one short block of shops. The walkways that line the road are graced in part by running wooden porches, and the facades of the buildings make Hollywood's back lots look like the fakes that they are. Cattle and oil are the mainstays of Meeteetse's economy, but it does glean the odd dollar or two from tourists hungry for chicken-fried steak or too tired to drive on to Cody. The town has an air not of anachronism, but of lack of interest in things modern. I believe Meeteetse gives no special thought to the rest of the world, any more than a fisherman concerns himself with what species of fish he might find in any stream other than the one he's fishing in at the moment. Meeteetse crouches patiently along the highway, waiting for dinner to swim in from the north or south in shining cars with out-of-state license plates, as the locals slip in and out from east and west. The town fillets its daily catch and rolls it in the same flour and salt as the day before, regardless of how exotic it may be, and tosses it into the same old cast-iron pan to fry. Perhaps it smiles if a given meal is especially tasty, but dinner is dinner just the same.

I parked the truck under the car port at the A&W and went inside. An angular girl with a smooth, freckled, egg-shaped face hopped off her stool and hustled over to take my order. I had seen her there many times and never heard her utter more than "Your order?," but this time she planted both hands on the counter and leaned cross, squinted into my face, dropped her soft mouth open a half inch, and said, "Say, you're Emmy Hansen off the rig out by Bar Diamond, ain't cha?"

"Uh, yeah, that's right, I been in here before," I said, wondering what stretch of vanity possessed the girl to go without her glasses.

"Say, maybe you can tell us—hey Marla! Get over here!—what happened out there yesterday, oh, I'm Cindy Fink, glad to meet ya." She favored me with a coy smile and a sideways nod of her head. The stiff flags of her short, badly abused hair waved a greeting.

A second female of indeterminate age shuffled in quickly from the back room, rubbing the palms of her hands on her apron. She stopped across the counter and observed me unexcitedly through eyes of no particular color, making a noise like, "Hnnnn," her tongue protruding a quarter inch for a moment before it snapped out of sight.

"This here's Marla, my cousin, she's stayin' with me a bit—Jilly, the woman as usually's here ain't here so Marla's helpin' out, kinda."

I was so fascinated to hear a person with a Wyoming accent spit words out that fast that it didn't occur to me to reply to what she was saying.

Having paused long enough to inhale, Cindy continued. "So hey, it's all we been hearin' about all morning, like about Willie gettin' trampled out there and all, y'know. I knew him in high school, though he was a year ahead of me or so, just the same, this ain't so big a town you have someone here and not know 'um, though he lived out on the ranch and I lived here in town, just back there by the filling station."

I nodded my head, which was thickening with fatigue, and prayed for the return of Jilly.

Marla polished the counter top with the hem of her apron, never taking her eyes off of me, never blinking. I considered abandoning ship.

"So hey, what can I get ya?" Cindy asked, leaning forward onto the counter. "So was it awful, was it just terrible, I can only imagine, I've seen a dead body before, my grandmother when she passed away, but that ain't the same, hardly."

"A root beer float, Mama Burger, fries," I said.

"Grill ain't workin' that's why no one's in here but I'll get your float." Cindy twisted sideways from the waist long enough to say, "Marla," and pivoted back to me. "So I hear that new geologist lady found him, her'n' Chet Hawkins, ain't he a hunk, ain't she the luck, them Hawkins got all that land and oil and all, course ol' Garth he just inherited the whole spread, never had to work none."

Marla fast-shuffled down the counter to start on the float.

"Dollar twenty-six cents," said Cindy.

I paid up and Marla brought my float over in a big chilled mug while Cindy chattered away about Chet Hawkins. About two draws of root beer later, I heard a door sproing open and slap shut somewhere beyond the store room behind the counter. Cindy stopped speaking in mid-sentence. Her gaze turned inward with the speed and mastery of a Buddhist monk.

Slapping footfalls and heavy asthmatic breathing approached. Jilly was back. "Lo, Emmy, how's it with you?" she asked, her square face flushed with exercise. "Guess you been having your share of excitement out there, eh? Crying shame about Willie, ain't it?" She put her large hands on the counter and swiveled her head around to survey her terrain. When her eyes lighted on Marla, her lips tightened and she snapped her head back toward the store room. Marla shuffled out of sight and I heard her heft land on some protesting piece of furniture. Cindy meditated upon her fingernails.

"You got what you need here?" Jilly asked. A lock of faded blonde hair flipped down across one temple to her boxy cheekbones, and she tried to herd it back into place by puffing out of one corner of her mouth. "Grill's broke, so's I can't get you a burger. Be fixed tomorrow. So now, Emmy, I heard you went out with the boys when the sheriff went to get Willie. That was good of you. I hear that geologist lady was a bit put out, seeing a dead man and all."

"She did okay, Jilly." Why was I protecting Alix?

Jilly tipped her head forward and raised her eyebrows. "Yeah, I hear she was out for something of a Sunday ride with Garth Hawkins' boy. What do you know. Looking to find herself a cowboy, is she?"

I managed a sly wink as I sucked at my straw.

"Ain't that strange those boys should make such a fuss over Willie," Jilly went on. "They never treated him so good when he was alive. Especially that Wayne. Hell, they was in a fight here out back of the Cowboy Bar not two weeks back. Now, that Bill Kretzmer, he showed Willie a little more respect."

"Oh?" I said, trying to make it sound indifferent, even though my heart was suddenly racing. I'd never seen the two even acknowledge each other on the rig.

"Oh, yes. Why, he had Willie in here for a soda just before closing time. Several times," she added, to make it sound even more important. Jilly leaned forward onto her elbows and glanced toward Marla as if she shouldn't be listening, which she plainly was. "Sat way over there by the door and kept their voices low." She pursed her lips and gave me a knowing look.

This really was interesting. So Bill and Willie had met for a soda in the late evening, a time when most business between men was conducted in the local bars. Either Willie had one overwhelming sweet tooth, or the two had been trying to evade notice. "You catch any of what was said?" I asked, one eavesdropper to another.

Jilly flared her nostrils in frustration, trying to think of something good to add. It was clear they'd been successful in keeping their voices inaudible beyond their booth. "Well, when they was leaving, Bill said, 'Thank you, Willie,' like he was real grateful, but you know, he didn't look happy. He looked like his pet dog had died."

I was sitting there with my mouth open, and quickly closed it around my straw. So Bill and Willie had been confederates of some sort. I realized with a jolt that, odd as Willie's behavior had been the night Bill died, I had never for a moment thought he was doing anything wrong; just, well, disrespectful. So what *had* he been doing?

Jilly was talking along, filling the air with the sound of her own voice. ". . . and it's a sad thing for Dinah, Willie's little wife. She ain't but a girl. Real broke up about it. Got that little baby and all: gonna be rough for her without Willie." Suddenly Jilly straightened up and slapped the counter top. "Hey, you should go over and see Dinah, she be real glad to hear from someone who was there. Tell her how it was and all. C'mon."

I had my mouth full of vanilla ice cream and plastic spoon and couldn't speak, but I managed to pop my eyes wide in alarm. This was not the turn I wanted things to take at all: I was supposed to be an observer, not the main event, and much as I sympathized with Dinah, I was sure I had no place making her acquaintance on the day after her initiation into widowhood. But Jilly moved surprisingly quickly when she felt motivated. She was around the end of the counter and out of her apron by the time I had pulled myself together to swallow.

"C'mon," she said, "it's just down the street here."

"Whoa! Jilly!" I called, "I don't suppose she really wants a visitor right now, do you? I mean—"

But Jilly was already out the door.

There was nothing for it. I took off after her, cursing my mother for teaching me manners. I wished I had spat the ice cream out all over the counter.

Jilly's wheezing worsened. "This'll . . . be good for Dinah," she said, as she slapped her feet down the blacktop. "She's been taking it . . . real hard. Her ma won't let her . . . see the body. You . . . tell her how . . . it really . . . was."

Her hips pumped up and down below the hem of her

sweater as she marched toward a high, narrow, clapboard building with a square facade and a shallow porch. Inside the doorway, on which open knuckles of two hinges testified to the loss of a door, I could see the bottom of a stairway and two locked doors with tin numerals. Jilly huffed inside and stopped by the newel post at the bottom of the stairs, wheezing for all she was worth. I halted outside. Her asthma attack grew worse. "Oh, damn," she said, leaning onto the post. "I stuff . . . down three pills . . . and . . . nothing. Damn."

I waited passively, smelling the stale cooking odors and the faint scent of old, dry wood that gasped from the building. Upstairs, I could hear a baby crying in an echoing room.

Jilly's constriction gradually subsided enough that she could breathe through her nose, but she stood bent at the waist, her eyes gazing unseeing at the third step. She shook her head in frustration.

A door opened upstairs, unleashing the full volume of the baby's sorrow. A hushed voice issued from instructions regarding eating and sleeping. Footfalls worked the boards of the upstairs hall. A middle-aged woman appeared at the head of the stairs. She was a small but muscular woman, with stiff lips and wide-open eyes, wearing sneakers and a knit polyester dress. She clutched the hand rail as she descended, her rigid legs throwing her back and forth with the effort of walking. Lumpy red and blue veins were visible through snagged stockings.

"Oh, Jilly, it's you there," she said.

"Lo, Mary, just coming over . . . pay a call on your daughter. How is the poor dear?"

"Oh, not good, Jilly," she answered, shaking her stiff head. "She won't eat nothing. Won't stop crying, neither." She looked me in the eye, stopping two steps up, so she was looking down at me. "Terrible thing."

"Poor dear," said Jilly.

"Baby won't stop crying neither," Mary went on, still staring at me.

Jilly looked back and forth between Mary and me. "This

here's my . . . friend Emmy," she said. "Wants to pay her respects."

"How do, ma'am," I said, still enduring her stare. She said nothing.

"Emmy here . . . was out with Chet and . . . the boys when they brought . . . Willie in," Jilly said.

"Ain't that how always it is," Mary said, her words clipped and acid. "There's a Hawkins showing off in the middle of everything. More money than brains, I always said."

Just as I wondered how much longer she was going to bar the stairs, Mary launched herself down the last two steps and toward the doorway. "Well, you give her a try, then, see if you can quiet her down. It's a pity. I got to get back out to the ranch, feed her father. He'll be as cross as two sticks without his lunch." She proceeded out across the porch without a backward glance.

Jilly's lungs were still rattling hard. "Aw, hell. You go up without me," she said. "To the right." She waved one arm up the stairs.

"Oh, I'm not so sure—" I said. In fact, I had by now re-signed myself to visiting Dinah: once hurled in a direction, I have trouble turning around, but it was another world to con-quer to think of going up there alone. Jilly waved me through again, this time vehemently, and I started up the steps.

The stairs sagged slightly under my weight, groaning back as I raised my weight from one to the next. At the top of the stairs, I glanced back down at Jilly. She waved me on, like a sergeant bullying a fresh recruit through an obstacle course.

To the right, a door stood open, giving onto a room with a high ceiling and tall, narrow, quarter-paned windows bracketed by stiff white ruffled curtains. Hanging too high on the wall, I could see a familiar, cheaply framed photo-graph of a bride and groom. All was quiet.

"Hello?" I said.

A chair scraped across the wooden floor. Dinah's face appeared from around the door jamb puffy and dazed, but solicitous. "Yes?" she asked. She was tiny.

"I'm Em Hansen," I said. "From the drill rig out by Bar

Diamond Field. I came by to—" I stopped, wondering just why I had come by. It seemed an outrage to be here, troubling this poor delicate girl with the wad of Kleenex clutched in her hand.

"Oh, yes," she replied, in a thin voice. "Thank you for coming. Come in, please." She stepped back and indicated a chair by a steel and Formica table. As I sat down, she pulled a bottle out of a hot water bath on the stove and gave it to the baby who lay kicking and squalling in a playpen in the middle of the floor. She ran a hand along its cheek and swabbed briefly at its nose. Then, straightening with some act of will and dignity, she turned back to me. "I—I really am glad you would come."

"Listen, I'm really sorry about what's happened, Dinah. It must be terrible for you. Is there anything I can do?"

She looked up, her eyes swimming again. Her shoulders heaved once, and then stopped. I touched her arm. It was so *tiny*. She drew a deep breath, crammed her hands down into her lap, her lips set in a tight line. Presently they came open again and seemed to reach painfully for words. "Yes," she said, "there is, ah—something. I—they won't let me see— maybe you can tell me about—no, that would be imposing. I'm sorry." She quickly put the Kleenex back to her nose and started to heave with silent sobs.

Shit. I didn't want to be the one to tell Dinah what Willie's remains had been like: I'd rather be poked in the eye with a stick. But I dutifully surveyed my memory, trying to formulate a diplomatic version of the grisly sight.

"Well, he was—we found him lying in the grass, Dinah," I started, "and he mostly just looked like he was lying down. Peaceful, almost." My mind drifted away and back again. Dinah watched me closely, lips clamped, giving me the impression that she was bracing herself for a lie. I cleared my throat. "It wasn't nice to see him like that. He was a good man." I stole another look at Dinah. She seemed to be bearing up. "His face was badly hurt, on this side," I cupped one hand over the right side of my face. "But the other side was just as you'd remember him. His freckles, and his red hair."

A flicker of a smile played across Dinah's face; tears gathered in her pale eyes. "For the rest, Chet Hawkins had put a blanket over him—" I fought back the urge to say that he had looked like he was sleeping, which would have been an insulting distortion of the truth, "—and I've been told that his chest was pretty bashed up, but I really didn't look. We put him over onto the blanket as gently as we could, and wrapped it around him, and put him in the sheriff's truck." The worst was over. I began to relax. "It was a beautiful day, Dinah. It was a fine, wide stretch of prairie, near the top of a hill, with a view of the mountains. The clouds were wonderful, all billowing up for a storm, with a breeze. It was nice out there." I stopped, suddenly self-conscious.

Dinah began crying again, but this time quietly, and with sweeter tears. She sat straighter, her head high.

A load of questions hung in my mind, such as *When did you last see your husband?* and *Do you know anyone he had a gripe with?* But there was one question I had to ask. "Dinah, what was Willie doing in Bill Kretzmer's trailer the night Bill died?"

Dinah's eyes widened with surprise. "I don't know. He never told me he was there. I mean, I knew he was gone, but—you see, Bill used to come here if they wanted to talk."

That sat me up straight. "What did they talk about?"

"I don't know. They wouldn't let me hear." Dinah's eyes filled with tears again. I rose to go.

"Thank you for coming," she said, flashing her braces in a brave smile. "I'm really glad you did."

"So am I," I said, and meant it. I headed toward the door.

"And Em?"

"Yes?"

"Please—come again. Please." She looked slightly worried again.

"Okay," I said. I headed down the stairs.

I found Jilly sitting on the bottom step, her breathing considerably quieted. "How'd it go?" she asked, eyes eager.

"Fine, Jilly, just fine." I said, as I continued out the door.

11

I felt better, driving back out to the rig, than I had on the way in. Visiting Dinah had put Willie's death in its proper perspective: a member of the human race had died, not a troublesome member of a miscellaneous cast of threatening characters; and he had died with the dignity of leaving behind a mourner with a heart and a soul that would miss him. As Bill Kretzmer had.

I stopped the truck when I reached that bend in the road, and got out to take another look. The ruts and scars left by the rolling car were still plainly visible, and would be for months, even years to come. Only the random wanderings of cows and the slow work of the wind and scattered rainstorms would soften this record of violent death.

My gaze drifted up and down the road, plotting the trajectory of Bill's car as it would have come into the turn and leapt out into the wash. I fantasized proving to the world that Bill's death had not been an accident, but I needed some clue, some watertight line of reasoning—at least something stronger than a character reference. Not for the first time, I cursed my luck at having been born with a brain that functioned by thrashing for long periods in a mire, followed by a occasional split-second leaps to thrilling intuitive understanding. Whatever paltry evidence I had wasn't going to convince a sheriff who stiffened up every time a woman had the gall to try to help.

Why couldn't I have been born with a linear mind which coolly accumulated facts in obvious, predictable sequences? How much easier that would have been, how much nicer for my teachers in school, for my parents, for my employers. "Emily takes after her father," my mother once told my grade-school teacher, emphasizing her point with flourishes of her cigarette. "The Hansens are a fanciful people, forever floating about in the ether. Emily probably believes in fairies, like the Irish."

I looked over the brink where Bill's car had left the road. I would not walk down there again; I had gone once, to say good-bye to a friend. There was no sense in returning.

Instead, I walked to the other edge of the road and had a look at the inside of the curve, where the embankment sloped off a little less steeply, and scrambled down the slope. The upstream end of the culvert projected from the base of the slope. I bent to pull some tumbleweeds from its mouth, stuck my head inside, and gave a good hoot. It gave a so-so echo. Kind of dead.

A cigarette butt lay just inside the culvert. It had been neatly stubbed out, leaving a dark smudge. I picked it up: Marlboro filter, smoked down to a quarter of an inch from the white stuff.

I'd have to have been a moron not to have divined from this evidence that someone had sat there by that culvert and smoked that cigarette, and I was awake enough to consider this a strange thing to find so near a site of such importance, but that was about the limit of my intuition for the day. Like I say, my mind spends excessive amounts of time in the mire.

I stood up and looked about. *Some kid, hiding his habit from Daddy? Who knows.* My mind drifted idly, out of gear. I ambled about, kicking stones over with my toe, breaking a twig off of a sagebrush here, picking up a feather there. By and by I circled back toward the culvert, admiring the crisp imprints left by the waffle pattern of the soles of my sneakers.

It did strike me as odd that my foot prints were so clear but that there were no prints left by the smoker. *Well, I guess that means the cigarette was smoked a long time ago,* I reasoned. *Big deal.* But I did get to looking a little harder, or at least more consciously. Where had the smoker come from? If he had come down from the road, perhaps his prints were lost in the avalanches he had set off. I backed off from the slope to survey it as a whole. From where I stood, I couldn't see the surface of the road. It was at least five more feet above my head, and banked the other way, which was supposed to explain why Bill had gone over the far edge.

I backed off further. The sun had sunk farther toward the hills, casting its golden rays at a low angle to the slope, illuminating the road bank like a monument. Each stone and blade of grass stood out in stark relief, casting a long blue shadow to the east. On this unnatural shape, I saw something that my mind identified as equally unnatural: an interruption of the pattern of the grasses, from the bottom of the slope to the top, making a slight angle from left to right, as if the grass had chosen not to grow in a band two or three feet wide. My mind settled into a petulant chatter, badgering me for showing it something it couldn't understand.

I glanced over to the right, where my truck was parked. The route I had taken down from the road was similarly disrupted, if on a much smaller scale, but wherever I had placed a foot, a small pocket of blue shadow rested in the depression left behind. *Cattle? But what self-respecting cow would climb such a steep bank?*

I turned and wandered away up the draw in search of cattle tracks, and found some a hundred yards away, along a pathway with a much more gradual slope. They were clear and distinct, and turned up draw, not down. A ways further up the draw, they were joined by the tracks of a lone unshod horse. These tracks were indistinct, more difficult to make out, and caught my attention because the only horses I would expect to see within the fenced portions of a working ranch should be shod. Perhaps it was a marauding stallion from the herd of wild horses that lived above on the BLM land.

As I returned to the embankment, the sound of a truck broke the stillness of the afternoon. I couldn't see the road in either direction from where I stood, but could tell the truck was approaching from the direction of the rig. The sound grew louder and louder, but I couldn't see it until it was just pulling to a stop up on the curve, behind mine. It was a beat-up tan pickup. I glanced at my watch. *The day tower coming off; is it after four already? The evening tower must have been ahead of me on the road as I drove in.*

Frank and Emo stepped out. A moment later, a second truck carrying the other three men from the shift pulled up, Emo squeezed in, and it rumbled off down the road.

Now, this was all I needed—to be caught poking around in the middle of the scene of a death. I realized too late that I had picked a time for my investigation with too much traffic, and I had left my truck in too obvious a place. Maybe I felt noble about what I was doing, but I knew better than to trade in my low-profile status for a big bull's-eye target to hang around my neck.

"Everything okay?" Frank called, his voice carrying easily to me on the afternoon breeze.

"Yeah."

He waited a moment. When I said nothing further, he asked, in a quieter tone, "What you looking at?"

"Um—" *What was I looking at?* I was tired enough that I just stood there with my mouth hanging open. I finally thought up an excuse, but it was too late: Frank had started down the slope, following my own steps. He moved easily, his shoulders rolling rhythmically to maintain his balance. He walked quickly right up to me, then abruptly looked away. He looked all about, at the ground, at the sky, at the hills beyond us.

"Pretty out here," he offered, almost in a whisper.

"Yeah," I muttered, knowing I wasn't earning laurels as conversationalist of the year. It was easy for me to talk to the men when we were on the rig, where we each knew our places in the pecking order and had business to hash over, and the social amenities began and ended with oil field humor. But here, on the short-grass prairie I held so dear, in the privacy of my off-duty hours, I was stripped naked of convention and I felt the social breezes keenly. Frank was suddenly real, and I didn't know how I felt about that.

He smiled, just a flicker of a smile that kept his teeth hidden, and stuffed his hands into his pockets, then pulled them out again and picked at the dirt deeply ingrained in his calouses. Suddenly aware of this gesture, he smiled again, this time showing a modicum of teeth, stuffed his hands back into his pockets, and said, "Well, just wanted to make sure you're okay and all."

I smiled. I still couldn't think of much to say.

"And, um—" he went on. "Oh well, I guess that was it." He smiled once more and turned to walk away.

"Frank," I said, suddenly not wanting him to leave. I was embarrassed. He had taken the trouble to be kind and I had been a complete boor. I felt compelled to patch up whatever of his feelings I might have bruised. He turned back. I fished for something to say. All that came to me was the one subject I wanted to speak about least. "Any word on the rig?"

"About what?"

"Um, about Willie." *Shit.* "You know, about what happened. I just came from town, but I didn't hear anything there."

Frank's face crumpled into a frown. He leaned forward from the waist, his shoulders thrust up beside his ears. He studied the ground. I cursed myself for my choice of topic.

"Don't know for sure yet," he said. "Least ways, haven't heard from the sheriff. Course, Ed Meyer's out there telling us what's what." He smiled at that and shook his head. "That guy . . ." He leaned down and picked up a blade of grass. "Well, anyways, Ed says it's an accident with a horse, all right. Says Willie was just a dumb kid couldn't get anything right. You know how Ed is."

"Yeah."

"Course, that's a pile of crap. I've known Willie all his life. Pretty sharp kid, always was. First in his class out of high school, you know that?"

"Yeah."

"Yeah," Frank echoed, his eyes far away in reminiscence. "And dead at nineteen. And Bill, too. What a waste." He tore the blade of grass in two and threw it on the ground.

I said something polite. We started to stroll toward the bank, reaching it right where the weird interruption in the grass cover was, and started up.

"Shit!" Frank said, slipping onto his hands as his foothold slid out from under him. " 'Scuse me, Em. This bank is loose."

"Yeah," I agreed. I was sliding, myself. We looked at each other, down on our toes and our hands like a couple of football players, and scrambled up the bank laughing, slipping and sliding, until Frank happened to cut to the left, into the grass, where he found firmer footing. We clambered on to the top and stood catching our breath. The sun was low over the mountains to the west, backlighting the few clouds. I straightened up, breathing in the sky.

Frank smiled broadly. "I've always liked it out here," he said.

We were quiet for a while, sharing a moment of peace; and for a little while, neither one of us was worried about a thing in the world.

12

Howard was up on the rig when I got back to the trailer. He had gotten only two samples plotted on the log. Cigarette butts littered the floor, and someone had been eating nacho chips all over the top of the plotting desk; a few broken chips had fallen out of the open bag and onto the heavy paper of the log, leaving oily stains. I mumbled, "You bore me, Howard."

Too tired to cope with getting ready for bed, I grabbed the orphaned bag of chips and flopped back onto the settee, numbly stuffing the chemical-coated wonders into my mouth. The bag was down to small pieces, which quickly made a gummy mash across my tongue and down into the crevices of my back molars. I studied the seams in the vinyl ceiling.

Ed Meyer climbed into the trailer.

"Hi, sweetie," he said. "Gettin' comfy there, eh? I like that in a woman, ha-ha-ha."

I froze, nacho-chip-stained fingers halfway from the bag to my mouth, knees gaping. I had slid down so far in the seat that I was lying down more than I was sitting up. *I didn't think I was trying to look seductive*, I thought, quickly straightening up. I swung the mouth of the bag his way, offering him a chip.

He grinned and shook his head and slowly strutted over to the settee, dragging the heels of his lizard-skin boots. As he lowered himself onto the seat next to me, he said, "I'll tell you what you *can* give me, ha-ha-ha-ha-ha."

He draped an arm lazily across my knee, letting it dangle

so that his fingers just brushed the inside of my thigh. Anxiety and the beginnings of shock spread through me.

"You know," he went on, "I been wantin' a chance to get to know you a little better. Good-lookin' little girl like you out here with no one to keep her happy."

I willed my leg to move, but it just lay there, apparently paralyzed. Something wailed silently within my head. Ed regarded me through half-closed eyes, his lips twitching faintly in advertisement of his thoughts. His other hand moved slowly up his thigh.

Finally heeding my call, my leg pulled away from him, and I reached down to scratch my ankle as an excuse for moving. The high ground gained, I moved quickly, rising and crossing to the sink and pouring a glass of water. An electric water pump thudded on. "God, I was thirsty!" I said.

Ed rose, his head rolling back, eyes closing further, and started toward me.

The door banged open. Johnny Maxwell stood on the ground, looking in. "Ho, Ed!" he said. "Mud man's out here. You said you wanted to talk with him abut this change you ordered."

"Right," Ed said, abruptly changing his momentum toward the doorway. The mask of his features flicked from Irresistible Male to Overworked Executive as he passed Johnny and strutted away, a cigarette already moving out of his pocket and toward his mouth.

Johnny gave me a wink and closed the door.

I blew out one long, ragged breath, my diaphragm a knot between stomach and lungs. *Why can't they just leave me alone?* My teeth clenched with anger at the memory of Ed's touch, and clamped down tighter with a thought that wasn't new: *Why did I let him touch me?*

I longed for bed, but couldn't handle the idea of getting out of my clothes just then. No lock on a bedroom door seemed strong enough. I leaned my head against the cupboard for a while, trying to get a grip on my tangled feelings. Through the window I watched as Ed climbed the stairs to the doghouse. All too soon, he reappeared and started back.

I headed for Alix's trailer, thinking fast for an excuse. I could ask her what this mud change was all about. Sure, that would work, I'd just chat business with her for a few minutes, until Ed left the site. I found I was enthusiastic about the mud change. *Maybe the new mud won't settle out as fast, and everyone's job will be easier. Maybe that's why they're changing it, in fact.* The mud change meant one of two things: either they were expecting to drill into superpermeable rock, which would suck the mud right into the formation, or Ed was at last admitting he had run the wrong mud. The pessimist in me started squawking away about how Ed Meyer could be self-serving even when it came to mud changes. What the hell did he think he was doing, running expensive experiments on this job?

Alix seemed serene and fully recovered from recent events, her good old business-only self. She sat at her kitchen table, teapot steaming, scribbling away at her notes. She motioned for me to take a seat and as I took off my shoes, she smiled.

"I hear we're mudding up," I began. "What's the occasion?"

Alix's mouth sagged open that telltale quarter inch. "We are?" she asked.

"Yeah," I said. I was confused. The wellsite geologist is usually one of the people making the mud decisions, or at least one of the first to know.

"What, you mean for the Sundance?"

"Well, maybe. That's where we are, isn't it?"

"Shit," she said.

I had no idea that Alix knew that word. Then I smiled, figuring it must mean she was starting to relax around me a bit.

"That asshole. He's supposed to keep me informed." She ran a hand through her excellent hair. "Oh, well." She rolled her eyes.

This was confusing. Without thinking, I said, "Didn't I

overhear you suggesting to Ed that he change the—" I stopped myself.

Alix stared at me for a moment. "Oh, that's right; that was the evening you slept in the next room."

"Yeah."

She smiled grimly. "Well, yes, but that was just some garbage I stuffed into his ears so he'd cut the nonsense. I thought he was so drunk he wouldn't remember." She tossed her head back and laughed ruefully.

"He probably doesn't. Remember where he got the idea, I mean."

She sighed. "I hope not. Jesus God. Well, maybe it's actually needed. Surprise, surprise." She shrugged.

About then the door opened and Ed Meyer climbed in. Alix observed him with calm detachment. I flinched, in spite of myself.

He lounged with his weight on one leg and took a long drag on his cigarette. "Just thought I'd mention that we just heavied up the mud for the Sundance. Just thought you'd like to make a little note in your little book," he said, flicking the ash on the floor. He strolled across the room and back in a lazy approximation of pacing, never taking his eyes off of hers, never blinking. He loosened his sinuses.

"Thanks for the word, Ed," Alix said, in a voice that conveyed nothing of the surprise or irritation she had just expressed to me. Her tone expressed only relaxed professional communication and courtesy.

I was amazed. Her cool was fully arctic.

Ed took another lap around the tiny room. He flicked his ash again. He watched Alix. She smiled the beatific smile of the Mona Lisa, pleasantly aloof, self-esteem intact and gallons to spare.

Ed took one more lap around the cramped room. The tension built in me even if it didn't in Alix, until I realized what Ed's performance was all about: he had a considerable amount of mud on the soles of his boots, and he was systematically tracking it all over the floor. I wondered if Alix had noticed. Surely *this* would get to her.

"So when do you think we'll hit the Sundance, rock jockey?" he asked her, smiling a little screw-you smile. He glanced at her clipboard.

I suppose he was expecting her to have to dive for the cover of her notes. Predicting when you're going to drill into the next layer of rock is a black art. Thicknesses can vary so much from well to well that most geologists, especially young, inexperienced ones, sweat big bullets over such computations, and recalculate several times when pushed for a number.

"Nine feet." She said, stifling a yawn, and added, "Pardon me," in the quick mumble of unconscious manners.

Ed hesitated a fraction of a second, momentarily without a comeback. "Right, kiddies," he said, glancing at me for the first time since he had come into the room. I believe I stared back at him fairly blankly. He turned and left the trailer.

Alix snickered. "You were right. He doesn't remember," she said. "What an ass; he'll blow the budget."

For a moment, I just stood there, frankly staring at this woman who took the economic future of a whole town so lightly. I didn't know whether I was more repelled by that or impressed with how she'd handled Ed. "How'd you do that?" I finally asked.

"What?"

"Make that call on depth to the top of the Sundance."

"Oh, I just checked it a half hour ago. That's my job."

"Yeah, but . . . well, how sure are you of that depth?"

"Not very. This is my first well out here, after all. And the nearest well is a quarter mile away." She shrugged her shoulders. "This is a new part of the field we're trying to open up."

"But what if you're wrong?"

"Then I'm wrong. A few feet here or there won't make much of a difference in the grand scheme of the universe. I've made the best guess I can from the data available. Worrying isn't going to help me be more accurate." She looked at me quizzically, as if to ask, *So what's your problem?*

"But if you're wrong, Ed will give you unholy shit."

"And? That's not a matter of great interest to me. It has nothing to do with getting the job done."

"Is that how you can stomach his propositions?" I said, and immediately wished I had controlled my tongue. She hadn't exactly tolerated his behavior, after all, and this time, I was sure I had crossed the invisible boundary that she had set between us.

Alix's blue eyes cooled five degrees. "How I can what?"

"Sorry," I murmured. I gritted my teeth, praying that she'd teach me just a little of that cool, hating her for keeping it to herself.

Half a minute passed. I was just about to give up and leave when she said, "Oh, is he starting on you?"

I gritted my teeth. "Yeah."

"Welcome to the club. You have my permission to ignore him."

"How?" I asked. "Shit, he thinks he's God's gift!"

Alix flicked her hand in a gesture of dismissal. "The moon is full. The man has fantasies. Ignore him."

Ignore a hand on my thigh? "Yeah, but—"

Alix's tone grew impatient. "Look, he's predictable: he's got a couple of favorite acts. Don't get cornered. There's the hand on your knee game: don't let him sit next to you. There's the come-to-dinner-with-me game: you're busy. There's let-me-give-you-a-lift—worst of them all, because you have to hear his life story: take your own car." She smiled. "Reassure yourself that it's nothing personal. There isn't a woman in the office younger than his mother who hasn't gotten the treatment."

My heart sank. The callousness of her words hit me like a brick, reminding me what a slow-witted patsy I was. I took a little dig at her. "Is coming in here with mud on his boots another favorite act?"

Alix shrugged.

"Doesn't that bother you?" I asked.

"I suppose it's meant to. This trailer belongs to the Company, not me. I prefer the floor clean, but other people have to use it."

"How can you stand it? If someone spits in your face, do you think it's raining?" I started to tremble, and fought to conceal it.

She smiled mildly. "Em, get a grip on yourself." She raised her elegant hands and laboriously explained what seemed obvious to her, ticking the points off on her long, tapering fingers. "Look, I'm the geologist on this job. He's the chief engineer. On this site, he ranks me. In the Company chain of command I'm not directly answerable to him, but he still ranks me. Two out of two. I've been out of school less than a year, master's degree or no, and he's been in this business since I was in kindergarten. Three out of three. He's simply paid more of his dues than I have, and is my superior as far as this job goes. So what if he's an ass? I don't fight facts of nature. Were I to waste energy on him, I would grow old before my time. Of course, if we go head to head on a point of geology, rather than engineering, he's got another think coming." She turned back to her work once again. "If Ed Meyer wants to be a small person, I can't stop him. But if he must behave like a child, that doesn't diminish me. If I fought him, if I let his behavior matter to me, then I'd be no bigger than he is." She drained the last gulp out of the cup.

I wanted to believe that she was wrong, naive, a dreamer. But mostly I wanted to get away. I made myself a silent promise never, ever again, to get myself caught fencing words with the likes of Alix Chadwick.

As I rose to go, she added, without looking up, "And we'll be in the Sundance when you come on at midnight."

13

Somewhere in there I managed five hours of sleep before going back on duty. Dreams crowded my rest: long walks over tiring obstacles, unnerving people who wouldn't go away. Bombscapes devoid of life. My mother's footprints in the snow among the sagebrush. I awoke thinking of interlocking patterns of tracks on dry earth. What had I been dreaming? I reached back into the void of unconsciousness, but couldn't find the thread of reason. I lay blinking in the darkness for a while, listening to Howard snoring gently by the plotting table. My eyes watered as I got my bearings in the fog of fatigue that filled my body.

Alix had been off by only two feet in her prediction for the top of the Sundance Sandstone, and the bit was now chewing merrily through the sandstone after its long, slow fight through the shales.

I must have looked as bad as I felt, because Frank Barnes asked me if I would like him to get Wayne or Bill to catch samples for me while I got more sleep. I turned him down, figuring it was a bad idea to risk snoozing on duty with all the strange things that were happening on this job, and in retrospect I'm glad I stayed awake. It meant I was alert at ten when Sheriff Lewis drove up to the rig.

Ben Lewis took his long step down out of the Blazer and headed straight for Alix's trailer. Little that I had any desire to cross paths with him, I fought off a weird urge to go help Alix, even though she obviously needed my help like a fish needs a bicycle.

The men on the rig found things to do so they could

watch Alix's trailer. Frank appeared at the top of the dog-house stairs and waited, eating an apple in his brooding way. Johnny Maxwell stood like a sentry on the step of his trailer, sipping coffee.

When he was done with Alix, the sheriff commandeered Johnny's trailer and called each of us in for questioning, one at a time. Johnny and Frank came into my trailer when the sheriff was done with them. "Your testimony is about to be requested," Johnny said, smiling sadly.

"Need I ask what this is concerning?"

He lifted his coffee cup and took a sip, winced, and spat back into the cup. "Shit. I hate cold coffee. Nope, you needn't ask."

Good. The sheriff knows it's no accident. "So, they've found something a little irregular about a certain body found at a certain location near here?"

"It's hard to get a straight answer out of Ben. I guess he takes his job pretty seriously. Don't let the nice man bully you."

"Here comes Alix," Frank said.

All eyes were on her as she left her trailer and strode across the yard, clipboard in hand. She stepped into the logging trailer with her usual brisk movements, nodded pleasantly to everyone, and bent over the log, checking my plot. "How are we coming here?" she asked me. "Any gas kicks in the Sundance so far?"

"No," I said. *Well bowl me over, Alix. You've just been questioned about a possible murder case, and you're asking about gas kicks? Hello! Anyone home?* I glanced at Johnny. His eyes seemed a touch wider than they had been a moment before.

Frank lowered his brows and stared at her. "What did the sheriff have to say?" he asked.

Alix blinked. "He asked me about finding Willie's body."

"And?"

"And I told him what I know, which is not much."

The two stared at each other. Frank looked away as her

gaze dropped. She began grooming the cuticles of her left hand. Johnny took his cap off, ran a hand through his hair, and popped it back on again.

"Yep," said Frank. "Old Ben can get a bit rough sometimes."

Alix stiffened slightly and turned back to me. "So the Sundance is just wet here?"

"No, it looks tight; no porosity or permeability." When Alix looked blank, I added, "You know, as in no pore spaces in the rock means no oil."

"It's always tight in this field," Johnny said, studiously gazing out the window at nothing.

Alix's eyes widened. So much for the confidence act. "Well, Ed—"

"Tight as a tick," Frank said. "Won't hold oil, or drink drilling mud, for that matter. But what Ed Meyer wants, Ed Meyer gets." He sipped his coffee.

About then Wayne thumped his fist on the side of the trailer. "Your turn, Emmy!" he called. "Let's not keep the nice sheriff waiting!"

My stomach tightened. I made an attempt at taking a deep breath and headed for the other trailer.

14

Ben Lewis sat tall in his seat by the kitchen table in Johnny's trailer.

"Thank you for coming over, Miss Hansen," he said, indicating a seat. He observed me with his goggling eyes as I slid into the bench across from him. His hands rested on the table beside a spiral-bound pad that was turned to a fresh page. A pencil lay neatly parallel to the edge of the pad, which in turn lay at a right angle to the edge of the table. His stiff Stetson hat lay on the other side of his hands, neatly lined up so that the front of its crown faced me as squarely as he did.

I smiled timidly, immediately furious with myself that I couldn't just level an Alix-type gaze at him.

"You spell your name H-A-N-S-E-N?" he asked, watching me closely.

"Yes, sir," I answered. *What is this, a test?* My stomach tightened further. I felt like I was sitting in the principal's office.

He picked up his pencil and wrote each letter carefully, in capitals. "And it's Emily." He put a comma after Hansen and wrote my first name in lowercase letters.

"I go by Em."

He nodded, printing "calls self Em" neatly, the deliberateness of each movement grating on my nerves. "Now, Miss Hansen, I have a few questions regarding the death of Willie Sewell. This is routine, in cases of death by unnatural, er—violent causes. You understand?" He paused to make certain that his words had found their mark. I nodded.

"Good. Now, I'd like to know, firstly, where you were on the afternoon and evening of this past Saturday, April the eighteenth."

In the state of nerves I was suffering, the sheriff's line seemed too cliché to bear. I tried not to smirk but just wound up making a weird face, pulling my cheeks back like I was a cheerful chipmunk caught in a wind tunnel with its mouth open. The sheriff's eyes got even larger.

When I spoke, my voice came out a bit squeaky. "I was here all that time. I didn't go into town at all on Saturday. After I got off, I took a short walk down the road, then went to sleep at around four. I got up at midnight, went on duty. I was on duty until the following noon, but you were here by then."

"I see. This walk you took. Where did you go?"

"Not far. Just down the road to the west about a mile. Just stretching my legs."

"You were alone?"

"Yeah."

"Do you walk alone often?"

"Yeah. Nothing special, just get off by myself for a few minutes." Paranoia sprang full-grown in my heart and mind.

"I see." The sheriff's face was nearly expressionless. "Now, Miss Hansen, will you please describe the last occasion when you saw Willie Sewell alive?"

"Well, it was Saturday, just after noon. I remember because I was just finishing up for the day, handing the work over to Howard. Willie came to the logging trailer to see Ed Meyer."

"Ah. And what did he want to see Mr. Meyer about?"

"About a problem with a well. Number 17-1. The valve was screwed up."

"And how is it you happen to remember the well number, Miss Hansen?"

This formality shit was really getting on my nerves. And since when was it a crime to have a good memory? I clenched my teeth, wavering between fear and rebellion. I was just about to start getting sassy when I realized that was just what he had in mind, so I took a deep breath and got myself under control. Maybe Alix's coaching was starting to rub off on me, after all.

"I remember because I logged that well when they drilled it last year," I replied.

The sheriff nodded, inscribed a note. "I see. And how would you describe his mood?"

"Willie? He seemed frustrated. Defensive. I would be too in his position—dealing with Ed Meyer, that is." My mouth was running away with me again. I took another breath. "He's kind of like that most of the time anyway. Was, I mean." How hard it was to speak of Willie in the past tense. Wasn't he in my thoughts now even more than when he was alive?

The sheriff went on to ask me when Willie had left, and with whom. I told him.

"Now, Miss Hansen: about Sunday morning. The Hawkins boy took Miss Chadwick for a ride. Did you see him arrive?"

"Yes. It was ten 'til nine."

"You're sure of that time?"

I stiffened again. "I make frequent notations of the time, Sheriff. It's part of my job to pay attention to drilling speeds." Why did I feel like I had done something wrong?

"And which way did he come from?"

"I didn't see. But he had his horse trailer with him, so he must have come over the main ranch road from his house, south of here. You know, the road that swings south just before you come into the field here."

"So you didn't see him approach."

"No, I was in my trailer here, working at my desk. I can't see much more from that window than the next trailer—Alix's—and the near side of the rig." *And surely you don't suspect Chet!*

"I see." He made more notes, leaving me stewing in my own juices as he carefully made each rising line as straight as cat shit. "And so you didn't see which way they went when they left."

"No. But I presume it was over the north road, like we went when we went after the body."

"Thank you, Miss Hansen. I believe that will be all."

You can't stop now! We're just getting to the important part! What about the condition of the body? And that's not all I can tell you! I stayed in my seat, hoping he would ask me just one more question, any question. But he didn't look up. He sat turning the pages of his notes, apparently cross-checking everyone's statements. "You may go now. Will you please get Mr. . . . . ah, Howard?"

"Mr. Blain. Yes sir," I said, cranky as hell and completely confused. I rose, pausing for just a moment longer. He didn't look up. I left.

When I got back to my trailer, the boys had Howard up and mostly awake, although still in that part of his waking-up routine where he coughs and rattles his adenoids a lot. Johnny got him onto his feet and hustled him out of the trailer with Emo following in his wake lecturing Howard on the importance of telling all the facts, just the facts.

That left me alone with Frank. He was still leaning on the counter by the coffee pot, swirling the now-cold coffee around in his cup. He nodded. I nodded. He looked into his cup. I stared at my hands.

I was beginning to get used to Frank. He didn't usually have much conversation to him, but he seemed to be looking out for me, rather like a big, patient watchdog that lies down by the door to your room and misses nothing; rather comforting, after the exasperation of dealing with the sheriff. By and by I found myself telling him what had happened.

"That sheriff really knows how to get to you, doesn't he?" I said. "I felt like I'd done something illegal."

Frank smiled a small, mirthless smile. "Yep. Ben's like that. He sure takes his job seriously."

"And he doesn't let you ask any questions, either, does he? I mean, it's 'We are on the hot seat here, Young Lady, and we are answering questions, not asking them.' " I imitated the sheriff's goggling stare.

Frank smiled again, this time with laughter in his eyes. He really had a gentle face, when he wasn't brooding.

He said, "What did you want to ask him?"

I shrugged my shoulders, trying to look like it wasn't anything important, but Frank trained his gaze squarely on me, waiting for an answer. After a glance or two into his intent grayish eyes, I crumbled. I said, "Well, it was something I saw when we picked Willie's body up. I just wanted to make sure the sheriff saw it."

"What?"

"Oh, there wasn't any blood on the ground under the body. I mean, here's a guy covered with blood, face and chest all smashed up, but there's no blood on the ground. And Alix said the body was face down when they found it."

Frank put one hand up to his face, began massaging his sinuses, his eyes closed. "It could have soaked into the ground."

"Yeah, but there wasn't any dirt or grass sticking to him, either—to the blood on him, I mean." The look I had taken was a fleeting one, as short as I could manage, but sights like that stay with you. "It was just dried blood. I just wanted to ask him if he'd noticed."

"Shit." Frank folded his arms across his chest and stared out the window. He started to rock ever so slightly back and forth, back and forth. It frightened me. Here was that dark well with no bottom again. Here was a man in pain.

"You okay, Frank?"

He looked over at me as if startled out of sleep. "Yep," he said. Frank shook himself the rest of the way back to the present moment. He said, "Em, let's us go talk to that Ben about this thing," and grabbed me by the elbow and led me to the door.

We found Howard just coming out of Johnny's trailer, a peevish frown on his face. He was mumbling something about getting wakened from a sound sleep for "some sort of bullshit about a punk kid didn't know his ass from a horse's hind end." He just about staggered right into us. "Sorry, Frank," he muttered, shambling away toward one more hour's oblivion. Frank opened the door for me and we went inside.

The sheriff looked up from notebook, pop-eyed as ever, placed both hands on the table as if ready to spring, and barked, "What is it, Frank?"

Frank didn't look impressed. "Ben," he said, "Em here's got something to say that bears listening to."

The sheriff swung his goggle eyes my way. "Miss Hansen?"

"Ah . . ." My voice took a vacation. *Hell of a start, Em. Why not take up public speaking? You're a natural.*

"It's okay, Em," Frank said, so quietly I barely heard him.

My voice returned. "Mr. Lewis," I said, slipping unconsciously into his formal speech. "I noticed something on Sunday which I'm certain you noticed, but I just wanted to make sure."

The sheriff made a show of opening his notebook again to my page.

Look, asshole, you're not making this any easier. Finally mad enough to quit caring if I sounded like an idiot, I got the story out, filling in the business about the lack of dirt and grass stuck to the blood, then took a deep breath and told him about finding Willie in Bill's trailer.

The sheriff rubbed his eyes, breathing deeply.

Frank said, "So what's this about, Ben? You've found something else, haven't you?"

"Damn it, Frank, you know I can't—"

"Ben, there ain't a man out there right now thinks it was an accident anymore, after the way you've come in here with your official act, and now this shit about Willie making midnight visits to people's trailers."

The sheriff looked at him for a long time, but his eyes stayed inside his head this time: his look was harried, not bulldozing. Then he spoke: "This is not good. I've scraped a lot of kids up off the highway. I helped fish that boy out of the canal up Hart Mountain, when his horse fell in and pulled him through the irrigation siphon. Aw, hell, we get them fools shooting each other at the Cowboy Bar; it's not like folks don't die in these parts, or get pissed off and kill each other. But this one just don't make a whole hell of a lot of sense, and that's worrisome."

Frank nodded. He sat caved forward, his elbows on his knees and his hands dangling between them, sharing Ben's silence. I pulled my presence even further inside, hoping they would forget I was there and say more.

Ben spoke as in a trance. "His chest was crushed by horse hooves, all right, but that ain't what killed him. The autopsy showed little flecks of red paint on the victim's skull. And traces of crude oil. The rigor mortis had been broken at his hips and shoulders. And there's some question of which way up the body was when the blood coagulated in the arteries. Just didn't look right for any trampling by wild horses."

Caught up in the trance, I said, "Unless they've taken up as roustabouts and like turning bodies over. All the horses I've ever ridden seem to like to stay the hell away from dead flesh. Spooks 'em good. No, sounds more like some-one hit him with a pipe wrench. I wonder how the body was moved—there wasn't any blood in his truck."

The sheriff popped his eyes at me, ready to bring me into line, but then slipped into thought, his eyes receding into his face like twin camera lenses focusing out to infinity.

The sheriff ordered us to keep mum on the whole mess and left the rig, heading back out to the site where Willie had been found. Frank suggested that I go along, but the sheriff stared him down, saying it was better I stayed out of trouble. Frank stood beside me with his arms folded tightly across his chest and watched the Blazer bounce off down the road and swing to the northeast.

"Funny duck, isn't he?" I said. "How'd he get into law enforcement?"

His expression slid into dark brooding. "He was in the service. Military Police. Viet Nam." His fingers grew tense, pressing into the flesh of his arms.

"Oh. Sorry."

He looked into my eyes, his face revealing a grief that couldn't be contained, his eyes searching my face, taking in small details at random.

My chest tightened. I tried to think of something to say, but words slipped in my mind, out of reach, floating like echoes in a canyon, hollow and faint.

"I better get back to work," he said abruptly, and headed for the rig.

Frank's sadness left me reeling for a moment, but then the rest of his words caught up to me, and I stood quietly, savoring them, taking in the strength of the sun's warmth on my face. *He says I've got a head on my shoulders,* I thought, over and over, *And he says I know how to use it.* The thought was strange to me. It tickled. It slipped around on me like a big thick warm sweater that belonged to someone much larger. I hurried to my trailer to finish up my work. It was almost noon, and I suddenly felt in the mood for a nice long walk in the spring sunshine. I needed time to think.

15

The weather is changeable in Wyoming in the spring. One day the sun shines and the air is still, warming the earth and starting the grass to growing. In the afternoon, a snowstorm can blow down out of the northwest, lacing the ground with winter, showing me why the summer birds haven't yet migrated up from the south. The winter hawks stalk stranded rodents across the white, filling their bellies for their own journeys north.

Much as I love the vast, open space of the short-grass prairie in any season, the spring is the most hopeful time, and the easiest to survive. In winter, the winds dominate the landscape, carving the thin snows into streamlined waves of ice, packing the flying crystals into the fur and flesh of wandering herds of antelope and elk. Cattle huddle in the river bottoms, cracking through the blisters of ice for a freezing draught, gathering around lonesome bales of hay dumped by red-cheeked ranchers. Wheat fields lie frozen for months on end, dreaming of the splendor of green shoots to come. The mountains exalt in their ragged might, drawing the snows together in white robes that will dwindle to hats in the summer's blaze to come.

The summer's heat sometimes exhausts me, settling into the wide intermontane basins with a merciless weight, blinding me with the glare of a tall sun unmoderated by atmospheric moisture. Water becomes a sacred emollient, as volumes of it pass daily through my pores, leaving so quickly that the sweat seldom pauses long enough to be visible on my skin. Armored grasshoppers hang motionless in the glare from blades of grass, and rattlesnakes await the cooler early morning hours to hunt. Afternoon thunder-showers rumble and crash, trying almost daily to dwarf the endless prairie with their might, but until the sudden cool of evening comes, the ground is only briefly moist.

Now it was spring, a season struggling between ex-tremes. I pulled on a thick sweater, a denim jacket, and a wool cap against the freshening breeze, stuffed a sandwich and a couple of carrots into my pockets, and set out across open ground toward the nearest hills. I felt good. The bur-den of special knowledge was off my mind, balancing re-sponsibility with duty performed, loosing me to enjoy the private things I like to do. *What is it, Tuesday?* It had only been ten days since Bill Kretzmer's death and three days since Willie's, but it felt like much longer, so much had I been absorbed by events, so little time had I spent in the privacy of my own company.

My mind played back the events of the past days like a newsreel, ticking off the high points and the low. I had met Alix, one of the most interesting and galling women I had ever come up against. Dealing with her reminded me of too many losing situations I had found myself in at prep school back East, where I had been the one lone low-bred hick in a sea of Alixes. I huffily assured myself that I was not just jealous, that in fact there was something unethical about her.

I shifted my thoughts to Chet Hawkins. Now that we were getting to know each other a bit, something more than a passing acquaintance seemed increasingly possible. He had been friendly during the crisis over finding Willie, downright intimate at times. The electricity of his blue eyes had infused me with a delightful warmth. I speculated cheerfully that he might just be noticing me at last, that my cool-headedness during the emergency had made a favorable impression.

I thought about Johnny Maxwell and Frank and myself, thrown together in a mutual commiseration society, swap-ping pots of coffee as events unfolded around us. I liked this camaraderie, but at the same time I was starting to feel uncomfortable with it, with Frank especially. How many times had it proved dangerous for me to get too close to people I couldn't avoid when I needed to? Johnny was companionable in a way that left me room to protect myself, but Frank was beginning to stir me up, punching through my carefully constructed wall of reserve, visiting me in places I held as emotionally private. At the same time, this intrusion left me looking for more. I shrugged my shoulders hard to rid myself of the thought.

I had reached the collar of sagebrush that flanked the striped hills, and I zigged and zagged between the blue-green branches, raking my hands roughly through the leaves here and there to coat them with the aromatic oils, which I rubbed across my nose.

I scrambled uphill through bands of maroon and blue-gray earth rilled by the flash rains and melt-waters of the seasons. Near the summit, great blocks of sandstone lay tumbled to and fro like the abandoned building stones of a lost temple. I ran my fingers along the sweeping cross-strata etched into their surfaces. I checked one for rattlers. Finding no one home, I climbed on top and sprawled back onto its concave surface to soak up what heat it harbored from the spring sun, pulled a carrot from my pocket, and crunched happily away.

For several minutes I mapped the clouds that skidded toward me over the Absaroka Range from the Yellowstone Plateau. After a while the wind shifted, bringing me the whiff of sulfur from the heavy crude oil of Bar Diamond Field, and the faint growl of the rig motors.

I could see most of the field from where I was. Some pumpjacks humped away at their work, others stood still, held at bay by time clocks until more oil filled the holes. Here and there, a workover rig lolled beside a disassembled pump. Jumbles of filthy holding tanks stood beside outlying wells. Pipelines ran every which way, some gorging on the heavy, tarry crude, others carrying water to injection wells from the pumping plant, a large corrugated metal structure near the center of the field, full of roaring pumps and huge pipes crusted with mineral scale and dripping water. To the south lay the entrance to the ranch, with its huddle of buildings and cottonwood trees. I could see several long, bare lines of fencing whose thin strands of barbed wire bullied the dreaming cattle into staying put.

The Hawkins 4-1 stood north of the field. Bill said the new wells would revive production of the foul, sulfurous crude and make the field economically competitive once again. For some reason, the first one we drilled didn't amount to anything. I hoped the Hawkins 4-1 would prove him right, but I had to admit I wondered about his plan. For decades the Bar Diamond Field had rendered up its wealth like a gentle cow coming in for milking, but now it seemed tired. If Bill's scheme didn't pan out, a great many lives would change, as one by one all the oilfield workers were laid off and moved away, heading toward some city in hopes of a new beginning, leaving their aging parents behind to shake their heads in poignant memory of simpler times.

Life looked strange to me; the economic vantage point of the oil patch has the odd, miniaturizing quality of looking the wrong way through binoculars, reducing everything to a vignette the size of my wallet. The values of commodities are like that; we make money, or we don't make money. Back before 1973, I was as complacent as everyone else, not caring where the oil Dad put in our truck came from. We dried up America's most economical oil reserves as we lazily let our appetite for inexpensive fuels lead us into economic addiction, and more and more oil was imported from the rich fields of the Middle East. Then in 1973, the OPEC nations met and tripled the price of oil, snapping the soft rug of complacency out from under the consumer market.

With the wild surge in market prices over the following decade, the American oil patch was revived. Hot young geologists like Bill stepped briskly into the arena, brandishing fresh oilfield maps still reeking of ammonia from blueprint machines, facing off against the wildmen in the board rooms and the investors' meetings, slapping a pointer down at some favored spot and saying "drill here!" with all the cheer of kids on Christmas morning. Bar Diamond Field and others like it enjoyed a brief renaissance, at least until oil prices started to sag once again. Blackfeet Oil worked over its tired old wells, fitting them up for a waterflood, a project that would pump water down half the wells to bolster flagging subterranean pressures, pushing the oil toward the others. As prices sagged further, even the waterflood made barely enough oil to keep production costs in black ink. So now, in a last-ditch effort to stay solent, Blackfeet was drilling the 4-1.

It was Bill Kretzmer who sold Management on the idea of a few new wells in the rich Tensleep Sandstone, a great victory for him. His efforts had rallied investors to pay for this new well, which would be drilled and tested with all the most modern techniques. In Denver, the investors and the Board of Directors were rubbing their hands together, daydreaming about the profits their gamble would bring them (this time for certain, yes! they could feel it), the avid light of the professional gambler shining in their eyes. But now Bill wasn't here to find out if his brainchild would produce oil.

Here stood the oil rig, the hungry child of their imaginations, still chewing its way into the rolling grasslands. Bar Diamond Field covered almost seven hundred acres, not huge as Wyoming oilfields went, but not tiny, either.

I stood up and began climbing the rest of the way up the hill. The long ride of Tatman Mountain and the absurd twin turrets known as Squaw Teats punctuated the random assemblage of hills and valleys. To the east, I saw an antelope sneak underneath a line of barbed-wire fencing to feed alongside fattening cattle. I thought of the few herds of wild horses that still roamed beyond. I had seen a few of them once, during an especially long walk: they had stood downwind of me, a quarter of a mile away down a long ridge. We stood quietly, facing each other for a several long minutes. I had been so inspired by their presence that I called to them; but at the sound of my voice they turned and vanished beyond the crest of the hill.

As I stood on the hillside remembering this, the sheriff's four-by-four bounced into view from beyond the rise. He pulled a little closer and flashed his headlights in summons.

16

As I reached his truck, the sheriff said, "Would you care to show me where that well is that Mister Sewell was having trouble with?"

I considered giving the surly son of a bitch the Bronx cheer, but my new-found status as an expert witness had gone to my head. I climbed into the Blazer and said, "The fastest way to the 17-1 is around by the main road. I'll tell you when we get to the right turn-off."

"Can you explain the well numbering system to me?" the sheriff asked as we rolled down the road.

"It's called the 17-1 because it's in Section 17, just like the one we're drilling now is the 4-1, because we're over in Section 4."

"What does the '1' signify?"

"That's the rest of Blackfeet's numbering system. Just signifies the order the wells were drilled in each section. There are scads of other wells in Section 17, but they were drilled by other companies before Blackfeet bought the field. Every company comes up with a different way of numbering wells."

"And they're named 'Hawkins' because they're on Garth's ranch?"

"Yes, the 4-1 is. He owns the mineral rights. The 17-1 is the 'Warner 17-1.' Hawkins still owns the surface rights as part of his ranch grazing lands, but he sold half the minerals off. These things get complicated. But I'm just the mudlogger. I don't know exactly what the royalty sheet looks like."

"You seem to do all right for 'just a mudlogger,' " the sheriff said.

That took me aback. Surely he didn't think flattery would get *that* far with me. "Well, I'm Wyoming born and bred. And I've seen the lease map that Bill Kretzmer had."

"Oh? Does Hawkins own most of the rest of the acreage?"

"There's a quarter-section in 8 that belongs to someone named Travis. Hawkins has the surface rights to the whole area, like I said, but not all the subsurface mineral rights. For the rest, it's real chopped up. The map looks like a bulletin board at the supermarket. As far as this new area they're drilling, the east half of Section 4 is BLM land, so if this new area proves out, any wells there would be named 'Government 4-whatever.' And the Government would get all the royalties. Presuming, of course, that Blackfeet can lease the rights."

"Hm. Does Blackfeet have all of the lease rights to the field?"

"No. The royalty owners got together and agreed to have Blackfeet manage the field. There's your turn to the 17-1." We had driven around the north end of the field and down two thirds of the length of the western boundary. The road to the Hawkins 17-1 branched out to the left and ran down a gully. Two cows stood in our way, their stupid snouts turned our way in defiance, protecting their young. The cow to the right chewed placidly behind dribbling lips.

"C'mon, ladies," the sheriff said, tooting his horn. Both heifers turned and ran straight down the road, flushing the calves along ahead of them. Our procession continued in this manner for several hundred feet, until one calf had a brainstorm, kicked its shining heels into the air, and dashed off to the right. The others followed, stopping five feet off the roadway. One heifer fixed a gaze of moronic contempt on me as we passed.

The road dead-ended by the pump jack that serviced the 17-1. The heavy counterweights swung around and around as the enormous "horse's head" loomed up and down, up and down, drawing the sucker rod out of the well over and over again. The unit stood about ten feet high, and rested on a cement pad about fifteen feet long. It looked for all the world like the front end of a giant black grasshopper. A chain-link fence surrounded the pump, the motor housings, and the storage tanks.

The sheriff descended from his side of the Blazer and wandered about, examining the unit from various angles, widening his eyes here, squinting there. "Now, what was it Willie was having trouble with that he came to Mister Meyer?" he asked.

"Ah . . . I think it was the metering valve. That would be over there in that housing." I opened a gate in the fencing and passed through.

The sheriff paused for several seconds by the gate, his arms tense above his gun belt. "Don't they keep this thing locked?" he asked.

"Apparently not," I answered. "I guess the fence is to keep the cattle off. But you think they'd just use barbed wire, in that case."

"You're always thinking, aren't you?" The sheriff actually smiled. It was an odd effect: his mouth curled up on each end, but his eyes didn't join the party.

"Well, anyway," I said, "as I recall, Willie said he had already fixed the valve once, but it was broken again."

"Any idea how long since he fixed it?"

"No . . . no, I don't recall."

"Maybe he didn't take very good care of it."

"No, that isn't the case."

"Now, how do you know that, Miss Hansen?" he asked, his tone solicitous. He was getting downright sweet.

"I can just see by how smoothly this thing is running that Willie knew his job," I said, pointing at the shining sucker rod where it rose and dove into the ground. "Just look at that rod. See how it moves up and down: it doesn't chatter side to side or make much noise. That means Willie was maintaining it well, keeping it adjusted so that it wouldn't wear out as quickly. You see, a new pumping unit costs thousands of dollars. A new wellhead's a mess. This whole collar can work itself loose, break the cement seal, everything. I don't know what that would cost. Willie took pride in his work."

"I see. What does the rest of the equipment do?"

I was beginning to have a good time showing the sheriff around. I began to tell myself that he was maybe kind of an okay guy, that he was only an asshole when he was interrogating witnesses or trying to order people around. So what if his face didn't work. "Well," I said, "this pipe carries the oil off to the holding tanks. This is your free-water knockout, to split off the water that's produced with the oil. This is the storage tank. And I think this would be Willie's valve."

"It records how much oil is produced?"

"No, it registers how much is pumped off from the holding tank and trucked away."

"Why do they have to truck—" The sheriff's question was cut off by the sound of a car door slamming. We both turned quickly, I flinching with the surprise, the sheriff bugging his eyes in the first maneuver of counter-attack.

"Now, what's my favorite girl mudlogger and the good sheriff doin' out on my pumpin' unit?" Ed Meyer asked, grinning widely underneath a pair of sunglasses. He lazily brought his cigarette up to his lips and took a long, sensual drag, stretching his spine like a cat. "Can I he'p you with any little thing?"

I wet a finger. He had come up downwind of us. Smart. To arrive that quietly, Ed must have rolled the car up behind us with the engine cut. Hard to do in a car with power steering and brakes.

Ed and the sheriff held their poses, one pair of dark glasses facing off against another. As the seconds ticked by, the silence gained weight. I grew stiff. Ed took another drag. The sheriff waited.

Ed backed down first, making it look magnanimous, grinning even more wildly. "I was wondering if maybe you were wanting to apply for the job that's goin' vacant, here. Ha-ha-ha-ha-ha."

I sure was getting sick of that laugh.

The sheriff rested his thumbs on the creaking leather of his heavy gun belt. A .357 Smith and Wesson revolver shifted on each hip. "Well, now, Mister Meyer," he said, "as long as you're here, maybe you can answer a few questions."

I watched Ed closely.

"Mister Meyer" waxed chummy. "Aw, well, of course, Sheriff, anything I can do to help." And then waxed concerned, sincere. "All jokin' aside, this is serious stuff happening here. I'm sure we all want to get to the bottom of it, figger out just what went wrong for old Willie and get the poor boy laid to rest."

The sheriff continued to stare.

Ed took another drag on his cigarette. "And then all get along with our work," he said, more forcefully.

I wondered how long this duel was going to continue. I couldn't tell whether Ed's tactics were getting him anywhere with the sheriff or just getting him further into the soup. Several drags later, Ed said, "So ask, Sheriff."

The sheriff turned to me. "Miss Hansen, you'll excuse us?"

I dutifully wandered off a few paces and turned my back, careful to head straight downwind. I hardly missed a word.

"Mr. Meyer, would you begin by telling me where you were this past Saturday afternoon and evening? Just start with the moment Mr. Sewell came to find you in the logging trailer."

I wished I could watch. Ed's expression must have been a pleasure to behold as the sheriff let him know he had already been checking up on him.

"Oh, why, he just came to report to me, as usual. I require that of all my people, Ben," Ed's tone grew confidential, man-to-man. "Got to run a tight ship. Let's see, he wanted me to see what he had been doing since the last time I had inspected his work, so we took a little tour.

Merle Johnson came with us. After that, I drove back to Meeteetse, had a little dinner, then back up to Cody for the night."

"Back up a bit, Mister Meyer. Just what did Willie want to show you?"

"Why, the usual. We toured the wells he looked after. This one, as a matter of fact."

Do tell, I thought.

"Was there anything amiss with this well?"

"Why, yes, as I recall, there was. Ol' Willie had a few problems with this well. We all have, as a matter of fact, ever since we drilled it. It never has produced like it oughtta had. Course, that Willie was a little green. Hired the boy myself, figgered he'd make a good hand, but you never know."

"But what was the specific problem this time?"

"Aw, a little valve trouble. These things are always breakin' down on you."

Bullshit.

"Did you fix it?"

"No, as a matter of fact, it's still broken. Course, we'll have to just quit pumping the crude off this well after a while, if we can't get someone on it, 'cause eventually the tank'll fill up. But not right away. Like I said, this well doesn't produce all that good."

"Did you and Mister Sewell argue about anything on the afternoon in question?"

"No."

"Any words at all, Mister Meyer?" The sheriff let his voice trail off dramatically, leading the witness not too gently toward a more complete reporting.

"Aw, just what a man has to do to keep his employees in line, Mr. Lewis." Ed's voice was chummy, almost clownish.

"I see. And you were in Mr. Sewell's truck as you examined the wells?"

"Ah, ye-es . . . yes we were, come to think of it."

"How long did the tour take you, would you say?"

"Oh, forty-five minutes, an hour."

"And then you went into Meeteetse?"

"Yes, we were good and hungry by then, so we all went in and got a bite at the Blue Ribbon Cafe."

"You went in Willie's truck?"

"Ah . . . yes, I guess we did."

"How did you get back to your own vehicle?"

"How did I . . . oh, let's see. It was a few days ago now. Oh, I remember. Merle had his car there in town, so he and his hand, Tim Cochrane, ran out and picked it up for me. Then I left for Cody."

"That sounds a bit complicated, Mr. Meyer."

"Oh, well, ah, that's how we did it, though. Will that be all, Sheriff?"

"Just one more question. When was the last time you saw Willie alive?"

"Why, just then, at the Blue Ribbon. Sad to think that might have been the poor boy's last meal. Eh, Sheriff?" Ed's voice grew so sweet and sentimental that if my ears had been teeth, they would have rotted.

"What makes you think it was, Mr. Meyer? His body wasn't found until the following morning. He could have eaten his supper and another breakfast by then."

There was a pause.

"Mr. Meyer?"

"Oh, well, I mean, it just might have been his last meal. Well! You know, I'd be proud to think I bought a fellow the lunch that he took to the grave with him. Ha-ha-ha-ha-ha?" The laugh sounded idiotic, almost frantic.

"I believe that will be all, Mr. Meyer. Perhaps you could move your car, so that I can take Miss Hansen back to her residence."

I rose and turned, hoping for a glimpse of Ed Meyer with shit-eating misery on his face, but he was too fast for me, already back in his car and starting it up. I joined the sheriff in the Blazer.

"I believe I have a young lady here with the ears of a jackrabbit," the sheriff said, after we got underway. "What

I mean, Miss Hansen, is that you certainly seemed to know when the conversation was over. What I mean is, I didn't have to raise my voice to call you over to the vehicle here. What I mean is—"

"Right," I said. "I'm sorry, sir. I suppose I should have gotten farther out of earshot."

"Or upwind instead of down?"

"Yes sir," I breathed.

The sheriff pulled the Blazer over to let me off where the road branched toward the rig. "Miss Hansen, before you go, might I make a suggestion?" His voice was caustic, sarcastic.

"Yes sir?" I glanced sideways at him. His face was impassive, devoid of emotion under the reflective sunglasses. I clutched the door handle tightly.

"Don't ever try to make your living playing poker. You don't have the guile. Now run along and try to stay out of trouble."

Fury filled my veins. I had every right to care about what had happened to Willie and Bill. I had every right to want to be involved, to make a difference. Sure, I had opened my big mouth and spoken my thoughts, but how dare he play on my vanity, pumping me for information, all charm and ain't-you-a-smart-one-ma'am, and then tell me to get lost? He could take his ego and stick it where the sun never shined.

I was at last angrier at someone else for asking me to speak than I was at myself for having spoken. And the sheriff's words had backfired: instead of leaving go of the investigation, I was now determined to have my part in it. I wanted to know who or what had killed these two men, and why. An excitement, an interest in what was happening in the world, infused my spirit in a way that I hadn't felt in ages, lengthening my stride and squaring my shoulders as I walked to my trailer.

I scowled openly at Howard as I traversed the cramped confines of the trailer to the refrigerator. He regarded me much as he always did, with rheumy eyes, his expression static and bland. I snagged a can of pop and a tortilla from the meager stores I kept in the refrigerator, heated the tortilla over the burner of the stove, and slathered peanut butter on it. Tortilla and peanut butter: the white woman's contribution to Mexican cuisine. Howard's expression assumed a trace of pain. I smiled at him as cruelly as I knew how and left the trailer.

The sun was still fairly high in the sky, although slipping away behind the afternoon clouds that formed along the peaks of the mountains; but to me it was mid-evening. My day should have been coasting down, relaxed and peaceful. I should have been looking forward to a good night's sleep, or afternoon-and-evening's sleep, depending on your orientation, but I was much too cranked up and angry to relax. I hopped up on the fender of my truck and munched viciously on my tortilla.

17

Alix emerged from the doghouse on the rig and trotted down the stairs, clipboard in hand. The metal steps sang *thung! thung! thung!* as the soles of her boots hit the treads. She said, "So, you're a detective now, I hear."

"What?"

"Ed Meyer's up in the doghouse. He said you're teaching the sheriff how pumping units work, or some such." She smiled expectantly.

I decided to deny it. "He's mistaken," I said.

Alix rewarded me with a quizzical smile, clutching her clipboard in both arms in the manner of a matronly grade school teacher waiting patiently and with equanimity for an explanation from a tardy student, but I was feeling so damn powerful in my anger that I just imitated her smile right back at her.

About then Chet rolled into the lot in his truck. Alix shifted the clipboard into a one-handed hold tight by her side, her spine flexing to reveal a more inviting presence between chin and navel. This maneuver was not lost on Chet as he crunched on his parking brake, hopped out, and came toward us, his long legs carrying him toward us with elastic strides. His eyes were on Alix every step of the way, happily grazing along the warm curves between her collar bones. *Outgunned again.* She was the only woman I had ever seen on a drill rig who had enough guts, power, or outright brass to leave more than the top button of her shirt undone. And on her, it wasn't a shirt, it was a blouse, damn it.

Chet slid a hand up Alix's side, from the elbow to a

place that must have been a little ticklish. "Free tonight?" he murmured.

"For what?" she asked, perhaps a shade too innocently.

"Oh, you know," he answered, good cheer boiling over like a runaway pot.

"Well, yes . . ."

"Meet me down at the pumping plant?"

Alix rolled her eyes. "Okay. Say, six o'clock?"

"Six o'clock it is," he said. He leaned forward lazily on one foot and kissed her on the cheek. I was stunned.

With much the air of having just finished a conversation with any one of the rig hands, Alix turned and went abruptly into her trailer. Chet and I found ourselves standing in the yard, staring at her closed door. Chet turned to me and his face lit up with a smile. Then he reached forward and squeezed my arm. It felt marvelous. He said, "So, ah—Emmy, what's up?"

I'm sure the grin that spread across my face was plenty foolish.

"Nice to see you, too," he said, playfully opening his bright blue eyes wide.

"Ah, yeah. Nice to see you," I said, cheerfully embarrassed. My heart did a triple gainer.

"You ride quarter horses, right?"

"Yeah. Barrel racing. Love it."

"You'll have to tell me more about that some time," he said, as he wandered off to his truck and left.

Half a minute later, Alix re-emerged from her trailer and we had just resumed our conversation when Ed Meyer came down from the rig to speak with her. Her clipboard returned to full armor position in front of her breasts.

"Alix, honey, there's something just slipped my mind to tell you up on the rig," Ed began. "There's a meeting you need to be at in town this evening. At the Pitchfork Restaurant, about, oh, six o'clock. That'll give time for drinks before dinner."

"Oh? I'm not sure I can make it, Ed," she replied, her voice light and airy.

Ed's face tightened, and he barked, "Well, I'm sure you can." When this drew no visible response from Alix, his tone stiffened to that of a parent lecturing a slow child. "Now, you see, this is a business dinner. The representatives from a couple of the supply companies are going to be there, and they're expecting to meet you. We have to maintain friendly relations with these people."

"Gosh, Ed," Alix said, "I thought they had to maintain friendly relations with us."

Ed stiffened further, pulled a cigarette out of his breast pocket, and lit it with dramatic flourishes. He said, "Just see that you're there, young lady," threw the match on the ground, and marched off toward my trailer.

"I'll try," she called after him, emphasizing the second word. Ed shot her a look of pure acid as he yanked open the door to my trailer and stepped in.

Alix turned her attention back to her clipboard as she walked away toward her trailer. I think I heard her say, under her breath, "But don't wait up, Eddie Honey."

18

The blue shadows grew long as I steered the truck over the road to town. A yawn fought its way out of my face. I had waited for Ed Meyer to leave my trailer so I could go to bed in peace, but an hour passed, and he had shown signs of staying until it was time to head out for his dinner party. Instead, I got into the truck and headed toward town to console myself with a root beer float. After the way he had touched me the evening before, I couldn't face the thought of undressing and climbing into bed when he was in the trailer, even if there was a closed and locked door between us.

A few hundred feet after I turned onto the main ranch road from the oilfield road, the truck tugged at itself, hesitating for an instant on its way up a shallow grade. I figured I must have hit a rut, but half a minute later the truck lurched again, harder this time. After I crested a rise, the truck smoothed back into a happy roar down the road.

It occurred to me to check the instrument panel anyway: *Temperature okay, electric okay, gas . . . SHIT!* The truck coughed twice more and died, rolling to a halt as I steered it to the side of the road.

"Fuck you!" I screamed. "Fuck you, Howard! The nerve! Bringing it back from town on empty! You asshole! You unmitigated, drunken, flaming, spherical asshole!" I slumped down in the seat, thumping the steering wheel a good one with my fist. My hand began to throb. *Well, that's it,* I thought. *Things can't get any worse from here. I can relax now.*

Minutes passed. I laid my head against the window and watched the late afternoon breezes riffle through the short, stiff grass. A meadowlark blessed the air with its song. I wondered how long it would be before the crickets emerged and sang. I wondered what the hell I was doing working on a drill rig, living in a shoebox with someone whose brain was so pickled he couldn't even remember to fill a gas tank.

It was three miles back to the rig, and it would be getting dark soon. My heart sank at the prospect of making the hike, of how cold I'd be when I got there. I considered sleeping in the truck, figuring I could curl up in the front seat and set a good, private night's sleep and worry about getting gas in the morning. At my leisure. *To hell with work,* I thought. *Fuck all of this. I'll sleep here until midnight, catch a ride into town with the evening tower, and mail my letter of resignation from Meeteetse in the morning. Then I'll just hitch hike up to Yellowstone, check into the lodge, and go back to sleep for a week or maybe two. Or maybe, just maybe, it would be all right to go home.*

A funny peace settled over me. I knew full well I didn't have the balls. *Balls? If I had balls I would have thrown Ed Meyer out of my trailer. Why, if I'd been born with balls, I'd be a member of the big fraternity! I could get a lot better job than this chickenshit deal, and never again lay eyes on Ed Meyer or Howard Blain, or anyone the hell else! No balls? Hell, that's the whole problem in a nutshell, isn't it? Nutshell?* Laughter hung stillborn in my throat.

Maybe I could go home, said a tiny voice deep within. *I just can't keep this up. I can't make it. Maybe it would be all right to go home this time.* The thought hung in the air like a wraith.

The sound of an approaching car wore into my consciousness. In the rearview mirror, I could see the source of the sound: a big fat bronze Oldsmobile. *Shit! All right, so maybe I'll get a ride to the gas station and get back to work like a good little girl, but does it have to be fucking Ed Meyer?* I heaved myself up straight in the seat, preparing myself for the blow.

As the Oldsmobile rolled to a stop next to the truck in a shroud of road dust, Ed hit the button on his electric window control and the glass slid down out of sight, setting off tiny avalanches of the fine buffy-grey pall of dust that was already settling on it.

"Well, well, well! What's goin' on here, little lady? Anything the matter?" His words popped around me like soap bubbles, drifting away on the evening air.

"Oh, just looks like I'm out of gas here, Ed."

"Well, you just hop right on in here, we'll get you fixed up in no time. Just roll you right on into town."

I began giving serious consideration to Yellowstone again. "Oh, no, really, Ed, I wouldn't want to put you to any trouble."

"No trouble at all. What'cha gonna do, just sit out here all night? Hah? Wait for the gas station to come to you? Ha-ha-ha!"

I was starting to get cold. *Shit,* I thought. *Shit in twenty baskets. What was it Alix said about never riding alone in a car with him? Oh, hell and God damn fuck.* I climbed out of the truck and dropped into the seat next to Ed, steeling my mind against knowing where I was and with whom, wondering why this happening to me.

He floored the gas pedal, racing the car down the rough road with the relish of a teenager, lounging back in his seat, a cigarette held high in one hand and the other casually draped over the top of the steering wheel.

He chuckled to himself. "Hey, this is just great!" he said. "I was just on my way into town to join the boys from one of the supply companies for dinner. You can just come along!"

"No Ed, I'm sure I should get back on out to the rig. I got to get some sleep."

"Sleep? Who needs sleep? It's settled then, you're coming along." He patted my knee with his cigarette hand, and then let it linger, tickling my knee cap.

Rigor mortis set in: I willed my leg to move away, but the committee of fears and worries that commanded my head locked themselves in debate. I tried to think what Queen Alix of the Imperturbable Self-Confidence might say, but it wouldn't come. My knee remained exposed, vulnerable. *You can't move it,* the committee said. *You'll offend him. You have no right to be so angry; he's only touching your knee. It's nothing. How do you really know what he means by touching you? Your anger is way out of proportion. And, finally, if you move your knee, he won't like you any more.*

After the next drag on his cigarette, Ed's hand came to rest against my thigh. It was a casual gesture, if you judged by the look on his face, but I knew his arm couldn't be any too comfortable at that angle. A sliver of my mind worried whether the coal on the end of the cigarette would fall off and burn me.

Slowly, like dragging a sledge through mud, I managed to move my thigh away from his hand and cross my legs.

Ever so casually, Ed lifted his hand to take another drag on his cigarette, and jabbed it into the ash tray. His now-empty hand rose to his head, and the fingers scampered through his hair. "Aw, shit," he said. "I'm so tired. I tell you, this is one tough job. I been up since six, runnin' around like who knows what, baby-sittin' these fools all day, and now I gotta be at it for another two–three hours, hashing out the details of the casing contract with these yay-hoos from Casper. Over dinner, no less. I tell you."

Words came out of my mouth. "I got to get back to the rig," I managed. "Get some sleep."

"No, no, no; you can't slip away like that! You just stick with ol' Ed! We'll have a good ol' time." He eyed me again, sucking his teeth, letting his lower lip slide provocatively down into a smile, the tip of his tongue slithering from left to right between his clean, even teeth. I realized with some surprise that he was actually trying to woo me. The very thought jammed the gears in my brain. A deer must be embraced by such fascination as it stands frozen on the road, staring into the headlights of an oncoming car. At length the gears started moving again and I said, as firmly as I could muster, "No, Ed, I'd love to come, but I'm just not worth a thing without sleep. Just gotta get back. Drop me in town, I can take it from there." I meant to sound like Alix, but the words came out kind of squeaky.

"No way, darlin'! You just let ol' uncle Ed take care of you! We'll have lots of fun. I'll bet you love a party. You just been a-waitin' for someone to say it's okay."

I opened my mouth to speak again, but he signaled me to save my breath. I looked out the window. The vast freedom of the open prairie swept past, remote and inaccessible, unaware of my plight.

"Boy, I tell ya," he said, his tone changing to background-level complaint, "I don't know when I been so tired. This job just keeps me runnin'. Before comin' up here, I was down on one of our wells in Oklahoma. I got this engineer down there supposed to be doin' the job on his own, can't get it together at all. Couldn't find his ass with both hands and a road map. He tries to run the wrong mud in a high porosity zone, plugs the thing right up like a whore! We almost lost the well. Ol' Ed's gotta go bail him out every time. I just told him, 'You swab that thing, boy. You swab it 'til your ass turns red!' He says the well's gone, we ain't gettin' it back. I tell him he's full of shit. He swabs. It comes back. I tell ya." He shook his head and raised his hand off the steering wheel to dramatize the extremity of his exasperation.

"Uhn," I commented.

"And I hardly seen my wife in the past month! I just been runnin', I tell ya. I won't hardly recognize her when I get home, she'll be such an old witch. Horny." He winked at me.

I cringed. This was worse than I had imagined. My eyes slid out of focus under the strain. My brain went dead. Dial tone.

"Boy, I tell ya. The old broad and I don't get along so well. I try to make her happy. We been married twenty years, ever since I got out of the service. She's tried draggin' me to one of them marriage counselors, y'know, one of them little pansies thinks 'cause he's got a fancy degree from the university and a shingle hanging out he knows how to live my life better'n I do myself. So I go to the asshole, just to get the bitch to shut up. He tells me it's all my fault, like I hate my own mother, or something. God, ain't she the bitch on wheels, though. Hell, I sure didn't go back to that little pig's ass. That counselor shit's just a load of crap, anyway. Hell, any marriage just goes dead after that much time, what's he expect? The old broad gets hit with the ugly stick, and you find out all that sweetness you thought you signed up for was just an act. But we got four kids to raise, so we gotta stick together. No choice about it. I tell ya, every time I turned around, she was pregnant. I look at her cross-eyed, she's pumped up like a nickel balloon. Shit. She wouldn't lay off me, though. She had to have it, all the time. Every night. The price I pay for being good at what I do. The price I pay." He hazarded a sly glance my way.

Meeteetse slid past in slow motion as Ed rumbled the car down the main drag, slouched in the driver's seat like a teenager on Friday night. I stared longingly at the Blue Ribbon Cafe, at the Cowboy Bar, at the A&W stand as they slipped past my view. I was Persephone, on her way to six months' tour of duty in hell.

The car swung west along the Pitchfork Ranch road, into the burning gold of the setting sun.

"Great little steak house up here," Ed said, lighting another cigarette from the coil in the dash. "Local knowledge. Looks for all the world like he's runnin' it out of a garage. Only open certain days of the week, and you gotta have reservations. Course, he has it open special for me tonight: private party." He turned and looked at me for a moment, observing me slowly, in detail. "Here," he said, pulling a comb out of his pocket. "fix your hair. I guess there's nothing we can do about your clothes."

I tried to think very small and far away.

The sunset's last faint illumination lay like gauze along the foothills outside the restaurant. Ed was right: the building did not at first glance look like what it was. We passed through a dim barroom paneled in weathered wood into a wide dining room with wagon wheels for chandeliers. "The boys" awaited us at the one populated table.

A large man with graying hair cut too short across his temples took a quick, sharp glance at me as he struggled to his feet, snagging the edge of the table with his gut on his way up. His shirt bulged over the ornate silver buckle on his wide leather belt. He smiled gaily between his rosy cheeks. "Good to see you, Ed! And who's your little pal here? Is this your gal geologist you been telling us about? Nice to meet you, ma'am, I'm sure," he called joyously, reaching out a hand as pink and large as a ham and pumping mine up and down with vigor.

"Well, hi there, Tom," Ed answered. "This here's Emmy Hansen, my little mudlogger from the rig. Our geologist will be along in a bit. Waiter, we'll have another to dinner here. Hi, Fred. Hi, Irv. Merle, you know Emmy." Each man nodded to me in turn.

I was glad to see Merle Johnson. At least there was one man here I could count on to have a measure of decency. I looked into his face for what traces of friendship I might find there, but found only his usual detached gaze. He put out his cigarette, rose, and moved his chair over a bit to make room to his right for an extra one that the waiter was bringing to the table. Ed sat down in the empty chair to his left, and as Merle started to sink back into the middle chair, Ed swatted him none too gently on the arm. "The little mud lump sits there," he said. "You can set yourself over there on the other side of her, if'n you're good. Ha-ha-ha."

Merle held my chair as I sat down. His expression never changed throughout this maneuvering, and I made a mental note that if I were ever roped into a mixed doubles poker game, I'd ask him to be my partner.

The waiter returned with a drink. "Scotch and water, rocks," he said, placing it in front of Ed. "Johnny Walker. Just like you like it. What can I get for the lady?"

"Good man," Ed said. "What a memory. Aw hell, what ya drinkin', Emmy?"

"Oh, nothing, thank you," I replied.

"Oh, no you don't," cried Ed, clipping my arm with the edge of his hand. "You ain't lettin' me down like that. You got to wet your little whistle, ha-ha-ha-ha-ha."

Tom roared with laughter. Fred and Irv joined in, shaking their heads and lifting their drinks for sips.

"Now, what'll it be, doll?" Ed continued.

I looked a plea to the waiter. "Just a Coke would be fine," I said.

"Coke, bull SHIT!" said Ed. "Get her a scotch and soda. Put hair on her chest, ha-ha-ha-ha-ha!"

The waiter smiled and disappeared.

My chair faced the windows, and I concentrated on the view of the world outside, watching the foothills fade and extinguish from sight as the rounds of drinks arrived and drained away through mouths and kidneys. I still had two thirds of my first drink left when the next came. As time dragged its pitiless feet, another round arrived, and then another.

Merle sat shrouded in quiet, watching the conversation as the alcohol cranked up the volume on Ed's voice. I managed to tune Ed out for a while, until he shouted, "That sumbitch never knew what happened to him! Well, now, I tell you, I set him straight," as he crashed through a story about some exploit or another, raising his hand high over his head in the international salute of forced fornication. As his arm descended, it found its way across the back of my chair.

Peals of laughter from The Boys.

Merle sat quietly, sipping his drink.

"Aw, Ed, you know how to tell 'em!" Fred rasped, hoisting his drink in a salute.

The monologue rambled on, a call-and-response of Ed-the-Magnificent to The-Boys-Who-Appreciate. I faded into dreamland, trying not to think about the arm behind my shoulders, thinking instead of billowing clouds with tints of blue skating above an endless prairie grassland of yellow, gray green, and palest violet. Jovial slaps to my shoulder jolted me back to the dining room for brief interludes. The minutes scraped by.

During a moment of abstract observation of reality, I noticed that the upper and lower halves of Ed's face were doing two different things, just like a game of cards I had as a child with which I could mix and match funny faces from horizontal slices. Ed's mouth was grinning, declaring the jubilance of his warrior-hero stories, but his eyes glanced furtively about, checking audience reaction and returning again and again to the unclaimed place setting on the other side of him. It occurred to me that the cocktail hour was dragging on and on as we awaited the arrival of one more dinner guest. My heart sagged as I remembered who was "supposed" to be joining us, because I had certain knowledge that she was miles away among the badlands, having an evening stroll with a tall cowboy with muscular buttocks and elegant legs, while I sat cringing next to a man I detested.

Why is this happening to me? asked a little voice in my mind. Was cocktail hour doomed to last forever? The scotch had begun to addle my brain, sliding me into reverie: I was standing on a heaving deck littered with the dead, alone on a wide, wide sea, with a albatross hanging around my neck. The albatross smelled of scotch, and kept wrapping a wing around my back. It had a voice like a crow. "Ha-ha-ha-ha-ha," it laughed, "Ha-ha-ha-ha-ha." Dimly, I realized I was falling asleep, be it from fatigue, alcohol, or self-defense, I knew not.

My awareness was jolted back to the dining room once again as the waiter appeared at the table with a chalk board listing the evening's specials. He crooned, "Can I get you another round, or did you want to order now?"

Fred came half alert, swiveling his jowls left and right. "No, not yet, we're still waiting for—"

Fred's sentence was cut short as Tom's elbow jolted the wind from his rib cage. "A little food sounds good to me," Tom roared, rubbing his hands together.

"Oh, yes!" Fred agreed.

"Yep! Say, I hear you got a great T-bone hereabouts," Irv added.

Merle shifted from leaning slightly to the right side of his chair to leaning slightly to the left.

"Nawww!" Ed said, waving his hands around over his plate, hushing the others up. His Oklahoma drawl was thickening, becoming slurred. "I'm sure she's comin'. She's jus' lost, or sumpin'. Give her a few minutes. Come on boys, let's have another drink." He snapped his fingers at the waiter in a gesture that took up half a yard of air space.

The Boys moved uneasily in their seats.

Ed's face contracted into less friendly lines and he leaned back in his chair, staring at each man in turn.

Merle sat relaxed in his chair, his hands folded loosely across his chest, staring into space. He spoke, but not much more than his lips moved. "What do you suppose, Ed?" he said. "You never know on a drilling project. That Alix is a conscientious girl, like you always tell me. I expect something's come up, and she's right there looking after it. Just like you ordered her to."

The Boys' heads bobbled up and down. They mumbled cheerful agreement.

Ed considered this at length. "Well, yeah. I suppose you're right," he allowed.

The Boys relaxed.

"Then let's get us some of them T-bones!" said Tom.

"Well, T-bones it is, then!" Ed hollered, his eyes joining his mouth in a grin. "Waiter, get us T-bones, and make 'em rare! Just saw that bull's horns off, wipe his ass, and run him on in here, ha-ha-ha-ha-ha!"

The Boys roared with laughter, slapped the table top.

Merle rose and headed away from the table, his expression as distant and unperturbed as ever. When he returned, he settled back into his chair and assumed the same posture, as if he'd never moved.

As dinner commenced, the conversation shifted gradually to the issue of casing pipe and other supplies for the well we were drilling. Tom asked, "Ed, have you thought any more about my offer?"

Ed said, "Waiter, my glass is empty." He stared insolently at Tom, his jaws slowly grinding his steak. "Yeah, I been thinking on it, Tom." He sat with his elbows propped to either side of his plate, his fingers interlocked. He clasped his hands one way and then another, apparently distracted by the light glittering from the stone in his ring.

"It's the usual deal," Tom said, forking a ragged chunk of flesh toward his mouth.

"And I'm not sure that's quite good enough," Ed said, knocking back a slug of his fresh drink and forking another hunk of meat into his mouth. "Gawd, this is good cow here."

Fred said, "I suppose we could raise you a percent—" His eyes moved my way and back again. "I mean, just let us know . . ."

Irv concentrated on performing surgery on his steak. Merle stared passively out the window, chewing his meat.

"It's the best casing pipe in Wyoming, Ed," Tom said. "You know we always get you the best. We always put you first."

"And you damn well better; otherwise you're shit out of luck. I just gotta think on it, fellah." He leaned back in his chair and lurched with a silent belch. His eyes glazed over for a moment, and he shook himself as if he had forgotten where he was; his steak half eaten on his plate, his drink permanently mounted in his right hand. Apparently forgetting all about the subject of the price of casing pipe, he started into a tally of his favorite barmaids of Oklahoma and Kansas: "Hey guys, did I tell you 'ere's this li'l broad in Okie City can carry the foldin' money 'tween her tits an' the change in her—"

I'd heard it before, one afternoon in the logging trailer. I stared fixedly at my plate. Every time I looked up, Ed was looking at me slyly, checking to see how his story was going over. Like he knew it was turning my stomach, and was both pleased and concerned that I might find him disgusting.

Beyond the barroom, I heard the front door open. The waiter materialized from the kitchen and slipped away to the bar to see who had come in, setting up a murmur of voices and a clink and thud of glasses on heavy mahogany.

I was just beginning to wonder why I was listening to all this, why didn't I just get up and leave and just start walking to Yellowstone, when I heard a loud, "Hi there!"

19

A tall, thin man strode toward our table with a drink in one hand and the other raised in greeting. He was so slender and loose-jointed I had the feeling that, in spite of his height, I could fold him up and fit him in a suitcase. Through the fog of my thoughts I thought he looked vaguely familiar, like I had seen him before.

Merle was on his feet. "Howdy, Stretch. What brings you out this way tonight?" They shook hands.

"Oh, why, just delivering a load of mud, is all, out of the Hawkins well. Why, hi there, Mr. Meyer! Y'all having yerselves a nice party here?"

Ed leaned back in his seat, his chin thrust upward. He said, "Yeah, and it was bein' a private party, until—"

"Hey, well then, I'm sorry Mr. Meyer! Didn't know, just didn't know that. Say, who's that over there? Emmy Hansen? The mudlogger? How you doin', honey? Past your bedtime, ain't it?"

His good will and humor were infectious. I felt a smile in my heart that I hadn't the strength to wear on my face.

"Yep, she's out kinda late," Merle said, "Ran out of gas out by the entrance road. Ed gave her a lift. Just haven't gotten her back yet."

Stretch whooped, "Well, hey there! I could give you a ride! I was just on my way out there, anyhows, with that mud!" He flung his free arm about in a sloppy gesture of *fait accompli.*

The drilling mud man. That was where I had seen him. "You just come on along with me!" he said, yanking my chair backward and starting for the door. He was so gleeful that I could think of nothing I'd like better than to do exactly as he suggested.

I was on my feet and after him faster than you can say, "saved by the mud man." And I didn't look back. I heard Merle call, "Thanks, Stretch," just as the door swung to behind us.

I didn't know this guy from Adam, but nothing could have gotten me to stay and take my chances with a drunken Ed Meyer. At worst, I figured I could have it out with this Stretch fellow by the front door and walk to town, ducking into the shadows if Ed came looking for me in his car, but as it turned out, I needn't have worried about getting to town in one piece.

When I got outside, I saw a familiar tan pickup truck parked front and center, with headlights on and engine running. Behind the wheel was Frank Barnes.

He pushed the truck door open for me.

"Boy, am I glad to see you!" I said, hopping in beside him. He grinned mischievously and ruffled my hair. I grinned back. As Stretch climbed in and slammed the door, Frank reached in front of my knees and slapped the truck into gear, and we were off.

Stretch howled, "Hoo-ee! That were a fun 'un! Went off like a charm!" He flailed me merrily with his elbow as he gripped his hands in a gesture of victory. "Best fun I ever had with my socks on!"

"What? What's going on here?" I asked. "Did you guys know I was in there?" Stretch kept on whooping. I looked at Frank. He kept on grinning. "Tell me?" I demanded.

"Aw, Emmy, this was great," Stretch chortled. "Ol' Frank and me was just fixin' to have us a bowl of chili down at the Blue Ribbon 'bout six o'clock. We thought we saw you goin' by in Ed's Oldsmobile, but we couldn't believe it. 'Naw, that warn't her,' I says. 'Sure it were,' says Frank. We was arguin' and arguin', back and forth like, and Frank here's gettin' all het up an' worried like, and we's eatin' our chili, and I'm layin' him a bet on it and all, and he's about to just get up there and go see for hisself if it was you, and I'm tellin' him to keep his shirt on, have some pie. Well, we go 'round and 'round, and by and by Miss Rita behind the counter comes over and says, 'Call for you, Mr. Long Bones,' and it's Merle, sayin', 'Y'all come up here and fetch Miss Emily, hear? Ol' Ed brang her up here and gots her ears smokin' with his talk. You tell him yer jes' on yer way to the well and could jus' do him this big favor like, savin' him haulin' her back out there.' I says to Frank, it *was* you after all! Frank had his truck a-rollin' like that." He snapped his skinny fingers. "Hoo-oo-oo-ee!"

The thought that Frank would hop in his truck like that and rush off to my rescue suffused me with a warm, rosy feeling, and I sneaked a look over at him again. He was still smiling, a bit more shyly now. I could feel the muscles in his near leg tense and loosen against my thigh as he worked the pedals with every turn in the road.

"Thanks, guys," I said. "Thanks for the rescue job."

"Aw shucks ma'am," said Stretch, "weren't nothin' a-tall. Aw, hell, did you see the look on Meyer's face when I snatched you outta there? Pure 'screw you!' "

Frank just smiled and kept driving.

I asked, "How did Merle know where to find you?" I was surprised. All the time, I had thought Merle was tuning out everything around him.

"Oh, he was at the cafe with us before he went up to the restaurant to meet everyone," Stretch said. Presently we pulled up in front of the Blue Ribbon and Stretch jumped out, waving and whooping and calling good night, and I thanked him for the tenth or possibly the eleventh time. Frank put the truck back in gear and continued to the gas station, where we filled a five-gallon jerry can with unleaded. When I got back into the cab, there was no reason to sit so close to Frank again, and I noticed that I felt a certain disappointment, which surprised me. We headed on out of town toward the rig.

During the drive back to where my truck had died of thirst, Frank and I talked about the warmth of the days we'd been having and about the crispness of the night air. The prairie welcomed us into its silent beauty, embracing us in her curves and hollows under the cover of darkness. As we left the main road, he quietly took my hand and said, "If that bastard so much as touches you—"

All at once, tears burned at my eyes. I wanted to cuddle close to Frank, say, *Yes, he's touched me, and nothing can heal it,* but all I could manage was, "Thanks, Frank."

As my truck came into view, I shifted back into my tough kid posture. "Back to the fun and games of life in the dead zone."

Frank swung his piercing eyes my way. Even in the dark, the sensation was like having two lasers focused sharply on me. This guy had a directness I was just plain unaccustomed to, an intensity that somehow left me frightened and fascinated and soothed all at the same time. I made a study of my fingernails.

"What's on your mind, Em?"

I shrugged my shoulders, vying for time as I tried to figure out which words to fit in the air between us. "Oh, it's all this business of Willie," I muttered. "And Bill."

"You think about it a lot?"

"Yeah."

"Can't you let it go?"

Now, that struck me as a bit righteous. "Hell, I just want to know who did it."

"You mean, who killed Willie?"

"I mean, who killed Willie and who killed Bill."

"What?" Frank pulled the truck to a stop beside mine, stamped on the parking brake, and cut his engine. "What do you mean, who killed Bill? Just because Willie went through his trailer doesn't mean someone killed him."

I sat in a sullen heap.

When he spoke again, his voice was low and gentle. "I'm sorry, Em. I get kind of abrupt. Please tell me."

What the hell, I found myself telling him everything that was on my mind about the deaths, from my first flash of apprehension when I heard that Bill was dead, right down to the well-tuned pumpjack on the 17-1 and the cigarette butt in the culvert by the bend in the road. We sat in the darkness of the cab with the headlights out and the motor off, while the night went on around us and clouds skidded across the starry sky. The lateness of the hour settled like sandbags on my tired shoulders.

Frank was quiet for a while, leaning on the door on his side, rubbing the tip of his nose with one finger. Having unburdened myself, I felt comfortable to let the silence sit. At length he spoke.

"Well, Em, you notice things, that's for sure, and I do believe you aren't telling me any kind of a made-up story. I guess I wasn't ready to see things this way. One killing is bad, but you can tell yourself it was manslaughter, just something that happened in the heat of things that someone went to some trouble to cover up. But two killings, that's premeditated." I heard him sigh. "I suppose you didn't tell all this to Ben Lewis."

"No, not all. Not by any means."

"Why not?"

I thought about it for a bit before I answered. Why hadn't I told him? Was it because I wasn't that sure of what I had seen myself? "Well," I said, "It's not so easy to talk to Ben as it is to talk to you, for one thing." *That's an understatement,* I thought bitterly. "I hoped he'd kind of get the drift for himself." I shrugged my shoulders. "He declared Bill's death an accident. If I'm right, he's going to be pretty damned embarrassed, isn't he?"

Frank didn't say anything to this. He just sat staring at me, and I soon felt conspicuously full of shit. After another ten seconds or so, the courage of my convictions crashed down in a smoking heap and I said, "Oh, hell, maybe I'm dreaming. If there was any reason to think Bill was murdered, it would have shown up in the autopsy, right?"

Frank slid down in the seat a bit, his hands rising to cover his eyes. I think I heard him say something like, "That son of a bitch," only it was really quiet, like he was sucking the air in instead of letting it out. I rested my head against the back of the seat and studied the clouds. After a half-hearted try at keeping my curiosity to myself, I gave up and whispered, "What did you say?"

"Ben Lewis," he said. "That horse's ass. I've had it with him."

"What do you mean?"

"Oh, Em, it's a long story. And not a good one. He—no, I shouldn't say. No point in it. Just suffice to say he wasn't any too decent about the way he handled Bill's accident— or whatever it was, and if he'd handled it a little better, maybe you wouldn't have to be all wound up in this like you are."

"What do you mean? Did he screw up the evidence?"

"No, he didn't. And I'm not sure he was wrong deciding it was an accident. It's just—well . . ."

"If you don't tell me, my imagination's going to run wild, Frank."

He brooded a while longer, looking at the palm of one hand and then the other. "Well," he said, "it's got to do with how he handled the body."

"Bill's body?"

"Yeah, Bill's. And Willie's, probably, if he got his way about it."

"What did he *do*, Frank?" My imagination was running wild, all right.

Frank struggled a while longer and then spat it out. "Oh, he just kept 'em for a while, is all."

"What d you mean, kept them? I thought Willie's went straight to the coroner's, and didn't Bill's go home to Denver?"

"Sure, but not right away. Em, he's just got this thing where he likes to keep bodies around for a while. You think he'd take them right up to the hospital in Cody or something, but somehow it seems to take him a while to get them there. Oh God dammit, he does a good job in most other ways, but this one thing—it just leaves us all wondering."

"But the coroner did go straight after Willie."

"Yeah, as soon as he got back from Billings, he picked it—Willie—up at Ben's house to take to the hospital for the autopsy. The coroner said he had Willie laid out in the barn, like it was a funeral home or something. The coroner gave him what for, and Ben told him, 'Oh, it's plenty cool here and everything, no problem.' " Frank looked at me in a muddle of embarrassment and tried to take his words back. "Aw, you never know. Maybe the coroner just said that. He could have been making it sound worse than it was."

"But you don't think so."

Between clenched teeth, he said, "No, Em, I don't."

"So what about Bill?"

"Shit. Excuse me, Em; I don't mean to cuss around you, but Bill was never taken to the hospital, as I heard it. His widow flew up from Denver to get him, and I guess it wasn't so great. She had him cremated right away, didn't have an autopsy, or anything."

Now I knew why Frank had been concerned about how Willie's body was handled. Or thought I did.

Frank squeezed my hand gently before I left him. I drove away feeling a strange mixture of exhaustion, excitement, and revulsion. Ed's behavior and my own inability to deflect it certainly made me sick and irritable, but there was something else—something about the whole evening that left me feeling manipulated, like I was someone's idea of an expendable little pawn. I was also beginning to have some feelings toward Frank. It was exciting, but it threatened to upset everything. It was one thing to moon over some unattainable cowboy who seldom even showed up, and another to have feelings about someone I worked with. Someone a lot more real. I'd had it. I drew the line. Too much of my world was on its ear. I had to get to the bottom of things, restore my balance.

Confusion mounted on me like a wave, looming bigger and bigger, and when I stepped inside the trailer, it broke. I took one look at Howard and started hollering at him for running the truck out of gas. He looked so startled that I got mixed up and went into the sleeping room, slamming the door behind me. I had never yelled at him before. In fact, I couldn't remember the last time I had raised my voice at anyone. I stood for a moment in the dark, trembling, the unaccustomed fit of emotion sliding about nauseously over the depths of my fatigue, pricking at feelings of impending doom and bumping up against the knowledge that I had to be back on duty again in just over three hours.

I kicked off my shoes, shucked off my jeans and climbed in under the sleeping bag, expecting to pass immediately into a bottomless, dreamless sleep, the kind of sleep that leaves you waking up uncertain of how much time has passed.

But as I lay there, I forgot all about Howard. My irritation at him, and everyone else for that matter, melted away like snow in the spring sunshine; and all that was left in my soul was excitement.

My eyes snapped wide open in the pitch darkness, and I was awake.

I rolled over onto my stomach, burying my face in the pillow. The noise of the rig rushed in my ears. I turned onto my side, pulling the pillow over my head, covering my eyes and my ears; but still my brain roared, like a big radar dish turning this way and that, trying to zero in on some strange signal.

I flopped back onto my spine, folded my hands beneath my head, and let my eyes search for traces of light in the enfolding darkness. A faint wraith glimmered around the heavy rubber-backed curtain that smothered the one window.

Gradually, I realized that it was as much my body as my mind that was alert. I felt a faint tingling in my legs and my belly that was more a buzz than anything else, as if a faint electric current was trying to flow through me but had jammed. Next I realized that I was breathing very shallowly, almost panting, as if I was anxious.

Am I anxious? I forced myself to breathe deeply. The first breaths came hard, like asthma, and my stomach muscles rebelled in horror, squeezing tighter and tighter. I concentrated on these muscles, forcing them to work like bellows. Gradually, the blockage broke and I found myself weeping, the tears disembodied from conscious feeling, and a sensation came at the base of my pelvis that I had forgotten I ever had.

It was an urge.

My thighs and pelvis wanted to be back in that truck with Frank Barnes, pressed against him in the darkness, seeking satisfaction in all things physical.

I forgot where I was. I forgot my revulsion for the man in the next room, and for a while I put pleasure before survival. My hands slid down my belly in the growing warmth of the world beneath my sleeping bag, seeking the center of the urge. I massaged myself slowly, peacefully, until the thousand jangled nerve endings calmed into a gentle purr, and I slid off into sleep.

20

In the hours before dawn on Wednesday I found time to organize my thoughts and observations. I put them all down on paper in a little notebook, and resolved to keep it with me at all times so I could add things as they occurred to me. I sat alone in the thin light of the single bulb over the plotting table, oblivious to Howard's ragged breathing and the incessant roar and grind of the diesel motors on the rig. I was tired; but fatigue rested on me like a mild weakness of my long muscles, as compared to the heavy, tearing burden it had been.

On the first two pages of my notebook, I wrote down the few observations I had that I could call clues. The first page was for Bill, and I wrote:

1. Found dead in overturned car (by Johnny Maxwell) Sunday, April 12, before midnight.

I didn't know the time Bill had died. I realized I would have to ask a lot of questions to fill in the blanks, but I kept writing.

2. Footprints of cattle, one horse, several people wearing heavy boots, misc. wild animals (observed next day)
3. Car traveled about 75 feet from roadway
4. Roadway a reverse-banked curve about eight or ten feet above arroyo
5. Papers missing from trailer
6. No autopsy—body cremated

This didn't seem like much evidence, even to me. Surely there was more I could write to make the list more impressive. I pondered for a while as I sipped coffee and ate dry Cheerios out of the box. Then I remembered Monday afternoon, when I had looked on the opposite side of the curve as I was driving back from town. I wrote that down, too, even though I hadn't any idea if what I had seen was anything at all, let alone involved with Bill's death. At least it filled up a few more lines in my book:

7. Marlboro cigarette butt in culvert on opposite side of roadway (fresh? not very old)
8. Grass growth irregular and dirt uncompacted on embankment opposite wreck
9. No footprints, but cattle and horse tracks in arroyo on opposite side of roadway from wreck (items 7-9 observed 9 days after wreck)

When I was done, I felt quite proud of the scientific detachment I applied to my observations, such as noting exactly when the observations were made. Page two was for Willie. I wrote:

1. Seen searching for something in Bill's trailer at 3 a.m. the night Bill died
2. Found dead on government lands near wild horse area, Sunday, April 19, circa 10:30 a.m.
3. Truck of deceased parked nearby, keys in it
4. Head and chest crushed
5. No blood on ground under body, and blood has no grass or twigs in it
6. Red paint and crude oil found on skull and scalp
7. Footprints of Chet, Wayne, Darrell, horses (no shoes), balding truck tires under and around the body (observed within a day of death)
8. Question exists as to which way body rested at death
9. Rigor mortis in knees and elbows but not in hips or shoulders

10. Last seen by me heading out to check valve problem on
   17-1 with Ed, Merle, Saturday, April 18, early afternoon

I was prouder yet of my detached description of the rigor
mortis, until I realized that I didn't really know anything
about the phenomenon. I knew that animals got stiff after
they died, but when I recalled memories of various pets and
livestock I had found dead on the ranch over the years, I remembered that not all of them had it. I couldn't remember
which ones were stiff, when they had gotten that way, or
why.

   Putting that aside for the moment, I started to write myself a list of things I could check on. This included:

1. Lunch at Blue Ribbon last Saturday. Willie, Ed, etc.
   What was discussed?
2. How did Willie get onto BLM land? Look for evidence.
3. Does Dinah know what Willie wanted to see Ed about
   on Saturday?
4. Time Johnny found Bill's body?

I thought I might be able to get somewhere with numbers 1
and 2 if I went into town after getting off at noon, and resolved to do so. I then started writing down information
about why I thought the prevailing opinions on how the
deaths occurred didn't make sense, but then decided that
these were not objective data. Instead, I started new pages
for subjective opinion.

Reasons Kretzmer "accident" explanation screwy:
1. Bill drove carefully, not fast
2. Bill seemed troubled

Bill's mood wasn't much to base an opinion on. I thought a
while longer, chewing on my pencil. Just what was it about
Bill's behavior, or anything he had said to me, that had
prompted such a strong gut reaction when I heard he was

dead? I was on the road to talking myself out of my own opinion for about the fifth time since his death when I decided instead to give myself a little credit for having a brain. Hadn't Frank said I had one? I pushed forward, closing my eyes and letting my mind run free, seeing where it might take me.

There was something about the accident site, my mind said. *You felt uncomfortable there. Why?*

Well, hell, someone died there. Someone I knew.

There was more.

I leaned back in my chair and stretched. The answer skated around just out of reach of my awareness, tantalizing me. It wouldn't come. Intuition sank out of sight into a bog of uninspired musings.

The only thing left to add was a list of suspects. To be scientific, that had to include everyone who had had an opportunity to kill Bill and Willie. Motive was important, too, but might be more difficult to ascertain. I wrote:

Suspects:
1. Ed Meyer
2.

Number 2 sat blank. Whom else did I suspect? Did I even suspect Ed? *Yeah, the son of a bitch. He's low enough, and he sure didn't like us poking around the 17-1. Not to mention the fact that he was one of the last people Willie was seen with.*

Who else had a stake? I considered making a list by category, which would include "Financial Interest" and "Personal Interest." Financial would include the Hawkins family, of course, and major contractors like the rig owner or Merle; but I couldn't imagine how that would figure in, because everyone was best served if the well was a success. Unfortunately, Personal included just about everyone else in town, including everyone from the rig, even Johnny and Frank. Not a comforting thought.

Then it occurred to me that the sheriff had been acting

pretty oddly. Just why was he so anxious to scare me away from the case? Was he killing people so he could have them over to his barn? With more than a little satisfaction, I added his name to the list. Then I tried eliminating suspects by thinking of who had *not* acted suspiciously at one moment or another. That didn't work very well, because even Frank had seemed bent on keeping me off the trail, stopping to talk to me by the road that afternoon and all. And was this story he'd just told me about the sheriff on the level? Perhaps he had made it up just to throw me. *No, not Frank!* Paranoia was beginning to rear its ugly head. In disgust, I wrote, "everybody else," after number 3 and tossed the pen down; but it looked downright inane. I tried deductive logic one more time, figuring there had to be someone completely beyond suspicion. This more scientific approach pleased the Zen enthusiast within me, and yielded:

Unsuspects:
1. Me
2. Alix (not here when Bill died)
3. Evening drilling tower (at rig when Bill died)

Then everything broke down, because I simply didn't know enough about everyone's movements. Furthermore, I saw a flaw or two in my logic: first, the same person didn't have to be responsible for both deaths; and second, a murderer didn't necessarily have to have been there at the time to have killed Bill. How did I know his brakes hadn't been tampered with or something? I closed my eyes to think.

Some time later my head dropped sharply to the left and I realized I had fallen asleep. I stared into space for several moments, trying to remember what it was I had been thinking when I dozed off, and I was just drifting off for a second time when I heard someone walk by outside, close to the trailer. I realized that anyone could have stepped quickly into the trailer while I was asleep and seen what I was writing. I didn't know who had killed Willie. It could be most anyone. From what I knew, there wasn't anyone I could safely eliminate.

I closed the notebook and shoved it into my shirt pocket. It stuck out like a billboard in front of my left breast. I pulled it out again and looked around the room for a safe place to hide it, but Howard's smudge marks told me there was no such place in the trailer; so I slid it into my back jeans pocket.

It was time to catch my next sample out on the shale shaker. As I stepped out of the trailer, the cold, crisp night air brought me wide awake. My breath formed ghosts and shattered with each exhalation.

The moon had disappeared behind a bank of clouds low in the western sky. Above my head the sky split open its bellyfull of stars, flickering white and palest blue and red and yellow. I traced the constellations, subconsciously at first, greeting their light in the darkness as I had for as long as I can remember. I found the bright stars of the Big Dipper, pouring their light toward Polaris, the navigator's jewel in the handle of the Little Dipper. Westward, the tight crown of the Corona Borealis blazed, the bright light of Vega marked Lyra overhead, and Cygnus the swan flew quietly nearby. Toward the eastern horizon, the great square of Pegasus galloped down the sky. *I'll pick a constellation to sing to,* I thought, *just like I did when I was little.*

Forgetting my sample, I walked away from the rig and up a low hill, until the lights from the rig no longer eclipsed the fainter stars. Casiopeia, queen of Ethiopia, emerged resplendent on her throne, and Cepheus, her king, held court nearby. Where was Andromeda, their lovely daughter, who was chained to a rock in offering to a sea serpent as punishment for her mother's vanity? Too early yet, not yet risen? *Andromeda,* I called to her gently in my mind; and then I found her, letting her faint tresses float across the Milky Way, longing for the season when Perseus would rise once again above the horizon to shine with her in the night sky, liberate her from the chains, and slay the monster that would consume her.

But Perseus was not yet risen. The loneliness of her vigil engulfed me in sadness, and I turned away. *Better to think about some other constellation tonight,* I told myself. *I won't think of Andromeda just now.*

The breeze shifted, bringing the rumble of the rig engines closer to my ear, and the rig lights glimmered like a mechanical apparition in the night prairie. A bittersweet melancholy settled into my heart: everything was the same and at the same time different, changed in some subtle yet fundamental way. *This has been home. for all it's been a raw existence and all that people haven't treated me kindly, it's been oddly safe. Now everything's changing. What's changing it? Murder? Alix?* The rig kept rumbling, probing its iron teeth into the earth. *You're different now,* it growled. *Go away. We're going to keep on drilling and we don't want you changing us.*

As I walked back toward the rig, I traced the faint pattern of Hercules, the hero for all seasons, between Lyra and the Crown. Much better, I decided: stars of strength for a night like this. I lifted my voice in a wordless hymn of friendship, of admiration for the hero, singing for his victory over the many-headed hydra as the cold fluorescent lights of the rig gathered me in and faded my friend from the sky.

21

At about eleven the next morning Ed Meyer rolled his Oldsmobile into the lot, followed by a man driving a heavy pickup truck with a trailer hitch. My stomach tightened as Ed strode toward my trailer, my shoulders tensed when the door slammed inward against the little drill bit. He left the door gaping and stared at me, cigarette flaring, his thumbs thrust into his pockets and his pelvis and chin forward of his navel. "So how's my little kinnie-gartner, who's gotta go to bed early?" he barked. "Doin' some nice work for your ol' buddy Ed this mornin'? Huh?" With a nasty smile spreading across his face, he moved slowly toward me, one hand rising from its pocket like a charmed snake, and slid it around the back of my neck. My shoulders jerked upward. He said, "Doin' lots of nice things for me today, I hope. Ol' Eddie *likes* it when you do nice things for him."

I squeezed my eyes shut, bracing myself against whoever might come next. The stench of stale smoke invaded my nostrils an instant before his lips pressed against mine, wetting my face with saliva. And then he left.

My hands moved of their own volition, grasping for an imaginary neck. God help me, I wanted to kill him. My breath came in shallow gasps.

Worse yet, it seemed that humiliating me was a trivial item on Ed's agenda for the day's fun and games: he had really come to the site to get even with Alix by evicting her from her trailer. The scuttlebutt that later circulated around the doghouse was that he had a well to drill in another field some miles away, and she was a big girl, she could commute from Meeteetse, ha-ha-ha-ha-ha.

Alix was still in her trailer, as was her custom, not coming out to acknowledge Ed's arrival on site. Consequently, her first clue that anything threatened her lodging came when the trailer lurched as Ed's assistant pulled the jacks out from under it, dropping its hitch onto the ball mounted on the back end of his pickup. Even then, moments passed without any sign of Alix at the door. I suppose she had been caught stretched out on the settee with her notes or a paperback, shoes off and feet up, drinking her high-class tea.

My eyes witnessed this lurch of accommodation, but the rest of me was preoccupied, still reeling from Ed's touch. My brain wailed at me, asking, *Why? Why didn't you stop him? Just when things seemed clearer, when power was within reach, you held still again!*

Johnny arrived at the logging trailer about then, all smiles; but when he saw me his face dropped, and he asked, "What happened to you?"

"I'm all right," I said, still wiping savagely at my mouth.

"Like hell."

"Forget it. I don't want to talk about it," I said, and rose to get myself another cup of coffee so I could turn my back to him. With the first sip, I swallowed the tears that threatened to spill down my cheeks; after two more I scrubbed my eyes with the cuff of my sweater and turned toward Johnny, looking something like normal.

He gazed at me for a while, as if checking to make sure I was still all there. Provisionally satisfied, he said, in a quiet voice, "This ought to be quite a show out here. C'mon," and glued himself as inconspicuously as possible to the window that looked out on Alix's trailer. I joined him and cracked the window open so we could hear. "She can't possibly take *this* one coolly," Johnny whispered.

"My money's on Alix," I whispered back.

"Name your odds."

"Five to four."

"Chicken."

Ed was leaning on the hood of the Olds, smoking a cigarette, enjoying his ringside seat for the show.

Alix finally stepped out of her trailer and looked left and right. she said, "Hi, Ed," and walked around to where the man was now connecting the wiring that served the tail lights and said "Hi" to him also. He nodded to her and kept on working.

"That's our girl," Johnny said, "What a performance. We are friendly, and just a touch curious. But definitely surprised. Pay up, Em."

"She gets points for face-saving," I retorted, wiping the last of the moisture from my eyes. "Cross my palm with silver."

"The vote's not all counted yet," he said.

Alix walked back over to Ed. "So, Ed, you going to let me in on this? Or am I just going for a ride somewhere?" She smiled deliciously, but I could see that her arms were stiff, her fingers tightly curled.

"Slick!" Johnny whispered. "Go for it, Alix, baby!"

"Points for humor!" I demanded.

"Nah. Pulse up, spine stiff."

Ed took a lavish drag on his cigarette and drew it away from his lips, gracefully carrying it out beyond the hood of his car before he tipped the ash onto the ground. "Better get your gear out of there, honey. I booked you a room at the Oasis Motel in Meeteetse." He regarded her through half-closed, insolent eyes.

She waited patiently for him to continue, her face completely calm.

"Mexican stand-off," Johnny said. "Who will speak next? Will it be our heroine? Or will the evil landlord back down?"

"Tune in next week for the thrilling conclusion," I said, praying that Alix would get serious and kick Ed in the balls.

Ed rocked his jaw to one side, slid his tongue slowly

across his upper teeth and down between his lower teeth and lip, then cleared his sinuses.

Alix waited. Her posture grew more relaxed.

"He's caving in," Johnny said.

"How do you know?"

"He's spending more time looking at his cigarette than at her."

Sure enough, Ed spoke. "Now, ah, Alix, my dear. It's just one of those things. You're just going to have to stay in town for now. This here trailer is needed elsewhere." And then, with a distinct edge, he said, "We all have to make sacrifices for the job."

Alix paused for about two heartbeats before she spoke. "Oh, I see. Well then, have your man wait just a sec, and I'll get my gear out." She smiled and trotted back inside.

"Let's call it a draw," Johnny said. "Wait! Hold the phone!" A truck rolled into sight on the entrance road. Chet, arriving just in time to save the heroine from the evil landlord.

"This just might be choice," I said. To be honest, I was torn: I'd just as soon Chet would walk right past Alix and come see me.

"Prepare to run for cover."

"Women and children first."

"In that case, I'm a children," Johnny said.

Chet parked his truck right next to the Olds, so that Ed had to crane his neck up to look him in the eye, touched the brim of his hat affably, and, folding his arms on the truck window, leaned out in such a way that his magnificent musculature filled the frame. "Ho, Ed," he said. "Nice day."

Lacking feathers to ruffle up, Ed crossed one calf over the opposite knee in an attempt to expand his size. He sucked his upper teeth and nodded, unsmiling.

Alix popped back out of her trailer, carrying a suitcase and her attaché. "Hi there!" she caroled to Chet. "Be with you shortly." She heaved her things into the trunk of her rental car and went back for another load, emerging the second time with her teapot and mug. She started toward my trailer.

We hustled away from the window and into seats by the kitchen table, and Johnny was already managing a thin whistling by the time Alix's footfalls rocked the trailer. Her eyes flashed with cheer and excitement. "Hi, mind if I hang my coffee mug here for a bit?"

"No problem," I said, gesturing toward the sink drainer. "Maybe you want to put that teapot in the cupboard."

"Thanks." She put her things up, winked at us, and said, "See you after lunch." We watched her vanish into Chet's truck, which rolled back out of the lot as the door on her side closed. It was delicious watching Ed's victory sour, but I hoped Alix would get gas from her lunch.

Ed Meyer lit another cigarette and took two long, contemplative drags on it before he slid down off the hood of his car. He took one more drag before he wandered over to the trailer and stepped inside, where his man had begun working to secure the fixtures for transport.

Half an hour later I had finished my day's work, shouted Howard awake, and headed to my truck for my fact-finding mission to town. A feeling of vengeance and exhilaration rose in my chest as I climbed in and cranked the starter, but as my hand went out to the gear shift, something made me pause, a confusing cross-riffle in the currents of my excitement.

I shut the engine down and trotted up to the doghouse. Frank looked up from the standing desk and smiled his quiet smile. "Got your jacket on. Going to town?"

"Uh, yeah," I answered. I smiled and stuffed my hands into my pockets.

"You catch this morning's episode in the soap opera?" he asked.

"Yeah. The Nielsen ratings are soaring."

Frank laughed, his face crinkling into a full-fledged grin for a moment.

I looked at my feet, shuffled back and forth a bit. *Why the hell did I come up here?*, I wondered.

Frank walked over closer to me, stopping about two feet away. He spoke quietly: "Listen, Em, you be careful in town there. I been thinking about it: I don't know what the hell's going on around here, but someone killed that boy, and maybe Bill, like you said. And here this morning, Ed's on the warpath. Em, I just don't trust that man." He scratched the back of his neck nervously. "Aw, hell, I don't know anything about this, but you know what I mean. I'd just hate for you to get caught up in something where you might get hurt, is all."

Frank's words turned in my head most of the way into town, putting my stomach askew. It wasn't just the risk that stirred me up: I wasn't used to anyone worrying about my well-being and personal safety, and worse, where the hell would I be if I got a crush on Frank? *Everyone will notice,* I worried. I'd never hear the end of it. *Frumpy girl mudlogger sets cap for moody, alluring driller over ten years her senior. Gets the brush-off. Instantly becomes local joke.* In frustration, I crammed my feelings into the most remote corner of myself where they couldn't hurt me and forced Frank out of my mind. I invited Chet in, but his arrival this noon had thoroughly burst my bubble of daydreams. Loneliness settled in my chest.

I did let myself think about Frank's words of caution, however. Although I felt I was taking reasonable precautions to evade notice, and had a lifetime's practice in low-profile existence to draw on, whoever had killed Bill and Willie was still on the loose and capable of killing again. Who was hateful enough to have done these things? *No one will put words to such speculation, because we do not bite the hand that feeds us, do we?* Only one name came to me, again and again.

Ed Meyer.

At the memory of Ed Meyer's touch, I gritted my teeth and stuffed it down deep next to my feelings, telling myself to be scientific, to make deductions from direct observation, not emotional bias.

22

Once in town I headed for the Blue Ribbon Cafe and took a seat at the counter. The waitress was a woman of unassuming countenance who could have been anywhere from thirty to forty, who always wore a bib apron and white short-sleeved blouse that fit snugly over arms the color and consistency of rising bread dough. She smiled a hello to me as I sat down, and snagged a pad and pencil out of her pocket to write down my order. She knew I didn't need to see a menu; I was a regular.

"Just chili today, Rita," I said. "No, wait. I better have a glass of milk with it, and extra crackers if it's spicy."

She smiled and took a sly peek over her shoulder toward the kitchen. Seeing that no one was in the doorway, she said, "I made the chili today, so it's edible." She winked. I winked back. We shared a giggle. I wondered how to get her to talk, to find out if she might have been the waitress on duty the afternoon before Willie was killed, and pump her for information.

By the time my chili arrived, two men had come in and solemnly taken seats at a table by the window. The waitress brought them glasses of water but no menus. Also locals, I thought, warming to my new role as Wyoming's answer to Sherlock Holmes. After she took their orders out to the kitchen, the waitress came back and leaned on the counter near me. "I hear where you got yourself waylaid by that Ed Meyer up to the Pitchfork last night," she said, her voice nice and low. Priming the pump was going to be easier than I'd thought.

"Oh, yeah," I said, rolling my eyes for effect. "Say, were you on shift here last night?"

"Yes, I was. Those boys sure scampered out of here in one hurry, when they got that call. I guess Merle says 'jump,' and that Stretch says, 'How high?' "

"Oh, is that so?" I asked, willing her to say more.

"Yep. That Merle keeps his boys ready to jump, he does."

This might be interesting. I knew very little about Merle, or any of his roustabouts, for that matter. Stuffing a spoonful of Wyoming's blandest chili into my mouth, I said, "So Stretch works for Merle, does he? I thought he worked for a mud company."

"Oh, yes. Well, not like you'd suppose. I mean, Merle got him his job, and well, you know . . . "

"You mean Stretch kind of owes him."

She winked. "I suppose you could say that," she said, laughing like the joke was on me.

Not to respond to this apparent dig, I asked, "How'd an Okie fetch up in this part of Wyoming, anyway?" *Perhaps there's a connection between him and Ed.*

Rita laughed again. "Oh, them rodeo brats is all alike. They wander. What's bred in the bone . . ." She laughed louder and hurried off to bring the men by the window their order. They joked with her for a moment or two and then fell back to their own conversation.

I pondered this new bit of intelligence, trying to see if it fit into anything. It didn't, really, except that it meant that I couldn't take everything Stretch said at face value. But come to think of it, there was a discrepancy. He said he was going to deliver mud and then hadn't. If he wasn't delivering mud, then what *was* he doing?

Rita drifted back my way. "So I hear where that Ed Meyer took and moved his geologist into the motel here," she said.

How did she know that so quickly? "Oh, was Alix in here for lunch?" I asked.

"Yes, her and Chet," she strung his name out long, making three musical syllables out of it. "But I heard from Wilma at the Oasis, last night." She stressed the last two words with evident satisfaction.

The Oasis is the only game in town if you're looking for a motel. If the establishment's name conjures in your mind a refreshing hideaway replete with palm trees and cooling zephyrs, think again. Rather, it is an all-American cinderblock and wallboard special, two stories high, with the requisite concrete balcony along the front and a few older cottages behind the office. The motel sits on the north end of town on the banks of the Greybull River, which has cottonwood trees along its banks, not date palms; and in the time-honored tradition of American motels, it was built right smack dab by the highway, so that the passage of heavy trucks can rock you to sleep.

"Is Wilma the woman that owns the Oasis?" I asked.

"Naw, Wilma's one of the maids, works there days. And sometimes takes the place nights, if the owners go off somewheres." Rita leaned closer to me. "You know about her and Ed, don't you?"

"No. Do tell."

Her eyes brightened. "Oh, them two's having a you-know."

"A what?" I smiled, looking as ignorant as I could.

"An affair," she said.

"No!" I tried to sound shocked. In fact, I was—at Wilma's taste in men.

"Truth," she said. "Told me herself. And you know, I think it's been going on some little time now. That Ed stayed there at the Oasis last summer, when Blackfeet drilled that other well, so I think that's when it started. A'course, I know because I know how to keep my mouth shut. You have to, in a small town." Rita leaned closer yet, lowered her voice to a whisper. "Tell a person like you-know-who," she rolled her eyes in the direction of the A&W, "and ain't nobody gonna have no privacy."

It occurred to me to wonder how I rated a top security clearance, but I wasn't going to look a gift horse in the mouth, even though this one wasn't telling me anything about Bill or Willie. Besides, I was already fully aware that Ed Meyer was a raging piece of pig shit when it came to his personal ethics. The only thing about this revelation that was remarkable to me was that someone would take him up on it.

I couldn't think how to steer the conversation smoothly to the information I was looking for, because I was aware that I was talking to a major town gossip. It didn't seem smart to let Rita know that I might have more than casual interest in her stories.

Rita left me again to take menus to a tourist couple who had ambled in from a big Buick with Wisconsin plates. When she came back, she said, "So I hear they're burying poor Willie up in Cody this Saturday. Family burial plot. Ain't that the saddest thing." She straightened the salt and pepper shakers along the counter top and adjusted the menus in their metal clip holders.

"You know, it weren't no horses that killed him," she said, one eyebrow high and the other low. "I wonder if it weren't that cousin of his. Never was quite right, you know." Gesture with index finger toward temple. "Always jealous of poor Willie." Squinted eyes, bitter tone.

This threw me for a loop. *Cousin? What cousin? You mean the timing of Willie's death could have been happenstance?* "Oh, really?" I said. "Tell me about it. What was this cousin's name?"

But Rita was off again to take the Wisconsin couple's order, leaving me with my head spinning with the thought that my intuition might be tuned in to Radio Moscow instead of the local station. Rita passed back through the kitchen and brought pie for the two men by the window, then returned to me. I was opening my mouth to pump her about the cousin angle when she said, "Ain't that old couple cute? They're here all the way from Washington."

"Washington? I thought they had Wisconsin plates on that Buick."

"Oh, no, they said Washington, I'm sure of it."

I struggled desperately to bring the quickly fragmenting conversation back where I wanted it. "I hear where Willie had his lunch here last Saturday," I said, and then, in a appropriately melodramatic tone, added, "the last day he was seen alive," immediately feeling a little disgusted with myself.

"That he did," she answered. "Course, I'm off Saturdays. I missed it." Dead end.

I heard an "Ahem." Rita twisted her neck around and saw the cook glowering at her from the doorway into the kitchen. She abruptly picked up a rag and started wiping the caps on the ketchup bottles along the counter.

"So do you think this cousin will be at the funeral?" I asked wildly, before she moved far enough away that I'd have to raise my voice.

"Which cousin?"

"Willie's cousin."

"Oh, I don't know," Rita said, vaguely. "Woops! Getting busy here, eh?" She was off again.

My patience was spent. I left four dollars under the edge of my half-eaten bowl of chili and rose to leave.

Outside, I glanced once again at the license plates on the Buick. Wisconsin. The frame around the plate read, "Kosciusko Buick, Madison, Wisconsin."

Washington, Madison . . . You know, one of them presidents. "So much for that witness," I muttered, as I walked away.

Where to next? Lucille's Cafe? The A&W? As I neared the A&W, two trucks pulled up, spraying gravel. Three young studs clambered out and crashed inside to pay court to Cindy. Marla sat by herself at the far end of the counter, and Jilly was nowhere to be seen. Lucille's looked busy, too, and I'd already had lunch. I kept walking.

The Mercantile was next on my list, a fine old dry-goods store on the corner across the street. The Mercantile sells everything from trousers to treble hooks and bubble gum to bee's wax, for what may seem like a handsome price if you aren't used to the cost of overhead in a rural store. I wandered up and down aisles crammed with flannel-lined jeans jackets and straw cowboy hats, lamp chimneys and bug repellent, boot laces and come-alongs, and decided to buy a pair of socks as an excuse for being in the store.

"Can I help you?" called a hoarse voice from somewhere behind the fishing tackle. I turned around and looked toward the source of the voice. Through the perpetual half-dusk of the Mercantile lighting, a glimmer of light reflected off the bifocal prisms of a pair of glasses, which appeared to float beneath a fringe of faded blonde hair. This specter hovered over a wooden counter, between displays of salmon eggs and spinners.

"Just looking for some socks," I said. "Spring coming. I'm about ready to get out of this wool."

A gentle tittering of laughter floated to the left and a more complete apparition formed at a two-foot stretch of open counter. The glasses, jowls, and hair came together above a Western shirt made of black-and-white plaid with metallic gold threads running through it as my eyes adjusted to the light. The ghost leaned forward onto the counter, cupped an elbow in her right hand and peaceably scratched an ear with the left. "Annual event, eh? Might try those ones with the green stripe across the toe. Kills the foot smell, if you're wearing work boots all the time," she said easily. "Don't have to wash them so often." The tittering laugh came again.

"Wash them?" I said. "I never wash my socks. I just wait 'til they're old enough to vote, and then I kick 'em out of the house; tell 'em to get a job."

"Tough girl, eh? Why'nt you come over to my house? I've got some old shoes I been trying to get rid of for years. Every times I throw them on the dump, they hop down and follow me home again."

"Oh, you just let me take them on, then. I'll take them with me out to that mean, nasty old drill rig and life will get rough. They'll head south. Last seen crossing the border into Mexico." I felt proud of that. I had maneuvered the conversation around to the subject of the rig, right casual like.

The woman behind the counter observed me in silence for a time, and then straightened up. I fiddled with different pairs of socks, wondering what she might say.

The next time I hazarded a glance at her, she had turned her face away, and she wasn't smiling any more. As her silence stretched into minutes, I paid for a pair of white socks with green stripes across the toes and left, wishing her good day.

Somewhat shaken, I crossed back to where my truck was parked, trying to think where I might head next. I turned my sights toward Dinah Sewell's apartment. *Well, this is a hitch, isn't it?* my brain muttered at me as I hiked down the side street. It was no fun at all to question—or should I say, try to question—someone who felt bad about what had happened. I felt guilty as hell about the sad look I had left on the Mercantile shopkeeper's face, and here I was heading up to the widow's home.

As it turned out, Dinah was glad to see me. I found her sitting at her kitchen table again, with the door standing open in pathetic hope of a visitor. The baby lay in an exhausted heap on the floor of its playpen, mouth open, drooling, mercifully asleep. I wished there had been flowers available locally, so I wouldn't have had to show up empty-handed.

"I'm glad you came, Em," she said, searching my face with faint hope for relief from her misery. "I been hoping you'd come again. Please sit down. Can I get you something to drink?" She moved slowly, dreamily, looking about as if she had to identify each item her eyes lighted upon, although nothing had changed since I had first seen the apartment three days earlier. *Three days? Is that all?*

Dinah brought me some Hawaiian Punch with ice in a green plastic cup. She sat down in her own chair and straightened the place mat in front of her. "How's it going with you?" she asked, moving the Tupperware salt and pepper shakers a fraction of an inch, aligning them more perfectly with the long axis of the table.

I was touched by such attention to manners in her time of distress. "Just fine, Dinah," I said, but then my conscience prompted me to spare her the trite sayings. "Except that I'm not getting a whole lot of rest. There's a lot been going on out at the rig."

Dinah's eyes came into focus. "Any news about who killed Willie?" she asked, her throat tightening around the word *killed.*

"I don't know much. The sheriff was out, of course. Asking questions. I took him around to one of the wells Willie pumped."

"The 17-1?"

"Yeah. How did you know?"

Her eyes were trained on the surface of my face, as if she were reading me like newsprint. "Of course it would be the 17-1. It caused him so much trouble."

"What kind of trouble?" Perhaps he had described the trouble with the valve to her more thoroughly or in a different way, a way that might cast some light onto his movements in his last days.

"The metering valve kept busting. He fixed it I don't know how many times. It just kept busting." She gazed away, scowling. Her voice sped up, scolding some unseen opponent: "And you know how good he was at tending things. He was wonderful. He could fix anything and it would stay fixed. It drove him nuts when that valve kept quitting on him."

"Did he say anything about why he thought it was broken, Dinah?"

Dinah's face crumpled into itself, imploding from woman back into child. She closed her eyes for a moment and I thought she might cry.

"Did the sheriff come and ask you all of this?"

"Yes."

"He's a bastard, isn't he?"

She broke into sobs. "Yes, and he can go straight to hell.

He didn't know Willie at all. He didn't believe me. He had no right. How's he supposed to find who did it if he can't even understand who it was that's died?" She stared pathetically at me through her tears. I moved around the table and sat down next to her, took her hands in mine.

"The sheriff upset me, too, Dinah. I think he's—" I couldn't think of a word stiff enough, so I said, "I don't like him, either," and left it at that. I waited at bit, letting Dinah pump more of her rage out through her tear ducts. Her tiny hands grew warmer with the release of tension. When she had calmed a bit, I asked, "Was it just the valve, or was there more that was going wrong?"

Her voice was tentative. "I don't know. He didn't tell me everything; never did. He just started going out there more and more. Started going out at night, too."

"Any special pattern?"

"No."

"When did he usually go?"

"At seven in the morning. He'd work 'til eleven-thirty, and then come home for lunch with the baby and me." A faint song came to her voice, and a smile flickered across her face. "It took him 'til noon or later to get here. Then he'd head back out at a quarter to one, come home at six. He'd do that five days a week, and a half day on Saturday. Sometimes we took a picnic out there on Sunday."

I hastened to keep her focused. "What would he do, the times you went out there with him Sunday?"

"Oh, he'd check on all his wells—make sure everything was running right. And on the 17-1, lately he'd started to climb up on the catwalk on top of the tank and shine a flashlight inside through this hole they have on the top. There's a lid on it. One time he pulled a long stick out of the back of the truck and let it down inside, and looked at where the oil came to on the stick when he pulled it out."

"Anything else? How about the most recent time you went out with him?"

"Oh, I went out with him last Sunday—I mean, the last Sunday before . . ."

"Yeah. And?"

"Well, he got out and put paraffin on the place where the valve goes together. At least, I think it was paraffin: it was whitish, came in a long brick. I remember he kind of heated it up with a cigarette lighter, and let it drip down in there where the threads on the pipe went together."

So Willie had put a paraffin seal on the valve and meter fittings. Had he suspected tampering? "Then what did he do?" I asked.

"That was all he did that day. I never went out with him again." Her voice trailed off, sagging back into sadness.

I pressed on. "What about the day he died? Last Saturday. He was gone longer than you expected." I immediately realized what an insensitive thing that was to say, and wished I could take it back. "I mean, did he say he'd be gone all afternoon?"

"He told me he might want to speak with Ed Meyer, that he might be late. I was walking the baby in town and Jilly said she'd seen them all having a late lunch down at the Blue Ribbon, seen them leave again after that, so I didn't start worrying 'til it was almost dark."

"Who all went back out with him after lunch?"

"Ah . . . maybe Jilly would know." Dinah's voice trailed off. Her eyes slid out of focus.

Oh boy, I thought. *Ask Jilly.*

23

I gritted my teeth and went back around to the A&W stand, hoping to find Jilly alone, bored, and forthcoming. If all else failed, I'd threaten to take my ears back down the street to the competition.

As I turned the corner onto the main street I spotted a small woman standing by the front fender of my truck, looking up and down the street in indecision, fluttering a couple of envelopes in one hand.

"Looking for me?" I called.

She spun about like a rabbit, half jumping. "Oh! Yes!" she said. "You remember me, I'm Evelyn Twitchell, from the post office. Bev over at the Mercantile said you were in town. This is your truck, right?" She smiled cheerfully, gesturing with the envelopes at me and the truck.

"Got some mail for me?" I was a little taken aback: I wasn't accustomed to having the postmistress run out onto the street with my letters from home.

Her excitement brought a flush to her fine, wrinkled skin, giving it a porcelain shine clear up to her froth of grey hair. "Oh, well, this isn't for you, exactly!" she said, looking at one of the envelopes as if it had miraculously appeared there only that moment. "Actually, it's for Bill Kretzmer, and of course, ah . . ."

"Yeah."

"Well! You see my problem! I don't know what to do with it! It came General Delivery several days ago, and I don't know what to do with it—oh, and here's one for you, actually, from your father—I don't know if I should send

Bill's letter on to that geology company, or what! I don't even have an address!"

I reached out and took my letter from her, turning it over to read the return address, which was written in my father's laborious hand. There were distinct prints of his thumb and forefinger in red Chugwater dirt, and a grime of dust pressed into the edges that told me it must have slid around on the dashboard of his truck as he drove to town to mail it and do the marketing. Inside would be his usual single page of news about the livestock and the weather, and the kind of evening it was when he sat down to write. And there would be a pitch for me to come home to the ranch. He'd be certain Mother was secretly longing for my company, just couldn't say so; or something like that. My jaws tightened at the thought.

When I looked up, the postmistress was on point like a bird dog, waiting for me to say something about the other envelope. Trying to figure out how to deliver a dead man's mail might be the biggest event of the week for her, and perhaps she was waiting for a statement from me about the man, or his death, that she could share with the next ten lucky visitors to her post office.

"Poor Bill," I said. "Can I help?"

She hopped up onto her toes as if the thought were new to her. She held the envelope in both hands, read it front and back again. "Do you suppose it's something that other geologist will be wanting? I just don't know, it could be important."

"Who's it from?"

"Oh!" She turned it back and front again, held it up to the light, seemed about to bring it close to her nose and sniff it.

I stepped over behind her and read the return address over her shoulder: *McCandless Well Histories, Casper, Wyoming.*

"Oh, yeah, I know that lady," I said. "Lucy McCandless. She works out of the Wyoming State Division of Oil and Gas. Private contractor. She looks up well data for you." It occurred to me that this might be something of interest. On the off chance that it was, I thought fast about how to overcome her remaining inhibition about giving me the envelope. I said, "I think this comes under the heading of company business. I could take it out to the rig for you. Give it to the new geologist. I'm sure that's the thing to do." I smiled again.

Evelyn Twitchell beamed back. "Oh, thank you!" she crowed, formally presenting the envelope to my care. "It's so sad, getting a letter I can't deliver because, ah—you know."

"Because the addressee is dead," I said, sliding into the sepulchral tones she so obviously craved. "Thank you, Evelyn. I'll see that it gets to her."

We smiled ceremoniously and she flittered back down the street to the post office. I stuffed the envelopes into my jacket pocket and headed into the A&W, bracing myself against the battle of wits I faced with Jilly. Jilly was peerless among gossips, although I got the impression that this achievement was of little comfort to her. Gossips can be a paranoid lot. *This time,* I vowed, *she won't get the upper hand.*

I was in luck. Both the boys and the girls had left. Jilly was there, leaning against the counter in a trance, her bulk draped toward me like a sack of melons. "Oh, hello there, Emmy," she said, sizing me up.

"Ho, Jilly. How's the asthma today?"

"Better, thanks."

"Root beer float, please."

"Thought you looked like a woman in search of the usual." She huffed off to the far end of the counter and started in on my order, grilling me as she went: "So how's the ruckus out at the rig? That sheriff been out there again?"

"No, haven't seen him." I took a deep breath and concentrated on my mission, abstracting myself from Jilly's pushy manner. *I stand on the bank of a stream, fly rod in hand, confident of an early strike. I cast out my bait.* "I'd say it was business as usual, but, well . . ."

"Well, I'd expect . . ." *A prize trout examines the line, regards the hook.*

"Of course, the way that sheriff carries on, we may never find out . . ." *I cast again. I let the elegant fly float down the riffle into the pool.*

"Do tell," said Jilly. "If that fool would just ask the people as know something, we'd get on with it." *The fish snaps up the fly, dreams glassily at the illusion of a tender treat.*

I play the line carefully, knowing this is a crafty old fish, that the hook is not irrevocably set. "I'll bet you could tell him a thing or two, Jilly."

She set my float down on the counter in front of me and took my money. "Yep, but he ain't asking me." She laughed bitterly. *Will the fish spit the fly out, leave me cursing on the bank?*

"That's stupid," I said, playing on her ego. "Here you were probably the last one to see him leave town on Saturday after he had lunch. That's damned important." By God, I was beginning to learn a little guile, after all, just slipped that in there like it was common knowledge. I prayed that Jilly had gossiped this point around a little, so she wouldn't realize I had talked to Dinah. A gossip can turn from a trout into a shark if it finds it's on the hook end of the line.

"You're damned straight," Jilly said. "But it wasn't just Merle and Hank. Ed Meyer was with them, too. Didn't you know that?" *The fish bites hard, leaps clear out of the water as the hook sinks home! I play it back and forth, tiring it out so I can bring it to the bank.*

"Oh, you mean they all came into town together and had lunch at the Blue Ribbon."

"Naw, I mean later. See, Hank was already here, but I seen them all come out together. They had Willie's truck parked on down by the corner here, and they all left together. I remember, because they looked like one of them circus clown acts, all loading into the cab of Willie's truck like that."

"You don't say." *Act casual,* I told myself. *Don't look too interested. Take another sip of your float.* "Do you remember who was driving?"

"Why, Willie was, I suppose . . . yep, something like that." Jilly was beginning to eye me with suspicion.

"And they headed back out the south end of town, out toward the rig?"

"Yep."

"Well, you probably would have noticed if he wasn't, because it was his truck." *Damned fish is disintegrating on the line.*

"Yep, of course he was. I would have noticed for sure if anyone else drove. Merle and Hank sat in the middle, and Ed got in last." She looked at me with her head cocked a tiny bit. "Right you are."

I perceived that my cover, if not exactly blown, was at least flapping in the breeze. I slurped at my float, readying the spoon for a speedy dive into the ice cream.

Jilly looked at me and I at her. She said, "So I guess they were on their way back out to the field. Who was the last to see them there?"

The fish is going fishing. Time to clear the bank. "I don't know, Jilly. I was off duty then. I never saw him after lunch." This was true. Someone had picked up Ed's car from the rig and driven it away during the afternoon. Had anyone noticed? Was it Ed himself? I had heard him tell the sheriff that he had stayed in town. But Jilly saw him leave town with the others after lunch. Who was telling the truth? And was it important?

Jilly's conversation drifted into a crepe-hanging session about the grim outlook for Meeteetse's economic future, complete with allusions to the occult and the macabre, suggesting that there was a curse hanging over Meeteetse, that someone might die each week for a while, you never knew about these things because why else would two guys with nothing in common die only a week apart?

I told her I didn't know, finished up the ice cream, and slid off my stool to leave. Jilly followed me to the door and took up her post like a sentry, watching the comings and goings about town, such as they were. Back at the Blue Ribbon, I saw Rita standing in the doorway in much the same pose. She flashed Jilly a look of pure bile.

I was halfway back to the rig before I remembered the letter the postmistress had given to me. It immediately started burning a hole in my pocket, sending smoke signals to my curiosity. I drove on, telling myself that it was not my letter, that it was none of my business.

But it's not Alix's, either, a part of my brain argued.

Thou shalt not open a letter that is not addressed to thee, answered its virtuous counterpart.

Spoilsport.

I have my integrity to think of.

Sure, but you want to know . . . Why not just pull over for a minute, and read dear old Dad's letter? It will only take a moment.

Well, why not? There's no real hurry to be back . . .

I pulled the truck over to the side of the road and pulled out my father's letter, and by George, the other just happened to come out with it so I tossed it up onto the dashboard lest I forget to give it to Alix.

That's right, give it straight to Alix, it's company business, my virtuous half said.

How boring. Toss Daddy's tripe aside and get to the gravy, said the other.

Virtue opened Dad's letter. As I had expected, it was three or four paragraphs outlining events on the ranch (not many), how pissed he was about the recent election of officers at the volunteer fire brigade, Mom said hello (she sure misses her little girl), and how was I?

I picked up the other letter and turned it over. It was a darn sight easier to contemplate than Dad's letter, and besides, I wanted to know what information was important enough to Bill Kretzmer in the last days of his life that he'd have it sent to him at the oilfield, instead of having it wait for him in the office. Or have his secretary deal with it, read it to him over the phone, or whatever.

By golly, it wasn't well sealed, was it? I fiddled with the edge of the flap, easing away at the small patches where the glue had adhered, and before I had really made a conscious decision, the flap was open and the papers inside were luring me onward like the Lorelei. I unfolded them and read the short message scrawled longhand on the first sheet:

Dear Mr. Kretzmer:
Enclosed please find information you requested by phone April 10 regarding Lone Spur Field. The records for 1973 thru June 1975 were not there. I believe that they have been illegally removed from the Oil and Gas Commission, like so many other things over the years. I enclose also my bill for services. You will note that there is a 25% surcharge for the rush job, as we agreed.

Sincerely, L. McCandless

I pulled out the other pages. There were three sheets besides the bill, all Xeroxes of a form entitled "Sundry Report of Oil and Gas Well," a standard submittal required by the State Oil and Gas Commission for every major change in well status. These ones announced plans to plug and abandon some new wells in Lone Spur Field, which lay about forty miles away and produced oil from the Tensleep Sandstone and gas from the Frontier Formation, just like Bar Diamond.

A rush job to look up abandonment records? That didn't make a whole lot of sense. I looked at the dates: 1975, 1976, and 1977. Ancient history. The wells would long since have been posted on any good map of the field, available on public record, and the well symbols would clearly indicate their status: drilled and abandoned. D & A: an open circle with four little spokes sticking out of it, like a chubby little compass. Eight spikes if it was a gas well.

I checked the billing page. For this, Bill Kretzmer had been willing to pay thirty-five dollars. I looked again at the date on the cover letter. For this, he was willing to pay thirty-five dollars on the day of his death?

I folded everything carefully back together, replaced it in the envelope and licked the flap to stick it shut again, readying it for Alix. I considered holding it out the window during the remainder of the drive to make sure it was completely dry before I got there, but figured that with my luck I might drop it out the window and Lucy McCandless would never get paid.

Alix was in my trailer, sipping some of her fancy tea and scribbling on her clipboard. She looked up briefly and nodded. Howard was nowhere to be seen: perhaps the company made him nervous.

"I saw the postmistress in town," I said, feigning a casual tone. "She gave me a letter addressed to Bill Kretzmer. She didn't know what to do with it, so I told her I'd give it to you." I tossed it onto the table beside her.

Alix kept writing. I fuddled around by the sink, not quite sure what to do with myself while I waited. At length she finished, put down her clipboard and stretched, a long, sinuous motion that worked her spine and rib cage. I waited, not staring at the envelope, just about writhing with the effort.

"Nice trip to town?" she asked.

I nodded.

"Things have been getting a bit tense out here," she said.

"Oh?" I waited for further comment, but Alix picked the envelope up in both hands, read the address and return address, and flipped it over without saying anything further.

I watched her at the edge of my vision, trying not to look interested, relieved to see that she didn't notice anything funny about the envelope. She read the cover note carefully, glanced briefly at the Sundry Reports, and stuck the bill in a pocket of her attaché case. The Sundry Reports she threw away.

"What was it?" I asked.

"Oh, I don't know. Just some well data Bill wanted." She picked up her clipboard and went back to her notes.

I wandered over to the plotting desk and affected interest in Howard's work.

"From this field?" I asked, rather proud of my misdirection.

"No, some other."

"That Bill sure liked to paw through the data," I said, taking another tack.

"Yes."

"Has he gotten any other letters like that one?"

Alix gazed at me, her eyes politely asking a question whose answer obviously didn't interest her.

I said, "Well, maybe he's got some others in those boxes of his. Shouldn't we look or something?" I hoped she'd tell me where Bill's files got to so quickly.

"Everything he left here went home to his wife." Alix looked elaborately patient.

Desperation came to roost. I said, "What did Bill hope to learn from looking at data from other fields? Isn't Bar Diamond the only Tensleep producer that Blackfeet has?"

Alix answered by simply lifting her pen an inch off of the page and looking up at me with a blank expression. She waited. Two heartbeats. Three. Four. Five.

I crumbled, blushing. "Sorry," I said. "I guess you got a lot of work to do."

She smiled a smile laced with just a trifling touch of condescension and looked back down at her work.

How I longed to fish that letter out of the waste basket before anyone else found it. But Alix showed no signs of moving. I huddled into the tiny cupboard known in trailers as the bathroom, brushed my teeth, and went to bed.

24

When I awoke at midnight to face the wee hours of Thursday morning, Alix was long gone. Having barked out my name just once to wake me, Howard was gone too, out the door and away in the truck. Another late night in Meeteetse awaited him, closing the Cowboy or the Elk Horn Bar, staring at TV and eating Beer Nuts to supplement his diet of ethyl alcohol.

I struggled into my jeans and hurried into the main room of the trailer, moving straight to the paper bag that served as a wastepaper basket, and dug into it in search of the note and Sundry Reports. A load of coffee grounds and some effluence from Howard's ashtray had landed since, but the Reports were still there, if somewhat stained and wrinkled. I smoothed them out and read the field name and well numbers one more time. Still, they meant nothing to me; but I folded them up and stuffed them into my cereal box, saving them anyway. Somehow, they had to be important. I sure wished I had Bill's files in front of me. *Who has those files?* I wondered, for perhaps the hundredth time.

As the men of the day tower arrived shortly before eight the next morning, they struggled into their coveralls and set to work amid a confusion of subcontractors who had somehow all shown up at once. Stretch was there, delivering the load of mud he had supposedly delivered two nights before; Merle Johnson was there with Hank Willard, delivering a new bit to replace the current one, which was evidently getting worn out; and the hole surveyor had shown up, readying to run a deviation survey while the drill string was tripped out of the hole for the bit change. When I put my hard hat on and wandered up into the doghouse to soak up some society, I was surprised to find an unusually large collection of hangers-on and droppers-by, all of whom were drinking coffee and generally getting in the way. The festivities even had an official clown: Wayne closed in on me, howling, "Hey, Emmy, know how turtles make love?"

I jumped aside. The bit trip was well underway. All eyes on the rig turned toward the drilling floor as Frank Barnes stepped forward and took over the brakes from Bud Holliday, and Frank's crew stepped into the spaces left by Bud's. Frank's crew seemed even smoother than Bud's as they fell into rhythm with the rise and fall of the huge draw works, hoisting the drill string out of the hole by ninety-foot stands. Bill and Wayne operated the tongs like telepathic twins, swinging these huge suspended wrenches in almost perfect unison, clamping them onto the pipe above and below the threaded connection between stands, bracing as Frank backed up the Kelley bushing to spin the threads open. Darrell moved up and back with the slips that held the pipe from falling back into the hole, his eyes always on the pipe, not needing to watch the others, confident in their movements. Eighty feet overhead in the derrick, Emo leaned into space from the "diving board" and slung a rope around the upper end of the pipe as the block hauled each stand his way, and then lashed the stands to the rig, leaning out into space at the end of the tether attached to his protective harness.

I glanced over at Frank, who stood relaxed but alert by the brakes, eyes on the block, muscular arms moving over the grips with the practiced, unconscious motions of a pianist in concert performance. His smoky eyes flicked suddenly my way and he nodded, his somber expression softening for an instant into a pensive half-smile. I bustled back down to the logging trailer. As I settled back to work, I listened with growing admiration to the smooth rhythm Frank made of the song of the brakes and block roaring and stopping, dropping and hitching. I worked peacefully, lulled subconsciously by this mechanical symphony, yawning now and then.

An hour had passed when the rhythm changed, alerting me that the motors were idling and the block had stopped moving. The bit was out of the hole. I headed up toward the floor again to get a look.

Ed Meyer had arrived in the doghouse. He stood with his hands on his hips, his neck craned dramatically to one side, cigarette dangling precariously from his mouth. The crowd waited. I took up a position strategically half-hidden behind a locker door. Just then, Merle and Hank staggered in off the rig floor with the bit.

Bits weigh a lot. It was about all I could do to lift that four-incher I kept in my trailer for a door stop. I can't lift an eight-incher, not on a bet. They are solid castings, twice as tall as they are wide, and they're just not going to blow away in the next wind.

The two men grunted, maneuvered, and dropped the iron mass, shaking the floor. Ed squatted down and pulled it over on its side to examine its cutting teeth.

"Shit!" he said. "Well, wait; get me some rinse water on this thing." Hank hurried out onto the floor for water while Ed and Merle craned their necks right down to floor level, squinting at the bit. The assembled masses looked on in silence, awaiting the verdict. I saw Johnny Maxwell straighten up from his usual lounging posture, instinctively shifting out of Ed's sight, his face set in a stiff mask.

Hank returned and doused the bit.

"Well," said Ed, "I guess we pulled it a bit early. But you never know for sure with these things. That's how it goes, ha-ha. Ha-ha-ha."

"Oh, yeah, look here," said Merle. "This tooth would have started giving you trouble right quick, Ed."

"Right. You're right, Merle. Oh, well, boys! Them's the breaks. We just won't tell the front office, eh? Ha-ha-ha-ha-ha?" Ed graced everyone with one of his most charming smiles, his even white teeth lined up like soldiers on parade day.

A thin chuckle ran through the audience. Johnny rolled his eyes slightly heavenward, and I could all but smell his brain overheating as he added a spurious bit run to the cost of the well.

"Okay, Merle," Ed declared, "go ahead and put the new bit on. C'mon, fellas, we got work to do." The party was over. The men shuffled back out onto the drilling floor.

At times when someone who ranks you makes a bad judgment call, it's best not to appear on the list of witnesses. I went back to my trailer with every intention of minding my own business, but Johnny Maxwell walked in, heading straight for the coffee.

"All in a day's bullshit," he said, saluting me with his cup. "Say, you got a special symbol you can put on the log that means, 'unnecessary bit run'?"

I asked, "So you think this bit run was a trifle premature, do you?"

"Premature? I hadn't even noticed she was pregnant!"

"That bad? How could everyone be that far off? Didn't the drillers have something to say about the change?"

"Nay, Lassie, this were the work of one man only, and he be none other than our own fearless Chief of Operations."

"Yon Edward, the Meyer?"

"Yea, verily." He raised his mug in a toast.

Ed had ordered a bit run to replace a bit that wasn't worn out yet. Ed had ordered heavy mud for a formation that didn't need it. Ed had appeared as if by magic when I showed the sheriff the 17-1, clearly wanting us to leave. Ed was crucifying his pipe salesmen for extra-special prices, with something fishy about the percentages. Ed was moving his geologist's trailer off site for another well that wasn't yet drilling, costing Blackfeet extra for Alix's lodging. If these costs didn't quit mounting, there would be no more wells.

And the original geologist was dead, in an accident that didn't quite add up.

And the pumper was dead, his head bashed in by a heavy object coated with crude oil.

"Johnny," I asked, "just what the hell do you suppose is going on here?"

"Damned if I know," he said. "I just work here. I only get a bonus if we come in under cost." His jaws tightened.

25

Two hours later, bad news came home to roost. I was in town having a bowl of chili at the Cafe when I heard about it, so I heard it from a man who had just heard it down at the gas station. He had heard it from Jason from the Lookout Ranch south of town, who had heard it over the radio telephone as he was leaving to come into town for gas. Jason had overheard a call from Frank, asking the operator to call Fuzzy McDowell out from Powell, which could only mean one thing.

Fuzzy McDowell is a subcontractor known as a fisherman, a man who comes out to the rig when disaster has struck. When something or everything has fallen down the hole. Dropped. Lost. Stuck. In the way. Can't get it out. Fuzzy has the tools and the talent for fishing lost drill pipe, wrenches, you name it, back out of the deepest of holes.

I quickly calculated where the men would have been in tripping the pipe back into the hole. It was almost two o'clock. The news might have traveled quickly or slowly—quickly, given the small town appetite for news; so the call from the rig came at say, one-thirty. I had left at twelve-ten, when Frank and his crew had been tripping the pipe in for, say, three hours. It had taken four and a half hours to trip out. That meant they probably weren't done tripping into the hole yet.

I feared the worst. Calling out the fishing crew before the bit is back on bottom means something really big and obvious has fallen into the hole, like maybe part of the drill string itself. If the pipe lets go during a trip, it drops until it either hits bottom or snags on the rough sides of the hole. It usually collapses, twisting hopelessly into something reminiscent of wet spaghetti but a whole lot more expensive.

The first thing that went through my mind was, *Poor Frank*. It's a really bad thing to lose the pipe into the hole; it reflects very badly on the driller.

Then I thought, *Poor me, for heaven's sake. What am I going to do for a job if this job gets shuts in?* I paid my tab as quickly as I could and hurried back out to the field.

By the time I arrived, there were enough cars and pickups parked around the rig to transport a small army. The owners of nearby ranches, off-duty roughnecks, and even a couple of hands who worked the Bar Diamond Ranch were standing around in the yard or sitting on the hoods of their vehicles, shaking their heads and commenting on the goings-on, their shoulders hunched as if to ward off evil spirits. They were gathering at the well because it was the only way they knew, within the cowboy's code of stoicism, to share their feelings in public. Gather and tell stories. Gather and be quiet together. Gather and watch the disaster unfold in the company of your fellows.

As a citizen of a town not unlike Meeteetse, I felt the echo of their pain. Once again they were gathering at the site of a death, but this time it was not the death of a countryman. This time they gathered to grieve a death that came by inches: the death of income, of possibilities, all the more painful in its incompleteness. If this well failed, for whatever reason, it would mean the departure of more people to look elsewhere for their living. This was the slow-moving death of community; the draining of youth from the land.

Frank stood right at the center of this pain. He had to answer to none other than Ed Meyer, who was becoming known throughout the Wyoming oilfields for making life rough on people who screwed up. Frank was the local boy, whom everyone had known forever. Ed was from some place called Oklahoma, where people talked funny. I looked up at the drilling floor. The tension there would be palpable.

I took the stairs to the doghouse two at a time. Just as I'd expected, the scene inside was about to snap.

Ed Meyer was in the middle of the doghouse shouting at Frank, who stood squarely in the doorway to the drilling floor, facing him like a soldier, chest out and hands behind his back. Frank's face was distorted in a mixture of rage and confusion, as if he were dreaming of sinking his fists into Ed's guts, but wasn't sure it would make him feel better.

Ed screamed, "What in hell you got in mind, droppin' somethin' that big down six thousand feet of hole? What, did you think you was testin' for bottom or somethin'? That's the hole surveyor's job, you second-rate rig pimp! You messed up good this time. And let me tell you, boy, you'll never get another fucking job in this business by the time I'm done with you."

Something that big. Not the drill string?

Emo paced up and back, up and back. Wayne and Darrell sat on the bench with their heads bowed. Merle Johnson stood stiffly in attendance beside Ed, gazing steadily into inner space, and Johnny Maxwell leaned into the corner over the standing desk, staring quietly into his coffee cup. I wondered distractedly what Johnny would do with his hands if he didn't have that cup.

I headed to the trailer in hopes of finding someone who could tell me what had happened. I found Howard sitting at the plotting desk, a small flask cradled tenderly against his chest. He didn't look up as I came in. Alix was stretched out on the settee across the end of the trailer, paperback in hand, reading. I wondered, *What book is good enough to keep your attention at a time like this?*

It was a strange scene: Howard drinking openly on duty, with the company man right there to see it, but I felt pretty stunned myself. I said hello to both of them—or perhaps just to the trailer, as I may as well have walked into a sitting room for the deaf and blind—dug through the cupboard for a bag of potato chips I keep squirreled away for emergencies and started stuffing them into my mouth.

When in doubt, eat. My stomach quieted. I said, "So, Alix, what the hell happened up there?"

She answered without looking up from her book. "That is not known yet."

That is not known yet. What a precise, seamless little answer. I cussed her out liberally in the privacy of my mind, but as I stared at the top of her blasé little head I found myself feeling sorry for her. *What a pity she isolates herself so,* I thought. From there I was just getting into patting myself on the back for being so damned big when this pity got really uncomfortable. There was something about it that threatened to explode backward into my face.

"All right, *when* did it happen?" I persisted.

"About one o'clock, when Frank got on bottom."

As soon as he got on bottom? What could be down there that would let Frank know he had a problem right away? And how did Ed get here so fast? "So Ed just got here from Cody?"

"Oh? Is he here now?"

Don't kid me. You know damn well he's here.

I could see I wasn't going to get much more out of Alix, and it would never have occurred to me to ask Howard. I didn't quite know what to do. I wanted to go for a walk to burn off nervous energy while I waited for the news, but I wanted to be nearby in case I could somehow help. *I owe Frank one,* I rationalized.

I could hear the rhythmic whir and grunt, slam and crash as the crew returned to tripping the pipe back out of the hole.

About an hour later, Fuzzy McDowell's truck drove into view, resplendent with all the trappings of the trade mounted on racks behind the cab. Fuzzy climbed out and yanked off his cap to rearrange his thinning hair, hitched his pants up toward a belly sufficient to fill his oversized plaid shirt to a taut smoothness. His hair looked no straighter when he was done and his belt immediately settled back to its customary position, but ritual is ritual. He pulled a couple of tools off his racks and labored up the steps to the draw way and out of sight behind the bunting that surrounded the drilling floor.

Then an odd thing happened: Ed and Merle came down the stairs, got into the Oldsmobile, and drove away. You could have knocked me over with a twig. I thought Ed would be up there making everyone miserable until the cows came home.

"Meyer's gone," I announced to my fellow zombies as I headed out the door. At the mention of the name, Howard jerked in his seat and slipped his flask out of sight in a fair bit of sleight-of-hand.

Up on the drilling floor, Fuzzy stood rigging a fishing tool to be lowered down the hole. There wasn't much to see. The upper two or three thousand feet of the drill string already stood in its lashings beside the derrick, and I had a bad feeling that the pipe would be there for some time to come. Fishing could take days or even weeks, and if they couldn't recover the pipe the hole might have to be plugged back and sidetracked, abandoning the portion that had something stuck in it.

Frank stood at the brakes, intent on his work. Now that he was back at work and no longer had Ed shouting in his face, he looked almost normal, his motions smooth and hypnotic.

Johnny stood by the standing desk. He sipped at an empty cup and then stared into it with disgust and declared, "I'm out of coffee, sport. Let's get out of here." At the bottom of the steps, I headed off toward my trailer, but Johnny snatched my sleeve, pulling me toward his. Inside, he flicked the propane on under a pan of water and hauled a jar of instant coffee down off a shelf. "Not as good as yours, but . . ." he said.

But out of earshot? I sat quietly and waited. The water made hissing noises as the pan heated.

I had never been inside Johnny's trailer before. It was sparely appointed yet cheerful, with a crocheted afghan slung over the settee and some Louis L'Amour westerns, a couple of John O'Hara novels, and a modest edition of Shakespeare's comedies stacked on the shelf above.

"Frank's been screwed here, kid," Johnny said. "I can feel it in my bones."

"What do you mean?" I asked. "And what about that fast exit Ed made? That was weird."

"Right." Johnny stared into space. His distraction unnerved me as much as anything. He meditated over the pan of water until it boiled, then made instant coffee, his jaws flexing vigorously. "You take it with cream, right?" he asked, holding up a jar of some concoction designed to make my coffee look right and feel right without tasting right. I declined and took it black. "Not as good as yours," he said again. "But."

We settled back into silence. As the minutes creaked by, I began to get the sensation I was sitting up at a wake. I glanced at my watch periodically, watching three-twenty-five turn into three-thirty, and three-thirty into a quarter to four. Frank would be off at four. The important thing was to be there when he was done.

By four, the evening tower had arrived. Verne Johnson, the evening driller, took a sorrowful look at Fuzzy McDowell's truck as he got out of his car. He bowed his head and marched up the stairs, lunch pail hanging dispiritedly from one hand.

Four-fifteen came and went. Johnny refilled the pan with water and turned the propane back on. The other four men from the day tower came down the stairs, crammed themselves into one of the trucks, and drove away.

Four-twenty. The water simmered and then boiled.

At four-thirty-five, Frank finally came down the stairs, his head bowed forward.

Johnny opened his door and waved him over. Frank came inside, and when he saw me, he smiled wanly and leaned against the door frame. He shook his head as Johnny raised the jar of coffee off the counter in offering, but nodded when Johnny opened his half-height refrigerator with the toe of his boot, revealing a six pack of beer.

"Did you hear Fuzzy say what I heard Fuzzy say?" Johnny asked.

"You mean, when he thanked Ed for the job?" Frank said.

"Yeah. Sound funny to you?"

"Well, yes and no. I suppose there were other fishermen as could have been called, but he was on the official roster Blackfeet posted by the phone. What I thought was strange was how fast them two took off after he said that. It almost looked like Merle was goose-walking Ed out of there, not the other way around."

"Like the tail is wagging the dog."

"Yep. But I don't know."

"Yeah."

The two men sipped their beers. I swilled down the last of my coffee.

Johnny handed me a beer and I pulled the tab. "Here's to bad luck," I said, hoisting it up. I am so clever in a pinch.

But Johnny looked at Frank and said, "I don't think this is just a matter of bad luck, Frank. What the hell's down there, anyway?"

"I don't know. Something big and hard. Like I told Ed, I just put that bit on bottom and knew I had company. Didn't even need to wait and see if I got any penetration. The torque was chattering around like all hell."

"What's big enough to do that? The drill string's still in one piece, ain't it? And a wrench would just hold you back. It won't make your torque erratic."

"Shit, Johnny, the only thing I could think of is a drill bit."

"A drill bit? Great. Yeah, that would do it. But they took that worn bit away with them this morning. The new bit didn't drop off while you were tripping in, did it?"

"No," Frank said, his eyes a bit wild. "That's why I stuck around, so's I could get a look at the goddamn bit when it come up. That baby was right there where I left it. I don't know what in hell's name is down there." He stared at the floor. When he spoke again, the weight of the world had descended into his voice. He spoke so quietly I could barely hear him. "I just plain fucked up. I thought I had my crew trained better than that. I thought we had our timing down just right. We were hot, tripping hotter'n a forest fire. I just don't know what's down that fucking hole or how the fuck it got there." The knuckles of the hand that held the beer went white. The can crumpled, spitting beer on the floor.

Johnny said, "Aw shit, Frank, come on. Think about it. I was in the doghouse—remember the commotion when that bit come up? It was like a circus act, like everyone was hustled into the doghouse to see the bit. No one was watching the drilling floor for a while. Shit, anyone could have walked out there and dropped anything they liked down that hole. I mean it. Someone's purposely sabotaged the hole."

As I sat listening to Johnny and Frank, a strange feeling came over me. A sickening feeling: one that said I knew something that I didn't want to know, and I tried ignoring it. Why not just stay ignorant of the absolute? But I wanted to know, and that was that; so I got up and started out the door of Johnny's trailer.

"Where you off to, Slick?" Johnny asked.

"Got to check something," I said. "Be right back." I hurried across the yard to my own trailer. Alix's vehicle was gone, as were all others except those belonging to the evening tower and Fuzzy McDowell. I pulled the inner door of my trailer outward, topped the step, and pushed the inner door inward. Sure enough, it whipped right around and hit the table. Crash. Howard cursed. I had my answer.

Frank looked up at me as I stepped back into Johnny's trailer. The late afternoon sunlight caught his eyes, lighting up to the softness of the green within the smoke. "What is it, Em?" he asked, his voice as gentle as a child's kiss.

"It is a drill bit, in the hole."

"How do you know?"

"Because mine's missing. The one I use as a door stop.

I'm sure it was there this morning, before, ah—every-thing."

Frank sagged. Johnny looked at Frank with *I told you so* written all over his face.

"So what we going to do, fellah?" Johnny asked.

"Piss. Nothing I can do. I guess we're going to have to plug that hole back and sidetrack it."

"It's not so simple as that. Em's probably right—aw, hell, you know and I know she's right, but I'm not going to Ed Meyer and saying, 'There's a drill bit missing out of the logging trailer, so that's what's down that hole.' He'd shit little gold nuggets."

"Ain't that the truth. But if it's true, it's true. Maybe he's the bastard that put it there."

"But he'll be saying you threw it down there! Use your head, Frank. The man's got a bad well going here, he's in deep shit with the big boys back in Denver, and he's got a twisted mind. You tell Ed Meyer that you're sure a drill bit somehow found its way from the inside of the logging trailer all the way up to the drilling floor and down the hole, and he's going to be all over you like a cheap suit. He'll say, 'So how do you know this, Barnes? Did you maybe throw it down there yourself?' No, I'd keep my mouth shut if I was you, Frank. God dammit, you didn't even give that new bit ten minutes on bottom before you started tripping it back out! What's it gonna look like, fel-lah?"

"Shit, Johnny! I got a job to do, and I don't go costing the company rig time while the thing sits there idling be-cause I'm afraid of some asshole ops engineer, company man or no. Fuzzy could be there fishing for days, or even weeks, and we'll never fish no goddamn bit out. You know and I know we got to plug that thing back and sidetrack it, so let's just get the hell on with it."

"All right, all right, listen: did you see it jump in, maybe? You want to maybe make yourself only eight inches wide so's we can dangle you down that hole by your foot and you can take a look? Someone could just as easily pinched the kid's bit for a souvenir. We're trying to drill through one of the bolts that holds the world together, for all I know!"

Frank got real quiet. His hands tightened into fists. The focus of his eyes receded to somewhere inside his head, until the tension in the man threatened to tear the delicate fibers of his soul.

I wished I could comfort him. My hands itched to touch the nape of his neck, where fine hairs curled against the warmth of his skin.

Johnny bowed his head. He ran his fingers through his short, wavy hair, forcing it into a row of cock's combs so tight they looked painful. He spoke very quietly. "Please just let me do my job, Frank. I'm the tool pusher here; I call the moves. I hate to say it, but we're going to have to cover our asses here for a while. For all I know Ed threw that bit down that hole himself. Heaven only knows what's going on here. It could've been anyone. So listen, fellah, I've worked with Fuzzy before. He knows his job. He'll try the magnet and then a couple tools, and then he'll call it quits pretty quick. He's not going to fool around, 'cause it would give him a bad name. He'll probably call for a milling tool and try to grind it out."

"That won't work."

"Right, but that's final. It's just a damned job."

"You have spoken."

"Yes, sir."

The little muscles twitched in Frank's face. A note of pleading leaked into his voice. "It was my tower. I got a reputation to maintain."

"You got a reputation that can stand a little fishing time."

There was silence for a while, and then Frank said, "God dammit, I want to know what's happening on this rig, Johnny."

"So don't we all, fellah."

So don't we all. As if he had heard my thoughts, Frank looked up and stared at me, a look that swallowed me whole. The power of his presence was growing on me, pulling me toward him like a narcotic. I looked into the grey-green depths of his eyes and knew he was thinking about me, and our talk in the truck two nights before, and the heat rose in my neck and cheeks. I tried to smile, but my mouth twisted around kind of funny. I wanted to say something that would break this tension, assuage my gathering feeling of helplessness. I said, "I think it's time I went to Denver and talked to Bill's wife."

"To who?" Johnny asked.

"Bill Kretzmer's widow."

"Why?"

I forced myself to turn and look at Johnny, concentrate on his face. "Just to get a look at his maps and stuff."

"Wait a minute, kid, what are his maps going to tell you? What's this all about?" Johnny asked.

"Um, well—"

"She thinks Bill was murdered, too," Frank said. "I'm beginning to think she's right."

Johnny looked at me like I was a painting. After a palpable pause, he said, "So what's the connection between maps and murder?"

Such a simple question, with such a hopelessly complicated answer. The truth was that I had been moving at random in my investigation, just snooping around in the corners that seemed most accessible. I said, "If they were both murdered, then it's highly likely there's a connection, and if there's a connection, it's this oilfield. Not just this well, because Willie didn't work on it. The whole field. So if the field is the key, I've got to see the maps. And Bill's notes, more importantly. You see, Willie suspected tampering at the 17-1. Willie was looking for something in Bill's trailer the night Bill died. So maybe they were working together to figure out what was going wrong with this drilling project."

Johnny's eyes were wide. "You're nuts," he said.

That hurt. I shrugged my shoulders, looked at the floor.

"I mean, to get involved," he said, in a kinder tone.

"So I'm involved. Maybe you'll keep that under your hat."

Johnny looked a little insulted. "Of course. But listen, kid, do you really have to drive clear to Denver? Can't you go to the district office up in Cody for that kind of information?"

"That would mean going to Ed, and I'm sure not going to Ed with this. Alix sure as hell doesn't want to get involved, so those boxes are all I've got to go on. He kept all kinds of stuff in them. Maybe he told his wife before he died."

Frank said, "Right, he was coming back from talking to her when he died. Phoned her the same time every night. You could set your clock by it."

Johnny still looked unconvinced, which was a problem because the tool pusher is top dog on the rig, and I needed his complicity if I was going to leave the rig for long enough to make a run to Denver. "Shit, Johnny, we have to try something. The sheriff's just out to collect bodies."

Frank's jaws clenched.

Johnny said, "How do you know what to look for?"

I was getting downright exasperated. I was just opening my mouth to whine or scream or gag when Frank said, simply, "You're forgetting she has a degree in geology, Johnny."

Johnny fixed his tired gaze on me. "Well, it's your bed time anyway, kid. Let's wait and see what Fuzzy says. If he calls for a milling tool, he'll be at it a while. But you go get some sleep. It's a long drive to Denver."

26

At midnight, I awoke to the straining racket of Howard trying to drive the truck away in third gear, and the more comforting sound of Johnny making a fresh pot of coffee out in the kitchen. He made a small ceremony of handing it to me, nodding and making something like the sign of the cross, and then handed me a set of keys.

"These are Frank's," he said. "To his truck. He's taken his house key off, but don't take that personal, kid; he'll probably just need it before you do."

I gritted my teeth in embarrassment, certain that my growing attraction to Frank must be tattooed on my face in red letters. "I'll drive Frank home tomorrow. He's asleep over in my trailer—that man paced until I thought sure he'd go right on through the floor boards."

"Thanks," I said, still listening to the painful protestations of the engine outside. "I guess my company truck isn't available."

"Right. Howard would get to whining if he had to rely on anyone else to get him to the bar, and just might do something pissy like call your boss. You wouldn't like that."

"No," I said. I fished a bowl and spoon out of the drain rack by the sink, reached my box of cereal out of the cupboard and shook some into the bowl, making sure not to dislodge the letter from Casper. Corn flakes. Breakfast of sleepwalkers. "So I take it Fuzzy's sent for a milling machine."

"Yup. You're in luck. We had one hell of a time finding one. Finally got one out of Salt Lake City. I figure the fellow in Salt Lake will be eight, ten hours getting here with it. Four, five hours to set it up and trip it into the hole. We'll be in Howard's shift then. Probably at least twelve hours before they give up, then another four, five hours tripping out again. That takes us through your next shift and into Howard's again, so I figure you got at least forty-eight hours to make your run. How long you need? I could stall it, maybe call for hole reconditioning or something. Maybe Ed won't miss you while we're running cement for the plug-back."

The corn flakes yielded listlessly to my teeth. I had forgotten the sugar, but my taste buds weren't awake yet, anyway. "Ten hours down there, ten back. That leaves me twenty-four hours. It'll have to do."

"Right."

We didn't say much more after that. I filled a thermos with coffee and got into my best pair of jeans and sweater for the trip into the big city, brushed my teeth, combed my hair, and headed out the door. I fired the engine and was off.

From the oilfield road I turned south onto the pavement of Route 120, glad to be starting the drive in the middle of the night. That would put me through that stretch of broad, flat, and lonely grassland between Shoshoni and Casper long before sunrise. You'd think that an old prairie dog like me would love it, but somehow those two hours of the drive drag on and on, and the sense of isolation eats me alive. It's just too empty. The few antelope and jack rabbits that try to scratch a living out on that plain seem half-sized against all that openness and far horizon, and what few towns you pass through are nothing more than a couple of shacks huddling miserably by the road.

The truck rode smoothly enough for something that looked like a refugee from a demolition derby. I had to take quite a swing at the gearshift to slap it into third and the clutch pedal was no shrinking violet, but the engine had a businesslike hum and plenty of power.

It was a dark night with a thick cloud cover, and seemed

darker yet because the dash lights didn't work. The only light was the bald reach of the headlights in front of me. I worried briefly that the clouds might portend a late snow from the east; but as I rolled along in the darkness all cares slipped away, and I began to feel exhilarated with the sense of journey. It was good to get away from the drill site after weeks of repetitive routine. The excitement of what I was trying to do had me sitting up straight in the cab of the truck, not even touching the back of the seat.

But before long the darkness began to close in on me, as if the sky was pressing lower. It had a hallucinatory effect. I fancied at one point that something extremely large was moving along the crest of a hill to my left. I knew of nothing that large that should be roaming the prairie at night, or for that matter at any other time, so I wrote it off to nerves, or tried to.

I decided to turn the radio on in hopes of getting one of those evangelical shows that broadcast out of Texas in the middle of the night, blessing me for eternity and asking for a few dollars here and there. They make good company for late-night cross-country driving, with their friendly voices and earnest message, and they say things that I differ with just enough to keep me a touch angry, which helps me stay awake. Besides, the radio lights might be on a different fuse than the dash, and I began to yearn for that happy little radio dial smiling its light at me from the vast darkness of the dashboard.

When I snapped on the left-hand knob I got a rousing load of static. The knob on the right did nothing. It spun this way and that, then gave up the ghost and fell off into my hand. I contemplated the static for a moment, staring into the minuscule radio light and trying to decide just how badly I wanted to listen. About then I thought I saw that big something moving out there again, and I decided I wanted to listen pretty damned badly. I slowed down and steered the truck to the side of the road, bringing it to a stop well off the shoulder in a depression below a low bluff of sandstone, and killed the engine and the headlights. After several moments of fiddling around trying to get the knob to stay on, I chewed up a bit of paper, jammed it between the knob and the post it mounted to, and tuned in the first station I came to. Darned if some Bible thumper out of New Mexico didn't try to save my soul straightaway.

I was just about to fire the engine back up when I caught something moving in my peripheral vision, this time entirely too close to write off to nerves.

It was just a hundred and fifty feet away, right by the side of the road. My heart raced in my chest. I held my breath and crouched down into the seat. The something moved off to the right, and I realized it was a small tank truck like the one Willie had driven when he collected the oil from the holding tanks. It was pulling onto the pavement from a place on the other side of the road. This was damn strange, because I couldn't see a side road coming in, and I knew the truck hadn't been sitting there when I pulled off. But stranger yet, it was running with its headlights off. And at one o'clock in the morning. It accelerated to the south, and as it reached thirty or forty miles per hour, the headlights came on.

It didn't take a brilliant mind to figure out I had seen something I wasn't meant to see. But what? And why? Who the hell would be driving around in the middle of the badlands hills in a pumping truck in the middle of the night with his headlights off? Some strange sport.

Apparently, they hadn't seen me. Frank's truck must have been almost the same color as the bluff, and the effects of a hard winter and a liberal amount of dirt must have completed the camouflage. Up-and-coming private investigator that I was, I swallowed the dregs of my terror, waited until the tanker was out of sight down the road, and pulled out behind it. I knew I wouldn't have any trouble catching up to it, because those units can't move but so fast in any circumstances.

I was wrong. I came around a curve and up and down two hills, but saw no pumping truck. I began to think it really had been a hallucination. I drove on a mile or two farther, and still no pumping truck. I pulled over and stopped, turned around and passed back, presently coming back to where I had started. No pumping truck. There was nothing for it but to give up and head on toward Denver.

But you can bet I wondered about it. If you have a situation where a certain pumper has turned up dead after sealing a metering valve with paraffin, and then you see an unmarked pumping truck rolling around in the dark of night with its headlights off, you'd have to be dead from the shoelaces up to miss the possibility that the two occurrences might be connected.

I kept driving south. I rolled onward through the night, falling back into the rhythm of the drive. I piloted my way through the rounded hills past Grass Creek, past Thermopolis, and through the Wind River Canyon to Shoshoni, where billboards lured me to the drugstore that boasted the "best milk shakes in the U. S. of A." I passed the sleeping drugstore and turned eastward, toward Casper. The broad wasteland of Fremont and Natrona counties slid silently by beneath the wheels of the truck as the light of the radio winked arhythmically to the strains of songs sung by cowboys in pain. They sang of lost love as I passed Moneta, and lost chances near Waltman and Powder River. The world quickened with the promise of civilization at Natrona, only thirty more miles to Casper. The late stars that danced on the horizon, presaging the coming dawn, were soon dimmed by Casper's lights. I sped past the sleeping suburbs and sluiced past the Hilton, the Holiday, the Ramada, and the Riverboat inns.

I turned off at the last Casper exit, found a gas station, filled the truck, and drained myself. The night attendant fumbled with my change, uncertain of his arithmetic. *This is an oil town,* his actions told me, *and any man with any wit, with half a brain, who can sign his name, is out making money in the oil patch.* He shook his head in frustration. I offered to help, but he snatched the money closer to his chest in defiance, counting it carefully, counting it aloud, nodding his head to each bill and coin.

I stretched my legs a moment longer, trying to shake out 165 miles' worth of kinks, and wondered if I might just get to Chugwater in time for breakfast with my father. Mother would still be asleep; it might be worth the risk. My heart skewed away from the notion, shunting my mind onto other thoughts. I climbed back into Frank's truck and turned its nose toward the road.

I pushed farther eastward, on Interstate 25 now, following the course of the Platte River as it sought lower ground on its way to join the Missouri, past Glenrock and Douglas, the home of the world's largest Jackelope. Roadside signs urged me to continue eastward across the prairie to Nebraska and then north to Wall, South Dakota, to visit Wall Drug, flagship of the world's tourist traps. Have You Dug Wall Drug? the signs said. I stayed with the Interstate, which rounded the end of the Laramie Range and swept southward toward Denver. On the radio, the cowboys' broken hearts gave way to the morning cow and pig report from Nebraska. Sow bellies up yesterday in heavy trading. Good weather predicted for spring crops. Wheat futures down.

Orin. Glendo. Wendover. Turn here for Guernsey. The sky brightened steadily. Wheatland next. The next would be Chugwater. What time? Six o'clock. Good time I'd been making. Father would just be getting up.

Wheatland ground past, brightly illuminated in imitation of a big city. Twenty-five miles to Chugwater.

A bright band of infant day spread across the eastern horizon, carrying with it the stirring of Nebraskans and Iowans and folks from Illinois. The band caught fire and blazed, brightest in the middle, erupting as the sun raised its burning eye to behold the west. Each bush, each blade of grass cast a shadow along the ground, feeling for the night, reaching westward to grasp it a moment longer.

Chugwater. I turned off, still undecided. I thought I'd just take a spin down the main street that runs through town. I could always continue on and get back onto the Interstate again at the other end.

As I passed the grain elevators and bald storefront of the Farmer's Co-op the rush of familiarity engulfed me. I turned off on a road that led west and headed for my father's ranch.

Three miles out of Chugwater I turned off the pavement onto a washboarded dirt road. The only indication that a ranch lies down that rutted track is a mailbox with fading yellow letters on it. Dad's let the track fall into such disrepair that you have to be driving a truck, or not care what happens to the suspension of your car, or be willing to drive at about four miles an hour for the remaining half mile or so to the ranch house. Dad never has cared too much for visitors, except his kids, who drive trucks anyway, and it's been years since Mother has driven. Since the night of my high school prom, to be exact; and that, I told myself, was why I was here. Once and for all, I was going to get an answer: was something wrong with the car that made her leave the road, or was she just too drunk to see the curve?

I bounced over the rails of the cattle guard and started up the rise that hides the house from the road. At the second line of fencing I saw that Dad had closed the barbed wire gate, which meant that the cattle or horses were in the near pasture. I got out, unhitched the gate and laid it aside; got back in the truck and drove through, then parked the truck and closed the gate again. First rule of ranching: if you find a gate closed, close it again when you're done.

As I headed back for the truck once more, I spied an old friend down the track. There, in the yellow light of dawn, with the waning moon setting to one side of her well-muscled flanks, stood Gypsy, my lovely mare, strong-hearted winner of countless barrel races, patient companion of a thousand afternoons. I whistled, and she trotted right up to me, forgiving as ever that I had been gone so long. What pleasure to hug her warm neck in the brisk morning air.

Gypsy raced happily along beside the truck as I bounced over the last quarter mile to the dooryard, and stood patiently by the last cattle guard, waiting for me to park the truck and come back to her for more hugs and to have bits of dried Russian thistle prised out of her mane.

Dad was up all right. He was just coming back to the house after feeding the chickens. When he saw the unfamiliar truck he stood stiffly for a moment, freezing like a fence post in his unathletic stoop. I waved, craning my neck away from Gypsy so he could see me.

He straightened up as fast as a man with a bee up his pants. "There's my girl!" he whooped. "You done come to see your pa! That's my Em!" He broke into a little jig, his rough hands flapping at his sides.

I ran to him, burrowed up against his chest and squeezed his bones as hard as I could. He thumped my back happily, still bouncing up and down a bit. The scents of hay and chicken feed assaulted my nostrils, and I knew I was home.

The sun flashed in the small panes of the windows of the ranch house as we strode toward the kitchen for some vittles, as Dad chose to call breakfast on this fine spring morning. He usually spoke in terms recognizable from Seattle to Bombay, but having his youngest child drop in without warning was a cause for celebration; and with celebration, he was liable to put away the vocabulary he learned at Boston College and flip into his ready reserve of Western jargon.

As had been his habit for as long as I can remember, he hung his jacket on the jutting end of the fourth log up from the bottom as we rounded the corner of the house. He always said that's why you live in a log house, so you have somewhere to hang things. He kicked open the heavy pine door, yanked a dog outward by the collar, and pushed me in. "Bacon and eggs it'll be for my little cowpoke," he crowed.

"Shh," I said. "Don't wake Mom." I wanted an answer to my question. Damn it, I was grown now, and I deserved a little information. The truth, even. But if Mother woke up, the subject would never leave my lips.

"Aw, hell, Em, that would take a nuclear explosion. You know she'll never rouse up before nine." He struck a match and tossed it underneath the kettle before he turned on the propane. "So what brings you? My, you're looking good to me, gal."

My lips tightened. "Just an errand to Denver, Dad. Thought I'd come by here and snag me some jerky, is all. I got to keep going." *I'll ask in a minute, I told myself. Give him a minute to think I'm here just to enjoy his smile.*

"Nah, you stay a spell this time, hear?"

"I wish, Dad."

My father shook his head, smiled at me with a coy longing in his eyes. He put a cast iron pan onto another burner and started peeling bacon into it out of a package from the refrigerator. A cat I didn't recognize wandered in from the next room and rubbed against his legs.

"New cat?"

"Oh," he said, "you know how these critters do come and go. A couple years they're good mousers, and then one day, whhhpt! Gone. Who knows where. This one come from Freddie down at the Co-op." Freddie knew a soft touch when he saw one. The cat hit Dad's leg with an audible thump, purring loud enough that I could hear him clear over where I sat. Dad dropped a tidbit of raw bacon directly into the cat's mouth.

The kettle boiled and I rose to make coffee. We worked side by side in silence for a while, enjoying the smells of bacon and coffee and the comfort of quiet companionship. The sun pushed higher in the sky, mingling with the branches of the cottonwood trees outside in the dooryard, as a flight of sparrows flittered about on their budding twigs. I looked at Frank's stubborn old truck in the driveway and found myself wondering what I was doing here, so far away from my compatriots in their time of trial. At the same time I wondered what dream of far adventure I had just awakened from, to find myself at my father's table just like any other morning. I shook my head to chase away this sleepy confusion. The truck sat resolute and obstinate in the driveway, demanding that I hurry to finish my meal and be on my way.

The sound of a toilet flushing deep in the house set me up on my toes and ready to leave on the run. I glanced reflexively at my father, who stood poised above spattering grease, his ear cocked to the same sound I had heard. "Early," he said. His face clicked into blankness, his eyes extinguished. He pulled the pan off the fire and fell silent.

My fingers tightened around my coffee mug and I shifted instinctively toward the outside door.

Soft footfalls approached through the house. A match spat into life and then clinked against an ashtray. I found myself praying that she would go back to bed, but knew that there was no hope.

"Why, good morning," my mother said, as she appeared at the doorway. "How nice to see you, dear." Her long body rested on one shoulder against the door frame, the lines fine and muscular beneath the papery silk of her dressing gown. The elegant bones of her face still stood proudly within her corrupted flesh, the red tracery of thin blood vessels in her cheeks still mistakable for rouge at first glance. She looked back and forth between me and my father, her eyes slightly narrowed above her sublime smile. "Having a nice little party?" she asked.

My chest tightened as it had so very many times before. I wondered idly if it was just an allergy to her cigarette smoke. "Hi, Ma," I said.

Dad busied himself with plates and forks and juice glasses. "Well, nice to see you up, dear," he said. "You sleep well? It's some beautiful morning, ain't it?"

"Isn't it," Mother said.

"Isn't it," Father echoed.

"Thirty-one years I've been in this house with you, Clyde. One would think I might have had a slightly greater impact on you." Her voice purred over the words, disappearing over the Rs and sighing over the vowels. *Thihty-one ye-ahs*, it said, bludgeoning us softly but firmly with her Yankee roots, indelible no matter how many years she might live with my father out in this imagined place in the sagebrush, so far from the white clapboard houses of New

England. She smiled cruelly, winking at me before taking another drag on her cigarette. She coughed.

"Sit, sit," my father said, herding us toward the table. He shoveled eggs and bacon onto plates and brought them to the table. Mother moved to the table and sat, her eyes on me every inch of the way. As she neared me, the reek of stale alcohol and cigarettes pierced through the friendly cooking smells, sticking to my face like cobwebs, pushing on my stomach.

"Eat, eat," Father said. He sat down next to me and squeezed my elbow. I looked at the plates. I had two eggs; he had one. His second was now on Mother's plate, along with half his bacon. He shoveled into his food heartily. I took a mouthful of mine and chewed, tried to swallow. Mother tipped her ash daintily onto the edge of her plate.

"What brings you to town?" she asked, twisting the last word with the irony of our distance from any city.

"Errand to Denver." I ate faster.

"Oh? May I know?"

"Um, for work. You know." I shrugged my shoulders.

"Yes, I suppose you can't tell your mother." Her voice cut with the last two words, ripped into me, spilling foul, stinking bits of her life onto my lap and spraying my face with bile. I stuffed two pieces of bacon into my mouth at once and tried to swallow.

"So, how's the well drilling?" Dad asked. His eyes rested firmly on his food.

"You look tired, dear," Mother said. "Are you letting them work you too hard again?" She fished a small silver flask from a pocket of her robe and poured some of its contents into her coffee.

"Well's going fine," I said.

Mother tapped her ash again onto the plate. Father finished his eggs and sucked at his coffee. I willed the last swallow of egg down my throat.

"Have to go, I'm afraid," I said. I rose from my seat, banging my knee against the table in my haste.

Mother looked up. "Your knee all right, dear?" she

asked, a wry smile flickering across her face. She stubbed
out her cigarette and lit another.

"Fine," I said.

"I'll walk you to your truck," Dad said.

"Just where did you find that thing?" Mother asked. "It
looks like the wreck of the *Hesperus*." She drank deeply
from her cup.

"Well, see you," I said.

Mother rose from her chair and came to me, patted me on
the cheek with a cool hand, took another drag on her cigarette. I looked up into her eyes for an instant. An invisible veil
dropped across them as she withdrew deep into herself, fleeing at the speed of light. She was still looking at me, but I was
no longer certain that she saw me. She leaned forward, presenting her cheek to be kissed. "Have a nice drive," she said.

I delivered the requisite kiss and left, following Father
into the dooryard. He held the door to the truck open for me
and asked, "Will we see you for your Mother's birthday?
Next month, you know."

Then it will be Fourth of July you'll be anxious about,
Father. And then Labor Day, and Thanksgiving . . .

"You never know with the drilling business, Dad," I said.
"I'm just on until they're done. Then on standby for the
next well. You know."

He smiled a self-contained little smile. "Well, you'll try,
okay? Your mother would sure like it."

"Sure, Dad." I kissed him and started the engine. "Dad?"

He was instantly on the alert, eyes locked on mine.
"What, Em?"

I stared at my hands. "I don't know, I—"

"Spit it out," he said softly.

"You know that time Mom rolled her car, and Uncle
Harry was killed?" *Sure, like how could he forget?*

"Now, what the devil brought that to mind?" he said, trying to deflect the question.

"A man was killed out by the rig. It was real similar.
Dad—"

"Now, Emmy, just put these things out of your mind."

"No," I said quietly. "I'm not a kid now. I want to know what made her car leave the road. It'll help us solve the question of this other guy," I added hurriedly, as if that was all the more important Mother's crash had been, just a key to another puzzle.

"Oh," Dad said, his face going blank, like he bought my line of illogic. "Well, she swerved to miss a coyote, see."

I wheeled on him, sticking my head out the window at him. "That was all? All these years I thought she was stewed."

Dad looked away. "Well, Emmy, there was that, too, but she would have made it home fine if that coyote hadn't crossed her path."

I wanted to spit. Just how far could my father go to rationalize things? "I notice she hasn't driven since," I said meanly.

Dad narrowed his eyes at me. "That's her preference," he replied hotly. Then he closed his eyes and sighed the sigh that always drains my anger into a puddle of guilty sadness at my feet. "Try to understand, Em," he whispered.

"I'm sorry I spoke, Dad."

Still sighing, he ruffled my hair. "Safe drive."

"I'll be careful."

He grinned. "That'll be a first."

I wheeled the truck around in the yard and headed out over the cattle guard. The ranch house grew smaller and smaller in the rearview mirror and then disappeared from sight as I crested the rise, and the sun burned heartlessly into my eyes. I pulled up to the highway, crossing the last cattle guard. Hard pavement again. *Away, away, away,* the truck sang, as it wound up through the gears.

To Denver. To get the job done, I thought, but my mind stayed on my father, and my mother. Why had she ever left the East? Was it such a good joke, to marry the cowboy from college? "Didn't work out for you, did it?" I shouted, into the quiet prairie.

27

The rest of the way into Colorado was a free-fall straight south along Interstate 25. By ten a.m., Denver spread out before me, languishing in visibly dirty air. Its tall buildings formed a knot of congestion seeding an invasive sprawl, like a rampant mold consuming a fading slice of bread.

I pulled off into a gas station and another and then another, until I finally found one that had a phone booth with a real live phone book in it. As I had suspected, Kretzmer was not a common name; but as the gods were smiling on me, it was in the book. I dialed the number and waited, patting the glass on the booth to coax the gods into smiling a little more and letting the party be home. She was. She said she'd see me, and gave me directions to an address on West Thirtieth Avenue.

I wondered what Bill's wife would look like. The serene, silver tone of her voice over the phone had been a surprise. Bill had been bristling and dark, with a voice that could saw through cast iron. I had never seen him in anything more formal than plaid shirts and jeans. Perhaps his wife would be one of those people who sound like a million dollars over the wire but look more like ten cents when you meet them: a man that gruff would have a raw-boned wife who put her feet on the table. At least, I hoped so. To be candid, the voice had me a bit unhinged.

But the feet of the woman who came to the door of the little Tudor-style house were not the on-the-table type. She was a rare and delicate flower with translucent skin and beautiful hands, and a strength of bone and slender muscle that moved with a near-unearthly grace. She examined me sadly through moist eyes, dropped her heavy lashes twice and looked away. "I'm sorry," she said. "It's just you remind me of Bill coming home from the oilfields, the way you're dressed. Come in."

I stepped into a room that beckoned me with quiet colors and rich furnishings. A florist's arrangement of chrysanthemums and roses sat aging on a low table, its withering petals the only note of recent loss visible in the room. "I'm so sorry about Bill, Mrs. Kretzmer," I said, glancing at my feet to make certain I was tracking no rural mud into this civilized setting.

"Call me Elyria," she said. "And please, come into the kitchen. The sunlight is much happier."

"Thank you, Elyria. That's an unusual name."

"My mother was Yugoslavian. Will you have some tea? Please make yourself comfortable. I'm glad you have come."

Her delicately chiseled cheekbones and the slope of her forehead spoke strongly of her eastern European heritage. The rest was, what? French? The effect teetered richly on the edge of the exotic. I thanked her for her kindness and took a seat by the kitchen table. A large grey cat materialized on my lap and made a small "pet me" noise as Elyria turned toward the stove, her well-draped skirt spinning with the motion. She lit the gas under the kettle and sat down across from me, smiling the slight, self-contained smile that is bred of good manners and self-esteem. The form definitely fit the voice.

I found myself gearing up into the best, most grammatical, most polite, most high-class English my mother had ever nearly despaired of teaching me. It came with a fusty awkwardness, saved as it was for state occasions such as visiting my maternal grandmother or other monuments to museum-quality class. "It is so kind of you to see me. I know you must want to be alone at a time like this," I said.

"I've been alone too much. I'm going back to work next week, gawkers or no. Please tell me how the well is going," she said, and added, "This well was terribly important to Bill."

"Well, that's sort of what I needed to talk to you about," I said, giving up any pretense at the King's English and slipping back into my Wyoming twang. "I'm wondering about what Bill had in mind for this well. It's important to—ah, the way we're drilling it." I decided on a chicken-shit approach to the whole matter because I was just that: chickenshit. Ever tried walking into a woman's house and saying, "I think your husband was murdered. Have any ideas why?"

Elyria tipped her head to one side and examined me as if I were an unidentified plant in a garden she was weeding. "Excuse me, Em, but isn't it rather unusual for the mudlogger to concern herself with the way the well is drilled? And to the extent of leaving her post and making a ten-hour drive?"

I felt my ears warming. "Yes."

"But this instance is different?"

I felt like a surgeon had just slit me open to take a look at my innards. I could see why Bill Kretzmer had loved her; the voice, the looks, the grace would catch any man's eye, but the lack of bullshit would capture that one man's heart and never let it go. She was waiting, burning me with her undivided attention. The cat dug its claws gently into my knee.

"Yeah. I don't know if you are aware there's been a second death on the rig."

Her eyes widened in alarm. "Who?"

"A pumper, named Willie Sewell."

She shook her head: she didn't know the name. "When?" she whispered.

"Well, it happened last Sunday, or probably the afternoon or evening before. And, um, y'see, it's been established that he, ah, died of unnatural causes; like, not accidentally." *Good show, Em. Your English is going to hell in a handbasket.* "Probably a blow to the head with a pipe wrench. His body was dumped out on the prairie and found the next day by the geologist who replaced Bill on the rig, Alix Chadwick. Well, that and a few other things got me thinking that something was not quite, ah—kosher about the way Bill died."

In the few moments during the drive I had dared wonder about the widow's reaction to this information, I had expected denial, tears, maybe a faint. What I saw was rage: quiet, deadly rage. If looks could kill, that genteel, delicate woman could have vaporized a brick wall. I knew the glare wasn't for me, but it took the oxygen out of the air just the same.

The kettle whistled on the stove. Elyria Kretzmer rose from her chair with a stiffened version of her grace and hammered through the motions of making tea. When she was done, she stood in the middle of the kitchen, looking down at the teapot in her hands as if she had forgotten something. In embarrassment, I looked away.

The teapot hit the back door with a gush of steam, china flying like shrapnel and water soaking the curtains. She wheeled on me, slamming her fists on the table. "All right," she said, her voice crisp and commanding, "All right." She panted, her teeth bared; seconds passed before her eyes were fully focused. "All right. Now I know why you're here. What do we do first?"

"Bill's files." My words tumbled out. "Did you bring his files home from the rig?"

"No."

"Do you know where they are?"

Elyria's face registered in turn dismay, loss, and then fury. "Those were his personal files. They should have come here with the rest of his things. I'll call the office." She grabbed the kitchen phone off the hook and punched in a number with martial precision. "Geology," she ordered into the mouthpiece, speaking in a clipped mixture of grace and command. "Hello, Sylvia. Elyria Kretzmer here. Fine thank you, much better. Yes, in fact you can do something for me. Can you tell me if my husband's work files have arrived back at the office? I believe they were shipped from the Cody office. Yes, thank you so much, dear, and thank you again for the flowers. You are all so thoughtful. I'll hold." She turned back toward me, her cheeks blossoming with the ripe flush of high fever, her rib cage moving in and out like a bellows under the soft fabric of her blouse. "The geology secretary is looking. Next question."

I was at a loss. "Did he keep anything at home?"

"Yes. A file of, ah, extra copies. Not er—common knowledge." She gave me a hard look, making sure I understood the gravity of what she had said. Geologists are not supposed to take proprietary information outside of their offices, but most do take bits and pieces. It's rather like a jeweler taking home the leftover chips of precious stones in his trousers cuffs; items that are of little value to the boss, but are stock in trade to the worker if he ever needs to take his labor down the street. I showed her both palms. Bill's indiscretion was safe with me.

The secretary's voice brought Elyria's attention back to the telephone. "Yes? What?" The color of her face darkened noticeably. She placed her hand over the receiver and turned to me. "She's switched to his desk phone. She says that no files ever came from Cody, that in fact the technician phoned the Cody office a few days ago and was told they never saw them. Wait—what?" She turned her attention back to the phone. "His desk, too? This is serious." Back to me, she said, "Sylvia's checked his file cabinet and his desk drawers. There's a lot missing. At first glance it appears to be everything Bill worked on in Wyoming."

"What?" That didn't make a whole lot of sense. Why take all of Wyoming?

Someone had lifted the office files, right under everyone's noses, without being seen. But who, and when? I ran down a list of everyone I could think of who might conceivably be involved, searching for the one who could have slipped away to Denver, gotten into Blackfeet's corporate offices without being noticed, and made off with a major set of files. Ed Meyer was the only one.

Glee swelled in my heart. The fantasy of nailing Ed

Meyer to a cross in a court of law consumed my consciousness. My mind careened wildly, building its castle of power to fantastic heights at terrifying speed. *Standing up in the witness box, I open my mouth and fire rushes out, consuming Ed Meyer in flames, burning first his hair and then his clothes, frying the flesh from his skull. He writhes, screams, begs for my mercy. The walls fly from the room—*

"Em?" Elyria's silver voice tugged me back toward consciousness. "What else should Sylvia look for?"

The grotesque volume of my hatred rocked me, frightening me with its ugliness, sluicing the filth and blame of the situation back at me, threatening to drown me in guilt for my capacity to hate. I stared at the palms of my hands. *What is happening to me?* I shrugged the fantasy off as quickly as it had come, but a sense of inadequacy lingered in its place. It was a moment before I could speak, and when I did, I was surprised at how normal my voice sounded. "Ask her if she can find out whether Ed Meyer has been in the office and when he's been in Wyoming during the last few weeks." *What's the matter with me?*

Elyria uncovered the mouthpiece. "Sylvia, this is quite important to me. Is there any way you can find out when Ed Meyer has been in and out of the office in recent weeks? His secretary keeps notes? Wonderful. Wait, try not to tip your hand: don't let her know you're checking. That's it! And I need to know as closely as you can manage just exactly what's missing. Yes, well—I'd rather not have to say why. You're a dear." Elyria hung up the phone with a slam and turned to me, her face a mixture of sadness and gratitude. "She's going to get right to it. What she's doing is against company policy, but she liked Bill very much. He was decent to her, it seems. And there are certain factions in that office." She set her jaw in a firm line, her lips narrowed.

"Let me guess. These factions are Friends of Ed Meyer, and Those Who Wish He'd Drop Dead." I quickly regretted my insensitive choice of words, but Elyria didn't flinch.

"And the second category contains most of the women who work in the office."

She said, succinctly, "Yes."

"And it is well known that Bill had no use for Ed and vice versa."

"Precisely."

"I guess we're thinking the same thought."

"Right again," she said.

We exchanged a long look. It was strange to begin to know, to really *know* that I was right, that Bill had been murdered; and at the same time it was awful to look into the eyes of someone who was in such terrible pain from the truth.

Elyria snapped her eyes off me and turned toward a doorway that led down a flight of stairs. I followed. At the bottom of the stairs we stepped over a large nondescript dog and into a small room with a linoleum floor that had been set up as a study. Technical books lined the walls. Two short file cabinets formed the legs of a long desk made of a hollow-core door, in whose empty knob hole sat a cup full of colored pencils. A rack of maps stood at one end and a stereo at the other. On the desktop lay a large map of Black Diamond Field and several manila file folders.

"What are we looking for?" she asked.

Shit, I thought. It could be a map, or a report, or a sheaf of notes, or just another Sundry Well Report with the important part red-penciled. Or maybe the only copy of what we need has been destroyed. I sighed. "What do you do for a living, Elyria? Are you a geologist, perchance?"

"Consulting economist. I do predictions of petroleum reserves and pricing."

"Oh." I had no idea what that meant in terms of her background. "Well, did Bill discuss his work with you much?"

"No. Or yes, after his fashion. Perhaps you noticed that he asked a great many more questions than he answered."

That was true. I cringed to think that, in all the time we had spent chatting about the Tensleep Sandstone, he had in fact never said anything of a specific nature about Bar Diamond Field. How easily I am led along. The sheriff's words about my poker-playing aptitude came back bitterly as I tried to think of how to explain to Elyria what I was looking for. "I'm thinking he might have known that something was funny about the way the field was being operated. Since he died, there's been a rash of unnecessary expenditures on the new well. The mud bill and rig time and bit bill are going to be outrageous, and the reason I could get away like I have is that someone apparently sabotaged the hole, kicked a drill bit down it. One mistake is bad judgment, two is coincidence, but three and four? Well . . ."

"You're wondering who's profiting, and if Bill might have known that."

"Exactly."

"I see. I was wondering why he had me show him how to calculate drilling costs. That's usually an engineer's job. I thought he seemed especially tense before this well." She shook her head. "I'll start with this drawer, you start with that." She pulled open a drawer and pointed me toward the manila folders on the desk. She turned toward her work after pausing for a moment to glance at a small framed photograph of herself and her departed husband swathed in plaid shirts and hiking shorts and standing on a high peak somewhere. Bill sported a rare grin.

I burrowed into the first file in the stack. As I worked, I glanced over at her only once. Her cheeks were wet with tears, but her hands moved systematically through the folders.

We worked with tense concentration for twenty minutes. It was appalling to think that I was looking at only a partial duplicate set of Bill's files. What we were searching through would have filled a large suitcase.

My stack of folders yielded nothing, so I started on the left-hand file drawers. The top drawer held reprints of several research papers on the Tensleep Sandstone. Many of the papers looked familiar, but there was one from the *Journal of Petroleum Technology* that was new to me.

Skimming it, I found that Bill had highlighted parts of it and made a few notes. On the second page he had written: "phone author re: Maverick Field." I remembered Bill's capacity for hounding people with questions, and smiled. On the back of the reprint was a notation that read:

Maverick at near virgin pressure after re-drill
Re-entered cable-tool holes with rotary tool
Tensleep not homogeneous as presumed
Cross-beds? Lupe and Ahlbrandt

I pulled out each reprint in turn, turning straight to the back pages, looking for similar summaries. Notes on a paper by Emmett, Beaver, and McCaleb for a field very near the Bar Diamond particularly interested me: they said that Tensleep Sandstone oil reservoirs produced more and more oil the closer the wells were positioned to each other, almost as if they were creating new oil. Weird. It blew the engineers' predictions all to hell. Bill had underlined half of the paper. Two particularly obscure notes read:

Untapped pockets
Which way was the wind blowing?

With that last note, I began to curse Bill for leaving nothing but undecipherable notes for the helpless dummies like myself who had to struggle along behind him. *Give me a break, Bill, you taciturn devil, I'm trying to find out who the hell killed you.*

Lupe and Ahlbrandt turned out to be a photocopy of one chapter of a book edited by McKee on the geology of sand dunes, past and present. Their chapter described ancient dunes which had turned to stone and were now oil-bearing rock. There was a bit on the Tensleep Sandstone, which Bill had highlighted.

My head began to swim. All I could really gauge from these papers was that Bill had found the Tensleep very interesting, which I already knew. Furthermore, it was evident that many people knew most of what Bill knew, and that they had put it all down in professional journals that were publicly available. So what was the mystery?

Mentally, I lined myself up in front of the firing squad, but before bidding them pull the trigger, I figured I was owed one last request. I interrupted Elyria. "Anything?" I asked.

"Nothing and everything. My husband was a bit too cryptic in his notation. Unreconstructed academics are all alike."

Shit. "Elyria, did Bill ever tell you anything he knew about the Tensleep that maybe no one else knew? Like a brainstorm he had or something. There's one paper here about the Maverick Field, an old field down in the Wind River Basin, drilled decades ago with old cable-tool rigs. When the field appeared depleted, some guys bought it for salvage and drilled a bunch of new wells using the newer rotary rigs. They say it came back in at virgin pressure."

"What does that mean?"

"It means that the original pressure that drove the oil out of the rock and into the well bore was still present in places all over the field. It hadn't been depleted except right around the older wells."

"I take it that's unusual?"

"Yeah. The pressure of the reservoir usually declines smoothly as you pump the oil out. Like letting the air out of a balloon, sort of."

"I take it that it's unusual for the balloon to find itself re-inflated?"

"Right, old fields are usually abandoned when the pressure gets too low. Except these Tensleep fields. They seem to work differently: there's something funny about the rock. You could drill a well and produce it for thirty years, and then drill another near it with a rotary rig and it'll come in gangbusters all over again. Most reservoirs, you can predict the rate of decline from the day you drill your first well until the day you haul the pumps off for scrap."

"But they always drill more than just one well. I've

never fully understood that. If all the oil can flow toward one well, why drill more?"

"You're an economist; it's easy. Imagine trying to earn your living emptying swimming pools with a soda straw: you can get the job done that way, but you'll make a lot more money using a couple of garden hoses. So they drilled a few dozen holes at Bar Diamond."

"Ah. The more straws you can get sucking at once, the faster you empty the pools, and the faster you can spend your profits—as long as the cost of drilling additional wells is adequately serviced by the increased cash flow, keeping the rate of return sufficient."

It took me a moment to absorb the economists' jargon. "Right, but here's how it usually pans out: the geologist finds the oil with the first well, then the job mostly goes over to the engineer to analyze the reservoir and figure out how many wells are needed and how far apart. A development geologist like Bill helps, but the engineers don't always listen to him. And in this case, they were re-drilling an old field."

"Yes, I remember a few things Bill had to say about certain petroleum engineers," Elyria said, dryly. Elyria had a flair for understatement. Some of the arguments I had heard on the rig would sear the ears off a brass monkey, on the way through to other parts of his anatomy.

"Yeah. Bill was invading Ed Meyer's precious territory. I wonder why Ed let that happen."

Elyria looked at me as if I hadn't been paying attention. "It had nothing to do with Ed. It was Bill's idea to buy up the rights to the field, and Bill sited the new wells and even designed the drilling program."

"You're kidding me. I can understand the geologist having something to do with recommending purchase, and maybe getting his two cents' in about well siting, but are you telling me an ego case like Ed let a geologist design his drilling program?"

Elyria said, "I understand there was quite a fight over it in the board room. Sylvia could hear it clear down the hallway."

A pattern started to assert itself. A pattern of a jealous

engineer wanting to make a hot young geologist look bad. But kill him? "Okay, so it looks like Bill thought Bar Diamond would come in with unexpectedly high pressures and extra oil on a re-drill. But the 17-1 was a dud."

. Elyria looked as though she might spit. "That's not exactly true. Bill said the cuttings looked quite good while you were drilling, but then the pressure tests were bad."

"Right, but my job was done before they tested. What happened?"

"Evidently nothing. Bill couldn't understand why it wouldn't produce—or rather, why the well was only marginally profitable. They had already spent the money to set casing and run pipe into it, so they went ahead and put a pumping unit onto it, to see if it might produce better after pumping for a while. It never did. It was a terrible disappointment for him."

I thought of Bill having to come home from the well and tell his beautiful and intelligent wife that his brainchild had been born retarded. It must have been a bitter day for him.

Elyria seemed to be sagging in the traces, her first surge of angry enthusiasm giving way to a pained fatigue, but I pressed her onward. "I guess that brings me around to the problem of how he sold the board of directors on the second well if the first one was a dud."

"That's easy to explain. They were already on the hook for the purchase cost of the field. And they are incurable optimists."

I smiled. "I think the word is gamblers. But try to remember: maybe he prepared a proposal for the new well, or something? Maybe he practiced it on you, even."

"No, he didn't. You know how Bill is. Was."

After another fifteen minutes of reading, I knew nothing more. I would need to see maps and new wireline logs and God knew what else. And of course, it wouldn't hurt a bit if, like Bill, I had a master's degree and five years' experience.

The phone rang again. Surprise lit Elyria's face. "It's for you," she said.

28

It was Johnny. "Got trouble," he said. "Big Ed knows you're gone, and he's throwing one bodacious shit fit."

In two seconds flat I went from calm but despairing to smoking mad and convinced of my competence. A few noises that weren't words came up my throat before I managed, "Just where does he get off? The rig's idling!"

"Makes no sense to this boy, either. He just reared up and started bawling about an hour ago."

"But I'm not even supposed to be on duty now. What's it matter to him?"

"Damned if I know. Look, I'm sorry kid. I told him you were on an errand for me, but he didn't buy it, like he wasn't even listening. He's screaming you're AWOL and says he's going to have your job for it. Now you know Ed—maybe his jeans are chafing him or something. There's a chance he'll leave it go as soon as something else ticks him off worse, but maybe you better just get back up here. See if he'll forget you were gone."

"Shit, Johnny, how'd he even know I was gone?"

"Oh, seems he went on one of his little Gestapo inspection tours. He got to looking at the log and asked Howard some question he couldn't answer, so Howard dumped it on you, saying you went off and left him in the lurch. You know and I know just what kind of bull roar that is. Ed was probably just trying to shake the old boy up anyway. So the next thing happens is Meyer's having such a good time he starts going through the whole logging trailer after Howard's rotgut. Hell if I know how he got off Howard and onto you, but when I got to the trailer to see what was cooking, Ed was coming out of the sleeping room right quick, looking like he swallowed turpentine or something, hollering about faithless women. Ah, hell, you can guess what all he was saying."

A chill ran up my spine. I grabbed at my back pocket for the little notebook.

It wasn't there.

It was in my other pair of jeans. In the trailer.

Johnny was still talking. "Want my opinion, Kid? The front office came down on Meyer's ass for running a lousy show out here, and you're today's burnt offering. Nothing like chastising someone else to make a man feel like a man. Maybe he thinks if he complains that he can't get good help, Denver won't notice what a load of horseshit this drilling job of his is."

Through my own fright, it began to seep through to me that Johnny might be the next one in line for incineration. Even nowadays, fired mudloggers can sometimes find other work, but I didn't know how things went for tool pushers. It touched me that he would take the time to drive into town to make a private call to me when he had such problems of his own. I said, "I'm starting to get somewhere with Bill's files," and wondered if I was right. I was only trying to cast a little hope his way, and it's possible a few more hours would have helped. For a moment I considered saying to hell with it and sticking right where I was, but there's nothing like being threatened with the loss of your job to make you want to keep it.

I didn't have to explain things to Elyria. She had divined the situation from my half of the conversation, and was already preparing to get me on the road. "You'll need something to eat, my dear," she called from half way up the stairs. "And if I have my way, you'll take a nap before you go. No job is worth falling asleep at the wheel."

Here was this woman being thoughtful of me, while I was letting her down and running back to Wyoming to retrieve my job like some slobbering hound chasing a stick! I wanted very badly to make it up to her, to magically compensate for Bill's death by serving his murderer up on a platter; to be worthy of her kindness and regard. I pawed rapidly through the files, hoping to find the one golden page that would answer all of our questions.

A few typescript papers in a file marked, "Not to Be Duplicated," came quickly to hand so I grabbed them to take along, figuring I might not have seen them before. There was a thick file full of more of the baffling Sundry Reports, all from fields in Wyoming and all highlighted where they were signed *Ed Meyer, Chief Engineer,* and what looked like beginning notes for a presentation on Bar Diamond Field, stuffed with view graphs and more cryptic notations concerning lots of dollars. I bundled them all together and looked for a map or two to take along. The one that was laid across the top of the desk was colored in, with markings showing who owned what; but a little more digging turned up a nice structure contour map and some cross-sectional diagrams, so I stuck them in with the files and made for the stairs.

Upstairs, I found Elyria scribbling on a pad on the kitchen counter. A sandwich lay half-constructed next to her. "I'm making a list of people to call for information," she said, without looking up. "Here, I hope you like ham and Swiss—I haven't had much in the house lately. You eat and I'll write."

"I'm not all that hungry, really."

"Nonsense. Sit down; it's unhealthy to eat standing up. Now then, I'll telephone my spies at work and see what I can discover. I have on my list to find out what it *should* cost to drill and produce those wells. There's the financial history of the field itself to be looked into, of course, but what about the people involved? Can you think of anything other than Ed Meyer's expense accounts?"

"Well, that's the problem. Other than Ed, everyone else with an opportunity is a local up there. I can't see how you could check up on them from here."

"Come now, my dear, think of the royalty owners. That's money: my department."

"Well, the map on the desk downstairs has their names."

Elyria had found me an old plastic zipper case of Bill's to keep the files in, after going through them and politely pulling out anything that looked like financial information. "My department," she said again, and, as I stood in the middle of the kitchen stuffing the sandwich down my gullet with one hand and unconsciously jingling the truck keys with the other, she scowled her disapproval and added, "Keep in touch."

By eleven p.m., I was having to slap myself to stay awake, but I was nearing the turnoff to the rig. I rolled down the window to throw fresh air on my face, and noticed the low bluff where I had stopped that morning to fix the radio. I slammed on the brakes. In all the intervening hours, I had forgotten about the pumping truck that had slipped onto the highway in the darkness.

A nighthawk flew up from the weeds as I pulled Frank's truck to a stop. The waning moon was not yet risen, but with flashlight in hand I walked the hundred yards back down the road to the point where I had seen the pumper entering and had a look. I was in luck. The wind had not come up during the day and the tire tracks in the soft dirt were still crisp and clear. They were easy to memorize: a fairly standard lug pattern in the front and double tires in the rear. Of the four rear tires, the outer two had the same interlocking S pattern as the front, with fairly new tread leaving a nice, sharp print; but the inner two were older and of a different pattern, more like a row of chevrons.

Panning the flashlight back into the grass away from the road, I could see that the tracks disappeared where they passed over a stretch of gravel cast off by the road-building crew, and then reappeared as faint traces of bent grass stalks leading back to a barbed-wire fence. It was plenty strange to me that a truck could magically emerge from the middle of a fence. I followed the tracks toward the fence. The soil passed into a hard pan; in the artificial light, it shined through the thinning grass like an old man's scalp. It was easier to see the faint pathway of bent stalks when I crouched close to the ground, fore-shortening the view. I was right at the fence line before I stood up straight and looked over onto the other side. There, concealed behind one fence post, was a set of hooks holding loops in the strands of wire. *My, my, my,* I thought. *So clever.* Normally, the three strands of wire making up the fence would have been continuous, held to the post by only three U-shaped nails. I pulled at the top strand and found that it came off the hook easily. That meant it had been opened recently, because as any rancher's brat knows, a gate in a barbed-wire fence that hasn't been opened for a while is a bearcat to contend with: wind and gravity will have worked at the fence, pulling the gateposts away from each other and leaving the gate as taut as a dead man's smile.

It didn't make sense to try to follow the tracks any farther in the dark; in fact, it would have been damned stupid, a nice way to kiss off living to old age. As these thoughts played through my mind, the hair stood up on the back of my neck, and I felt that someone was standing right behind me, just about to touch me, just about to—

I spun around and jumped sideways. No one was there. Something moved near my foot and I jumped, gasping for air. Only a ground squirrel. *God, Em,* I thought, *this is getting away from you.* The weight of twenty-three hours awake, over seventeen of which had been behind the wheel of a truck with stiff suspension, landed on me all at once and froze on contact to fear. I started to shake, and clamped my teeth so I wouldn't shatter into tears. I braced myself to hitch the top strand of wire up again, twisting awkwardly on feet that didn't want to point away from the roadway again, struggling against a wire that had suddenly turned into a twitching, writhing snake. The loop finally jumped back into place over the hook, exacting a toll in lacerated flesh from my right thumb, and I made a fast retreat to the truck, tense with the terror that something cruel and unstoppable was hard on my heels, ready to consume me into the perverse communion of the damned.

29

Amazing, the dumb things you do when you've come a little unhinged. Instead of heading straight for the rig and a place to collapse, like any reasonable person might have done, I drove into Meeteetse, hoping to find Frank still up and in someplace public. I needed the company of someone, anyone, who might be glad to see me, might chat with me until my fears subsided and I could sleep. *Maybe Johnny will be in town,* I thought, in my last conscious attempt at staying out of emotional trouble.

By the time I parked the truck, I had my need for companionship so well rationalized—I was just tired, right?—that I forgot all about the feelings I had for Frank that night he fetched me back from the Pitchfork Restaurant. I further rationalized that it was a long shot anyway, that he probably wouldn't be there.

I found him, all right. At that hour in that town, there are only two public places open: the Cowboy Bar and the Elk Horn Bar. Frank was at the Elk Horn, hoisting one with Rita.

Rita? Frank and Rita? The very thought disgusted me. But even more, I was disgusted with myself for having ever entertained the thought that Frank would want to see me, would care if I lived or died. Worse yet, Rita spotted me and waved me over to their table.

I stood there like a little kid facing the principal, hands folded contritely at my waist. Rita said, "Have a beer with us, Emmy. Ain't nothing to go back to the rig for. What you up to, anyway?"

Frank smiled, started to make room for me.

Like hell, I thought. *I may be a dumb shit, but I got my pride.* I made up some hasty excuses, like, "Aw, no, it's late. Gotta run. Get some sleep. You know . . . just looking for Alix."

Rita snickered. "Where you been? The lady geologist ain't hangin' out here with us common folk! If you want to find her, you best see Chet Hawkins. He's the man's got her undivided attention tonight, if you know what I mean." She cranked one shoulder up under her chin in a parody of the coquette.

No answers, no job, no man. My ears began to ring, and my stomach felt funny. Wanting nothing better than to find some quiet place to curl up and die, I hurried out of the bar and down the row of shops, listening to the hollow patter of my running shoes on the wooden sidewalk, forcing my eyes wide open so I wouldn't cry. I kept walking along the road after the sidewalk stopped, thinking dramatically that I would walk out onto the bridge over the Greybull River and look for the reflection of the moon in its icy waters. Forget that I knew damned well that the moon wouldn't be up for another hour: infatuation unrequited must be served with suitably melodramatic acts.

But I was even cheated out of my festival of self-pity. As I dragged my feet across the loose gravel by the Oasis Motel's parking lot, Alix's car sped in from the highway and ground to a stop in front of her room, and Lady Bountiful herself clambered out and hailed me merrily. "Hey there," she called, "Up past your bedtime, or awake early?"

Piss, I thought, *can't I even be a loser with dignity? Must I be cornered by the most sexually satisfied woman in Wyoming?* I stood stiffly where I was, certain that my looks could kill and hoping they would. I reckon that it was only because it was dark out that Alix got off easy, with only minor burns.

She walked toward me in the parking lot, passing a familiar Oldsmobile on the way, giving it a pat on the fender. "I see here Eddie's getting some, too," she said. She sidled up to me, more cheerful and animate than I had ever seen her, holding her hands together behind her back and playfully swinging her hips to and fro. She came closer and closer, much too close, loomed above me until she blocked out the lights of the motel, grinning, stopping only inches from my face. A wash of warm breath swept across me, imbuing my nostrils with its boozy message. She spoke in a quiet, predatory voice. "God, I love sex."

She might just as well have slapped me. "Fuck you," I said.

"What did you say?"

"I said, fuck you."

She stood without moving for several seconds, time beating away like heartbeats, studying me like an object set up in formaldehyde in a jar, while anger welled up through me and conquered what was left of my composure. I began to shake.

Her voice came coolly, like a clinician's: "What's eating you, Emily?"

"You damn idiot! Who do you think you're fooling? You think people don't know? You think you can just come here and behave however the fuck you please? Just what are you trying to prove?" I knew I was making no sense, but the words just tumbled out, yanking tears with them. Alix was frighteningly motionless as I shook and blubbered, carrying on like a maudlin uncle at a funeral until my voice finally caught in my throat. Now shaking uncontrollably, I bared my teeth at her with all the ferocity I could summon.

All Alix said was, "Get real."

"Get real? *I* should get real?" I was almost screaming. "What the fuck do you mean, I should get real?"

Detachedly turning me over with her words like an odd specimen, she said, "Really, Emily, I think you've been out here in the oilfields too long. If you're going to isolate yourself like this, avoiding reality, living out in the middle of nowhere in a barren trailer with a comatose drunk, then your perception of the world is bound to tend toward the paranoid."

"What do you mean, 'living with'!" I squealed, terrified that she might be right.

"Oh, come now, Emily. We all know how you love to hate Howard."

"No I don't. I never chose him. He just came with the job. Don't you understand? It's the only fucking job I could get," I whimpered.

She laughed. The scent of whiskey enveloped my face again as Alix leaned even closer, eyes luminous in the light of the motel sign, and whispered, "I hate to have to be the one to notify you, my dear, at this advanced stage of your life, but you're really much brighter than the job requires. Did it ever occur to you that you might be setting your sights a bit low, to avoid risking failure?"

My scalp turned cold. I forgot for a moment where on planet earth I was. My mind took me somewhere else for a while, and I certainly didn't want to know I was where I was, or hear what I was hearing.

Alix turned and walked away. She called, "Good night," softly, over her shoulder. I watched her until she disappeared into her room.

30

I sat in the dark for a long while, tears slowly ebbing, my thoughts wandering through the events since the advent of Alix. My carefully constructed world was crumbling, blowing away in a midnight wind. Even fully clothed, alone in my trailer, I had never felt so naked. I prayed numbly that I would be spared ever seeing Alix again, as if that would mend the pain in my heart.

My damning note pad was right where I had left it, in the pocket of my other pair of jeans. But I knew anyone could have looked at it and then replaced it, leaving no trace.

I leaned forward in my chair, my head between my knees. My mind whipped back and forth between the immediacy of physical danger and the ancient agony of my soul; back and forth like grinding surf, wearing away at what was left of my spirits. My mother was right, she had always been right: I was just another fool like my father, but without his charm. My mind was beginning to bend. Finally, exhaustion overtook me. I quit caring what happened to me. I resolved only to stay where I was, in the slender hope that I could avoid the final shame of being fired.

The next hours were a blur. I sat slumped over the logging desk, forehead resting on hands, trying to sleep without sliding onto the floor. The destabilizing effect of gravity woke me up every ten or fifteen minutes until I found a position stable enough to keep me from sliding off the chair; but then periodic stabbing cricks in my back took over, punctuating a smear of fitful dreams. I blearily remember Howard coming in sometime after three, and I remember the day's first light reaching through the windows. It's a mystery to me where I got the idea that it made any difference whether I spent the night uncomfortably unconscious at the desk or in something closer to sleep on the settee; there was no reason to suspect Ed would trouble himself to check up on me at that hour, and there was no reason to feel guilty about sleeping through duty hours when there was no work to do. Perhaps I thought I was proving something to myself, or to Alix.

Alix did come in once, at seven-thirty, in search of tidbits for the morning report. She woke me from a nightmare in which I stood naked, save for my underwear, and covered with oil on the drilling floor. I jerked upright as she entered, bracing myself for further confrontation, but Alix was her good old business-as-usual self. She said, "Good morning. Anything for the report?"

"Not much," I said.

"Worried about Big Ed?"

"Um . . ." That was about the last question I was expecting from her.

"Want some advice, free and for nothing?"

I said, "Sure." Now I was startled, and completely confused.

"Never apologize, and never explain."

Oh, sure, I thought. *Easy for you to say. Old third-degree sonofabitching Meyer's going to peel my fingernails back, and I'm going to just sit here calmly and not turn into a jabbering idiot.* Bitterness crowded into my heart, but I managed to keep my mouth shut, and she left.

By and by I found myself in meditation on what she had said, and a strange calm came over me. I grudgingly realized she was right about two things: that I didn't have anything to apologize for, and that indeed, I owed him no explanation. Besides, if I tried to explain to him that there was no need for me to be on the rig during the time I was gone, it would just be stirring his shit; and if I told him, "Relax, I just took a little spin to Denver in search of evidence to incriminate you," I could kiss off growing old.

And Alix hadn't seemed to hold a grudge over what I had said to her. Could it be she had been so drunk she didn't remember our fight? I doubted it. There seemed in her manner this morning a new feeling . . . of what? Camaraderie? A tinge more respect? I was astonished. Something like gratitude seeped into my veins, and I got up and stretched, tentatively ready to greet the day.

But my stomach kept churning anyway. By the time ten 'til eight rolled around, I had taken a spit bath and gotten myself up to the doghouse on some pretense or other, counting on safety in numbers when Ed showed up. I sure didn't want to let him corner me in the logging trailer again.

Thus fortified with the fantasy of security, I caught myself staring out the doghouse door, watching for Frank. I had been wrong about Alix; what about Frank?

Johnny caught me looking confused when the evening tower showed up instead of the day. "It's Saturday," he reminded me, "the day the shifts rotate. Frank and his crew are off 'til Monday, then they come on as the morning tower, not the day."

Wondering if I smelled like a bitch in heat or just looked like one, I said a silent prayer that my endocrine system would revert to its usual state of stasis something like immediately. But my scheming little ovaries were up and running again in no time, reminding me that I still had the man's truck. *You'll just have to take it to him, Honey,* they said, to which my brain retorted, *Fuck off, a girl's got a little pride.*

I never did see Ed that morning. Merle showed up a while later as his emissary, with instructions to keep milling for another eight hours before calling it quits if no headway was made. I returned to the logging trailer. Some time later, Johnny woke me from a cat nap as he stepped up into the trailer in search of coffee. He said, "Sorry to wake you, kid. Thought you were up."

"It's okay. How's the milling going?"

"Nowhere fast. I told them to start pulling it out around

seven o'clock," he said, "but Fuzzy insists he had cast-iron instructions not to budge it until Ed showed up this morning. Damned if Ed was so thoughtful as to let me in on that order. I couldn't even raise the son of a bitch on the phone. I figured I could wait maybe an hour, see if he shows up, but then I get Merle wandering out here calling the shots. Anybody ever heard of a tool pusher? They're supposed to know something about drilling." Johnny smiled a smile that didn't do much more than air his teeth.

"Where is Ed, anyway?"

"God only knows. I tried phoning him at the Cody office, but he's not there. They said try his motel there in Cody. No dice there, either. Even Merle claims he doesn't know. So here we sit, kid."

Then I remembered. "Ed's not in his room in Cody because he's at the Oasis in Meeteetse. Wish I'd known you were looking for him."

"What's that?"

"Aw, hell, Johnny, I thought the whole world knew about this one. He's shacking up with the maid. I saw his Olds there in the parking lot last night."

"Shit." The weight of the past days and weeks sagged Johnny's face. For a moment he stared glassily into his coffee, but an instant later the impression vanished and his usual cheerful expression reasserted itself. He said, "I bet that's fine with you, anyway. You can't be looking forward to seeing him, eh?"

"Nope."

"Don't worry, kid. Getting back here as quick as you did was half the battle. He'll have to find another scapegoat now." He punched me lightly in the shoulder. "By the way, I have a message for you. Frank came by to get his truck while you were napping, and said to ask you if you were free for dinner tonight. He'll be at the Blue Ribbon at six-thirty, if you can make it." He winked. "He *said* he wants to get your news from Denver.'

If hope springs eternal, then the repressed spirit rebounds at the speed of light. With a stay of execution granted and the prospect of dinner with Frank to look forward to, the day suddenly seemed full of possibilities. The sun had risen high in the sky, chasing away whoever was killing people by the dark of night, there was a strange set of pumper tracks from a disguised gateway in a certain stretch of barbed-wire fence to be investigated, and I was free to investigate.

31

The tracks left by the phantom pumping truck faded out three miles northeast of the fence over a long stretch of hardpan near a dry wash, and beyond the hardpan lay a broader, more established road, which soon brought me to a locked gate. The only thing for it was to give up and turn around, head back to the paved road via this larger road, and come back later with a BLM map, which would show roads and fence lines. But I had at least found out which way the tracks were heading.

I arrived back in Meeteetse near dusk, feeling the price of every bump and wash in each mile of road in the complicated little muscles of my back. My mind was fatigued with all the information it had to sort through; too many possibilities, too many false clues to weed out. Too many important pieces of the picture remained to be found.

A phone call to Elyria confirmed the obvious, that the cost of the new wells at Bar Diamond Field was way over estimate, within a hair's breadth of shutting the drilling operations down. She felt certain that the expenses were unnecessarily high, and that Ed Meyer was in it up to his eye sockets, but as yet she had nothing that pointed him up as a criminal. Proof of incompetence was not enough to take him to trial.

Six-thirty, an hour that had seemed cavernously distant all afternoon, was suddenly upon me, and I felt about as ready for my next appointment as a sky diver without a parachute. I dove into the women's room at the Conoco station to see what could be done to make me more presentable, cursing myself for not bringing a washcloth and a complete change of clothes. I had showered off and had put on my best jeans and shirt before leaving the logging trailer at noon; but now, staring into the poorly lit mirror in the gas station, I felt distinctly dumpy. My face looked just as ordinary and bland as ever, and my hair hung in pathetic, dusty hanks. I considered driving straight back out to the rig. It was damned confusing, after years of dressing like one of the boys to avoid their notice, to find myself wanting it. In the mirror I saw a soft-looking boy, not a woman. Where had my femininity gone? *Did I ever have any?* I wondered how Alix managed to maintain her womanhood in a world that seemed bent on beating it out of us, as a penalty for having the audacity to work in jobs guaranteed us by law. *How does she do it?* I asked myself, and an answer came: *Maybe she'll tell me some day.* I found myself smiling, shyly, at the thought that Alix and I might someday be friends. *Well, I can take at least one page from her book,* I thought, and I undid the second button of my shirt, revealing a section of throat that hadn't seen the sunshine in a very long time. I washed my face, combed my hair, and headed for the Blue Ribbon Cafe.

He was waiting for me outside the cafe, sitting in his pickup truck. As I pulled up, he nodded to me and stepped out, a little awkwardly, and tucked in his shirt tail, which wasn't out. "Hello, Em," he said, smiling his faint smile.

"Hi."

I had never seen Frank so cleaned up before, with his hair combed and town clothes on. His jeans fit more closely than his driller's work pants, revealing a tight musculature in his thighs. They followed sleekly to his boots, where they sat low, draping to the prescribed level, just tagging the heels. He said, "You look nice. You got the sun in your face today."

Dinner was easy after that. I had the good sense to avoid the chili, ordering the chicken-fried steak instead, with a milk chaser. Frank was as easy to talk to as ever, prompting me with questions about Bill's files and so forth. I quite enjoyed myself.

When we had finished our coffees and a couple of fine pieces of black-bottom pie, Frank asked if I'd like to head over to the Cowboy Bar with him, to have a beer. That stopped my clock. I asked, "What about Rita?"

"What about who?"

"Rita. You were with her last night. You know."

Frank squinted at me over his slow smile. "She's my cousin, Em."

"Oh."

I followed him out the door, across the road, and down the sidewalk. As it was Saturday night, the walk was lined with trucks sporting bug guards on their prows, gun racks silhouetted against the back windows of their cabs.

The Cowboy Bar is a home-town sort of place, but not for the faint of heart: a sign on the door requires that you relieve yourself of knives and firearms before entering. Inside is a wide-board floor with a row of high-backed booths along one side and a long bar with a big mirror behind it on the other. The high ceiling disappears into a smoky darkness. That night as always, the room was dimly lit, packed with sound, slithering with smoke. A few couples, dressed in their best hats and blue jeans and locked in slave-and-master embraces, shuffled and turned to the strains of crooner and slide guitar, a sad song that wailed from the jukebox at the far end of the floor.

We found a booth and ordered a couple of cans of beer. Frank sat jiggling a matchbook cover on the table top, passing it from hand to hand and then jiggling it some more. After a bit, he said, "Long as we're here, Em, would—ah—you like to dance?"

My mouth went dry.

He smiled quickly. "Well, only if you like to," he said. His mouth smiled some more but his eyes looked worried. "I just thought you might. Like to." He glanced away.

"Sure," I answered, my words sticking to my lips. "But only if *you'd* like to. I mean, you don't have to just for me.

I don't dance so well." I was beginning to blather uncontrollably. "Maybe you should ask Alix sometime. I'm sure she dances much better."

Frank looked back at me. "Alix? Why would I want to dance with Alix?"

"Because she's so attractive and classy and all."

Frank studied me for several long moments, and all the while a sweet, slow smile spread across his face, breaking away finally into a soft laugh. "Aw, Em, you funny thing," he said, shaking his head. "Alix is like them roses you buy in the store: real showy." He sipped at his beer, smiling at me over the edge of the can. "I hear some feller breeds them roses just for the bloom, just to make them so huge and red, and now he's bred them so far they no longer got any smell. They're so pretty, sometimes I buy them anyway, bring them home and put them in a jar on the table. But they ain't grown around here, Em; they've already been cut a while. It ain't long before they wilt. I even got dried flowers once, but they just gather a lot of dust."

"But roses are nice, Frank. Everyone wants them."

"Sure. How about you, Emily; you're like the wild roses that grow beside a stream I know, up in the mountains by Yellowstone. I try to get up there every spring, just to see them. This little rose—it's a simple thing, the same lovely shade of pink every time, and it's got a scent that smells the better for the miles I had to walk to see it. And you know, it only blooms a couple months, but then the leaves are pretty, too. And in the winter, I can think of it up there, in that cold, fighting off the winter with its spindly little thorns. And it's there every spring, each time I go back, blooming again."

The length of this speech seemed to have drained him of conversation. He said no more; just smiled even wider, chuckling softly, shaking his head at me. After a moment he rose and came around to my side of the table, extended his hands for me to take. I put my hands in his. *How warm.* They were rough and thick, the nails chipped and stained with crude oil. I followed him onto the floor, where he

chose a quiet space away from the jukebox. With his right
hand on the small of my back he drew me into the step,
sweeping me into the slow, sliding, swinging step of the
cowboy waltz. Warmth pulsed through my shirt from his
hand, transmitting his rhythm to my spine. With his left
hand he steered me around the outer edge of the dance
floor, throwing an extra turn in at the corners. On the fourth
turn, he pulled me closer to him. His voice came softly,
very close to my ear: "You dance well."

"Thanks," I answered, in a voice that sounded oddly
sleepy and far away. He was close enough now that I could
feel the heat from his neck radiating against my cheek, his
breath warm against my ear, and his strong thighs brushed
mine ever so slightly. The rhythm of music wrapped around
my brain, carrying me with its walking bass, working my
shoulders with its guitar. I closed my eyes. His cheek
brushed mine—by accident?—and then again with certainty.

The tune came to a close, the last few notes wavering on
the honey-coated strings of the slide guitar. With a shy
smile, Frank dipped me gently backward. I smiled back
from a bed of soft, woolly clouds, the aches in my back
gone, consciousness floating on a puff of smoke. *It's going
to be okay,* I thought. *Perhaps it's going to be okay to be a
part of this world.*

The jukebox slid into another slow song. We moved on
and on, the room slipping from sight. His hand warmed
against my spine, and he pulled me right up against his
stomach: I felt his ribs spread as he brought in his breath,
and he trembled sightly as he let it out, settling slowly into
a deep, rhythmic breathing. His thighs pressed firmly
against mine. I rode along against them, surrendering myself to the slow, sliding step. Heat coursed through my
body. A tightness burned in the pit of my stomach, pressing
down against my groin, pulsing with the beat of my heart,
exuding a hot moisture against my jeans.

When the song ended Frank held on to me. "Let's go
outside," he said, his voice a whisper. He guided me off the

dance floor with one hand, snatching our jackets off of our seats with the other as we passed our table.

Outside, the air was fresh and clear, washing our faces clean after the smoke and din of the hall. Frank led me across the street and into the darkness beyond the buildings, down to a grassy verge along the river. There, among the cottonwood trees, he dropped our jackets on the grass and pulled me to him once again.

32

During the small hours of Sunday morning, I dreamt once again that I was naked on the drilling floor, but this time I stood smiling, proud of my nakedness, my breasts, the swelling of my hips.

At ten, I was awake and sitting at the logging desk, dreaming of the few short moments Frank had spent holding me and kissing me, replaying the delicious moments again and again, when Merle drove into the pipe yard and dropped Ed Meyer off and the long-feared confrontation finally occurred.

Perhaps I dreamt that scene with Ed. Even at the time, it felt as if I were watching it in the movies, and not as if I was really there, experiencing it; if I had been eating popcorn and sipping over-sweetened Coke, the sensation would have been complete. It happened like this: Ed stomped in, gave me his absolute calculated worst, most insinuating, "There you are," to which I replied absolutely nothing. He blinked twice, bared his teeth, and tried, "Think you can fool ol' Ed, huh?" I gave him something approaching a beatific smile, a touch more forthcoming than the Mona Lisa's but far more innocent. Ed strutted and steamed for about another twenty seconds, and then gave up.

That was it.

The whole incident, for which I had taken the foolish risk of driving half asleep through a third of Colorado and clear across Wyoming and for which, during the past forty-some hours, I had subjected my stomach to a goodly ten quarts of extra digestive juices, had come and gone with all the impact of a random minute of TV violence experienced while flipping channels. I felt large and expansive, and I wondered what in blazes I had been so worried about. Shit, I was just getting to the point where I was enjoying the show.

About then Alix came into my trailer. I turned to her, a grin of thanks spreading across my face.

Ed wheeled on Alix. "Aha! I have a li'l ol' message for you, Darlin'. A Mister Garth Hawkins called me this morning and asked me t'give a certain one of my girl employees a li'l message. It seems that a certain occasion his li'l boy invited you to ain't a gonna happen. He said, don't go troublin' yourself to appear at the ranch this noon, 'cause there ain't gonna be no lunch served to no girl geologists. Hah! And from the tone of his voice, sister, I don't believe you better go around expectin' anything like no rain check. Get it? Ha-ha-ha-ha-ha-HA!"

Alix turned a shade paler. Her lips moved vaguely before organizing themselves enough to say, "Thank you for relaying the message, Ed."

"Oh, and one more thing: give me your car keys."

"What?"

"I'll be takin' your car for a while."

Alix was at a loss, for the first time since I'd met her. Her hand went jerkily into her pocket for her keys, but by the time she extended them to Ed, she had rallied a little, fixing a matronly glare on him that demanded, *Justify this action.*

Ed snatched the key and said, "I need the car, y'see. Don't be angry, girl, the company rents it, not you. Keep you out of trouble, anyway. Don't want you runnin' around all night lookin' for somethin' you might have just lost. You need your beauty sleep, anyways. An' Daylight Savin's starts tonight anyways, y'know, spring ahead, fall behind? Ha-ha-ha-ha-ha? I guess you're gettin' old, Alix honey, an' you're startin' to need those extra little hours of sleep, hmmm? Don't worry, ol' Ed'll look after you." He settled down into a seat and spread his knees wide apart, smiling his vulgar smile.

Now I had to wrestle with my conscience in one tearing hurry. My ego still counseled that I keep my distance from Alix, and I still wasn't sure I was any too fond of her. But this was different: Ed had knocked her and clipped her wings, and now showed every sign of sitting right where he was, drinking up every last ounce of Alix's humiliation. This was not to be tolerated.

This meant war.

I jumped up and stared dramatically out the window, then started for the door and yelped, "Ed, I think you're needed up on the floor, I see Johnny waving."

Ed vacillated for just a moment before following me. I ran, bent on reaching the floor before he did, praying that Johnny was indeed up there.

He was. I said I needed him to trump up something urgent and keep Ed up there with his ego distracted for a few minutes. Johnny nodded, smiling his cagey little smile. As Ed puffed through the door from the doghouse behind me, Johnny turned on his Men In Combat voice and started into something about the wear on the crown block. It was a slick move—there was no way Ed was going to climb a hundred feet of ladders to check it out, so he bought it. I vanished. I ran all the way back down to my trailer, bursting with good news and sudden camaraderie for Alix.

Just in time to see her disappear into Johnny's trailer and close the door, firmly.

All this left me with more time to think. I sat in my trailer with a cup of coffee, letting the rising steam soothe my eyeballs; and then the darnedest thing came to me. Here I had been living in fear of Ed Meyer for days, hating him, in truth flinching at the thought of him ever since he first touched me. But now that I had met him head on, my fear seemed a limited thing: I feared the loss of my job, and I perhaps feared the loss of my sanity if he ever touched me again, but I didn't fear for my life. He had walked into my trailer and caught me alone, and my stomach had certainly recoiled; but I had not feared that he might kill me.

Because I didn't think of him as a killer.

Was Ed honest? No. Decent? Hardly. Sane? Questionable. But violent, capable of premeditated, cunning murder? No. He was simply too much of a fool. Every ounce of his effort was focused on just one thing: buttressing the flimsiest ego in northwest Wyoming. I began to wonder how he had enough wit left over to make simple decisions on the drilling project, let alone act as chief engineer. Perhaps that was why his projects ran over cost. What the hell had I been thinking, suspecting him of murder?

I stared into my coffee, willing clarity to come to me. Perceiving Ed's smallness had removed a blockage in my consciousness, opening the way to further insight. It was as if a hole had been knocked in a wall, revealing a neighborhood that had been hidden from me, a neighborhood containing a whole universe of mundane reality, where things were neither black nor white but shades of grey, with even a few tints of color. It had the tightly focused clarity of a scene within an Easter egg; ordinary, complete in every detail, twinkling with the familiarity of a child's story right down to its moral content. I marveled, mentally squinting at it until my perception matured one more notch and I found that the neighborhood was not in fact tiny. It didn't stop five feet beyond the wall, it went on and on. It was in fact a whole world, and the wall had not been keeping it hidden from me, it had been tricking my perception, hiding me from the plain facts of my existence. It was I who had lived within an egg.

In the stillness of the moment, I could see that the wall was built not of brick and mortar, but of anger. With that knowledge the rest of the wall tumbled, leaving me keenly aware of the limitations that it had been built to conceal.

The immediate implications of my folly crowded into my brain like dirty wet dogs coming in out of the rain. Some impartial, scientific mind I had: I had let my emotions rule me just as Ed Meyer let his rule him. I had lavished all this time and energy trying consciously or unconsciously to assuage my pain by blaming Ed for the loss of a friend who had meant more to me than I cared to know. Worse infamy, I had sullied Bill's memory by confusing his loss with rage over Ed's injustices to me, seeking revenge instead of facing the enormity of my own rage and inability to defend myself.

The coffee grew cold in my hands. Tears blurred my vision as the sadness of a thousand losses touched my newfound heart. It was frightening to feel so much, to know so suddenly how much sadness was stored up inside, and I struggled against it, straining to take action rather than sit with myself any longer. Bill's gruff presence seemed to alight beside me in the trailer. I could feel him there, greeting me as a colleague, as a friend. "Do what you're good at," he seemed to say. "You're a geologist. Look to the stone. Look at the Tensleep; she'll speak to you."

Bill had known something about the Tensleep, something so profoundly important that he had kept it strictly guarded, something that gave him an understanding of current events that made him angry, and had filled his eyes with fear. Bill had a temper, but he hadn't blown the whistle on Ed for the simple reason that he couldn't connect Ed with what was going wrong with Bar Diamond Field.

I was just about to get up and fetch my note pad to start revising my notes when Alix stepped in again. She didn't look entirely well. She said, "Em, how about coming to town with me for lunch. I'm buying. Actually, the truth is I need a ride. In fact, maybe you could just lend me your truck, if you're not interested."

I thought I knew what was coming and I didn't want any part of it, but it wasn't my truck to lend her. "Sorry, Alix, it's my company's policy, I can't lend it to you." Looking at Alix's hang-dog face I felt guilty as hell, and added, "But sure, I could use a square meal." I waited. It came.

"I wonder if you'd mind dropping by the ranch on the way."

"No sweat," I said.

It didn't take much imagination for me to piece together her dilemma. Chet had always before met her at the pumping plant, or had taken her to town, but now he must have invited her to the ranch for lunch, a meeting that had the formal overtones of presenting her at court. Now she had been uninvited. Had Garth really phoned Ed? He might have, because somehow Ed had known about the luncheon. Or had Ed heard about the invitation by accident and fabricated the telephone call from Garth? It seemed suspicious that he had gone to the extreme of taking her car; after all, he didn't truly have her best interest at heart, and wouldn't have done it to spare her embarrassing herself. Perhaps it was all a scheme to mess up her love life. Should Alix go to the ranch, fearing further humiliation, or stay, and risk committing a faux pas of epic proportions?

I knew the Hawkins' ranch was very different from my father's before I even saw the main house. The cattle guard was broad and new, the road was carefully graded where it crossed over, and not a single rut was visible anywhere in the driveways; but as we rounded the turn past the row of cottonwoods that formed the windbreak, my mouth sagged open.

It is amazing what oil revenues can do for a homestead. Homestead, nothing: this was a castle among ranch buildings. A lush lawn led up to the broad, lavish expanse of the main building, with its sumptuous double-doored entryway surrounded by moss rock and its immense walls of glass opening the westward rooms to a sweeping view of the Absarokas. Heavy, honey-colored exterior beams jutted at an angle to the front of the building, supporting a prow-shaped overhang of shake roof. I had never seen a shake roof on a ranch house, nor a ranch house with such an energy-squandering expanse of glass. I stopped the truck short of the dooryard, humility dictating that I keep myself and my muddy truck away from the formal entrance. In fact, I drove the truck clear over by the main barn, adjacent to the bunk house, where I felt more at home.

Alix climbed out of the truck and slammed the door, incensed, I suppose, that her entrance had been marred. I watched her go, wishing I had not gotten involved, feeling acutely visible, vulnerable, and just a touch nauseous. I tried skulking down in the seat out of sight but felt more silly than anything else, and soon opted for getting out of the truck and sitting on the back bumper, out of sight of the house.

No one was about, and no cars or trucks were visible, so it was unlikely that anyone was nearby. I began to relax. It was another balmy day, with a gentle breeze carrying the scent of warm horses and moldering hay past my nostrils. I reckoned that the horses must be quartered in the main barn, and decided to have a look at the Appaloosa while Alix was about her errand. Surely one quick look couldn't be considered rude. I stepped toward the barn, breathing in its earthy odors, feeling as welcomed by the dark expanse of its doorway as I had felt shunned by the gleaming brass door plates of the house. One step, two, another, and another, into the oat-flecked interior of the barn, watching with pleasure the dance of the dust motes in a shaft of sunlight from a high window, feeling the well-trampled dirt of the ground beneath my feet, smelling well-oiled tack leather, now tobacco on a man's breath—

I jumped involuntarily and spun around, stepping backward and away from the source of the scent, my heart pounding in my ears, dizzy with the surprise of finding another human beside me in the close, dusky air of the barn.

I strained to see him. As my eyes adjusted to the darkness, I saw first the reflection of daylight in his eyes, no higher above the earth than my own; then his skin and teeth resolved from the gloom, stained and worn with hard use and little care. His grizzled chin gave way to a neck poignant in its narrowness. He raised a leathery hand in salute and displayed two additional teeth in a shy approximation of a smile. His narrow build caved in where the faded fabric of his flannel shirt met his jeans. A thin grunt escaped his nostrils.

"I'm sorry," I said, embarrassed by my fright over this

least threatening of all creatures. "I just wanted to see the horses. I didn't think anyone was here."

He bobbed his head forward in a welcoming gesture.

I asked, "Are you the wrangler?"

He nodded his head enthusiastically, turned around, and pointed to the name tooled into the leather at the back of his belt. Jimmy.

I said, "Glad to meet you, Jimmy."

He bowed a fraction of an inch from his waist and gestured for me to follow him deeper into the barn to a long row of stalls, each resplendent with a new gate. It was becoming evident that the better part of the inside of the barn had been gutted to make way for this very fine and expensive system of stalls, each sporting a little brass plaque with an equine name engraved on it. A horse snorted as we neared the first gate, lifting its tall neck over the railing in hopes of a treat. It was an elegant, handsome quarter horse easily seventeen hands high, a mahogany bay, beautifully groomed.

The wrangler pointed to the brass plaque. *Rommel,* it said. Rommel, the desert fox. Beneath that in smaller letters were the names of his sire and his dam. I said, "He's beautiful. Whose is he?"

Jimmy grew fretful, his hands moving about in an effort to describe a very big man. My brain clicked into consciousness and I realized, *He can't talk. He's mute.* I ventured a guess, sparing Jimmy's efforts. "Mr. Hawkins'?"

Jimmy nodded and ran his hands lovingly down the animal's neck, happily accepting fermented nuzzlings in return. I joined him in stroking the warm, satiny hide. "You take wonderful care of him, Jimmy."

Jimmy grinned.

"Are the other horses out to pasture? I don't see Chet's Appaloosa."

Jimmy nodded *yes,* Chet's horse was out, and an ambivalent side to side over the disposition of others. Waving me farther on, he showed me gates marked Whitney, Dream Girl, Apache, and Jake. Jimmy pointed over the gate at

Jake, whose sorrel nose was deep in a bucket of water. Jimmy pursed his lips and made a kissing noise, calling his friend forward to be admired. *Mine,* he gestured, smiling proudly and thumping his own chest, *this one is mine.*

I smiled in admiration, nodding and holding my hands wide apart in a gesture of grandeur, falling into the quiet spirit of Jimmy's pantomime, and ran my fingers across Jake's velvety lips, scratching lovingly at the few bristly hairs that grew from the soft, springy flesh. The horse favored me with a harrumphing blast of hot breath.

I could hear by heavy shiftings of hay that there was a horse in the last stall, but there was no plaque on the gate, and its occupant stayed alluringly out of sight, chewing quietly. I moved to the gate to get a look and saw a smallish pinto stallion, rugged and well-formed, but wild and inelegant in his grooming. He swung his head balefully around and studied me with one gaping brown eye.

"Ain't he something!" I said, breaking the silence. "An Indian pony, looks like."

Jimmy smiled proudly, nodding and making a big gesture, pointing south, way south, repeating the movement several times, eyes focused far beyond the back wall of the barn.

With a suddenness, I knew what he was trying to tell me. "It *is* an Indian horse. From the reservation?"

Jimmy nodded rapidly.

"Indian trained? Is he shod?" This was unusual, to see a reservation horse in a white man's barn. He was classic, a creature straight out of a Remington painting, his mane and tail hanging long and shaggy along his muscular flesh. Jimmy unlocked the gate, moving inside to show him off, and lifted one hind leg to display a well-cared-for but unshod hoof which struggled and nearly kicked him. The horse moved suddenly, rounding on him, and burst out into the wide dirt floor of the barn. Jimmy emitted a weak giggle and chased after him. As the horse reached the bright opening of the barn, he clapped his hands together. The pinto stopped abruptly and gazed at him, waiting. Jimmy pursed his lips and sucked inward, making a quick, sharp whistle, like a marmot's. The pinto reared up, thrashing the air with his hooves until Jimmy whistled again, and he dropped to the ground. Jimmy clapped three times, and the horse came toward him at a run. He pointed back at the stall, and the horse trotted in and stopped. Jimmy grinned, shaking his head with pleasure. He fished a lump of carrot from his pocket and palmed it to him, patted him on the neck, and closed the gate.

I was in love, overwhelmed by this superbly trained horse. I asked, "Whose is he, Jimmy? Is he just being stabled here for a short while?" The second question was a stupid one when I compared this humble pinto and the brilliant conformation of the stallion in the first stall, but I was embarrassed at asking Jimmy another question he would have trouble answering and hastened to replace it with one requiring only a nod or a shake of his head.

Jimmy smiled, shook his head no, and pointed one index finger repeatedly downward, toward the floor.

"Mr. Hawkins owns him?"

Again a shake of the head, less vehement this time, the head tipped a bit to one side, and the pointing gesture repeated hopefully.

"But he stays here."

Happy nods.

"Someone always stables him here."

Big happy nods. Jimmy headed abruptly for the front of the barn, urging me to follow. Right by the brightness of the entrance, he disappeared into a shadow and reappeared as he switched on a light, revealing the doorway into his small but tidy sleeping quarters. On a table near the door was spread an assortment of bridles, several rags, and bottles of oil and brass polish. This was the warren from which he had so suddenly materialized as I first walked into the barn. Jimmy pulled open a drawer in a plain pine bureau and pawed through it, scrambling for something that would answer my ill-considered question.

I said, "It's okay, Jimmy. It's none of my business, anyway."

Jimmy straightened just long enough to signal *keep your shirt on* and went back to his task. At length, he came and stuck a battered photograph into my hands.

The horse was not in the picture. Instead, there were other horses, three of them, each carrying a man. One was certainly a pinto, not this pinto, but on it sat a man of Indian blood, dressed in a satin Western-cut shirt; on the left, a second horse and rider, but the man was white. Jimmy jabbed a rough finger at him. This man was also decked out in rodeo finery—black pants, hat, and black satin shirt—but there was something familiar about him. I took the picture out of Jimmy's hands and moved it into better light. There was a shadow cast by the man's hat, obscuring most of his face, yet there was something about him, in his stiff and muscular bearing, in his withdrawn observation of the camera. Was this someone I knew, or was Jimmy trying to point to some famous rodeo cowboy? I turned the photograph over, and found the inscription, "Cody Stampede Rodeo," and a date almost twenty-five years past. At closer inspection, there was something familiar about the third man in the picture, too. With a laugh, I said, "Oh, this is Mr. Hawkins! I didn't know he was a rodeo man!" Jimmy nodded some more, fluttered his hands at the wrists to say, *sort of*. We both laughed, Jimmy's a thin hiccuping. I said, "Well, I used to ride rodeo," fluttering my hands at the wrist; *sort of*. "Actually, I was some okay at barrel racing. But tell me, who is this other fellow?" Much as I knew I was asking a question difficult for Jimmy to answer, there was something about the unnamed white man in the photograph that begged me to know him, begged me to uncover a trace of history twenty-five years buried.

Jimmy fretted, rocking from foot to foot, flailing the air with his fingers, trying to conjure the name from the dust motes as if they were chimes that could sound a code. He dodged sideways, grabbing a can of salve off of a shelf, and pointed at the brand name, his eyebrows working where his tongue could not. *Champion,* it said; *Champion Brand Salve.*

"He was a champion, twenty-five years ago?" I asked, but as Jimmy's face brightened, my heart sank. *I was just a baby then, I thought, and Cody is the far corner of the state from where I rode. I know nothing of the rodeo champions in these parts.* But as I opened my mouth to ask what event this man had ridden, Alix called me from the yard, an edge of nerviness pulling her voice up a note.

"Emily! Where have you gotten yourself to? Emily!"

Flustered, I handed Jimmy his photograph and hurried to the door, calling, "Here, Alix." I started to add, "Just looking at the horses," but remembered Alix's own words— Never apologize, never explain—and instead said, "What's up?"

"Oh. Ah, Chet's not here just now." Her face was bright in a feverish way. "Let's head on into town and get our lunch."

The words, *Bounced you, did they?* came to mind, but I said, "Of course," waved good-bye to Jimmy, and climbed into the truck.

The suffocating weight of the ranch house slowly receded in the rearview mirror as I piloted the truck down the road toward town. Alix chattered away about the weather, the milling job . . . anything except Chet Hawkins.

33

My mind was only half on what Alix was saying. The other half was laboring hard with the ghost of recollection that Jimmy's photograph had summoned. Who was the third man? The weird thing was that he looked like Chet, only heavy-set, but he didn't look like Garth. Some little file clerk in the back of my consciousness was squeaking, *What's a matter with you, you can't read this big, fat message I'm holding up? You need maybe semaphores? Pay attention!* An intuitive mind can be such a pain in the ass.

Alix, having decided that the A&W's brew wasn't strong enough for her, had dragged me to the Cowboy Bar, where we sat in a booth eating Polish sausage and swilling beer. Her first beer became two, then three, then she switched to vodka. A ball game popped and hissed on the big color television set over the bar, watched only by one wiry old cowboy with a cigarette burn in the brim of his hat.

I was getting really irritated at Alix. Perhaps it was remnant anger from what she said to me Friday night. Or maybe it was really anger at myself for getting caught up in her spoiled afternoon. Worse yet, after all my pissy, jealous thoughts toward her, I hated to watch her crumble. Whatever the source of the irritation, I felt sorry for her and couldn't muster the bile to desert her. So I sat, trying to decide if I could summon interest in a piece of beef jerky from the big jar on the bar. My stomach answered with an uncomfortable pressure against my belt.

I decided to phone Elyria on the chance she had made any progress; but my pockets yielded only three pennies and a fifty-cent piece, so I headed to the bar to change some folding money. Before I got there, a man who was all belly girth and pencil legs strutted in and commanded the bartender's attention.

"A round for the house!" he crowed, in a garbled, growly voice. "Dis be a red-letter day, m'man! Dis be d'day Garth Hawkins, *de* Misser Hawkins, done paid me up his debt. Whiskey for d'men! Beer for d'ladies!"

The bartender's eyes and mouth sagged open, and rocking his head back so his nostrils had a good view too, asked, "Eh? What's this, Verne?"

"Dis be a day among days! C'mon!" He slapped a twenty on the bar. Verne turned to me and asked, "You joinin' me, young lady?" I shook my head. "Phil, what you be drinkin', m'man?"

The wiry cowboy gurgled and tapped his glass on the well-oiled wood, intent on the bottle of his dreams, which nestled among its brethren against the mirror behind the bar.

The bartender asked, "You had a bet on with Ol' Hawkins, eh?"

"You be correc', my man, you be correc'. Bet him on d'Super Bowl clear las' January, and dis be d'day he finally paid up. Three fingers of Misser Daniels, if'n you please, sir."

The bartender poured. "Eh. I thought ol' Hawkins was better'n that with his bets. An' thought he paid up, too. C'mon, Verne, this is April."

"Naw, Elmer, is like I bin tellin' you. Used to was he paid right up, but nowadays, he bin hangin' onto it for a bit. Course, he bin bettin' bigger, too; maybe he don't carry dat kind of jack around on him, heh, heh."

"Eh? Twenty bucks? C'mon."

"Twenty? Haw! Be slidin' yer eyes acrost dese 'uns!" Verne said, spreading his wallet wide. Enough green to make a fair-sized salad yawned from its leathery maw.

Phil whipped his shot of whiskey back and stared. "Boy howdy, Verne, how's about I drink what the lady ain't?"

Verne raised an imperial finger in largesse and nodded at the bottle that housed Phil's poison. The bartender poured. "So ol' Hawkins is back from Vegas already? He must have won big, eh? An' how'd you find the funds to risk to stake like that yourself, boy? What if you'd lost those dollars instead of won them, eh?"

"Aw, he bin back three days. An' it warn't nothing—you should'a seed d'odds he laid me on dat dere ball game. I kep' sayin', no, y'ain't got a bet. He keeps sayin', how 'bout dese here better odds, and dese here'ns better yet, until I'd a bin a durned fool t'say no. Yep, he bin dyin' for a bet. Dat boy got d'fever."

"But he just left a week ago today. I thought he usually stayed down there a week or more, eh? Another round?"

"Three fingers, if y'be so kind. Well, I know, but dere y'has it. He bin sayin' dat new airplane flight from Cody t'Denver's connectin' straight to Vegas, purty as y'please. Sure y'don't want nothing, miss?"

I had been listening so intently, trying to make out his speech, that I had forgotten my earlier mission. I said, "Yeah—ah, no: all I wanted was some change for the phone. Thanks anyway." The bartender made my change and I headed back to the pay phone by the bathrooms, trying to reconcile disparate images: Garth Hawkins, the big cheese rancher with the huge house and shiny new stables and immaculate trucks; Garth Hawkins the rodeo dilettante; Garth Hawkins, the local Force To Be Reckoned With; Garth Hawkins the gambling man, riding with the jet set to Las Vegas. *Must be nice, to have oil pouring out of the ground you sit on.* But something didn't fit.

Elyria caught the phone on the first ring. "Oh, good, it's you. I've got something! I've got something! My spy at Blackfeet got into the land records, and guess what she found!" She rushed right on, not giving me a chance to guess. "Your main land holder, Garth Hawkins, is out of the picture! But I'm getting ahead of myself. I got to looking at the land map on the desk, and thought I'd check it against the records. It would seem Hawkins still owns the surface rights, but all of his mineral rights were recently transferred to a John Gunnard."

Visions of new stables and trucks and an expensive house swam in my head. I had wrongly assumed that Hawkins made the purchase from an overflowing income, but maybe it was from the sale of his capital assets. I said, "Wait a minute. Who is John Gunnard? Never heard of him. He's not local."

A cruel chuckle issued from the telephone receiver. "That's the plum, my dear. John Gunnard is most certainly not local. He hails from a little hamlet called Las Vegas."

"Las Vegas?"

"Yes. It would seem Mr. Gunnard won the mineral rights in a card game."

What? "That's crazy!"

"Gamblers aren't known for their sanity, my dear."

"Hawkins wouldn't bet the rights!" But as I said that, I remembered Verne's words: *the fever*. Elyria's information clicked into place, locking tightly into a pattern, and I knew she was right. *Then how is he keeping up appearances?* "Are you sure Gunnard didn't purchase the rights? I was just out at Hawkins' ranch today, and it's looking plenty prosperous."

"Absolutely certain. My spy's credentials are flawless." She sounded deliriously pleased with herself.

Sure, Mister Hawkins, let the world think you're still top dog. But how does this involve you in murder? How does killing a geologist and a pumper in a field you no longer own benefit you? I should think if you wanted to kill anyone, it would be Gunnard.

"What shall I investigate next?" Elyria asked. The martial tone was back.

Keeping ahead of her was getting rough. "Any luck on Ed Meyer's expense accounts?"

"Oh, yes. He was definitely in Wyoming when Bill died, and you already know that he was there when Willie Sewell died. Other than that, it looks padded: is sixty dollars a day a reasonable food budget for rural Wyoming? Seems high."

"Shit, yes, it is: especially when you consider he's getting most of his meals for free from the contractors. I wonder what he's hiding. Petty larceny? I wouldn't put it past him. He's such a shit, that would all be in a good day's sport."

"Or a mistress?"

I just laughed. It seemed Ed's little secret was no secret anymore. But was being caught dallying a motive for murder? I thought not. And deep in my bones, I felt that all of this was just a haze obscuring the one thing that tied everyone together, be it a ranch owner, a pumper, a geologist, an engineer, or his phantom mistress: the oil in Bar Diamond Field.

34

As I walked back to the booth, I found that my shoulders were bunched up with tension. I hated seeing Alix cave in and climb into her cups. As I sat down, she gave me a shrug, as if to say, *What the hell,* but I felt an unaccustomed pity forming in me, and wondered which one of us was truly the more isolated.

Then the front door to the bar swung open. Ed Meyer walked in with Stretch in tow, marched right up to Alix and brayed, as loud as he could, "Alix, my dear, here are your keys. So I hear you got yourself out to Hawkins' anyway. So tell me, sweetheart, how's it feel to be dumped by the local boy?"

I jumped to my feet, ready, perhaps, to hit him, but Alix still had words left in her to protect herself and the vodka spoke them. She narrowed her eyes, drew her lips back from her teeth, and said, "Watch what you say, Ed. I have nothing to hide around here, but you sure do."

I backed away from the table. Ed took one long hard look at Alix and stormed out of the bar. Stretch chased behind him, arms flapping like a seagull.

Alix wobbled to her feet and headed into the rest room, bumping the door open with her shoulder. I slumped onto a stool at the bar and ordered a glass of water.

The ball game sputtered along. Verne mumbled cheerfully to the bartender, something about weird folk from Denver. After five or ten minutes of it, I decided to rejoin Alix at the booth, the fatalist in me resigned to take its chances sitting next to a lightning rod.

But she wasn't there. A search of the bathroom yielded no longlegged female geologists, and she wasn't visible anywhere up or down the street. I headed down to her room at the Oasis, but the lights were out, the door was locked, and her car was gone, which worried me. She was certainly too drunk to be driving.

I considered finding Frank, in hopes that he could help me find her, but dismissed the thought because he was due on the rig at midnight and might therefore be sleeping. I was standing in the middle of the street, uncertain what to do next.

Something quiet but insistent pulsed within me at the same pace as my heart, now grabbing at it, now speeding it up. Fear. The tension in my shoulders wouldn't go away. Things were just plain getting out of control. *Clean up this mess, and I'll leave you alone,* I said.

The sound of an engine tapped at my consciousness. The sheriff's Blazer appeared at the north end of town and bore down on me, breaking my inertia in favor of the safety of the sidewalk. As he passed each break between buildings, shafts of late afternoon sun winked across his windshield, obscuring his face with glare. I dodged to the east side of the street to avoid meeting up with him, but he pulled right across and parked facing the wrong way on my side of the street. His window slid noiselessly out of sight into the door, leaving me looking up into the forbidding reflective green of his wire-rimmed sunglasses.

"Staying out of trouble like a good little girl?" he asked, sarcasm oiling every word.

In reply, my voice came fainter than I bade it; but I managed a terse, "Hello, Sheriff." *Never apologize, never explain.*

The sheriff's cheek muscles contracted, wasting a stare underneath his dark glasses. He cleared his throat in an offensive way and said, "I'm saddened to hear, Miss Hansen, that you have been visiting the Hawkins' premises without an invitation. If you are too headstrong to mind your own business, perhaps you will convey the message to Miss

Chadwick that when there is a wrongful death investigation underway, it is considered prudent to mind your own business, so she better confine her movements to the rig and her quarters here in town. Surely *she* has some sense." The window slid back up into position as the Blazer pulled away.

I cracked, all my newfound self-assurance and insight disappearing like dew. It was one short block to where my truck was parked; in no time at all, I could be at Frank's. I was halfway down the block, moving fast, when providence spared me some distance: Frank's truck pulled into view.

We converged in front of the Blue Ribbon, and I suddenly found myself without words. I had never outright gone to someone and asked for help before. I must have had some sort of insipid smile on my face, because he opened his mouth and shut it a few times, looking back and forth between me and the cafe. His facial expression could not be described as one of joy at seeing me; in fact, it was more like irritated confusion. "Em," he said, looking downright bothered, "Em, I want to talk to you, but ah . . ." He looked away toward the cafe again.

He may as well have punched me in the gut. A whining little voice in my head said, *He didn't really care for me, he was just horsing around last night.* I tried to shout it down, but my brave new world was crumbling to dust, and I automatically started to cut my losses and save face. I made an apology, *and* a goddamn explanation. "I'm sorry," I said, "I just needed to get at the maps and stuff I left in your truck."

"Yeah, okay. It's unlocked." He went inside the cafe.

I felt like frozen shit. I reached into his truck, grabbed my packet from under the seat and went back to my truck, but had only the strength to drive it around the corner, where I parked in front of the laundromat and bawled like a baby.

There's no privacy in this world, not really. Emo struggled out of the laundromat about a minute after I parked the truck. He fixed his fevered eyes on me and froze, staring like a statue. I cast my eyes down at the packet and pulled out a file and started to read. He moved away.

Well, now that I was there and had the packet and had no chance of privacy or dignity, the packet became a reasonable thing to focus my aching heart and mind on.

The first thing I pulled out was one of the technical papers Bill had found important. It was a photocopy of an unpublished manuscript by a Laura Babcock, something about permeability testing in the Tensleep Sandstone. I didn't know what importance it might have, but I thought, *Well, maybe this being unpublished and all, it gave Bill a leg up on the competition.* I proceeded to try to read it.

It was pretty heavy sledding. I read through the first page three times before even a word of it sank in. It was a whole mess of gobbledegook about taking one-inch plug samples from drill core and testing them to see if there was any correlation between how the rock was deposited and what the permeability and porosity were. Original research. Science at its most slumberific.

I was on the third page of the manuscript before I got smart and remembered to turn the whole thing over to see if Bill had made one of his summaries on the back of the last page. Sure enough, he had. Taped to the back was a photograph from a paper by some guy named McKee, showing the insides of a sand dune he'd carved open at White Sands National Monument. I'd never seen that before. I always figured that the inside of a sand dune would be just this blank, homogeneous face, but in fact it was full of really obvious layers lying at about a thirty-degree angle. It made sense, once I thought about it: a dune migrates as sand scoured by the wind from the windward slope avalanches down the leeward slope. That would form just what I saw, cross-beds. They looked pretty much like a bunch of cedar shakes I'd seen once leaning up against a wall of a house waiting for the roofer, and it looked *exactly* like the cross-beds in the cliffs of the Tensleep Sandstone where the road goes through the cut between Shoshoni and Thermopolis. Big, sweeping cross-beds, each lamina an inch or so thick, marching along the roadway like, well, shingles. I felt a little silly and wondered why I'd never made the connection myself. Surely Bill had told me enough times that the Tensleep had been laid down as a sea of sand dunes beside the sea.

Below McKee's drawing was another one that Bill had drawn. It was a deceptively simple little block diagram, a wonderful, clear, concise picture that told me all at once what he had in mind for Bar Diamond Field. It showed McKee's cross-beds again with the third dimension drawn in, this time with the permeability values from Babcock's tests superimposed, a big arrow meaning lots of permeability (oil flows well), a medium-sized arrow meaning lots less permeability (oil doesn't much want to flow), and a tiny arrow meaning almost zilch permeability (hang it up, this rock's tighter than a bull's ass in fly season). Because of the way the laminations formed when the wind blew, oil that found its way in millions of years later would flow well parallel to the dune slipface, poorly normal to the slipface, and vertically not at all.

Permeability. The degree of ease with which oil can flow through the minute spaces between the grains of sand in rock. The diagram triggered in me an immense leap of intuitive understanding. I became engrossed in Babcock's manuscript, drinking up every word and bit of data presented, my understanding of how oilfields work growing geometrically.

I realized that I was grinning. Bill had been one smart geologist. He had read these papers and figured out that the Tensleep Sandstone was not, as engineers like Ed Meyer supposed, a huge homogeneous layer of sand waiting to have its oil drained out in an orderly fashion. No. It had a *grain* to it, like wood or fish scales or fur on a cat.

I dug further into the packet. I found a small map of all the wells in Bar Diamond, with a red arrow marked *wine* and a series of blue lines at right angles to it marked *maximum permeability*. I could easily see that there were lots of places where there was no well between two of the blue lines, no well to drain the oil from the rock along its grain. Whole regions of the field were left undrained, rich in oil at virgin, untapped pressures. It was a simple, brilliant analysis.

As if from divine applause, a gust of wind rocked the truck, snapping me back from this reverie to the tender, mundane reality of Meeteetse. My heart lifted in love for this little town with its humble citizenry scurrying in and out of its laundromat, rushing to clean their coveralls for one more day or night working on the drilling rig that would prove Bill Kretzmer's brilliance for all to see.

That is, all would see Bill's brilliance *if* the 4-1 came in gangbusters. The 17-1 had been all but a dud. Where did that fit in Bill's theory?

Ripping back into the packet, I pulled out Bill's well file for the 17-1. Perhaps he had scribbled some note, left some clue.

I didn't have to look far. The top page was a photocopy of a rather extraordinary intra-office communication, dated just a week before we had started drilling the 4-1:

Bill:
Your statement in the board meeting this a.m. that mud acid ruined the 17-1 is so much self-serving bullshit. The engineering department is sick of being your whipping boy every time you lay an egg.
Ed Meyer, Chief of Engineering

Scrawled across the bottom of the memo was Bill's reply:

Ed:
You assholes dump mud acid down another one of my wells and I'll nail your nuts to the city gate.
Bill Kretzmer

Mud acid. What was mud acid? It sure sounded important. Had Ed Meyer run another one of his weird muds in the 17-1? I hopped out of the truck and headed for the pay phone in the laundromat to try Elyria again, in hopes of unleashing her spies and snoops into the bowels of mud chemistry. As the phone rang, I looked at my watch, and was surprised to find that it had gotten quite late.

Elyria once again answered the phone on the first ring. She sounded breathless. "Oh, Em, it's you," she cried. "You surprised me. It's exactly nine-thirty, just when Bill always phoned."

"Sorry."

"No, it's all right. Oh, wait a minute, it's actually ten-thirty—I was looking at a clock I haven't set forward yet. I'm all confused."

"What?"

"Daylight Savings started this morning. I was up working on the files at two, when it happens, and I thought I'd changed every clock in the house. I've hardly slept. More to report: Sylvia has prised some information from the receptionist. Our Mr. Hawkins paid Blackfeet a visit this Monday morning past—we are not certain why—and he was in the reception area when the receptionist arrived. She was surprised to find him there, and he was clearly surprised to be found, as she was early that morning."

"How odd."

"Yes, how odd."

"How did he get in? Were there other people there?"

"No, she's the early bird who unlocks the offices. She questioned him, of course, and he claimed that Maintenance had let him in. Maintenance is now gone for the weekend, but you may rely on me to check that statement first thing Monday. My bet is he had a key, and it's not hard to guess where he got it."

Hawkins? My mind raced. "Did she happen to mention if he was carrying anything? An attaché case, perhaps?"

"Nothing, my dear, except a very large suitcase."

"Don't we wonder what was in that case."

"Yes, don't we," she said, in a voice that was slippery with satisfaction. Then her more military tone returned and she said, "May I ask what you telephoned about?"

I had forgotten all about the mud acid, and told her about it.

"Mud acid?" she asked. "Just one moment, I have an engineer over here helping me scrutinize the specifications and cost estimates for the wells. I'll put him on." She sure did know how to marshal the troops.

A deep voice boomed over the wire. "Sure, I know about mud acid," the engineer said. "It's used all the time. It's a hydrofluoric acid treatment used to clean out the perfs."

"You mean the holes they blow in the well casing?"

"Yeah. I thought you were a mudlogger. Am I speaking over your head or something?"

"I'm usually gone before they case the well," I said, somewhat testily. "The casing pipe trucks are usually arriving just as I leave."

"Oh. Yeah, well okay, they cement the steel casing pipe into the well bore so it doesn't collapse and all."

"Right."

"Then they lower this gadget into the hole that shoots a bunch of bullets, like, through the casing. Otherwise, you'd have a nice hole in the ground with no way for the oil to get through."

"Right."

"So but there's crud in the rock that makes it not let go of its oil even after they shoot the perforation holes through the pipe. All that nice drilling mud you've been logging sets up like a cake of dried oatmeal all over the inside of the well bore. A little hydrofluoric washes it out of the perfs real nice."

Something didn't tally. Bill had gotten angry over a routine procedure? "If mud acid is used all the time, why would Bill bitch about it being used in his well?"

"Well, I don't mean *all* the time. There are times where you wouldn't want to use it, like if you were working in dolomite: the acid would cause the magnesium in the dolomite to precipitate out into the worst snot that ever plugged a well. But you're drilling in sandstone, sister."

"Like hell," I said, now certain why the 17-1 had been a

failure—in fact, what had been *done* to Bill's well to *make* it fail. Pieces of the picture snapped into place, flashing like neon signs, pointing the way toward bloody murder. "The Tensleep Sandstone is full of dolomite," I told him. "It's the cement that sticks the sand grains together."

Ed Meyer had washed Bill's brand new well with glue.

I had a feeling, deep in my guts, that I knew what else had happened to the well. A dead pumper who had put paraffin on his valves and an unmarked pumping truck moving darkly through the night spelled only one thing: the 17-1 had been killed, but not killed dead. Whoever had dosed it with mud acid had known just how much to use to gum it up temporarily, maybe just the parts of the rock right where the perfs had been blown through from the casing pipe, maybe just enough to make it produce very slowly. The rest of the rock had been left unspoiled. The preliminary tests on the well would indicate low production rates, and Blackfeet would expect little of the well, keeping it pumping only to pay back its investment, never bearing the expense of running a pipeline to such a marginal producer. It would be kept pumping only a few hours a day, to reduce wear and conserve power, the time clock set to draw up to the surface only the paltry volume of oil the tests had indicated should be expected.

That same someone who knew how to douse the well could then go back into the well with another perforation gun, shoot himself another, deeper set of holes, and the well would make oil like a fool. Such a scoundrel could jimmy the valve and the meter and pump volumes of crude oil into the holding tank when no one was looking, then haul it away in unmarked pumping trucks on moonless nights.

Who was that someone? Ed? Certainly, he had ordered the mud acid. He wouldn't be pleased if the pumper, or Bill for that matter, began to catch on to his scheme. But wait, Ed was on record as fighting Bill's proposals tooth and nail. Was that all a front? Had he bad-mouthed Bill day after day just to make it look like he didn't agree with his plan, just so he could douse the well and then steal its oil? Was Ed that clever, or that gutsy?

Perhaps he hadn't done it alone. He would have to have a confederate, someone local, someone who could slip onto the ranch with a pumping truck unseen. Someone who needed the money badly. That someone might be Garth Hawkins, the man who had been seen hauling a suitcase load of what were probably Bill's papers out of Blackfeet Oil's offices.

After I hung up the phone, I got back into the truck and sat staring at the steering wheel, my body numb as my mind raced along slamming pieces of the puzzle together. *I'll get you, you son—* A face appeared suddenly at my window.

35

I jumped clear out of my skin. By the time I realized it was Johnny standing there by the truck, my heart rate had nearly tripled and my skin was damp. I cursed, the low-level fright I had been harboring for days finally reaching the flash point as I realized how thoroughly I had left myself exposed. Whoever was shrewd enough to figure out this scam, and to get to Bill and Willie, would most certainly have spotted me by now. In panic, I stuffed the thought out of sight, and snapped, "What do you want?"

Johnny came around to the far door of the truck and opened it. "Sorry if I surprised you," he said. "It's just that Frank's been looking for you." His eyes danced.

I could feel the heat rising in my face. "Sure, Johnny, but he seemed to be busy with Stretch."

"You dumb bunny, he's trying to shake Stretch down for some information on this pile of shit's been happening. What, he run you off? Come on, buck up. He may not have pretty manners, but he was probably just trying to protect you, keep you from view while we try to sort this mess out. I'd say he's dreaming, judging by what a stubborn old mule you are, but there you have it, the boy cares about you."

Now I was downright mad. I was sick to the gills of men trying to tell me to run along and behave myself when there was anything the least bit chancy going on. "Since when do I need Frank to wipe my nose?" I asked.

Johnny's face tightened with exasperation. He said, "Mind if I get in? You and me need to talk."

Something about Johnny's tone of voice brought me up

short. I was starting to rebuild that brick wall of mine, and was amazed to find that I really didn't want to. "Get in," I said, between my teeth. In my present state of nerves, I wondered about letting anyone, even Johnny, corner me in that truck or anywhere else. *God, you're getting edgy,* I thought. *Surely you don't suspect Johnny.*

Johnny settled into the seat and stared out the windshield. "I don't think you quite understand what Frank's been through, Em. The Nam done something to him. Done something to a lot of guys. Maybe you're too young to remember."

I was bewildered. I had oil wells on the mind, not military history. I couldn't imagine where he was headed with this line of conversation, but I told my mind to shut up and listen.

Johnny continued. "Frank won't talk about it, of course. I got some of this from the sheriff, who was over there the same time, in the Military Police, and some from a few other folks in town. You may not believe this, but Frank was a real hell-raiser in his day. Boisterous. Talkative. He had a brother two or three years younger who idolized him. Joined the army right out of high school and begged for Viet Nam because that was where Frank was. Well, it seems Frank was down in Saigon celebrating his twenty-first birthday, having hisself one hell of a fine weekend's leave, when his little brother got killed up there in the bush. Seems Frank got real quiet after that. Seems he's been real quiet ever since." He paused for emphasis, glancing sideways at me to see if I was getting the drift. I wasn't.

I said, "So he misses his brother?"

"I guess it's a whole lot worse than that, Em. I don't know if you'll understand this, being a woman. And that's no put-down. But darn it, kid, girls and boys just aren't wired quite the same way. If you were a man sent to some weird foreign country, you never been out of Wyoming before in your life, and your ma told you to look after your kid brother like, and then wham! he's dead, right there while you're goofing off enjoying yourself, things just aren't the same."

"Frank thinks he's responsible?"

"It's not so simple as all that. Of course he wasn't; some Viet Cong plugged his brother. Frank wasn't even in the same unit—there was nothing he could have done to protect him. *But he wasn't there,* Em. He was off duty, relaxed, enjoying himself. The stress he was under, everyone was under, in that stupid war, over there getting shot at for no reason we could possibly understand, it was horrible. None of us came back the same boy as went over. And Frank; well, Frank came back hurt inside. I guess you could say he's still grieving, Em."

"For his brother?"

"For everyone. And there was more. There's—a lot going on here just now, in this town. It kind of brings it all back up. You see, Ben Lewis was an M.P. there in Saigon, like I said. He had a special duty. He—" Johnny left off for a moment. This was quite a long speech for him. He stuffed more tobacco under his lip, took a deep breath, and said, "Ben was in charge of the morgue. He guarded the bodies. All the boys that got killed in country got shipped out through Saigon, in body bags, and old Ben, well, he just loved that duty. Had 'em arranged, kind of—the bodies, I mean—laid out in a special way and all. Ah, it was pretty strange." The memory of Frank's concern for Willie floated back into my consciousness, this time with new meaning. "Well, anyway, Frank went there to see what was left of his brother, before the body was shipped back to the states. The way I heard it, the boy was riddled full of holes. The one that killed him was a bullet in the back of the head. It came clear through and out one eye. It seems Ben had run a stick through the wound so it wouldn't rot shut, like this was some special feature he wanted everyone to admire. Frank told him to take it out, and he argued, and the guy who told me this said neither one of them was making any sense. Well, like I say, that was kind of it for Frank. He could have gotten home for the funeral on emergency leave, but he decided to stay in country, went up to the bush with his unit. Didn't take another leave until he was out of the service."

I was still mad. "Why can't Frank tell me this himself?"

Johnny actually looked irritated for a moment. "Because, goddammit, you're not the easiest woman in the world to get close to."

All I could think of to say was, "Oh."

"Frank's over at the Blue Ribbon now. Maybe you want to drop by and see him in a bit."

That was asking too much of me, to be Frank's buddy. I wanted to grab Frank, to hold him as tight as I could, to crawl right inside of him; but to care for a man with a well of sadness that deep and dark? I exploded. "Just what the hell am I supposed to do, Johnny? I can't—"

He cut me off. "You dumb shit! He's nuts about you. What are you waiting for?" He cuffed me on the shoulder as he climbed out of the truck and disappeared into the night.

I tried to get up, but I knew I couldn't walk into that cafe and brazenly sit down at the table with Frank, any more than Frank seemed able to come to me. I put one hand on the handle, trying to summon up the will to open the door, but stopped short when another shape loomed up by the glass. This time I didn't even have the energy left to jump.

It was only Stretch. He knocked on the window, gesturing for me to crank it open, but as I slid the glass down I realized that he wasn't smiling his usual daffy smile. "Jesus, Em, you seen Alix?" he asked, his eyes bright with worry.

"No, not since a couple hours ago. She left me high and dry at the Cowboy Bar."

Stretch's agitation sent his lanky body into a jerky dance. "Aw shit, I been lookin' all over for her. Chet's left for Casper and asked me to get this message to her, an' I couldn't give it to her at the bar because of Ed, so's I went 'round to her room but she ain't there, an' the manager says she done gone out some time ago. Said she done got a message this afternoon from Chet hisself sayin' meet him at the 'usual place,' took the message to Alix herself over by the bar; what's'a matter, ain't Alix showed up? So I gets real worried like, 'cause I knows he never left no such message."

Stretch's long arms were flailing so hard and his speech was coming so fast in that wild Okie accent of his that I was quickly getting confused. "Wait a minute," I said. "Slow down. Maybe there's a mistake. Maybe he left that other message before he called you, and just forgot to tell you. Like now he's just breaking off a date, or something."

"Shit, Em, I'd like to think that was it, but you know I been awful worried what with all these people dyin' and shit, and here's Alix goin' off down that same road, and the manager says she was drunk when she left, and well . . ."

"Tell me, Stretch! What else?"

"Aw, shit, I don't want to get involved, Em, maybe he'll kill me too." Stretch looked like he was trying to climb out of his skin.

"Who's *he*?"

I could see the whites of his eyes all the way around his pupils as he said, "Meyer. Ed Meyer." He licked his lips.

"What the fuck you trying to tell me, Stretch?"

"Aw, shit, Em, the truth is I think I seen Alix git into her car and drive out south of town, an, an, an, aw, Em, Ed Meyer followed her. I caught this glint in his eye like I never seen before, all cold and mean, and calm, like he had something on his mind, like he was gonna—"

Just how wrong had I been about Ed Meyer? Had I been fooled by a fool? There was no time to think it out. Alix was in trouble, and I was likely the only one who knew where they met. I said, "Stretch, you go get Frank, will you? Get Frank and meet me at the waterflood plant. That's where they met. That's where Alix and Chet used to get together. Run!"

36

Alix, Alix, Please be all right. I willed the truck faster and faster over the rutted road, pressing my foot harder and harder on the accelerator pedal, which was already flattened against the floor. A jackrabbit skittered from a clump of grass by the roadway, fleeing my headlights, my reaching headlights, which searched and grabbed at the hidden landscape, waking up dark spots among the sagebrush as the truck catapulted down the road. Suddenly, I was in Bill Kretzmer's turn.

The truth pitched and yawed, breaking into a sideways slide for twenty feet before it snapped back onto track. I downshifted and drove on, screaming at myself. "You dumb shit!" I hollered, "How you going to help Alix if you roll this fucking truck?" I slowed, breathing deeply, for the first time taking a moment to think, to plan.

What was I going to do, out there in the dark pocket of the pumping plant, in this dark hour of the night, if Alix was truly in trouble? What could I do?

I can save her, somehow. He might rape her or beat her. And what if I was wrong, and Ed is a killer?

But how about you? another voice asked. *If he would harm her, he would harm you, too.*

I had reached the turn that would take me to the pumping plant. *Will Frank know this is the right turn?* I crunched to a stop, grabbed my flashlight out of the dash, switched it on, and dropped it out the window to the edge of the road, its yellow beam pointing the way, bright in the gloom of the overcast night. I drove on. Over the next rise the pumping plant loomed into view, its heavy moan of motors and laboring iron arms already audible a half mile away, calling through the night.

A hundred yards short of the final turn-off to the pumping plant, I stopped the truck, idled in the middle of the road, uncertain if I knew what I was doing. Was Alix really in any trouble? Ed was no real threat to her. *She's always handled him before.*

But what if he is a killer? Does she know how to handle that?

My brain rang with conflicting evidence, teemed with false signals, buzzed with static. I forced it to be quiet, to idle like the truck engine, to await clarity. I leaned on the steering wheel and breathed deeply, staring out across the remaining ground to the plant. Darkness crowded the headlights.

Someone killed Bill and Willie, came a thought, dressed simply, waving no other signs.

There is danger.

My heart thumped loudly in my chest.

The engine of the truck purred. Through the open window, I could hear cattle moving sleepily somewhere nearby. I wished the moon would rise so I could see. I slipped the truck back into gear and moved slowly forward, rolling toward the turn-off. The illumination from my headlights swayed and bounced as the front wheels of the truck dropped from the grade of the larger road to the smaller, and cast a pale and callous light across the face of the metal building, marking the black maw of the open doorway starkly. Alix's car sat off to one side. Beyond the edge of the building, I could see the reflective gleam of one tail light of another car. *Ed's?*

I pulled the shift lever out of gear and let out the clutch, letting the truck roll to a resting place among the ruts of the drive. Nothing moved. I waited.

I was marginally aware of a slight tingling in my hands and fingertips, a sensation not unlike a faint electric current moving through them. My breath came shallowly and my

eyes strained farther and farther open as every inch of my
being tried to detect what was out there.

Something moved near the edge of the building, beyond
the reach of the lights. I switched the headlights off,
squeezing my eyes shut for several seconds to hasten night
vision.

Nothing. Minutes passed.

A trace of sound whispered past my ear: a mewling, a
tiny sound of distress, almost swallowed by the deep crashing of the pumps. I strained to hear it; switched the engine
off, the better to hear.

Someone is out there.

The open door of the building tugged at me. Was it Chet,
awaiting his assignation after all? A maintenance man?
Who? Possibilities whisked through my head like ghosts. I
held my breath, praying that it wasn't Alix.

The sound came again. A cry, a tiny call of anguish,
piercing through the thrash and groan of the pumps.

My breath whistled between my teeth as I slowly, carefully, swung the door of the truck open and lowered my
feet to the ground. My pulse sounded in my ears, much too
fast, rickety and racing, rising like spindrift on a cold
ocean. I eased forward, keeping to the dark-on-dark shadows in the diffused and dampened starlight among the few
sagebrush, crouching down, my knees and hips moving
smoothly as an oiled bearings, my senses reaching, scan-
ning the darkness for direction.

The sound was pitiful, pleading.

I moved forward more quickly, my heart pulling me toward the sound, my skin reading the darkness like an in-
frared sensor, reading cattle, reading mice, reading only
one other human.

Thump! A heifer lurched to her feet behind me, outside
my peripheral vision, struggling away from me in alarm,
rousing three others. My body twitched, awash in adrenaline, my mouth dry, my breath laboring; my eyes tried to
take flight from my face, straining to see more, to resolve
the dark forms of the cattle from the sage; my hearing

dulled, crowded by the roar of machinery. I straightened, instinctively raising my ears higher above the ground to listen for the cry. I held my breath, my ears pounding with my blood, and—

Whzzing! The skin on the back of my neck read the closeness of another human a split second ahead of the sound of air parting before the swing of metal, just in time to drop low and run, racing along the side of the building, footfalls coming behind me, crying for cover, screaming syllables without form, can't run fast enough better hide, around the far corner

A door

Through it, eating the night with my eyes, devouring

Every scrap of information

Place to hide, save me, *please, please*

Down below the catwalk into the pit between the pumps, my feet in cold, oily water, squeezed in between the crashing rocker arms of the pumps, my head twisted sideways so they won't hit me with the falling stroke, my back pressed against frigid concrete, the only warmth the fine spray of crude oil and water spewing against my chest from a leak. Inside the building, inside the insulation of the walls, down inside the concrete well with the motors, the noise of the pumps is deafening.

A horse. I had seen a horse as I turned the corner. A horse standing far away from the building, its great mottled white patches floating in the starlight.

The pinto, awaiting his master.

Grit spilled onto my head as its master moved past my head along the catwalk. Adrenaline shook my body, wracked my muscles with spasms that tightened into pain. I rolled my eyes upward to behold my enemy, squinting so the faint light of distant stars sifting through the dirty windows wouldn't reflect off the whites of my eyes. I couldn't see him. I twisted ever so slightly to look—

The arm of a pump skinned my nose, shocking me with its quick, uncaring stroke.

The sound of the front door slamming shut, snapping

locked against its heavy metal frame, dimly met my ears through the roar of the pumps. My enemy passed along the opposite side of the pit, moving with a thick grace, oozing like a shadow. He was dressed entirely in black, his hat, his satin shirt, his pants, his boots. His face was blackened with charred cork, its features unreadable in the darkness, only a few bits of white flesh missed by darkness reflecting dimly in the diffused starlight. Only his hands stood out clearly, clutching a three-foot-long pipe wrench, vaguely red and oily in the darkness. I stretched my consciousness, trying to know this feral human, this animal that hunted me in the night. He was eerily familiar, yet lost in time.

Here, shifted in time, was the third rodeo cowboy in Jimmy's photograph. Arrived by horse from—where?

The ranch.

Was this Garth Hawkins? No, his companion. The other one in the photograph, who kept an Indian-trained pony in the stables. Who could ride a horse like that? A rodeo rider, a champion—

Where had I seen a champion's belt buckle recently?

The pony was unshod.

Unshod, like the tracks near the curve in the road where Bill died. Like the tracks near Willie's fallen form.

My enemy crouched, twisting his neck and torso to peer up into the shadows among the rafters, shifting the wrench over into one hand to balance, now planting the other on his knee and twisting stiffly.

Merle Johnson! Recognition poured into me, snapping into focus, the template of patterns fitting perfectly together as I saw all at once that this antique cowboy from an aging photograph was one and the same as a quiet, polite, solicitous man who kept the company of a fool, the better to snatch up the gold that fell from his pockets. The perfect cover: hide stealth in plain sight within an unassuming exterior beside a braying ass of a man, virtue appearing to wax in the quiet as it waned in the loud.

How tidy. Ed, a slave to an ego so crippled that he would pay any price, deny any weight of reality, just to have a friend forever beside him. Ed, so distracted by his uncertainty of self that all anyone had to do to steal the key to the throne was to keep Ed company.

Merle's teeth flashed white within a perverted smile, all facade vanished, his eyes dancing with unwholesome pleasure as he lifted one hand to his mouth. He poised his weight almost seductively, and made the sound—the mewling sound, the little *help-me* sound that had lured me out of the safety of my truck. Shame rained cold through my body, saturating me with the sure knowledge that I, too, was such a fool as Ed.

Like a nonsensical machine, my brain raced onward, snapping little pieces of the puzzle into place from the recesses of conscious thought. All Ed's decisions had been cleared with Merle. Merle had become the access to all oilfield contracts with Blackfeet Oil, all decisions to buy equipment, to set casing, to test production. How easy it had become for Merle to call for unneeded procedures, filling his coffers with unnecessary jobs done with overpriced materials and equipment. It wasn't Ed who was taking the kickbacks, it was Merle. And when that wasn't enough, he enlisted his old rodeo buddy, Garth Hawkins, hooking him with his vanity, stealing back the oil that Garth had gambled away.

It all fit together, down to the last detail. My wandering bloodhound of a brain leaped across a final critical threshold of understanding. Here was a man so supremely arrogant that he had finally been seduced by his own game, pushed it too far, and been noticed. Bill Kretzmer had spotted the deceit, had compared notes with the pumper, had perhaps given Merle one look of wrathful knowing. Such knowledge must be done away with, must be snuffed from Merle's clever world, and Merle knew how to snuff it. He had ridden his marvelous horse through the night and waited, smoking a cigarette, for a worried geologist to return from making his nightly call to his wife, so predictably—hah, here he comes now—and had raced that horse perilously up that bank, ripping the grasses from their roots, rising like a juggernaut in the path of the oncoming car. Just as my mother had been pushed past the edge of her capabilities by a coyote, Bill had swerved to miss a man on horseback, a man who followed him over the far side and made certain he was dead, twisting his neck past the breaking point with arms made strong as steel from bulldogging steers in a hundred rodeos, from laboring ten thousand days in the oilfields. This man had just as coldly murdered a red-haired boy who was trying to be a man, crushing his head with a pipe wrench, and then folded his stiffened body over the marvelous pinto, breaking the rigor at Willie's hips and arms to fit him more securely. He had tied the pinto with Willie's body to the back of Willie's truck and taken them out into the badlands, grotesquely signaling his horse to trample the lifeless form before he rode the animal to its home.

The shoeless horse. Disappearing tracks and crumbling embankments. Unshod hoof prints beside both bodies.

And now this man who killed those who came too close to discovering him, this heartless killer with the beautiful horse, was after me, unable to stop himself in the machinery of death his greed and vanity had set in motion. Stalking me, searching slowly through every inch of the rumbling building, enjoying it very much.

How had he caught me?

I squeezed my eyes shut and prayed. *Please Frank, hurry!* But as I sent my prayer, I knew he wouldn't be coming, because Stretch wouldn't have given him my message. Stretch was Merle's man. Stretch had lied about Alix. Alix wasn't in any danger; she was probably passed out in her motel room, sleeping it off, like anyone with any sense would do. And Ed was probably a few doors down, lolling around on top of his mistress, feverishly submerging his weakness in the oblivion of her embrace. The monster who stalked me had requested Alix's car keys through the unwitting Ed so that he could make duplicates for his assistants to bring Alix's car out here, have the originals returned to Alix in front of me, so I would leap at his bait.

Trembling wracked me, tearing painfully at my knees,

which struggled to hold my weakening body the last half-inch above the oily water. I wept silently with fear and sadness, not wanting to die. I had to escape. Any moment, Merle might snap on the lights just long enough to spot me without drawing the attention of anyone who might be passing by. I screwed up all my courage and then bobbed up once, glimpsing his position, sensing his motion. Another twenty seconds and he would be as far from my position as I might hope, but still too perilously close to the back door.

I bobbed up once more, and he saw me. I jumped up with the next rise of the pump arm, its uncaring metal snatching at my left heel, tearing at my skin as I streaked toward the door, slamming it behind me with every last shred of my strength. It crashed open again, reverberating off the sheet-metal wall of the building, the roar of the pumps again spilling out into the night.

I ran toward the horse, clapping my hands three times, saw him turn and consider me, saw him start to move, saw him start to trot. *Please,* I willed, *come to me, faster, save me.*

My hair yanked backward as a hand snatched at me; short, thick fingers raking my scalp as they closed. The horse hurried closer. I heard a thin whistle and the horse reared up—higher, higher, impossibly high. As the horse rose up, I fell to the ground, yanked backward by my hair, dizzy with fear. Hooves danced around me. I pursed dry lips and whistled once, begging him to stop. I rolled wildly, bounced up and ran, clapped my hands, confused now, trying desperately to remember the horse's code. Hoofbeats closed on me and I turned, leapt upwards onto the thundering animal, grasping for its mane. My grips sank home beside the heaving neck and I rounded him, turning him back toward my enemy.

Merle's teeth flashed with vicious glee just before he calmly pursed his lips to signal the horse once again. As I watched him, all my fear melted to rage, a deep, roiling fury at the twisted soul who stood before me.

I kicked the horse into a gallop, charging directly toward Merle. As Merle whistled, I whistled, too. In confusion, the horse thrashed its naked hooves in the air, dancing on its hind legs, then crashing to the ground again and again. My body snapped violently with the horse's motion, my wet, oily fingers slipping further and further down each strand of wiry hair, my slippery legs twisting helplessly around the giant neck. I tried to whistle, but the motion ran though me like a drug, knocking the last ounce of will from my body. I fell.

The horse wheeled, rising above me. My lips pursed; my whistle floated far away, somewhere beyond the buzzing in my ears. The horse was also floating, hanging motionless for a moment before his hooves fell a final time, landing softly to either side of my chest, pinning me by the fabric of my shirt.

"Ho, now," Frank's voice called, "quiet now, away here." He leaned against the animal's neck, pushing him backward and away. The horse snorted, stepping precisely not to harm me. "Emmy, my God, Emmy," Frank said, "are you all right?" He crouched down and touched me tenderly, afraid to move me.

"I'm all right," I managed, shock sweeping through me.

Frank took me in his arms and lifted me gently to my feet, brushed tears from my cheeks with one thick and calloused hand, which traveled next to my hair, my neck, and met its mate behind my back. He pressed his cheek against mine with a sigh, and held me close. "I looked for you at the rig but Howard said you hadn't come back yet. So I figured I'd better check out that flashlight by the road. I never thought I'd find this."

A thin moan brought my attention back to Merle. At first I could barely see him. The shadows seemed to swallow him into the earth, but his eyes shone dully in the moonlight, brighter now than the ruined satin of his shirt. He summoned the strength to raise one arm just far enough to view it, and held it, quivering with pain. The sleeve was torn and hung in ragged strips. His lips moved, as if in sleep, a look of great sadness settling into his face. "My shirt," he said, in a voice barely audible. "My shirt."

I reached down and tried to smooth the tatters. The cloth was cold to the touch.

37

Warmth spread through my body, pressing toward a coldness in my soul I feared might never leave. Warmth from the fresh cup of coffee that Johnny had given me, proffering it sweetly, as if it were a chalice; warmth in the faces of the people in the room; warmth flowing from Frank's flesh into mine, as we sat cuddled on the settee in the logging trailer. With one great strong arm around my shoulders, he squeezed me closely to his side. The thick, rough fingers of his other hand wandered through my hair from forehead to neck, over and over again, their slow ministration transporting me to some place slightly fuzzy, until the unquenchable cold in my soul ached against the warmth. The manic buzzing of voices in the room receded, melting into a pool of sound that added to the massage, sounds popping like bubbles in a ticklish pool of release.

The trailer rocked with the gain of one more body. Night air washed through, sucking heat and cigarette smoke outside, refreshing my face, *Sheriff*, the voices buzzed. *What news, Ben? What can you tell us?*

I opened my eyes.

Sheriff Benjamin R. Lewis stood before me, feet planted squarely, hands on hips, eyes set on medium bulge, hat shading the main overhead light from my eyes. He stared at me and shook his head. "She looks shocky. Get her feet up." Someone scraped a chair across the floor and lifted my feet onto it. My head began to clear.

The sheriff spoke again. "My dear Miss Hansen, I won't ask if you have the sense that God gave geese, because it's more than obvious you don't. It might have taken me a bit longer than you to solve our little mystery, but it would have been better for your health if you had kept to your job here and let me do mine. It's what I'm paid for. I did tell you to stay out of trouble, you'll remember, on at least two occasions. You could have saved yourself one hell of a fright, and right now you could have been in your own little bunk asleep, instead of sitting up here with this sorry bunch."

Titters all around. I realized the sheriff was almost sort of smiling at me.

Frank spoke: "You should've tried asking her instead of telling her, Ben. Em don't bully so good; I think it just makes her more determined." More laughs. "So tell us, Ben, how's it look?"

There was a hush: all ears and eyes turned toward The Law. "Merle's dead, boys. That horse drove some of his ribs right through his lungs. The medical boys did what they could, but that was the end of it for that old cowboy; his heart quit before they got him into the ambulance."

My arms tightened and I started to tremble all over again, as the all-too-recent sight of what had been left of Merle Johnson rammed its way back into my consciousness. "There now, it's okay, Em," Frank whispered, but I could feel his pulse grow faster, too. Tears started to form in my eyes again, but sweetly this time, and just for a moment. It came to me that it might be all right to cry, that perhaps at times like this, holding in the tears was like putting a brick back in the wall.

As if on cue, the sheriff whipped his hat off and waved it around the closeness of the room. "Okay, boys, everybody out. Johnny, Frank, you stay. Someone take Frank's place on the rig for a while, okay? Thank you, boys." The rest of the evening and morning drilling towers shuffled out of the trailer, grumbling that they had a right to know, some taking backward looks at me that spoke of sympathy. The sheriff told them to keep on moving, that they'd get their story. When they were gone, he descended an inch as his undersized legs folded to drop him into a chair. He said, "I tell you, teach a horse to trample a human, and you might better keep your distance yourself. Well, it saves the taxpayers a trial, but I for one would have liked him to answer a few questions. Just how and when did you get on to him, young lady?"

With the sheriff interviewing me in such a genteel tone of voice, I wondered at my foolishness in recent days, thinking him incompetent, uncaring. Embarrassment and confusion left me wishing I could give him a satisfying answer to his question, maybe tell him I had arrived at my knowledge through brilliant deduction instead of blind meddling and wild-ass intuition. Finally, honesty seemed like the best policy. I said, "I can't say I knew it was Merle, I hadn't really gotten that far, but it all fits together now. I just knew it wasn't Ed. He's too preoccupied with keeping his paper-thin ego together to have any time left over to go 'round arranging complicated murders, let alone pulling off big oilfield scams. I imagine you'll find him right about now down at the Oasis Motel, shacked up with the chambermaid. I'll bet Merle had it rigged so she'd receive Ed whenever Merle wanted him out of sight or unavailable, and without an alibi he'd care to admit."

"What theft are you talking about?"

"Bilking Bar Diamond Field. If you'll phone Bill Kretzmer's wife in Denver, she can show you how Merle overcharged Ed for every job he did. I'll bet he was charging Ed for things he didn't do, too. It's funny, because Merle helped me out once, got me out of a dinner up at the Pitchfork I didn't want to be at, so I thought he was a nice guy. But he did it so smoothly that I began to wonder." I paused, momentarily too angry to speak. How easily I—and everyone else in this community—had mistaken the cool, measured actions of a parasite for kindness and humanity. How many years had Merle clung like a tick to his "friends," never quite taking all the blood, so that his host would keep feeding his desires?

"Keep talking."

"And the way this whole business with the fishing on the rig got my attention. It seemed Merle was making the decisions." I got up and pulled the Sundry Report out of my cereal box. "At least, now I know what this was all about. Bill was on to them. When I first saw this, I couldn't figure out why Bill wanted such a mundane bit of information from another field, but here it is in black ink: Broken Spur Field. Three wells plugged and abandoned. Engineer, Ed Meyer. You can see here Broken Spur is operated by a different oil company: must be where Ed worked before Blackfeet, and I wouldn't be surprised if they bounced him for suspicious handling of funds. I found a whole wad of these reports in Bill Kretzmer's personal files at his home in Denver, and the funny thing was that the signature varied. It didn't dawn on me right away, because I was in a terrible hurry, but it was like two different people were signing Ed's signature. It looks like Bill just kept ordering more reports as he found out which wells in which fields Ed had worked on, hoping to find one where the forger had slipped up and signed his real name: Merle Johnson. Merle's probably been doing Ed's work and making Ed's decisions for him for years."

The sheriff shook his head. "How does Merle profit from making the wells expensive? He's a workover man."

"He got kickbacks. If he got Ed to hire Stretch to supply the mud, for instance, he got a piece of Stretch's take. Maybe he owned the mud company, under a dummy name. Maybe he even got a percentage of rig time, because someone threw my pet drill bit down that hole. All the time he's setting Ed up to take his fall for him, if worse comes to worst." I couldn't believe it. I was actually clearing Ed's name. Sort of. Guilty? No. A wise manager? Hardly.

The sheriff said, "All right, as long as you have all the answers, how did you know about the oil theft? It was taking me and half the law enforcement officials in Wyoming to piece that one together, after what I got out of Dinah Sewell. And I'll have you know we were getting there, young lady."

My head was beginning to pound. "Dumb luck. I saw the tanker. I tracked it around to the south end of the ranch."

"Tired of living, Miss Hansen?"

"No." I was not about to admit in front of these people just how consummate a fool I really was. Besides, just because I have delusions of being invisible doesn't mean that it didn't take a very shrewd mind like Merle Johnson's to catch me nosing around.

"And?" prompted the sheriff.

"And I talked to Dinah, too. She told me about the paraffin seal Willie put on the valve, so he'd know if anyone was messing with it, and she told me about how he'd started to check the tank levels, to see if anyone was pumping them off. It was a major slip-up, I guess, for Merle to let Ed hire Willie, but no one's perfect."

"So you think Merle was involved in the oil thefts, do you?"

"Yeah. It just follows, don't you think?" I was beginning to get embarrassed.

"Would you be so kind, Miss Hansen, as to share the basis for your speculation?"

"Yeah," I said, my eyes starting to close under their own weight. "You might want to go round up Jimmy, the Hawkins' wrangler. He can't speak, but I know he can read and he can probably write. He's a simple old guy; they probably ignore him."

The sheriff snapped his fingers in front of my face and I opened my eyes. "You passing out on me? You ain't making much sense."

"It was the oil theft that really confused me, because it's tough to move a tank truck around in an oilfield with people coming and going at all hours around this drill rig. It would be really hard to pull it off as an outside job, but then, why would Hawkins steal his own oil? And Chet was riding out here like he was still heir apparent to an oil fortune, courting the Company Woman and all. Business as usual. But I kept seeing horse's hoof prints wherever a body showed up, and not just any prints. These were from an unshod horse, but the prints weren't rough enough for a wild horse. Besides, the wild horses don't come down onto the ranch, they stay up on the BLM land. So I went looking for a local horse with no shoes, and I found Merle's pinto.

"Garth probably figured Jimmy was so cut off from the world he wouldn't tell anyone what was up, but it was Jimmy who showed me how the pinto was trained. He loves the horses he cares for: they're his family. I bet if you go tell him what Merle did with that beautiful Indian pony, he'll tell you all about the comings and goings on that ranch, little activities like midnight tank truck runs through his dooryard and which dark nights the pinto went out for a ride and came back exhausted."

The sheriff shook his head. "This is all a bit hard to believe about old Garth. We were starting to investigate him because this is happening on his ranch, but I hadn't pegged him as a man of crime." He went to the other end of the room and poured himself a cup of coffee.

It was all coming clearer. Garth wasn't immoral, he wasn't big enough to have any real morals at all. The only thing big about him was his pride. But Merle knew what he was doing, and he had a system in life. He studied people, learned their habits, their weaknesses. He picked on the people he was closest to, or maybe he got close to them because he could pick on them, and chummed up to people in positions of influence who had weak egos. Like Garth, his old pal from rodeo days, gambling addict and heir to the richest ranch in the area.

The sheriff paced back and forth in front of me, sipping his coffee. "Continue," he said.

"Okay. Hawkins needed his cash flow from the oil to pay for his showy horses and his fancy new trucks and stables, not to mention that house. Vanity is a progressive disease, just like compulsive gambling. So he got in bed with Merle Johnson Enterprises, stealing back the oil he'd gambled away. Merle set it up so folks would think the well was a lousy producer, so no one would miss the oil they stole. They'd jimmy the valves and reset the time clock on the

17-1, and then they'd pump it off in the night and haul out over the back way through the ranch. When Garth found out his son was making time with the company geologist, the close scrutiny made him nervous; he put a stop to their romance fast. He panicked when he heard she was coming out to the ranch. Chet's kind of a cream puff anyway. You see, it all fits together."

The sheriff had finally gotten out his little notebook and was scribbling away. "So those two old boys were out thrashing around in the dark, getting their hands dirty with an oil well?"

"I didn't get a look at who was driving that tank truck."

Frank cleared his throat. "Try Stretch," he said.

"Stretch?" asked the sheriff. "You mean that mud feller?"

"Yep." Frank's eyes started to burn with rage again, only this time the feeling was right there at the surface. "That squat-to-piss son of a bitch must be Merle's man. Em sent him to get me before she headed out to the pumping plant. He came to get me all right: kept me sitting right there in the Cowboy Bar, talking my ear off with that damn Okie palaver of his. Didn't say a word of Em's message. I finally just left him squawking, 'cause I wanted to see her before I started work. I seen her flashlight by the turn but didn't know what to make of it 'til I got clear to the rig and found she wasn't there. Lucky for Em it's the last Sunday of April."

"What?" The sheriff was looking at Frank as if he was hallucinating.

Frank smiled again. "The time change, of course. Daylight Savings. We started an hour earlier than we would have under standard time. That son of a bitch Johnson thought he had it timed so no one would be passing through the oilfield when he bumped our little detective off, but he forgot to set his watch forward."

38

It was almost eighty degrees the day the well came in. The waning fingernail moon was setting over the Absarokas, and a soft breeze carrying the scent of the warm prairie played through the trailer, riffling the papers on the logging desk and messing up the shining perfection of Elyria Kretzmer's hair. She smiled at me, brandishing her excellent teeth, when I looked up from the first Tensleep Sandstone cuttings sample and told her. And then tears collected in her already shining eyes.

"It's a well," I said. "And a good one. Bill was one smart geologist. Come over here to the microscope; just look at the oil streaming off these cuttings—this part of the field's never been drained. Look here: see all that black stuff? That ain't ink, my dear." She took my seat and stared into the binocular eyepiece, but I knew she couldn't see a thing, so thick were her tears.

Funny how things work out. Here we were, just a couple of women from the oil patch who had gotten to know each other in the damnedest way, sitting around on a fine spring day watching an oil well come in. The success of this well was going to make her life softer, because Bill had nailed down overriding royalties on the wells he proposed, and as his widow, Elyria had inherited them. But that's not why she was crying. I think it had more to do with remembrance of what was, than happiness for what was to be.

Even in her sadness, it felt good to sit with Elyria. She made it easy for me to practice something I was just learning: how to be close to another human being. It was pleasant.

Perhaps, after all, it is time for me to join the world, to find my place in it. All these years I've felt like a beggar at the servants' door, wishing the Alixes of the world would give me just a little bit of what they had in such abundance. Now I find I have what I need, and it's been right there inside me all along. I still keep losing sight of this knowing; but on that day, as Elyria and I sat in the trailer watching the first cuttings from the Tensleep turn Bill's theories into facts, I enjoyed one of those rare, clear moments of vision, a moment of waking during the long, fitful sleep of my soul. Perhaps I would travel ten more sleeps before such clarity would visit me again; but for that moment, I was content.

Sometimes I still wonder if the price of knowledge is too high, or if there might be a less costly way of learning. Two men were lost to us, and even now the smallest things can bring to mind the horror of the night I brushed so close to death myself; but what's done is done. Nature sometimes teaches lessons on a scale too large for me to grasp; but perhaps, it is a part of learning to protest the teaching.

Materially, the Tensleep had yielded another bounty to me: I'd just been offered a job. A nice one, that would pay a lot better than mudlogging, and afford me more respect. The president of Blackfeet Oil was in Meeteetse that day for the same reason Elyria was—to give evidence at the inquest—and he had come by that morning to have a look at his well and make a few announcements to the assembled employees and subcontractors of Blackfeet Oil Company. Anyway, he asked me if I might be interested in replacing Bill as Blackfeet Oil's geologist for Wyoming. He said that with a mind like I had, he'd much rather have me working for him than for his competition, and he said it right there in front of everyone.

I'll have to think about it for a while. It would mean moving to Denver, which is a long way from the pure, endless skies and windswept prairies of my heart, but this particular piece of prairie has too many memories attached to it now—especially that place near the waterflood pumping plant.

On the positive side, it would be a chance to better use the brain people keep saying I have, and I'm sure I wouldn't miss Howard. And even if Alix didn't need me to save her from an aging phantom cowboy in the wilds of Wyoming, she's said she wouldn't mind my company in Denver, while she mends a heart that got itself bruised a bit by a young one.

Chet did come by to see her a few days ago, to see if she still cared, but I don't suppose she does; I heard her saying something about boys who let their daddies run them around. I couldn't quite catch it all, because the wind kept shifting that day.

I thought for a moment that I'd have to reject the job offer on account on Ed Meyer. Life's too short to spend working with that slimebucket every day, and of course Ed was standing right there with everybody when the president asked me to consider it. But then Ed announced that he was leaving the oil business. It seems Ed had decided (through whatever method of decision-making; there's been some speculation around the Blue Ribbon Cafe that Blackfeet Oil buries its wounded) to tender his resignation and go into chicken farming back home in Oklahoma. How small the giants when they tumble.

You could about have knocked me over with a feather. I was once again frozen and speechless in the presence of Ed Meyer. The president smiled cheerfully as he assured Ed that the company would miss him. Alix, ever perfect in her manners, offered him her hand to shake, although by the look on her face she was keeping silent so she wouldn't start laughing. I guess there were too many people watching for Ed to let it go at that, because he stepped forward and tried instead to kiss her on the cheek, like he was giving her a consolation prize or something. Well, old Ed lost his balance and trod on her foot, making himself look pretty darned silly, and once Alix's mouth was open to shout it stayed open to laugh. She laughed long and hearty, like Ed had done it just for her.

If I took the job, I might miss Johnny, although he says he'd see me on the very next well Blackfeet drills. It seems he's gotten a sweet little promise to go with the pat on the back that Blackfeet's president gave him that day.

I know I'd miss Meeteetse. I understand Denver has a million or so inhabitants, but where in that tangle of humanity would I find the likes of Dinah, or Emo, or the postmistress, or dueling gossips like Jilly and Rita? Besides, Denver has too damned many streets.

Most of all, I'd miss Frank. He says I shouldn't worry: he'd see me on the wells and he says he'd come to visit me as often as he could. He says I should follow my kismet (whatever that is), but I wonder if I shouldn't just follow my heart.

For the near term, I won't have a problem sorting out my heart from my destiny. As soon as the well is completed, Frank and I are heading out to Yellowstone with our backpacks and hiking boots to visit a certain stream where a wild rose grows; and we're not coming back until we damn well feel like it, if ever.

AUTHOR'S NOTE

For those interested in historical notes, in the spring of 1981 I sat three Tensleep wells in Little Buffalo Basin Field, one of several oilfields near Meeteetse, Wyoming, as geologist for Amoco Production Company. I was dining on Polish sausage and watching the big color TV at the Cowboy Bar as the first space shuttle returned from space and touched down at Edwards Air Force Base. Nineteen eighty-one also saw the turn in the oil boom set off by OPEC in 1973, and by 1982 the industry was already contracting sharply. It is of the economic crises that have followed that crash that I write.

In certain ways, the oil patch has changed since then. The bottom has completely dropped out of the price of oil, putting me and a dizzying percentage of geologists and engineers out of that line of work, but that's about what I always expected in a boom-and-bust, commodities-based industry. With the crisis in the Persian Gulf, oil prices temporarily bounced a little higher, but so far investors have been hesitant to bet their money on prices so strongly overshadowed by political maneuvering.

In certain other ways, the oil patch is just like it always was. The oil can wait, just as it has for all the sixty million or more years since it first matured out of its source beds and migrated into the Tensleep reservoirs.

Meeteetse is just about the same. I'm sure that, save for the name on the gas pumps and the quality of the streets, it would look much the same as it did to Amelia Earhart when she fell under its spell in the 1930s and bought land in a nearby valley to build a cabin retreat. A few shops have closed, others have opened. The old stone bank is now the home of the Meeteetse Historical Society. The Blue Ribbon Cafe stands empty, and there's a new motel at the south end of town, but the Mercantile still sells everything from socks to fishing lures. There never has been an A&W stand in town, though—I borrowed that from a half dozen other little towns around the Big Horn Basin—and there is no Bar Diamond Ranch or Field. And of course, all the characters depicted in this book are entirely fictitious, and no detail of any one of them is meant as an affront to the citizens of Meeteetse, who welcomed me kindly to their bend in the Greybull River.

Em Hansen returns in

A Fall in Denver

by

Sarah Andrews

Turn the page for an
exciting preview of this next mystery,
coming soon from Signet. . . .

1

If I had seen the body fall past the window, I wouldn't have taken the job. At least, that's what I kept telling myself, but maybe I would have rationalized my way around that, too.

In hindsight, the first day on that job was full of omens, and the body was hardly the first. If I'd been wiser, I would have tucked tail and run the instant the brown cloud that passes for air in Denver turned to acid on the moist parts of my face, burning my eyes and leaving a foul taste on my tongue. But no. When Gerald Luftweiller hit terminal velocity outside that twelfth-floor window, I was sitting with my back to it, so instead of witnessing the penultimate instant of his life, I was taking in the exquisitely tanned and shaven face of J.C. Menken, president of Blackfeet Oil Company. Menken was giving me his "welcome aboard" speech, just getting to the part where he favors the new hire with a congenially arrogant smile and compliments himself for hiring "such a keen mind—another company asset."

Old J.C. had been lounging back into the soft leather of his chair before the body fell. When he saw it, he sat up abruptly, but moved to cover his surprise by leaning onto his desk, as if that was where he'd been heading all the while. His face writhed through a bizarre bit of gymnastics, concealing shock before it arranged itself into a display of rational detachment.

"Damn," he said, his tone conversational, "looks like another suicide. That's two in a week—there was one off the Radisson Hotel last Thursday. These people, they can't seem to think up a better option than killing themselves. Now, if I found myself in tough circumstances—" he smiled at the thought that he, Josiah Carberry Menken, would ever find himself in such straits—"I'd certainly think up something better. A man can always head out for the South Seas and spawn illegitimate children with a dusky-skinned maiden. Suicide, Jesus Christ. And worse yet, it starts a trend and you get two or three together. I can't imagine having that little self-respect: not only killing myself, but being unoriginal in the way I went about it."

"Someone's committed suicide?" I said, rising from my chair. I pressed my face to the glass, but couldn't see the part of the sidewalk straight down, only the adjacent curb and street. Traffic below had stopped in a weirdly skewed pattern. There were people running around like ants do when you rip the top off their nest.

Menken said, "Sit down, Emily."

I kept standing. "Are you telling me someone just *fell* past this window?"

"Oh, forget it, forget it," he answered, his tone becoming somewhat paternal, a touch irritated. "Come, sit down."

In my confusion, I did as he said.

"You must forgive me," he continued. "I forget that you're not a city girl. I might have forgotten, what with this elegant outfit you're wearing. I must say, it becomes you." He smiled, perhaps a shade more broadly than was quite decent.

Tensing, I thought: *Is this why he hired me?* I forced a self-assured smile. Had I misunderstood him?

"In fact," he went on, "I hardly recognized you. You look so different from the way you did in Wyoming. I had in my mind's eye the picture of a young woman dressed like she was on her way to a rodeo. I could see, of course, how intelligent you were. I said to myself right away, 'J.C., you must hire this girl; she's going to waste working as a mere mudlogger. Make a geologist out of her. Bring her to Denver, where you can keep an eye on her.'"

Perhaps I was only some barely animate trophy after all. I exhaled quietly. I wasn't used to being noticed, any more than I was used to wearing a skirt. I glanced down furtively at my new suit and pantyhose-encased shins, in fear that my mother's long-discarded Bostonian heritage was erupting through my Wyoming upbringing like a demon seed. Confused, I focused back on the room. And that window.

Drawing a deep breath, I tried another tack: "Um, excuse

me, sir, but what exactly did you see outside the window just now?"

"Yes," he said, "I told myself, 'J.C., wits like hers are hard to come by; it doesn't matter how they come packaged, it's the raw intelligence that counts.' Although, I'm most pleasantly surprised at the way you've turned yourself out. Most professional."

"Huh? Um, ah—I'll try to live up to the challenge, sir. I sure appreciate your giving me this chance."

Menken beamed. "I'll be watching you. As a matter of fact, I'm intrigued with this intelligence of yours. A woman's intuition? Eh? If you have any more of your sharp little insights, I want you to report them directly to me, Emily." He flashed me a million-dollar smile, shining with self-satisfaction.

My own smile sagged somewhat. It appalled me that he could refer to the impromptu detective work I'd done in one of Blackfeet's oil fields in Wyoming as "having a sharp little insight." And while I could adjust to being called "girl" by the company president, especially a man almost old enough to be my father, I wasn't sure at all how I felt about becoming his pet female. And worse yet, was I doomed to being called Emily, my whole unabridged antique moniker?

"Ah, my friends call me Em," I ventured.

"Eh?"

"My friends—" The phone rang.

"You'll excuse me, Emily," he said, waving one large, perfectly manicured hand over the phone. I rose to go, but before I was even on my feet, he had pressed the receiver to his ear and swung his mammoth chair away from me in dismissal, his universe already perfectly adjusted to the loss of one of its citizens.

2

That left me standing outside Menken's door, feeling like I had just gotten off a train in the wrong dimension. *You misun-*

derstood him, my mind informed me. *No one fell past that window.*

Menken's executive secretary looked at me expectantly, fixing me with an impersonal gaze. I stood staring into her middle-aged, I've-seen-it-all eyes, my mind flooding with questions. Nowhere in my fantasies had my first hour as a professional geologist included death. My hands began to tremble.

The secretary's almost-smile became politely bland. "Personnel has some papers for you to sign, Miss Hansen," she said, in a low, growly voice.

"What?" At length, I realized that in this climate-controlled office, twelve stories above street level, the news, whatever it was, had not yet reached this woman. *That's right. Her back is to the window. She didn't see.*

Somewhere in the middle of this, my mind registered the fact that someone years my senior had just called me "Miss." Was this what it meant to be a professional? People were going to treat me with respect?

Much as I liked being treated like a superior being, the experience also came with a twinge of guilt. I opened my mouth to say something sociable. What came out was, "There's been some kind of accident on the street." I gestured toward the window beyond her shoulder, immediately wishing I had chosen a more neutral topic.

Her smile began to congeal. "City living. You'll get used to it, dear." She nodded toward the hall. "Third door on the right," she added, as she swiveled her chair back toward her computer.

So give me a break; not having seen the guy fall with my own eyes, I began to figure I had dreamed it, or misunderstood Menken, or something. When in doubt, do what is expected of you, right? So I just got back on that train, hoping the next stop would make more sense.

I counted doors to the right until I found Personnel.

Personnel gave me her canned welcome and led the way farther down the hall toward my office-to-be. She moved quickly for someone leaning backward in an affected slouch, somehow maintaining her balance on needle-sharp heels while rolling her mighty buttocks beneath an emerald-green knit. I cast furtive glances left and right into the bull pens and offices we were passing, trying to catch glimpses of my new colleagues. Personnel chattered along about my retirement plan and health benefits in her high monotone, finishing with, "Fill out these forms, that's your desk in there, you share the office with Maddie McNutt, good luck."

Good luck? Maddie McNutt looked harmless enough, but perhaps I had mistaken the nonemphasis in Personnel's voice, and it was the forms that were dangerous.

My office mate sat thrashing a map with an eraser, all but tearing the paper in her vigor. She was a muscular little unit, blessed with a wild head of black curls and dressed to stop traffic. No demure East Coast tweeds for this lady; she liked stripes: big, wide, sharp-edged green and pink stripes, running all up and down a dress that fit like paint. As she scrubbed the map, the stripes worked back and forth with gusto, twisting and jumping over her body. She finished her job with a spray of eraser crumbs and a resounding thump and hollered, "Take that, mother fucker!" in a lusty, West Texas drawl, leaned back, and smiled at it cheerfully. By and by she looked up and turned that smile on me.

I felt moved to speak. "Ah, hi, I'm Em Hansen, I guess I'm your new office mate."

"Y'all sure?"

"Huh?"

"Take your time," she said, and went back to work.

This scene wasn't in my hotshot-geologist-goes-to-Denver fantasy, either.

Half a minute later, I was still standing on the threshold between my fluorescently lit beige office and the fluorescently lit beige hallway, the sheaf of papers Personnel had given me growing damp in my hand. I eyed my desk, whose hard, immaculate beige surface seemed to rebuff me. Some little flywheel in my brain was spinning, whining around and around in annoying complaint. It was a little voice, surprisingly like my mother's. It said: *It's time you toughened up, Emily.*

Right. So I walked over to my assigned desk, lowered my body into my assigned beige swivel chair, and set to work on Personnel's papers.

That kept me busy all of ten minutes.

I sat fidgeting. My mind kept straying down the hallway to Menken's office, wondering what he had seen outside that window. That good old mind of mine consumed itself with the image of a body falling, growing smaller and smaller as it plummeted toward the street. I longed for a radio, so I could at least get a news broadcast, find out what had really happened.

I considered asking Maddie McNutt what to do next, or maybe broaching the subject of whether or not someone had just jumped out of one of the windows of our building, but just then she got up and left the room.

After another ten minutes I couldn't stand it any longer. I got up and marched right out of the office, caught the elevator to the lobby, and hurried to the front door, just in time to see two police cruisers and a van pull away from the curb at Seventeenth Street. Yellow caution tape fluttered in the morning breeze, and a uniformed cop was signaling people, hustling them across the street to avoid an obstruction that was just out of sight to my left. People shuffled by slowly or stood staring, their mouths twisted in disgusted fascination. I started out the door to get a better look past the caution tape, but stopped when I saw two men in dark suits hunched down over the sidewalk, examining a great, dark stain.

On the way back to my desk I discovered, mercifully, that Blackfeet had a little kitchenette stocked with big, heavy mugs and all the strong, black coffee a person could gag down. I wished I had something stronger yet to flavor it with, to help me forget what I'd just seen.

At last news began filtering through the office. Some of the other inmates of Blackfeet Oil gravitated into the kitchenette to get the lowdown. They eyed me frankly and I introduced myself, a little thrill of excitement rising within me. *This is it, I'm a professional geologist meeting my new colleagues.*

Their eyes dimmed like shutters closing. Oh, you're the new geologist, they said. Hi.

I pulled back and eyed *them.* They were a tense bunch of people with softening waistlines and uncomfortable-looking shoes. As the conversation got rolling, they turned out to be pretty blasé about the demise of Gerald Luftweiller, the man who had dived past J.C. Menken's window. Lots of no-shits and you-don't-says went back and forth.

I began to wonder if these city folk were just as cold and alienated from one another as I had always heard. They began retreading dead baby jokes as Gerald Luftweiller suicide jokes. Okay, the oil business has always been full of sick humor, but this was the limit.

I asked if anyone had known him. I meant it to sound righteous, and it did. All I got for my trouble was a lot of *huh? . . . well of course no one knew him, did you, Scott? Me? Oh, no. No. Did you, Angie? Ah, no . . . no, people like that don't know anyone, know what I mean? I hear he was an accountant or something, worked for Love and Christiansen up on sixteen— not even thirty and a burnout already—you know, those people are always a little weird, look at numbers too much or something. Hey, did you see the sidewalk? Oh, yeah, and how about that hole he made bashing the glass out of that window? That sucker must have hit hard, man! Shit, yes, the janitor told me, and like, he talked to the janitor on sixteen where it happened, and he heard from someone who was standing right there, man. . . .*

Through a slight ringing in my ears, I heard details of the scene on the sidewalk. . . . *couldn't identify the body at first, but he had a map of Hat Rock Field in his pocket, with Love and Christiansen's logo on the title block. Hat Rock? Yeah, soaked him up like a blotter, they had trouble reading it. No shit?*

I escaped to my office.

From that moment I began to develop a thing about Gerald Luftweiller's death. A fascination, almost, a bit like my cousin Lester's interest in cats. You see, Lester was asthmatic as hell, but he'd hold my brother's cat on his lap and stroke its fur, wheezing away in defiance, just to prove to us older cousins that his weakness was not a limitation.

Now that I think of it, I was even crazier than cousin Lester. I wasn't just being tough, I was being a full-blown martyr. I was the good guy in the white hat, riding into town to call Gerald Luftweiller's enemies out of the saloon for a duel. Call it rage against the heartlessness of humanity. Call it sympathy as a subversive activity. But don't call it empathy. I wouldn't want to know that about myself.

So that's how the whole thing got started. One hour after becoming a real live geologist at Blackfeet Oil Company, I began collecting information about a dead man. I opened a mental file, and called it the Gerald Luftweiller Case.

3

The ancient dog whined softly as Elyria bent to give him his morning kiss, then he staggered across the kitchen to the food dish to await his breakfast.

"There, you sorry old thing," Elyria said, emptying a ration of kibbles into his bowl. "Just the item. Very nutritious. Yum, yum. Eat up."

The dog groaned. I kept my silence. I figured I could put up with Elyria's morning ritual, as long as she was being so generous as to put up with me until I found a place of my own.

Elyria straightened up and ran a hand through her taffy-colored hair. She looked how I would have looked I'd had any say in the matter: hypnotic eyes and fabulous cheekbones reigning serene over a slender, impossibly graceful carriage. At ten or fifteen years my senior, it was she who drew the stares as we walked down the street, not me. So much for the American youth cult.

I spilled coffee on the Wednesday morning *Rocky Mountain News.* "Sorry," I said, mopping the spill with my placemat.

Elyria set a bowl of granola down in front of me. "Relax. Eat this. It's good for you."

"Yum, yum?"

Elyria raised a shoulder in mock haughtiness. "Be like that. Don't let me care."

I ducked my head and smiled sheepishly. Elyria was one of the few people on earth who knew how to care about me without giving me a total screaming case of claustrophobia. Way back in April, when Menken offered me the job, she had given me one of her matter-of-fact nods and said, "And you'll stay with me until you're settled."

Normally, I'd have been a mite shy about accepting such a lavish invitation, but by the time I was ready to take the job, I knew she needed me, too. As busy as Elyria was with her work, her evenings had been lonely since her husband, Bill, died. That was how we'd gotten to know each other, after all: investigating his murder. It had made us fast friends.

And for my part, I needed her more than I cared to admit. Much as I'd always liked my solitude back home in Wyoming, where alone meant being out there in the wide-open spaces with the rest of creation, I was damned nervous about living alone in the city. Perhaps that was why I'd cut things so close, arriving in Denver the evening before I had to report to work.

Elyria glanced pointedly at the newspaper as she took her seat at the table. "Looking for news of your falling man?"

Of course, I was. And my search was rewarded: A terse paragraph at the bottom of page one carried the headline, SECOND MAN FALLS TO DEATH. It gave the dead man's name (Gerald Luftweiller), his place of employment (Love & Christiansen), and the surprising information that the police had yet to rule his death a suicide, continued on page twenty-two.

I turned the damned pages so fast I tore a few, but that was the end of the juicy stuff. The rest of the article just said that he was twenty-seven—a year younger than I—and that he hailed from Haverford, Pennsylvania. Luftweiller was a graduate of Haverford College, and was survived by his parents and two sisters, all of Haverford. I didn't get much from that, but I speculated that he was the only member of his family with enough sense of adventure to leave the old hometown. That presumption didn't fit with my preconceived notions about accountants as a personality type.

"What does it say?" Elyria asked. "Come on. Here I drag myself in from a business trip at midnight and find the strength to ask you about your first two days at work, and all you say is, 'Someone jumped out the window, things have to improve from here.'" She was exaggerating, of course: I had waited up and told her everything, lingering over details of Menken and Maddie and all the others.

"You don't really want to hear any more about this at breakfast, do you?"

Elyria gave me one of her don't-patronize-me looks. "Come now, Em, there has to be at least a paragraph on the poor man. Let's put him to his rest."

"Well, there's more here than the *Denver Post* had yesterday morning, but it doesn't say why he did it. Or *if* he did it, for that matter."

Elyria came and read the article over my shoulder. "Hmmm, Love & Christiansen, they're not in good shape financially."

"Really? This guy was one of their accountants. Maybe he was falling on his sword."

"Or just celebrating the equinox," she said, dryly.

I glanced at the date at the top of the page. She was right, it was September 24th, two days after the equinox. In the confusion of starting a new job, I had forgotten to celebrate it myself. "What does jumping out of a window have to do with celebrating the equinox?"

"First day of fall, dear."

"That's sick, Elyria."

"Mm-hm. I've been in the oil business too long." She lifted a spoonful of cereal to her lips with her pinky crooked in mock elegance. "I'm sure you'll figure out who or what killed this man. It didn't take you long to find out what happened to Bill."

I was Bill's replacement at Blackfeet. Working as his mud-logger—a lowly subcontractor's technician—on two of his wells in Wyoming had been my entree to Blackfeet Oil Company. For years I'd dreamed of getting a chance to really use my college degree in geology, and Bill had redoubled my longing by making the work look fascinating. Now here I was facing a third day of twiddling my thumbs at an empty desk. "I'm just bored, Elyria. If I had anything to do, Gerald Luftweiller would have been a sad but fading memory by lunchtime."

Elyria's look grew sharper. "They haven't given you anything to do yet?"

"No." It had been more glamorous to skip that detail during our debriefing of the night before.

"Who's your boss?"

"Someone named Fred Crick. But he's out of town, and he left no instructions for me. I spent Monday reading the company policy manual, stocking my desk with paper clips, and trying to look important. I spent yesterday reading the paper."

"Sounds stimulating."

"Yeah. It was a big moment when I got my first memo. Something earth-shattering like, 'Words To The Wise: President Menken's parking space in the basement parking garage is reserved for President Menken's Mercedes only. All other vehicles will be towed.'"

"Sage advice. What marvel of office acumen sent that around?"

"It was signed Irma Triff, executive secretary, or chief valkyrie, or whatever she is. I filed it in the wastebasket under H for who cares."

"You have all the makings of an executive."

The dog collapsed in the corner and sighed. Elyria looked pointedly at the clock over the stove. "I'd offer to drop you at work, but I'm heading out to Golden this morning. A little business at the School of Mines."

"That's okay, the bus is pretty quick."

"And so environmentally conscious."

The truth was, I didn't own a car of my own. Or a truck, which would have been my preference. I'd always driven my father's truck, or one belonging to the mudlogging company.

I drank the last of my coffee and hurried out the door to the bus stop, trying for the first time to jog in high-heeled shoes.

At the office, there was still nothing for me to do except drink more coffee and make a study of the way the steel girders that formed the floor sent shock waves clear into our office, up through my chair, and into my spine as cranky-looking people stalked by in the hallway. I didn't like being reminded that I was sitting over a hundred feet above terra firma on what re-sembled a stack of old 45-rpm records on a concrete skewer dressed up with fancy glass. It fascinated me that the damned building even managed to stay upright, considering its con-crete taproot was only sunk in mungy old river gravels.

I dusted off my pristine desk, rechecked my supply of paper clips, and tried to look confident. As usual, Maddie had her mind firmly trained on her work, and my attempts at striking up conversations with my other new colleagues got me nowhere in a hurry. Damn it, it bothered me that they wouldn't talk to me. *I thought I was a professional now, a member of the club. Is there some secret handshake I'm supposed to know?* I caught myself staring down at my brand-new white-collar uniform, wondering if it was too new. I flicked a piece of lint off it to cover my awkwardness, and wondered mo-rosely why I'd ever left Wyoming. I missed the clean air, I missed the open sky, and I missed my boyfriend, Frank.

Toward noon, I discarded the preoccupying question of why I'd taken the job for the greater mystery of why I'd been hired. There were layoffs throughout the industry. Why had Menken hired me, when there clearly was nothing for me to do?

By two o'clock, I was so bored that I was ready to pack my tweed suits in mothballs and leave town, when a skinny little guy in tight jeans scuffled into the office and brought me my first assignment. "Crick says, 'Look this field over, evaluate this new drilling location,'" he said. He unloaded a thick file and a rolled-up map onto my desk as if they were hot to the touch. I thought, *This is it, cowgirl; saddle up and say your prayers.*

The orange label on the tab at the top of the file said LOST COYOTE FIELD. I had heard of it; gas and light crudes in a Cretaceous-aged sandstone, about three thousand feet below surface, eastern Wyoming. A strong discovery in this time of severely limited exploration budgets.

"Ah, just what am I supposed to do with this?" I asked.

"I already said." He vanished.

"Oh. Right." *You little twink.* To Maddie, I said, "Who was that?"

"That's Fritz, the technician who works with us geologists."

"Oh."

"Ain't it sad when cousins marry?" she added.

"Sure," I said. I was learning to take Maddie in stride. I stared at the file. *How am I supposed to do this?* I'd been on plenty of drilling rigs, but I didn't have a clue what went into deciding where to drill.

I turned the file around and flipped it open to the middle, riffled through its contents. No revelations, just a bunch of memos with technical gibberish about casing pipe, and so forth. The memo on the top of the stack clasped to the first division of the file folder was signed by some dude named Peter Tutaraitis.

I sighed, wishing it had been signed by Bill Kretzmer, Elyria's late husband, my departed mentor. If Bill had worked this field, he would have made so many notes I'd know the field backward and forward by lunchtime. How I wished he were here. But then, if he were here, I wouldn't be here, and . . .

My mind began to wander again, musing on the good old days with Bill, and my boyfriend, Frank, out among the sagebrush. Simpler times. High plains. Endless horizon. Wyoming. Lonely life, but making sense. Two hours' drive north of Denver, life becomes real. I could be home by dinnertime. . . .

Maddie sneezed. My mind crashed back to Denver, to my new clothes, my new title, and to the job before me. *Screw it,* I thought savagely, *screw them all.* I started reading through the file.

The pages were clipped in chronologically. A glance at the earlier memos told me something about the history of the project. Blackfeet had acquired the lease and drilled the wildcat discovery well about two years earlier, and had thus far drilled ten more wells. The credit for the discovery belonged to this geologist named Peter Tutaraitis. So why wasn't *he* evaluating this goddamned location?

"Hey, Maddie," I asked, "who's this . . . Pete . . . ah, Two-tar-ray-tis? Did he leave the company or something?"

My office mate straightened up and stretched in the day's answer to fashion, which featured rather large polka dots, two of which barely missed being too well placed on her bosom. "Naw, he's still here. And you pronounce that 'Tutor-itis,' like a rash you get from teachers."

"Does he still work Wyoming? I thought the territories were pretty clearly drawn here."

"That's the story. Used to be a little looser, but the big dogs got to rearranging the kennels a couple weeks ago, and got all formal about who sniffs whose ass. Big Pete's California now."

Roughly translated, that probably meant Management had drawn a few boundaries on the map, reassigning Lost Coyote Field to me, and maybe there was some politics involved, and maybe this guy Tutaraitis had an ego. I said, "So when in doubt, I call him Pete?"

Without quite her characteristic volume, Maddie said something that sounded like, "When in doubt, don't call him."

"What?"

No answer. This was very interesting: it was the first time Maddie had been anything but screw-you and fully in charge. I flipped back to the first memo, to see if I could reconstruct the drama written between the lines.

No luck. The filed seemed overly tidy, devoid of marginal notes, calculations, or work sketches. I wondered what kind of a geologist this Tutaraitis guy was, if he didn't fiddle with his data any. Either this guy was so damned sharp that he could keep it all in his head, or he was asleep at the switch.

There were some large blueprinted sheets folded up in a pocket at the back of the file. I pulled them out and unfolded them. They were a bunch of graphs, plotted to show oil and gas production over time, with annotations indicating when various wells had been brought on line. The production rates looked pretty good. Damned good, in fact. But something had sure turned down Maddie's voltage. And Fritz, the inbred technician, had handled the file like he needed oven mitts. Odd. I dug through the rest of the file, trying to find a good old-fashioned, cross-sectional view of the oil field, a stratigraphic correlation from well to well that would show me something about the rocks from which the oil and gas were flowing. There wasn't a single cross section in there. Odder yet.

I tried again: "Can you tell me anything about this field?"

"What field is that?"

"Lost Coyote."

"Nope. Wouldn't want to crowd your job security, sweet peach."

That stung. I was trying to think up a suitable rejoinder when I heard a voice at the doorway announce, "Committee, ten minutes." I looked up to see an engineer named Scott Dinsmoore leveling a look on me that said, *Yeah, you.* Maddie looked up and observed him dispassionately.

"Huh?" I said.

"Committee meeting in ten minutes," Scott repeated. He looked put upon, tried to puff up his slight frame to fill a greater portion of the doorway.

"Cool your jets, Scottie," Maddie drawled, "that's just Emmy's word. 'Huh' means lots of things to her, like in this case, 'Roger and acknowledge that, big fellah, see y'all's ass in committee.'"

"Who asked you, McNutt?" Scott shot her a look of pure disgust and departed. Maddie smiled beatifically and bowed her raven curls back over her work.

How I envied Maddie's cool. I counted to ten, hoping she'd look up and at last take pity. Finally, at great cost to my pride, I cleared my throat and said, "Ah, what's Committee?"

"Do what, honey?"

"Okay, honey," I said, trying to match her tone of amiable defamation, "in this case 'huh' means 'what the fuck is Committee and what the fuck do I do when I get there?'"

Maddie straightened, reappraising me. Then she slapped down her pencil and came over to my desk. "All right, now: Committee's where y'all's taking this well proposal. All the dogs get together and have a good scratch and figure out which cars to chase. Piece of cake." She pointed at one of the wells on the cross sections. "See here, this last well they drilled ain't producing so good as the others, so y'all's supposed to tell 'em if the company's outta its furry little mind to drill this one out here."

"But I only just got this file half an hour ago."

"So?"

"So how am I supposed to tell them anything? I haven't had time to get to know the geology worth shit."

"Honey bun," said Maddie patiently, "that ain't the point. This field spits hydrocarbons like a motherfucker. See, in this case 'good' is a relative thing, so all's you have to tell 'em is calm down and drill. And then if they don't want to drill, they don't drill. It's just a matter of form. These boys is just sitting around in the committee room all day jerkin' off anyway."

"Huh?" I said, with gusto.

"Justifying their salaries, love duck."

"Oh."

Maddie raised a polka-dotted shoulder coquettishly. "You might want to take a look at that map, so's you can practice pointing out the well locations."

I gave her one of those *I-knew-that* looks.

"Y'all knock 'em dead, I just know it." She gave me a merry wink and went back to her desk.

Bracing myself with a deep breath, I slipped the rubber bands off the map and unrolled it. I had to move everything around on top of my desk to accommodate the size of the unrolled map, arranging my stapler and tape dispenser to keep it from rolling up again. At first the map didn't tell me much. Just a spattering of black dots signifying existing wells—eighty-acre spacing, it looked like—a big orange sticker in the shape of an oil derrick in the proposed location, and dashed lines for our minerals lease boundaries, marked "Blackfeet Oil Company." But then I shifted the stapler to unroll the map a little farther, to see how far west the lease went, and found something interesting.

The adjoining lease belonged to Love & Christiansen, Gerald Luftweiller's employer.

More interesting yet, the lease comprised Hat Rock Field, whose map Gerald had taken with him to his death. I imagined the pattern of wells before me drenched in blood.